I0601557

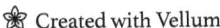 Created with Vellum

COMING SOON

BY AARON D. SCHNEIDER

War-Torn (Book 2 in The Warring Realm)

War-Sworn (Book 3 in The Warring Realm)

Visit www.aarondschneider.com to sign up and receive notification as soon as these titles go live (2018).

THE WARRING REALM, A PREQUEL

WAR-MARKED

CHOSEN FOR
A WAR THAT IS NOT
HIS OWN

AARON D. SCHNEIDER

I dedicate this book to my father, a man who does not view doing the right thing as easy, but necessary.
Thanks Dad.

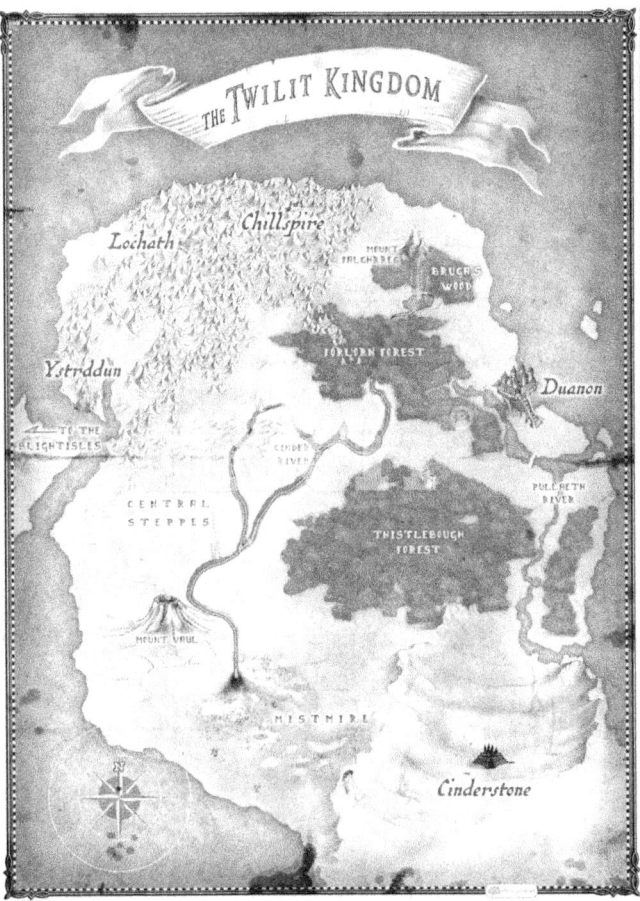

WAR-MARKED

THE WARRING REALM, A PREQUEL

Can I go home in March? March!

— Tom Waits

"Son, we live in a world that has walls, and those have to be guarded by men with guns."

— Colonel Nathan R. Jessup

"When d'you think that he'll come back?"
Not with this wind blowing, and this tide.

— Rudyard Kipling

PROLOGUE

The smell in the cave was thick and syrupy with the coppery sweetness of blood.

Three pale shadows moved between patches of twilight peeking through cracks in the cave roof, light on their feet as dancers. Their lithe forms picked their way over the broken corpses and pools of blood, until they came to the back of the cavern. The shimmer of dying sunlight did not reach this patch of blackness. Swaying like willows in a ghostly wind, the pale shadows coalesced into something more solid. Measure by measure, the shadows began to change.

In the narrow gap between the last light and absolute darkness, the shades thickened into three impossibly tall and delicate bodies, two softened by slight feminine curves, the other possessing a male's triangular ratios. With ginger steps they moved to the brim of the pool of darkness and stood poised with eyes of molten silver, peering into the black.

Something huge seethed in the dark; a suggestion of

movement, various hues of darkness coiling about themselves.

A scraping like files across rough stones sounded through the cavern and then a wet growling sound. Four points of red light, one pair atop another, formed in the midst of the dark and regarded the three figures coolly.

The masculine figure padded forward, his long-sinewed form garbed in sculpted plates of black glass. The crimson lights narrowed.

"Where is your quarry?" he asked in a voice like a bass bell reverberating in the cave.

"Not here," hissed a hungry whisper from the dark.

"You have failed," the male figure pronounced with a lofty rise of his chin. "You have not met the conditions of the pact, and so find yourself pronounced oath-"

The cave network's corridors shook with the force of a ragged roar.

"I AM NOT FINISHED!"

The three withstood the furious sound with hardly a flinch, but their white silk hair was tousled in the gale of carnal wind that came with the sonic assault. A corpse leaning upon a rough-hewn wall slid to the side then pitched forward. The wind stank of blood and split entrails. Congealing pools of vitae rippled and fell still.

"You were to bring him to us by the turning of our moon," the male figure said, condescension's drawl curled the corners of his lips. "He is gone and you have less than a day to acquire him. You cannot fulfill the pact."

The darkness seethed further, and sound like millstones grinding together in utter rage flooded the cavern. The grinding dragged on for several heartbeats as the three stood in utter, inhuman stillness, and then another necrotic breeze blew. This wind was a tamer, defeated sound.

"More time," the hissing voice breathed. "I beckon for more time to acquire him."

The male turned and looked to the taller of the two females, her skin and face as unmarred by age as any of the three yet with eyes that spoke of an age unfathomable. Those eyes stared at the four points of light and her head gave the slightest of nods.

"More time can be afforded by the pact," the male declared, turning to the twitching black. "But what is offered to restore balance?"

Another long pause. Another defeated sigh.

"The next spawning of my children shall be sworn to your service," the dark whispered. "For more time to acquire the human, I offer this to balance the pact."

One more nod from the timeless matron and the male turned, tracing silvered symbols which burned in the air before evaporating. In the eye-searing brilliance of the dying symbols, a face could be glimpsed around the four points of light, now shrunk to cringing eyes set in a face of tusklike mandibles and crowned with a spiny mane.

"The pact is amended," the male intoned. "A year and a day is given you to bring the human to the Gloaming Court, unharmed. In return, the next generation of your children shall serve the Gloaming Court."

The darkness rippled and there was a torrent of blood-soured wind. More corpses were jostled by its passing, and some thickening blood pools were churned enough to spray staining tendrils out from their banks. Then the air was turgid again, and the blackness at the rear of the cave lost its heavy potency.

"Do we truly have a year before the Gythraul move on Ystrdduun?" the male asked the matron. "Ceterum Cinis has marshalled his legions and the others are said to be doing likewise."

The matron turned from the empty corner and raised one elegant hand to a spear of light surrendering to the inexorable grip of night.

"The fiend's children will provide the distraction we need," spoke the other female, a clear and soft soprano song. "With their attention turned upon the darkling's get we should have the time necessary to acquire the human and stem the tide. Perhaps he will even be the one to put an end to this war. He thwarted the fiend, after all."

The look upon the male's face could best be described as incredulous, but he continued to watch the matron, grinding unspoken arguments between his teeth.

"Come," she said at last, with a voice as rich and dark as Solomon's Mines. "We must go. The die is cast either way."

Without further conversation they stepped within the burning shaft of light and vanished, leaving nothing but silence and a deepening dark in a hold of the dead.

1

Despite what you might think, I am sort of happy to be sitting here with some 31-Bravo investigator making me wait for him to finish looking at my file and my report. Even sitting here, trying not to sweat like some water-working rookie, is better than spending another day doing nothing, because that has been my life for the last two weeks.

They say that "hurry up and wait" is par for the course when you serve, but in the past six years that I've been a soldier with the United States Army I have never, ever been as bored as I've been in the last two weeks. I went from tracking the Taliban, or T-Man, through the poppy fields of the Helmand province, to being stuck on base here in Baumholder, Germany, with nothing to do all day except get paranoid at the way the MP's keep looking at me.

All because I was honest.

The investigator, a man who introduced himself as Officer Wakes, is almost done with the file, and through the whole thing his face hasn't changed. I can't help but think that is a bad sign. If what he is reading is what I think he is reading, then he should've had some reaction–shock or incredulity–something that showed he was surprised. The fact that he just finished reading my report of what happened in the tunnels of the White Mountains of north-eastern Afghanistan and has barely blinked means this guy is either jerking me off and he already knew what happened, or he's so burnt out from dealing with shell-shocked soldiers that drudgery is all he can handle, and this just won't compute.

Either way, this guy is not going to be on my side. Still, it's better than another day puttering around the barracks.

"So, Lieutenant Lucius Bollham," he says, like he wants to make sure he's talking to the right guy. "That's quite the story I just read."

Dear God he sounds like my father, in all his professo-rial condescension. He scoots the folder away from himself on the table so that it sits halfway between me and him. A not so subtle power play for dominance, just like dear old Dad. Except Dad probably would have used something a bit more pompous than read; "perused," maybe.

Regardless of phrasing I knew what he was saying. *Story*. Yep, this guy is either trying to provoke me or he doesn't give a shit if he does. Permission to treat the MP dick as hostile, your honor?

"I simply reported what happened, sir," I say, keeping my eyes on him and my voice flat.

I already threw myself on top of that landmine on the table between us, back when I put it all down in debriefing, and now the thing is finally starting to go off, a little bit at a time.

"Oh, I never said you didn't," Wakes smiles, like he scored a point on me. His incisors jut out from behind his tight-lipped, smug expression, and the similarities to a rodent are hard to miss.

"The question that comes to my mind, Lieutenant, is: what are we going to do about it?"

The response is automatic, like a reflex or that one dog who slobbered when he heard the bell. I might be embarrassed by how fast it came out of my mouth if it wasn't so true.

"That's above my pay grade, sir."

All of this, everything that happened, and what to do about it, is way, way beyond me.

"Maybe," Wakes muses, and then extends his hand to tap one white, square nail on the folder, twice. "But, for now let's pretend, you and I, that what we have to say about all this matters. Do you think you can do that, Lieutenant?"

All right, now I don't like him. Up until now, I just didn't trust him, but now that the rat-smiling, ball-squeezer decides to be condescending. I decide there is more here than just professional scrutiny. This guy is an asshole.

"I am not sure I understand what it is you want me to do, sir." I say coolly, because I really don't know what the point is, and I am not going to give this guy anything unless I have to.

"Well, if what you saw and heard in the White Mountains of Afghanistan is true, then shouldn't we notify all field commanders to be advised?"

He's fishing for something.

"If you say so, sir." My peripherals pick out the folder between us. I can just make out that the file is open to a series of photographs with blocks of text beneath. It takes an ungodly amount of effort to keep my face turned toward Officer Wakes.

"What about the intelligence agencies?" he asks, like he

is piecing it together out loud. "They should definitely know. And probably, we should inform our various allies in the region. Don't you think they should know what was going on in those tunnels?"

"Liasing with other armed forces has never been my forte, sir," I put a little more force behind the title this time, hoping to express that whatever motivation he was looking for I didn't have.

"No, but you are witness to something extraordinary, right?" he asks, seeming to warm up to this little show, as he races towards the punchline. "I mean you, Lieutenant, you've been in the Shit. Three years enlisted, kicking ass and taking names, then officer training, then back in the Shit. The stuff you've seen would blow people's minds, even before this."

Wakes taps the file, trying to snare my eyes into looking down.

"Hell, now you've got world-class, grade-A, X-Files stuff in this little folder right here. This is the kind of stuff that will get you a meeting with the Joint Chiefs and the President, isn't it? This is the sort of thing that you run to some little Hollywood pussnut who is going to make a movie and get you laid from here to LA. I mean, the amount of civilian beaver you could rack up would be historic, a big, strong guy like you."

And there we are. It took Wakes longer to get around to making the assumption, but I knew we'd get there eventually.

"I just reported what happened, sir."

"So you're telling me that you don't see the potential here?" He gives a disbelieving shrug. "All the stuff I just talked about doesn't interest you at all?"

This is a test. He is trying to figure out how much of a

liar I am. If I level with him a little then maybe, just maybe, he'll think I've lost it instead of being some opportunistic sell-out.

"Honestly, sir?" I search his eyes, which seem more like masks than windows into what passes for his soul.

"I would hope that goes without saying, Lieutenant," he grins, ticking off another point for himself.

I pause to iron the angry folds out of my voice.

"I am not looking for a cash-out option, because there is no out for me."

Wakes continues to sit there in silence, so I decide to lay it all out.

"Sir, I am a twenty-seven-year-old college dropout who has spent the last six years of my life becoming fit for war and nothing else. Hell, I even got some bullshit degree along the way so I could be an officer and keep doing this. I've trained and fought hard to be a soldier. I've gone through three childhood best friends, two engagements, half a dozen brothers-in-arms, and if you put me stateside now or six months from now or, hell, five years from now, I would be as clueless at making something of my life as I was when I first signed up to serve. As far as family, I've got cousins I don't know and a father I wish I didn't. There is no home for me to go back to, no happy welcome with family and friends. Just a self-righteous prick in an empty house. I am in 'the Shit,' as you put it, sir, for good. I have nothing but this."

I finish with a gesture to the file in and then a sweep to the four walls around us that sit snugly in the MP station in Baumholder Army Base.

The burst of honest, unguarded speech done, I feel almost winded and settle back into a seat. I hadn't even realized I was leaning forward.

"Nice speech, Lieutenant," is all Wakes says after a while, and the silence stretches.

Officer Wakes looks me up and down. I can tell there is some kind of formula running behind the dark mirrors that he uses for eyes. Internal calculations as he weighs every word, every twitch of my face. It's so intense I swear you can hear his gears clicking.

I almost jump when I do hear a clicking sound, then I realize it's his square nails snapping over each other as he rubs the pads of his thumb and middle-finger together.

"Suppose you never get to that Hollywood bloodsucker, huh?" he asks with a rhetorical flourish. "Hell, what if you don't even get so far as the shrinks that've been called in to assess you when I'm done here?"

I watch Wakes's stare go inhumanly blank, and there is a drastic change in temperature. I have to suppress a shiver as I stare into a pair of snake eyes as a monotone voice begins its situational diagnostic.

"I'll cite this as classified at a level so deep, no sane person would ever want to know about it, and then have you shoved into a crate with a black bag over your head. The next time you see anything is when some voice behind a glaring light starts asking you questions that make no sense and you can't answer. There begins your mind-breaking experience with enhanced interrogation and utter hopeless-ness. There is no money, no fame, no hordes of naked women. Only you and the certain knowledge that it will only stop when you have been so wrung dry that the voice behind the light puts you out of your misery or spits you into a hole to be forgotten."

This is hardly the first time I've been threatened by another officer, even by one who seems to have the juice to back up what he is saying, but damn, if Wakes isn't one of the best at it. The utter lack of venom in his voice, the way he almost sounds bored while giving me the rundown of how far he is willing to go is more convincing than any snarling threats could be.

"Sir." I fight like hell to keep the tremor in my belly out of my voice. "I am just trying to tell the truth."

The snake eyes don't even bother to blink away the explanation, just lets it slide off their flat surface.

"You still want this report to stand?" Its not a challenge, not even a curiosity. He is a damned machine waiting for input, as uncaringly patient as the terminal primed to launch the bombs or abort the launch sequence with one keystroke or another.

I finally look down at the file.

In camera-flash starkness I see the terrified faces of dead men, ugly and garish in splashed shades of red. Men trying to scream for help with throats torn out are hardly photogenic, even after death has stopped their gagging on red froth. A few hardly have faces, the violence having been less exact, or just angrier, just open meat and bone to the soft palate. I didn't know the men's names except for one, but I felt the pain of loss for each face.

After all, those men are the reason I am still alive.

"Sir," I finally manage to say around the knot that sits in my throat, raising my eyes to look the viper in the eye. "I don't have a choice."

"Why is that, Lieutenant?"

"Because," I answer slowly, to keep my nerve and stomach in place, "I just reported what happened, sir."

That's it, game over, drop the bombs, and preemptively call off the search for survivors. I am done.

Officer Wakes pins me to the back of my chair with his stare for an eternity and one more heartbeat before his eyes slide down to the file and the color printing of those unfortunate corpses. I listen to the mental abacus clack away as neurons spark with possibilities that I probably don't want to know.

The fingers *kah-click* again and he reaches out and slides the file closer to himself. I think he is about to close it and signal for someone to pop the bag over my head, but instead he starts flicking through the papers in the folder.

"What was your mission objective that day?" he asks as his pace through the pages slows. "What was your platoon's role in the operation?"

"Support, sir," I manage to choke out, my mouth having grown so dry that my tongue is stiffening on me. "The German forces had planned an assault on the complex and the 29th was told to provide containment support in case any hostiles tried to rabbit when they went in to flush them out."

Wakes settles on a page, and scans the contents. "What was the full purpose of the German operation?" A finger traces a line on the page.

"Through coordinating their own intelligence with some of our Local Nationals they had located a complex in the mountains that acted as a supply depot for the area's insurgents," the information came out like a familiar liquid from a well-worn vessel. "They had good evidence to suggest that eliminating the complex would effectively defang the insurgents. Capturing the complex was their objective, and keeping the perimeter was ours."

"Your platoon did not follow the operation plan, though?" he asks without bothering to look up from where his finger rests.

"No, sir." I sag another inch into my chair, the weight of the memories bearing me down.

"Why is that?"

Curiosity, no judgment. We've crossed a threshold of some kind.

"Well, sir," I breathe slowly, feeling the past settle fully across my shoulders. "One of those LNs was a young man named Nasrullah. He had given us good intel a few times, and the men had formed a kind of attachment to him..."

2

Mae'r pyllau'n torri. Dewch arwyddion, dewch draw, dod â gweledigaethau.

I can see nothing, my Queen.

Patience.

Yes! There--I see mountains in a rough-hewn country. There are men among the boulders and crags. They are armed and seem to be waiting.

Do you see HIM?

They all seem much the same, my Queen. No one seems to be leading them, and they are so scattered across the rocky ground, all hardly moving . . . could Mothe Gwiddon have been wrong?

It would be the first time in nearly two thousand years--

Wait! They are looking down the slope and some of them seem to be pointing to something, near where the mountainside opens to a cave. There are corpses before the cave. This seems to agitate them.

Is HE there? Can you see anyone directing the warriors?

Yes, there he is! He seems to be giving instructions to his warriors through some device and with hand signals. They move

quickly, changing positions around the cave. One of them is
directed by him to go forward.

Just one?

Yes, I... I think he is using the spyglass mounted to his weapon
to look at the cave and the bodies.

Reconnaissance?

Perhaps... The scout's face is grim... angry... and he is saying
something into his own device...

"Yep," Shaw confirmed as he sighted down his spotter's
glass. "That's him."

I could feel the current of the announcement rippling
through all of my boys as the confirmation came. It was the
gathering potential energy that comes before the first punch
that starts the riot. I should have said something, something
to check that building force, but damn it! Nasrullah was a
good one, and now he was gone.

He was just a kid, really, not even eighteen yet, but he
was tired of the T-Man taking its pissing matches out on the
neighbors. Nasrullah didn't deserve to be lying there in a
shallow ditch, especially when he was put there by pricks
who knew what it meant to a good Muslim boy like him.
Right then, if those bastards were in front of me in shackles
with an entire UN war crimes tribunal behind them I would
have put two rounds in each of their heads without a
moment of hesitation. I didn't just want them punished,
didn't just want them dead; I wanted to look them in the eye
while I did the deed.

And I wasn't the only one.

"We've got a clear path down the slope, sir," Sergeant
Feng said over the radio.

Feng, like some subtle human thermometer, was always
able to tell me what the men needed without actually telling

me what I had to do. I trusted him with more than just my life; I trusted him with the men I had under my command. So if Feng was telling me we had to go before the boys came undone in a bloody storm of indignation and pent-up frustration, then by God, I had better listen.

"The Germans are supposed to be making their entrance into the complex--" I began, but then, as if on cue, the sound of gunfire and explosions echoed across the mountainside.

Still, that wasn't much comfort as I heard some of the men in my platoon starting to shuffle and edge down the slope. I was about one shot away from things spinning completely out of my control. The reputation of the German military was nothing my men would have trusted most days, let alone for a case of revenge.

"All right, listen up," I growled, funneling my anger at Nasrullah's death and my fear of the situation into a ferocity that I hoped carried through radio waves. "We are going to advance down the slope toward the complex entrance, but so help me, if one of you breaks containment cohesion or opens fire without a confirmed enemy contact, your balls are going to take a permanent vacation inside your ribcage."

A chorus of affirmatives and we were off to a series of maneuvers, dashing and crouching behind cover, keeping our weapons trained on the mountain gully trenched in sandbags.

I had Shaw and Petralis, our resident designated marksmen, sit on some rock spurs flanking either side of the opening. They gave regular updates, but so far nothing even twitched.

Our advance went so smoothly that by the time I looked around and had everyone whisper their check-ins, we could nearly post some grenades into the trenches. I had hoped for communication from some of the German forces, confirmation that they had neutralized the enemy position and were in the caves. Knowing that there were enemy casualties and that advancing into the caves would create a friendly-fire nightmare might have given me the leverage to put the brakes on all this.

But the only thing that told us that Germans were up to anything was the sporadic sound of gunfire and the occasional dull thump of an explosion. No communication, just the perpetual confirmation that on the other side of this rock, violence was being done.

It might seem like my boys were out to lunch or that I was a piss-poor platoon leader, but you have to understand who we were and what we had been doing. We had all served more than one tour here in Afghanistan, and had all started full of piss and fire until the reality of the war we were fighting sank in. As we endured orders that made no sense, we watched the populace we were supposed to protect bounce back and forth between embarrassingly hospitable and cruelly hostile all in the same day, sometimes in the same person. Then we went home to a country that couldn't decide if we were heroes on an unreasonable pedestal or pawns in some military-industrial complex farce. It was a madhouse carousel yet none of us found a way to jump off the ride.

We were wound up, angry about it, and these bad guys-- because that is what they were, no matter what bullshit you hear from some philosophy professor--had just killed a young man we called *friend*.

Justice, righteous or otherwise, can be a terrible force, and right now it was riding us hard to the mouth of that cave.

Except now that we were at the doorstep, there was no one there.

The miniature embankments built from stacked sandbags and sheet metal lashed to pallets stayed untended. There was only a narrow ditch, where Nasrullah's body lay among others, that stretched horizontally between our position along the rugged slope and the mouth of the cave.

"Hold position," I growled into the radio. "We can't let--"

Sounds of movement came from within the cave for less than a second, and then people were pouring out. Handfuls of men, all armed but intent on nothing but getting out of the cave. Some threw wild looks over their shoulders but most just ran, skittering out of the cave and vaulting over their entrenched barricades.

The sudden appearance had stalled the last words in my throat, and that kept me from snarling a command to hold fire. In that space of a heartbeat, someone popped the first shot.

I never found out who it was, but it didn't matter. The first shot hadn't even begun to echo across the mountainside when it was joined by the chattering roar of an entire platoon opening up.

The first four men went down like perforated sacks, their legs giving out as their momentum dragged them forward to pitch face first into the ditch. A few more fell behind them, one sprawling onto the ground to squirm and scream, but the rest crumpled to the ground like marionettes with cut strings. The others must not have been totally green, because they went for cover pretty quick when the bodies started dropping.

"Fire discipline!" I spat into the radio. "Check your targets, damn it!"

Somewhere in all the thunder of rifle fire and the

screams of that one poor bastard writhing in his own bloody dust, I found time to hope we weren't totally screwed. I took a deep breath and checked the bodies on the ground, and yes, they were all T-Man pricks, or at least people armed and dressed for the part. That, at least, was a relief. I couldn't tell you the number of brothers who got jammed up because they opened fire on some moronic friendly coming around the corner at the wrong time.

More surged out of the cave, like ants out of a kicked-over mound, but these men seemed to get the memo and hunkered down almost immediately. I heard the throaty yet precise chuff of Shaw and Petralis's Crazy Horse rifles, and I watched heads snap hard sideways in red eruptions before the rest of them could make it to cover.

"I want suppression on that cave, now!" I roared before snapping a few shots off to keep a pair of hostiles ducking behind their sandbags. "I want them terrified to come out. Shut it down hard!"

Seconds later Lopez and Schwartz had the 240's chattering, turning the cave mouth into a cloud of moondust. Half a dozen unlucky pricks walked into that storm and got themselves stitched up and down by the incoming machine gun fire. The tide slowed to a trickle after that.

I took another breath. We were still within the limits of operation protocol, and as far as I could see, we had T-Man between a rock and those German sons-of-bitches.

Some sporadic fire started coming our way, but it was mostly blind, and the few brave enough to rise up and fire over the entrenchments learned to keep their heads down, if they kept their heads at all.

Because the terrain we had scuttled down was so rough, we were left with an elevated and well-defended position. We had them exactly where we wanted them. A few grenades and some more disciplined fire, and we'd wrap up avenging Nasrullah with a pretty bow.

"RPG," squawked a voice voice over the radio that sounded like Petralis. Before I could think, the *whump-pop* of a rocket-propelled grenade tore through the chatter of firearms, and a good hundred yards up the slope from me there was a burst of fire and fury that set my ears ringing.

Half a heartbeat later, and with two more percussive pops we were showered in a stinging spray of fractured rock. I heard Jules snarl out a blistering string of curses next to me as he rolled back deeper behind a crop of rocks, knuckles digging at his eyes.

"Grenades!" I spat through a mouthful of dust. "I want those cocksuckers blown out of their holes!"

Plink, plink, plink, and then spouts of debris, human and otherwise, shot into the air, chased by brief flashes of fire. More screams, pained and some crumbling into sobs, rang out in the uneasy quiet left after the chain of explosions.

"Everyone check in," I ordered as I kept low and looked to see if there were any targets left on the ruptured enemy fortifications. "You all got the parts you came here with?"

A chorus of names and affirmations began to cycle through, and nothing seemed to stir inside or outside the cave.

"I've got all accounted for," Feng assured, just before another volley of explosives tore through the air from inside the cave.

A trio of explosions ripped across the slope. I heard a moan of pain before the whole platoon thundered in retaliation. A flurry of salvos from rifle and machine gun chewed up the mouth of the cave, but the only thing hit seemed to be the rock face.

"They're tucked behind a bend," Shaw barked in my ear,

his frustration dragging his Kentucky drawl into a snarl. "Shitballs just leanin' out to take potshots!"

"Can you draw a bead on them?"

There were several long seconds during which a few shots were snapped at the yawning cave, until someone reminded them to stop wasting ammo.

"No," came the eventual answer, the sound short and heavy. "I could reposition, but that's goin' to put me right in the belt of where they've been blowin' shit up, sir."

Damn it! Nothing could just go easy.

"Hold your position, Shaw," I said as I racked my brains for a way out of this snafu.

We'd gotten too close, and if we tried to narrow the distance they might hit us with a face full of grenade since there was no knowing if they were holding anything back for us to be stupid. If we tried to back it up and draw them out, you can bet they were going to hit us with everything they had, and besides the risk to the platoon, there was the real risk of losing containment. I wasn't going to let one of those bastards escape if I could help it.

I looked over and saw Jules sporting a nasty patch of cuts across his face, one eye half-hooded and bloody. He saw me looking at him and flashed me that wide, white grin of his, all the more stark for the blood streaking his dark face.

"All still in one piece, Luce," Sergeant Feng reported, his use of my nickname telling me that my right-hand man was keeping his head despite the snafu we were in. "But Kinder and Hobbes got some surface cuts that look ugly, and Rimada blacked out for a minute, so I'm watching him."

I had maybe seconds before they nutted up enough to launch another round at us. How many could they have in there? Did we press our luck and hope for the Germans to pressure them out into the open? Could we afford to take that risk? Why were those Kraut bastards not communicating with us?

The mountainside opposite us sprawled up and around the cave, and I was just forming a plan when four more RPGs tore across the slope.

My whole body curled as small as I could make it, I scrambled across the slope toward Corporal Mueller and Specialist Lopez.

"Your squad ready to dig us out of this shit?" I hissed at Mueller's shoulder as I hunkered down next to him.

"Well," the unshakable Corporal said with a soft New Orleans lilt, "Lopez here does have 'im a mighty big shovel, sah."

Lopez, big and broad as an old oak, hefted his 26 pound 240 like it was a squirt gun, and the cold look in his eyes would have made even the hardest meat-eating grunt think twice.

That was enough for me.

"Tether yourself to my ass and follow me up and around that place where that ridge comes up parallel to the cave," I pointed with barrel of my service rifle. "Once we get up there, Lopez and the rest of the squad are going to unload on those assholes until you're in the black."

"You don't have to come, sah," Mueller started to object, but I cut him off with a look.

"I need a better look around," I said, just in case he thought about bringing it up again.

He knew better than to push it further.

"Feng," I huffed into the radio as I stalked toward the edge of the boulder we were taking cover behind. "I am taking Mueller's squad up and around the crest on the northern side of the mountain. On my go, I want you to have the rest of the platoon unleash a metric fuck-ton of fire on that cave. If one of those T-Man pricks sticks his head out, I want the Germans getting splattered on the other side of the damn mountain!"

There was second's pause, and I knew Feng was considering arguing with me.

"On your go, Luce," came the Sergeant's resigned reply.

I double checked to make sure Mueller's squad was ready to go. Then I gave the order.

"Give 'em hell, boys."

We took off just as they did.

This was not disciplined bursts of fire meant to chew up an enemy with a steady voracity. This was total war, apocalyptic measures of more than two dozen Army grunts pouring all their rage and will into an all-out onslaught.

The enemy couldn't have fired on us even if they were brave enough to stick their heads out, because the dust and shivered splinters of rock would have made blind pincushions of anyone who tried.

We made good time across the rocky ground. We scrambled, hopped, and downright hauled our asses over to that rock face, and then sprawled out across the ridgeline.

"All right, Feng," I roared into the radio. "Back it off enough so we can see what we're shooting at, you beautiful, overachieving bastard!"

The fusillade slackened, and the air began to clear. In the space of a single heartbeat, the scene went from a haze of pale dust clouds to a knot of less than a dozen cowering behind a lip of rock with a stockpile of arms next to them. If I had given the order to press forward it would have been four flavors of Armageddon.

Mueller's squad didn't need the order to fire, but the last thing I saw before they did was the faces of those men crouching with their hoarded weapons. Dark eyes bulging in terror, they seemed to hardly notice the bullets flying past their faces, and instead kept peering into the dark behind them. It may have been my imagination or some subconscious lip-reading hallucination, but I swear I heard gasped words.

Jinn!

Shaitan!

Iblis!

Then Specialist Lopez unbridled the 240 and that mustang of a machine gun punched round after round through their flesh. He probably could have done the work on his own, but the rest of us refused to let him have the fun.

More than half their number were down and bleeding out before they even saw us, and the rest only got to see our muzzle flares before the ground was slick with blood.

"This one's for Nasrullah, you cocksuckers," I breathed, then put another round down-range into some prick with a launcher held across his chest.

The shot was lower than I wanted and bored its way through his belly. He fell to his knees and screamed. An ugly part of me, a part you don't tell others about, drank in that scream and paused for half a second to savor it. That cry, right then, felt like Justice. I should have put two more into him, ended it right there, but God help me, I wanted him to suffer just a little more. For Nasrullah, for Jules, for me.

In that brief pause, my victim fired his RPG.

In a slow motion that only comes when you are certain you are about to die, I saw the rocket streak by, too high and wide. Whipping around hard enough to make my neck pop and eyes water, I watched the explosion detonate on a spur of rock thirty feet above us.

I could have whooped for joy, but the sound would have choked in my throat.

With tormented slowness, the spur above us began a cracking, splitting descent. Tons of solid stone twisted and slid downward, turning so the impact tumbled across the entire ridge line.

"Rockslide!" I screamed loud enough to make my ears crackle. "MOVE!"

Bodies moved around me as pebbles and then fist-sized rocks began to rain down.

I scrambled up the ridgeline, onto the part of the mountains over the cave complex, racing and scrabbling when something hit me from behind.

I bounced across stone–and then gravity was dragging me downward.

A dark crack yawned in front of me, and then I was falling into it with stones pelting across the back of my head as I tumbled into the black. I hit something hard as I fell, and then the black was all that was left.

3

"If that was the end of the report I wouldn't be here," Officer Wakes interrupts as he leans back in his chair and raps on the metal door behind him. "You want some coffee, Lieutenant?"

"Water would be appreciated, sir," I say as I realize how incredibly dry my mouth is. And we haven't even gotten to the tough stuff yet.

The door opens with a booming clang and an MP sticks his head in.

"Coffee, black, for me, and a bottle of water for the Lieutenant, if you would, Rawls."

Rawls gives a curt nod as he scuttles off to get Wakes's drink order. Wakes, already turned around, is staring at me as though expecting me to say something.

"O-oh," I stammer stupidly as I remember what he said before. "End of the report? How could that be the end of the report, sir? I fall into a hole in some cave in Afghanistan. The End?"

"That could certainly be the end," he says, like he is explaining where you go to get your mail on base.

"Impetuous officer in the US Army disappears in a rockslide during a firefight -- seems pretty simple. Like you said, you are estranged from your family, so no one would come looking for you. It is a simple solution to what doesn't need to become a complex problem."

There it is again, that threat hanging overhead. Bag 'em and don't bother taggin' 'em, because he's never coming back.

"What about my platoon, and my COs in Helmand?" I ask, knowing in my gut he already has an answer, but hoping against hope it gives me light in all of this.

"You mean the poor bastards who were stuck with you after your old Regiment refused to keep you around?" Wakes shrugs and stifles a yawn. "I don't think they'll miss you."

That's right. The son of a bitch is yawning.

"With respect, sir, you really think no one in my old unit is going to ask about me?"

"No," he says with just the barest shake of his head. "Why would they? More than half think *you* were the thing in the cave, and the rest just want to get as far away from crazy as they can."

And if they're delivering a package you'll have to sign – like it's nothing at all.

I fight the urge to sink my face into my hands. My head feels so heavy right now. I just want to lie down and close my eyes, but then something whispers that if I do I might see the *thing* again. Suddenly even sleep doesn't sound like a comfort.

There is a single, gong-like knock on the door, and then Rawls is there handing a steaming cup of coffee to Wakes and putting a bottle of water on the table.

"Thank you, Rawls, that'll be all," Wakes says with a nod and a little hoist of the styrofoam cup.

"Yes, sir," Rawls replies and then shuffles back through the door, sparing me what I think might have been a glare, but it is hard to tell. When a man's fugly, you can never be sure if he's pissed or if that's just his face.

"I don't think Rawls likes me, sir." I comment dryly as I twist the cap of my water, which feels tepid even in my hands. Figures.

"I am not sure he likes anyone whose ass he can't kiss to get ahead in life," Wakes replies distractedly as he squints down at the papers in the file and sips his coffee. "And even then he's just pretending."

I hope Rawls is listening, but I don't have time to ponder the possibilities when Officer Wakes taps the file.

"Yeah, right here," he says with a subtle shade of satisfaction. "Corroborating reports from Sergeant Jonathan Feng and Corporal Baptise Mueller that you were in fact trying to evade a rockslide when a boulder clipped your back and you were lost from sight. It was their belief, at first, that you had been buried beneath the rockslide. But they were mistaken, it seems?"

The question hangs there for a second before I can muster up an answer.

"It might have been... cleaner, if I had, sir," I say, unable to keep the bitter notes from playing out in my tone. "But no, I was not buried in the rockslide. I fell through a crack or breach in the cave complex."

Wakes eyes me over the lip of his cup.

"And just like that you found yourself in the bowels of an enemy stronghold? Must have been thrilling."

I should be used to Wakes's attitude by now, but he is

just that special kind of asshole that you can never really adjust to.

"You must be one meat-eating hard case, sir," I retort, not trying all that hard to dial back the snark. "A lowly grunt like me--I was just scared, with a nasty headache, in a hole that stank like FAN in an Afghan July."

Wakes pauses, his cup halfway to his lips.

"FAN?"

"Feet, ass, and nuts, sir."

His eyes seem to flatten out and, I am considering if I should apologize or at least pretend to, when something like a smile tugs at the corners of Wakes's mouth.

"Sounds like a charming spot."

"It wasn't going to get any nicer," I tell him, the almost-smile giving me the barest glimpse of hope as I fall into the dark memories. "But before anything got batshit crazy, I had to get myself unstuck..."

4

Is he still alive?

I don't know... I see nothing but dust and stone. I feel the spell pulling me down into the dark under the mountain.

If that darkling has fouled this...

Peace, my Queen, I can see him--he is breathing. He is alive within the mountain!

The mountain where his enemies are? Has he been captured?

No... the vision is difficult... cramped. I think he fell within one of the cracks in the mountain. He is alone in the darkness. He seems trapped in a narrow cleft in the rock.

Trapped? Is he injured?

It is hard to tell. He is more ragged from his fall, and there is some blood, but it seems only from small scratches and scrapes.

Is there a way out of the crevice? Will he be able to escape?

I... I am sorry my Queen. All I see is walls of stone.

I came to in the dark, but to my horror I realized I was trapped.

I groped around and felt nothing but rough rock. The

straps of my field pack were tight and kept me pinned against the wall. I reached up and found my helmet had been knocked off and ran a finger over a raw gash where the straps had been torn off. I was pretty sure that some rocks had fallen in after me. I ran my fingers over my crushed my pack--and therefore me--up against the side of the crack. I tugged and pulled, but other than an ominous rumble and clatter of pebbles from the rock above me, nothing happened.

I had never thought of myself as claustrophobic before, but right then, pressed against hard stone and with nothing but the dark all around, I found myself gasping and whimpering.

What if I was stuck here, buried alive until I died of thirst or lack of air? Could my boys find me before that? How were they going to find me down here?

Radio. My headset was gone with my helmet, but the radio itself was still on my pack strap. The position I was in made it difficult, but I struggled and strained until eventually I got to the radio on my shoulder strap.

"Feng! Mueller! You there?" I panted into the device, but there wasn't even the crackle of static.

"Lopez! Shaw! Petralis! Jules! Fucking anybody!"

I yanked and tugged the radio over, thinking maybe I had turned it off, but as I did, I felt the casing splintering in my hand, that little bit of strain pushing the failing machine beyond the breaking point. There is a soft *plink-ka-plink* as more pieces fell away into the dark, the last chimes of what seemed my best hope. I felt the cords of panic tightening around my chest and throat until my breath started to come in sharp, wheezing gasps.

Trapped. Buried alive! I'm going to die down here!

Get your shit together, boy!

That hard internal voice, which sounded like my grand-father's craggy rasp, cut through the panic and fear. This wasn't the first time I'd heard it, but each time was a special kind of shock–something which hit me hard enough to knock me out of my tailspin. Five words, and I realized how stupid I was being.

With enough wriggling and squirming, I discovered that I had room to move a little, though it still seemed like there was only rock in this triangle space I was wedged in. Still, not being squashed against one side seemed like a good idea, so I started to work at it.

I got a little bit of movement, but quickly realized part of the gear harness was pinched in the fallen rocks and it was only when I got my M7 bayonet knife free that I was able to cut the straps and get free. That left my water and some spare ammo trapped under a ton of stone, but at least I could move and stretch a bit in my claustrophobic space.

As I stretched, I realized I still had my flashlight, and thank you God, it still worked. With a click and a blast of glare, I got to look around at a space between rock walls and compacted rubble that I couldn't quite turn around in. Up above me the space narrowed after about a foot until it reached a place where a boulder, as big around as my shoulders were wide, sat wedged and waiting.

With nothing but stone and dark all around I couldn't even begin to guess how deep I was.

I thought I could still hear rifle fire, but in the enclosed space, my own breathing sounded so loud, and every move I made scraped at the rock, so I couldn't be sure.

With no way up, I decided to look around my feet, hoping to find my rifle, but instead I found something even better.

About six inches from my foot was an opening in the

wall of the crevice. I couldn't see where it led, if it led anywhere at all, but I didn't hesitate. I started to worm my way down and through that narrow gap. I paused with my head and shoulders sticking out of the hole shining the light around one more time to make sure there was nothing else I could salvage.

Nothing.

So with only my flashlight, my M7, and a few odds and ends in my pockets, I clicked off the light and began my ass-first crawl through the dark.

Now I don't want to give the impression that I'm so balls-to-the-wall hardcore that I wasn't terrified the whole time I was shuffle-squirming my way backwards through that worm-run; it's just a matter of degrees. I was scared that I was going to wriggle myself into a spot where I would get stuck or, hell, even squirt myself into some bottomless abyss. As much as that though, I was exponentially more scared of just squatting there in that upright coffin of a crevice. In that trap, one of two things would happen: either that rubble shifted slowly, and inch by inch I was crushed into paste, or I slowly succumbed to dehydration and in my agonized fevering I opened my wrists with my faithful M7. Either way, that's not how I was going out, not if I had a choice and a chance.

So on I went for what seemed like hours, but was probably less than half of one, until at last my feet felt around and there was nothing there. I puckered up with fear, convinced this was the part where I slid inexorably into the dark and hellish anus of the world. When no such doom occured, I inched my way back a little farther, and then a little farther still -- and then my feet hit a solid stone floor again.

With a desperate speed, I squirmed out and then found

myself crouching on stone floor with enough room around me to stretch out my hands on either side and above without feeling anything. The air stank of many men living in close proximity.

Now, with enough room to take a breath without my ribs scraping stone, I had a chance to assess my situation and remember that as far as I knew, I was still in an enemy stronghold, cut off from help, and armed with only a flash-light and knife. I needed to find a way out, fast and quiet, and then rendezvous with some friendlies. I was hoping for my boys, but I would have taken the Germans at this point.

I took a couple deep breaths and then held it so I could listen a spell, and then repeated the procedure a minute later. I heard nothing.

That was worrisome, but now that I was free of all that rock closing in on me, I was feeling unrealistically optimistic.

I clicked the light on and made a survey of the room in which I now found myself. The eye-stabbing brightness of the flashlight punched through the dark and revealed pallets stacked with plastic-wrapped boxes arranged against uneven walls. A sweep of the flashlight picked out what looked like a plastic shower curtain stretched over a rough portal.

Good, another way forward -- but first I was going to take a peek at the insides of these palletized boxes. A quick slash and I was able to pluck out a colorfully sheathed square of everybody's favorite dehydrated noodles, garlic and herb flavored. I stuffed a few into my pockets and then stalked over to the doorway.

Slowly, carefully, I leaned out and saw a hallway which I probed with the beam of my flashlight. Thick bundles of electric cable ran along the far wall, junctioning at regular intervals with work lamps, none of them lit. The hallway stretched around a corner on the right hand side and seemed to split into a T-intersection on the left.

I smelled something metallic on the air that I should have recognized.

It was only as I moved into the corridor that I saw the blood pooled and streaked across the floor.

I've seen a lot of blood–from accidents and battle wounds–and after a while you get used to seeing the patterns from the different ways it's spilled. The floor was slick with the stuff, but I'd never seen it in smeared puddle like this before. My best guess was that someone had dragged the corpse of an animal they had done a piss-poor job of gutting. Heavy streaks of blood were punctuated here and there by wide splashes.

My mind raced back to those fragments of sound my brain had snared right before the world exploded and I was thrown into a hole.

Iblis. Sháitan. Jinn.

I'm not all that familiar with Islam's teachings, but when one of the terms rhymes with Satan, it doesn't take a linguist to put two and two together.

All those hostiles pouring out into the open. The way they seemed determined to push through an obvious killing ground. The terror that was so plain on their faces. The damn lights being off. The floors covered in fucking blood!

This wasn't the Germans pushing in from from the other side. This didn't make sense for anything I'd ever seen in this charlie-foxtrot of a war.

Then, as I stood there with the flashlight beam juddering and twitching more with each second I stared at the blood, I just knew it. It was like in a dream when something impossible or crazy happens, and you just understand what it means or why it happened. When the rabbit pops out of Grandma's ear--wearing a hockey-mask, no less--it all just makes sense. It was kind of like that, only without all the detached haziness of a dream.

At that moment I knew the truth. Someone bad--someone scary--was running around inside this mountain. Someone who didn't follow rules. Someone that even these jihadist, seventy-virgin-chasing sons of bitches were scared piss-less of. And here I was stuck in the middle of it, in the dark, with only a knife and a flashlight.

Could things have gone any more sideways?

A piercing shriek, followed by a series of yammered cries, sprang from multiple voices, and then a staccato tune of sporadic AK fire seized my heart in my chest. But it was the sudden, prolonged silence which came afterwards that killed any thought of plucky heroism. There had been no responding burst of fire, no striking blast of a clearing grenade; nothing that I knew of on this earth could put down armed men so fast.

I ran–or at least I tried to–because immediately I stepped into something slippery, and my feet splayed out beneath me. I heard a popping sound in my hip as I went down. I slowly pushed myself back up with the arm I hadn't fallen on.

The metallic scent in my nose and on my lips were like spurs to a horse.

No disciplined clearing your corners or scouting doorways for me as I took off. I just ran as fast as I could with the lurching gallop I'd acquired in the fall.

The screaming and shots had come from the right, so I instinctively bolted for the left and took that arm of the T. I raced down a corridor with what looked like more shower curtain doors and then hit another intersection. This one branched in three directions. I stood at that crossroads, cursing under my breath before I gulped down more air and took off down the left-hand path.

More curtained rooms flew by, and here and there I spotted solid doors framed in against the rock. Some hung open, and I crashed through them as I rounded corners, but most were closed. Here and there I saw an arm or foot sticking out from under a plastic curtain dripping red. Others had dark, wet lumps that may have once been men, but I had no time to give them much attention; I had to keep running.

I am not sure how long I ran or when the corridors started widening, but it was while I was wheezing with exhaustion and plowing through a wider chamber that I smashed into a living human being.

"Was zur Hölle!?!"

The two of us went down together in a tangle of limbs, curses and growls erupting from both of us as we rolled across the cave floor. My flashlight and M7 both flew out of my hands, which was just as well because right then I was fighting on raw instinct, and my empty hands hammered and ripped at my ensnared partner. He screamed and fought back, and I snarled and fought harder.

"Halt! Stop!"

Pairs of hard hands descended on me, and before I could shake them off, I was pulled upward, struck squarely in the face, and then thrown to the floor. The blow to my skull was still vibrating my world when a booted foot came down sharply on my chest and then slid up to my throat. With my eyes watering from the first blow and the suffocating pressure of a boot on my neck, I looked up into the black abyss of a rifle barrel.

All around me were nearly a dozen flashlight beams.

Some swept this way and that around the wide room, but most stabbed down toward me. In their light I could see the gleam of more barrels aimed in my direction.

A storm of quick, guttural barks in a familiar language flew around me. I think they were trying to whisper, but adrenaline and the acoustics of the underground made that impossible.

My fingers scraped and tugged at the boot on my neck, fighting to buy just another quarter inch of breathing room, but then the barrel was jammed up against my face, and my cheek was mashed against my teeth. I froze.

"*Dummes Arschloch!*" came a sharp hiss from just beyond the gun barrel and its world-eclipsing light.

"*Holt! Schreibber!*" called another voice, softer and a note higher, but heavy with authority.

There were a few tense heartbeats, and then the barrel withdrew a second before the boot came off my throat. The flashlight beams silhouetting the rifle barrels lowered to create pools of illumination on the floor, and I could see that there were, in fact, men behind those deadly lights; soldiers in desert camo whose tri-colored flag I could just see emblazoned on patches at their arms. They formed a rough circle around me, some of them still facing outward in perpetual, sweeping vigilance. The rest watched me.

Slowly, gingerly, favoring my bad hip, I got to my feet, doing my best to keep my hands up, palms out. I knew that there was some protocol for being recovered by friendly forces, but in the long list of briefings I had to stay awake for, that one had seemed more trouble than it was worth. So instead of following the proper procedures laid down by the great leaders of the coalition forces, I followed a time-honored tradition of all US citizens meeting foreigners.

"A-me-ri-can," I said in over-enunciated English. "Any-body speak English?"

"*Arschgeige*," someone said, followed by a grunted chorus of "*Ja*".

"*Ruhe!*" came that soft, commanding voice. It belonged to a tall, thin soldier who stepped from the circle toward me. "I am *Feldwebel* Zorn, 234th Mountaineer Brigade. Please identify yourself."

For the courtesy in his words, his tone was cool and crisply measured, though I was glad to find that his accent wasn't too thick. I couldn't see his face very well in the backlight of the flashlights, but I felt his eyes weighing me.

"Lieutenant Lucius Bollham, 29th Regiment, 25th Infantry Division, US Army, sir," I said all in one breath, even though I still felt winded from my panicked run and the whole boot-slash-throat thing. "I was separated from my men in a rockslide and wound up in here."

Zorn nodded slowly, a tall, grimly contemplative specter, and then growled something in German into his radio. He paused and, after hearing nothing, shook his head. There was a subtle ripple through the men as the silence deepened.

"*Wir sind gefickt,*" a voice hissed out of the darkness.

I didn't speak a word of German, but I knew what the voice meant. It was the same tone that Samuelson had when he knew that sniper had him in the crosshairs, the same heaviness of speech from Pierce when he saw wires running from that parked car in a narrow street.

It seemed the Germans were having their own nightmare.

"Do you guys know what the hell is going on down here?" I asked, feeling the rumbles of unease. "I mean with the blood and the bodies. Doesn't seem like typical soldier stuff."

For one stomach-turning second I had a suspicion that these guys may have been the ones responsible for the horror show down here, but quick as it came, the fear left. Part of it was exhaustion, as I knew I couldn't keep running with a jacked-up hip, and the other part was just pragmatics. If they were the monsters, then there was nothing that I could do about it, and they would probably have killed me right then if they had wanted to.

"How do you have this?" Zorn said and I saw a long, lanky arm sweep across the blood smeared over my sleeve and face. "Are you injured?"

It was impossible not to notice the suspicion in his tone. Looks like I wasn't alone in wondering what was going on.

"I was running through the tunnels, and I slipped and fell," I said, hoping I sounded sincere.

"Running?" Zorn asked like the word was unfamiliar to him, and then his soft voice sharpened like a razor. "What did you see?"

I opened my mouth to respond, but then shut it. What had I seen? Nothing except what was around us right now. Blood, a few bodies and the dark. Nothing else. I felt a sudden flush of my own blood in my cheeks. When you are running through a pitch-black butcher's drain, you don't think about having to explain yourself, but now it seemed more than a little silly. I was a soldier, damn it; why had a little blood cost me my nerve?

Then I remembered the awful silence after the sound of terrified men fighting for their lives, and I couldn't lie to myself enough to be convinced that I had overreacted.

"I saw the casualties and then heard gunfire, and I had

lost my rifle, so I retreated," I said guardedly. I couldn't explain it, but I couldn't deny what my gut was telling me.

For a second I sensed the entire squad sizing me up, felt the tremble in their collective finger that crept back toward the trigger. Down here in the dark, with no allied witnesses, no nosy embeds, and not even the quasi-omniscient surveillance systems, they could end me just to cover their six. They wouldn't be soldiers if they didn't at least consider it for a second.

Even shaded in darkness, I could detect the quick sweeps of the German officer's eyes around the circle of his men. He was doing what I had done so many times. It was second nature. He was weighing their lives against the risks, running through the ways it would be his fault if things went sideways, finding a way to move forward despite all that.

I found myself not quite ready to like the Kraut, but I decided I could certainly respect him. A man who thinks about his men is not as common as it should be, no matter where you serve.

"You will come with us," the *Feldwebel* stated in a tone that brooked no argument from me. "De situation here is... unstable."

I nodded and looked around, squinting in the dark, until I spotted my flashlight and combat knife which I had lost in the struggle. Zorn didn't stop me, but I felt the rest of the squad shift a little as I bent to retrieve them, a subtle shift of awareness which I felt as much as saw.

Well, that wiped out any thought of asking them for a weapon to defend myself with. These boys were not in any mood to trust me, but right now I needed them to help me get out of here.

"I lost my radio, my service rifle, and most of my gear

when the rockslide threw me down here," I admitted as I checked my light with a few experimental clicks. "My platoon was covering the western approach where reconnaissance had found a secondary point of entrance or exit from the mountain. We could probably meet up with them there if you want to get rid of me."

I hoped I sounded reasonable rather than naively optimistic, but Zorn's head was shaking before I finished speaking.

"*Nein*, no good."

With a quick flick of his upraised hand paired with a sharp syllable in German, the squad was moving out, and I had to lurch along to keep up.

"What -- why?" I managed to puff as I fell into step alongside him. "Why is that not good?"

"The western egress collapsed–your rockslide, maybe." Zorn whispered with his rifle at his shoulder, barrel down in a soldier's war shuffle. "We confirmed two hours ago."

Two hours!

A twisting flutter swept from my stomach to my brain and back, but then I remembered that I had been knocked out. It was more than a little scary to imagine being trapped, wedged upright in that hole for so long, but right now keeping up with Zorn was taking all of my energy. I could find time to wrap my head around things when I wasn't limping through the dark.

I was gathering breath for a question about where we were going when the distant rumble of gunfire rebounded down a far corridor. This was disciplined fire, rifle bursts in steady succession–but before the first round of echoes died out the next round was becoming more erratic. You develop an ear for it, the sounds of war, and eventually you can envision the battle taking shape even without seeing it. That's why that silence was so terrible and that was why, even wheezing and grunting to keep up along-side my new-found protectors, I felt chills clawing up my spine.

I was listening to well-trained soldiers–professionals–being taken apart by something even as they fought back. And this was all happening without that something making a sound in return. That just doesn't happen.

At least, everything I knew told me it shouldn't happen, and a quick look around told me that these boys from the 234th knew that as well. Even their shadows were jumpy as hell.

Zorn hissed another command, and the squad arranged itself behind the best cover they could find around a bottle-neck into two tunnels. One of these was where the sounds of shooting were coming from. I slumped down behind some stacked bags of what looked like quick-dry cement, nearly at Zorn's shoulder, who had taken up a similar position to that of his men–down on one knee with his battle rifle trained on the bottleneck. It was more than a little reassuring to see so many barrels leveled at whatever might be down that tunnel.

"*Vogel, hast du Kontakt aufgenommen? Vogel, hast du jemanden gefunden?*" Zorn called into his radio headset. The only response was the fire in the corridor growing wild and random until only a single rifle could be heard from the tunnel.

"*Vogel?*"

That last desperate rifle fell silent, and a dreadful silence took hold, only intruded upon by our ragged breaths.

A scream shot up from the right-hand tunnel, and then silence again.

"Why aren't we withdrawing?" I said as softly as I could.

"Why don't we pull out of this hole so we can establish communication? Do you even know who is down here?"

It was a fair question. It seemed like these Germans had no idea what was going on either, and they weren't getting any communication even with working radios. For all we knew we could be about to open fire on friendlies who were just as scared as we were and then get taken out in the chaos by whatever group was doing all the killing.

Unless Zorn had some compelling reason to stay down here, he should pull back and get in touch with operational command.

"*Nein*, no good," Zorn said as he raised his head slightly to do a quick headcount of his squad. "We cannot do that."

The silence carried on, but I swear I could feel some kind of pressure building under my skin. Instinct, ESP, the damned Hand of Providence--take your pick, but I knew something was coming down that tunnel, sure as a bullet down a barrel.

"Why? Why not?" I snarled as I stared into the yawning darkness of the empty tunnel.

I needed him to answer before whatever was within that flashlight-pinioned tunnel exploded all over us.

"All exits are gone," Zorn said in an urgent voice which sounded like he felt that imminent pressure as well. "We cannot find them. The tunnels are *verzaubert*, bewitched. Every time where we should find the way out there is another turn deeper, or it is blocked."

Bewitched.

Iblis.

Suddenly aware of a pervasive stench, I realized the tunnel was no longer empty.

It was thick, a solid thing, and seemed to churn with an oily muscularity over, under and around itself. Matching its noxious aura, the thing released a sudden gust of charnel wind--a huge cannibal belch that reeked of blood and entrails.

My eyes watered, and I wasn't alone in choking back a gag.

As the world blurred around my tears, and I almost missed the four lights which winked into place in the utterly dark tunnel. With an arachnid gaze, they assessed every living thing before them. Then they narrowed, and I swear it was like they were looking right at me.

"Luciusss..." something sighed between a thicket of jagged teeth.

Several things happened at once.

Zorn, gave the order "*Feuer!*" and a squad full of fine Heckler and Koch battle rifles sent a heavy salvo into the dark. At the same time, another blast of foul air surged into the cave, and in the flashlight beams, I could see thin strands of red reaching out from the tunnel, a fine mist of crimson silk roiling out toward us, almost in slow motion. The two red lights blinked off on one side briefly, some alien imitation of a wink, and then all the red lights retreated down the tunnel. The rounds seemed to have no effect, not even giving the report or dusty evidence of striking the tunnel walls.

Had we scared it off? Hurt it? Did we do anything to it? Could we?

The only things that remained were some of those thin fibers of red in the air, as ethereal as free strands of hair floating on stale air.

"*Geht's allen gut?*" Zorn called softly and then began a quick, quiet succession of *Ja*'s as his squad checked in.

The last affirmative was when the floating strands, with an audible twang, straightened with a rigid tension under the flashlight beams. Four soldiers closest to the tunnel were thrown bodily toward the tunnel mouth. It happened so fast and with such bone-snapping force that no one had time even to cry out. Some of their comrades opened fire into the tunnel again while Zorn rushed forward to grab the nearest man. The four men were screaming, and I could see their hands clawing at their chests and arms.

Another twang, and they were dragged toward the tunnel like they'd been tied to the back of a speeding truck. Zorn fell back with a scream of frustration as the soldier he'd gotten his hands on was torn from his grip. The poor bastards gibbered and scrabbled at the stone floors or their own bodies, dripping in bloody strands of silk. It took only another second for all four to be drawn into the tunnel mouth.

The tunnel was barely wide enough for two men, shoulder to shoulder, so the four men were drawn over and under each other with bone-snapping force.

The screams ended before the rifles clicked empty, and other than the viscous streaks of red on the floor, the tunnel seemed unchanged. Once more, silence.

The black became solid again, and sanguine strings reached out toward us on a gore-scented wind.

Without a word or scream, I flew into a lurching run alongside the leftovers of the 234th.

5

Wakes doesn't blink for a long spell, his eyes just digging at me with mechanical focus.

I feel cold, and as I try to keep from shivering by crossing my arms tightly across my chest, I feel the hair follicles standing at parade-ground attention. My whole body feels like it is about to collapse into a shivering pile, like I'm running a fever or something, but I know I'm not sick.

"I don't know if you can understand what it means to run for your life if you haven't ever run like that," I breathe the words out, almost expecting it to fog out in front of me.

"You aren't just running scared, but knowing you are about to die, and running anyway."

Wakes throws back the last of his coffee and winces.

"Your whole body is electric, but everything seems to be made of molasses. You feel like you're about to collapse, which is almost appealing given how sick and weak you feel."

I stare at Wakes for a second and then slowly take a swallow of water. I've only made it about halfway through the bottle, but the stuff is getting even warmer. It makes my throat feel oily.

"I guess that's close enough," I shrug and arch my back, which gives a grinding pop of protest. "Any chance I can get up and stretch my legs? We've been sitting here for a while."

Wakes looks up from contemplating the bottom of his styrofoam cup, and I can see the internalized arithmetic rippling the surface of his eyes. Every crazy thing I just said is being weighed against my service record, and all of it filtered through the testimony of all the men they inter-viewed, American and German. I am sure the instructions he was given before he started looking at my case also play into it as well. Nobody is totally objective and free of bias--in life, and especially in the military. Everyone gets orders from someone, some force that pushes them one way or another.

I twist a little in one direction and then another as I wait for him to decide. In the little time I have spent with him, I've pretty much figured out that when Wakes wants to tell you something, he'll tell you when he is damn well ready to.

"Sure," he says at last, and then he is standing up in front of me.

I heave myself to my feet, and do another stretch to try to quiet some of the nagging creaking sounds in my back.

"You're moving like an old man, Lieutenant," Wakes observes as he gives a single sharp rap on the door. "Things catching up with you."

"Stupidity and service, bending me over a barrel, sir," I grunt as I straighten. "Drunken accident as a young man, and then an IED upending my ride a few years later."

"You should still be a young man," Wakes says right before the door clicks open with Rawls behind it. "We are going for a walk."

Rawls pauses, and you can tell the two parts of his nature, bootlick and asshole, are at war -- whether to comply or say something. Both sides must be really entrenched, because he just stands there for a good long while, his forehead knotting up like he's going to get a cub scout badge for it.

"You have something to say, Rawls," Officer Wakes says in a way that isn't really a question.

"No, sir," Rawls replies getting the message, and then glaring at me when I swallow a snort.

Rawls moves so Wakes can step by, but then he steps forward so that his beaky nose is close enough to sniff at my throat. Rawls, half a head shorter than me, looks up at me with a twisted sneer stamped on his already-ugly mug.

"Hold on, Lieutenant," he snaps, meeting my eyes defiantly. "You'll have to be secured with restraints first. Base policy for all detainees."

I clamped down on a wince in the dangerous proximity to Rawls's breath and face, and decide to just look over him to Wakes.

"Last I knew this was just an interview," I call to him from across the tops of Rawls prickly dome. "Has something changed, sir?"

Wakes, who had been walking down the hall, stops and turns with a hint of exasperation, like a teacher turning from the board to sort two troublemakers out.

"Oh, quite a few things have changed, Lieutenant," he says with a twitch of a smile gliding across his face. "But for now that isn't one of them. Stand down, Corporal."

Rawls's face puckers up until the comparison with southward parts of the anatomy is inescapable, but he steps back without a sound.

I contemplate dragging my due from him as a superior

officer, but decide I am too tired to waste time and energy on a shit like him.

Fighting to conceal the limp I get from holding one spot too long, I follow Wakes down the hall.

It is only a few more turns past steel doors and more sour-faced MPs before Wakes leads me outside to a small yard enclosed with chain link and barbed wire. Crack-stitched asphalt blankets the ground, and beyond the chain-link is a small sward of grass that terminates in another more imposing fence. Beyond sprawls the quaint city of Baumholder, cradled in the wooded arms of the Gartel forest.

It is cool without being cold, an autumn breeze nibbling at my ears and neck without too much bite.

"So close, but so far, eh?" Wakes intones as he pops out a cigarette.

I am pretty sure the base policy is set against smoking, but somebody like Wakes seems to be beyond such concerns.

He offers me a smoke from a pack that looks like some menthol blend I am not familiar with.

"Thanks," I say, taking the proffered cancer stick and then bending forward when Wakes produces a lighter.

I did some smoking when I was a teenager, but quit in college before I ever went into a recruiting office. I made it through six years fighting the T-Man without taking up smoking, but after all that talk about the caves I can pick it up again like I'm still sixteen.

We stood there for a few minutes sending up thin streamers of smoke, watching them unwind and peel away with each fresh breath of wind.

"So you and your old man don't see eye to eye?" Wakes asks as he stares through layer upon layer of fence.

I nod and take one more drag before I grind the butt out on the asphalt. I think wistfully of asking him for another--I smoked the first one too fast to enjoy it--as I scoop the remaining butt into my pocket. As I come up, Wakes graciously has one jutting free from the pack.

"Yeah, but that's just the tip of the iceberg," I say before taking a pause to light the new one and let loose a fresh current of smoke. "First time I had an original thought, my dad and I were at odds."

Wakes still hasn't bothered to look away from his contemplation of interlinked barriers, but he nods knowingly.

"Man of the house, tyrant king in his castle," he muses, almost like he is talking to himself. "Military man; got used to doling out orders and never stopped."

"I wish," I say through another jet of blue-grey vapor. "At least that would have made more sense."

Wakes turns and looks at me, and for the first time since we've met, I think he is actually surprised by something I've said. Given what we've been talking about, I don't know if that's really a comfort, but I decide to put it down as a point for me. It is at least a little fun to watch this guy have to reassess his assumptions about me.

"Really?" is all Wakes says, the question obvious in his tone.

I take my time in answering--one puff, two puffs, three puffs, four, but I eventually give another nod and a smile.

"My old man teaches sociology at Hycklar State University, Minneapolis. Been a professor there since I can remember."

Wakes gives a little chuckle and then flicks his spent cigarette to the ground.

"Ah," he says, and that shield of self-assurance has slid

back into place. "One of the "-ists". What's his flavor? Marx-ist, pacifist, anarchist?"

"A symbolic interactionist," I state flatly. "He spent my entire childhood trying to shove micro-sociological para-digms and a rational self-concept into my psyche. As a 'child of color', he would tell me, he didn't want me surrendering to so many negative perceptions of myself or, as he called it, 'over-correcting into destructive patriarchal norms.' "

"He's a whitey, then," Wakes guesses without really guessing. "Which makes your mother?"

How many times with this question? Good to know that even in the midst of a military investigation, questions of mixed heritage are still deemed relevant. Some things never change.

"Hell if I know," I shrug. "Absent. My dad said talking about her and dwelling on her was no good for me."

"He sounds like an ass," Wakes comments dryly.

"That's nicer than what I called him the last time we talked."

"Would have been fun to watch that show," Wakes says without a hint of mirth, and then taps out another cigarette. "Still, that all makes what comes next easier. When you don't come back from all this, the old man isn't going to dig around too hard. I mean, maybe the guilt will push him to be a nuisance for a little bit, but then his selfishness will drag him along and he'll tell himself that it's all just a natural consequence of your self-destructive life choices."

And mind your step as you exit... son of a bitch, he's cold.

Somewhere in all this, I gag on my smoke, and I'm left standing there hacking and wheezing. My little respiratory fit doesn't slow or stall a syllable of Wakes's prediction, and somehow through all my coughing, that steady tone remains perfectly audible. He is quickly becoming runner-up for the scariest thing I've ever met, and given my recent history, that's saying something.

The fit passes, but I still feel like I can't really breathe.

"What the hell do you want?" I wheeze.

Wakes stares at me long enough for me to catch my breath, and then taps ash from his cigarette.

"Right now, well" --he draws it out with painful consideration. "Right now, I'd settle for the rest of your story."

One more data point. He already knew the whole thing, already had read the report I gave nearly five months ago. Sure, it was just a piece of paper, but damn it, I told the truth. Nothing, and I mean nothing I was going to tell him was going to be any different than what was in that report.

Why is it so important that I tell him what he already knows?

My hands are shaking and I nearly miss my mouth as I try to take another drag.

"Fine," I spit to chase another blue-grey streamer into the cold clouds. "Let's pull the pin on this thing."

Wakes's smile is cold enough to put ice in my guts, but I am going to finish the story, and then at I can be done, no matter what happens next.

Just done.

6

He is running.

I expected as much.

You think he is behaving cowardly, my Queen?

Hardly. There is wisdom in flight, no matter what some, like our dear Uzran, might say. He is outmatched and is keen enough to understand that.

I am not sure it is quite as cerebral as all that. This no retreat. This is a rout.

I trust Mother Gwiddon's word. And it must be remembered that just as with Valoise, these are mortal men, my child. At the onset their worldview is so very fragile.

As you say, my Queen.

Trust me, my child. If Mother Gwiddon has found him out, then he will show us why in good time.

Assuming that it does not kill him in the process.

That... would be unfortunate.

With my limping run I had fallen behind the rest of them, and every stabbing step I took felt certain to be my last. I had lost my M7 and my flashlight somewhere along the way as I grabbed at the wall to support me when the pain drove me to a knee.

Somewhere in the nether regions of my brain a voice was gibbering about some abomination made of shadows and blood. That voice, given the chance, would have drowned out everything else until I just collapsed to the ground and surrendered, but in the basement of that low place another deeper will kept my body moving. Lizard-brained, you might say–nothing but a will to keep breathing and not die. That instinct was in the driver's seat for what felt like ages as I chased the flashlight beams ahead of me.

Behind me, the blackness boiled with movement I felt but didn't dare to look back at.

A few times the squad rounded a corner ahead of me, and for a few mind-breaking seconds there was nothing but the dark around me as I felt that thing coming up behind. I think I may have screamed through those moments, though I am not sure how I had the air for it. Then I careened around a corner, rebounding off a wall in ragdoll fashion and seeing the lights ahead of me again. I would put forth another burst of hopping, hobbling speed and maybe get a little closer for a second before fatigue dragged me down.

At some point we entered another large cavern, at the center of which a slender shaft of light shone. I'd never have thought a little light like that could mean so much to me. Right that second it did me absolutely no physical good, but it still became supremely important the instant I saw it. Light, sun, world: there was something beyond these caverns and corridors of blood and horror, and that tiny sliver of reality was what I needed to hold on to in the midst of insanity. And as I looked around, I knew I wasn't alone in that hope.

Zorn and the remainder of the squad had taken up a

kind of rough perimeter around the light and, though twitching and shivering, they held steady, weapons reloaded and ready.

I staggered forward, the true weight of my injuries and exhaustion settling across me, and I was crawling on hands and knees as I moved into the circle of vigilant rifles. I lay there for a few moments, just aware enough to note that the thing must not have been following so closely if it let us regroup like this. Still, that thought wasn't much of a comfort, considering our last encounter.

Could we even slow this thing down if we wanted to, let alone kill it?

I dragged myself closer to the light, some part of me desperate just to draw a kind of strength or comfort from it. I saw Zorn crouching next to the light on one knee, one hand held open in its raw glow. His head was down and I heard murmuring in his soft voice, the steady intonation of a well-known prayer.

"...*geheiligt werde dein Name; dein Reich komme; dein Wille geschehe wie im Himmel so auf Erden...*"

His tone was even, measured, though sometimes his hand shook a little as he took a breath. It was not the last gasped plea of a terrified animal, the kind of thing I've heard before from insurgent and soldier alike. It was the voice of a man drawing strength from a well-rooted source, from a well he knew to be deep and pure.

I was never comfortable around religion, in no small part thanks to my old man's insistence on poisoning everything with condescending critiques, but what I saw in *Feldwebel* Zorn right then made me reconsider my place in the universe, at least a little. I knew there was something down here that would give the Devil a run for his money, so maybe, up there in the light, was someone or something else worth meeting.

I had almost finished catching my breath when Zorn looked up and saw me staring.

In the glow of sunlight I could see a face that was lined and toughened with many years, but still held a youth and liveliness in its eyes despite the webbing of age that framed them. A small, genuine smile was on his thin-lipped face, and I saw an idea spark across his countenance as he looked up to regard the yawning breach in the cave roof.

"I think it is time for you to leave," he said, and then lowered his gaze to meet my eyes.

I sat up a little at first, fearful that somehow I was being blamed for what had happened, and then I realized what was going on.

"Hell. No."

The *Feldwebel*, still smiling, shook his head a little.

"You are unarmed and injured," he said as he rose to his feet and came to stand in front of me, passing beneath the light so that for a second, the short hair across his scalp was a sheen of gold crowning his head. "*Mein* squad will hold until you give all clear, and then we will join you above."

One long hand was offered to me, and with a groan of surrender I took it, leaning hard for support.

"All right," I said, again feeling an irrational but implacable sense of guilt come over me in his presence.

"*Gut gemacht*," Zorn said and then we both looked up.

"How am I going to get up there, exactly?"

"Your children play with the Legos, too, *jah*?" he said, and then swept a hand around us.

As I blinked away the after-image of my escape hatch, I looked around the cavern and saw a number of boxes, crates, and pallets. Some looked organized together in sections but others seemed scattered and cast about, like the former occupants might have been in the middle of a move when things went down. In some places containers were even overturned, and everything from bullets and bandages to baby wipes and barbecue chips lay spilled out in random spaces across the floor.

"It'll work in place of an actual good idea, I guess."

Zorn's smile broadened and he gave a soft little chuckle.

"*Jah*, it will have to! Quickly now; they will watch while we build."

Together we grabbed and hauled some of the sturdiest-looking crates we could manage and formed a base. Some felt like they might contain munitions and when we slid one into place, a metallic clink sounded inside. I tried not to think too hard about what that might be. The higher we went, the lighter the things we had to stack, as it became impossible for us to carry things together. Pickings got slim as we didn't dare go wandering too far from the light and the encircled soldiers, but thankfully there seemed to be just enough within reach.

I kept looking around, certain that at any second the red lights would appear in the dark, staring right at me.

It had called my name, hadn't it? Had I been the only one who heard it? Was this thing really coming after me?

Was this my fault?

Zorn slid the last box into place, and then held a hand down to me.

"Come quickly, I help push you up."

I took the hand and began to clamber up the precarious pile we had built. My guts twisted inside of me, and I felt that same certainty that it was getting closer, perhaps moving in now that it sensed that its quarry--me?--was close to escaping. It was coming and I was pretty sure that when it did, every man in this room would be dead.

"Zorn, I-I ," I stammered, breathing hard now more from fear than exertion. "I don't know how, but I think that thing is coming after me."

"Well, why else would it call you by name?" he snorted and then began to push me toward the next tier of boxes. "*Schnell*, no time!"

"You knew! But I-"

There was a cry from one of the sentinel soldiers and then a burst of rifle fire. Curses and cries of defiance rang through the echoes of futile shots fired.

"I would deny the demon its quarry," Zorn said with another small smile. "We are stubborn like that, *jah*?"

The bloodshed began as I got to the top of the pile with Zorn's help. I stole a glance over my shoulder and watched as two men, wrapped in those same damned crimson fibers, were dragged screaming into the dark where they were silenced with a wet, tearing sound. I snarled and spat at my own impotence as men died for me. It is a feeling no one should ever be comfortable with.

"Go! Go! *Schnell!*"

Zorn was perched precariously next to me, but above us the lip of the crack was within arm's reach.

I stretched up and grabbed the rough rock, not caring as it bit through my ragged gloves into the flesh beneath. I tried to haul myself upward, but the battering and fatigue were lead weights, mocking my strained effort. Strong hands propelled me forward and up, and I managed to get my head and shoulders over the lip. Jagged rocks gouged my arms as I tried to hook my elbows over the edge, curling my whole body to try to worm upward while my legs swung in open air.

There was no cry, but the strong hands were gone and that terminal tearing noise was close enough to set my teeth on edge.

Little by little I pulled myself upward until my belly was pressed to the opening in the cleft stone.

Panting and grunting, I began to raise up to finally pull my legs into the sunlight. Overhead I saw a clear and brilliant sky, lit by a midday sun that shone over the pale face of the mountainside. The stone was hot under my hands, and I looked down to see my arms and hands smoking.

It couldn't be that hot.

Then I saw that the wisps of oily smoke peeling off of hair-thin threads the color of blood. The air was thick with the smell of baked roadkill.

Before I could scream, a frightening strength hauled on the enmeshed fibers across my sleeves and my arms were yanked backward toward the crack in the rock. My head snapped forward as I fell onto my belly so that my head clipped a stone in front of me. A light of numbing brilliance dawned inside my skull and I was gliding feather-like back down into the dark.

Limp as a boned fish, I tumbled down the pile of boxes and landed on the floor, a splintered crate propping me up. Part of me was pretty sure that all of that should have hurt and was worried about the absence of pain, but most of me was just thankful for the break.

There I lay, on the edge of light and dark, when the red lights--hell, the *eyes*--emerged from the coiling black. They looked me up and down, wrinkling at the edges in the way that I am pretty sure is the universal look of satisfied sadists. Closer and closer those eyes crept until the fumes of dark began to unravel and smoke at the utmost edge of the light.

I could just make out the impression of a blunt wedge of

a black head, spurred and barbed with tusklike growths, all dripping with what must have been the blood of the 234th. My skin crawled and through the concussive haze I felt my heart quicken. Four eyes like gory pearls glistened within that forest of jagged points.

"Luciusss," hissed a voice that didn't come from the head but on a charnel exhalation from a long, segmented body that slithered and roiled behind it. "You have been... entertaining."

The words, carried on that putrid scent, left my whole body feeling sick and oily.

"But the game," it breathed, "the game is over... now, we finish this."

The fog in my head was clearing and my hands slowly spread across the floor to the crate at my back. Something cold and hard met my hand.

"What are you?" I managed to choke out, as my fingers closed around a thin, metal cylinder, and one finger felt the prick of its tapered end.

The bloody, black head crept closer and its long, chitinous body seemed to quiver with anticipation.

"I am old," it whispered. "Older than names, older than the petty tongues of men. But enough; I have amused myself enough. You have places to be."

I might have asked where, but as I watched, the quivering intensified, and then its head began to split open, gaping like an open wound. Within were black, ichorous walls of pulsing meat from which sprouted lines of bony fish hook teeth.

"In you go," it purred on soiled air, and then rushed forward.

My muscles screaming in protest and my bones grinding like unoiled gears, I threw myself to the side and swung my arm up the packing nail clutched like an ice pick. Long spurs raked burning trails across my chest and shoulder as the plunging head went past, but I drove that nail into part of its bifurcated throat, twisting and grinding the point deeper as it punched through carapace and into oily flesh.

A hiss, like a thousand eighteen wheelers letting off the brake pressure, exploded from the thing and didn't stop as it began to thrash, carrying a stream of curses, only a few of which I understood.

"Chwistyn'ffug... Rotwhelp... Feoil'lofa... Apeseed... Cac Domhain... Whoreborn!" it shrilled, lifting me bodily as I held onto the nail and dug deeper. "Traitorstone, thrice damned, Traitorstone! Deceit and damnation. Traitorstone!"

It mewled and babbled, but I couldn't understand most of it, some because it was in words that hurt my ears to hear and some because I was being thrown around the room like a slipper in a dog's jaws. Things popped and clicked, and more than once I think I hit stone, though if it was ceiling, floor, or wall I'll never know.

Then suddenly, in the middle of all that, the spinning world became bright, and on instinct alone I let go of the nail and went spinning through the air. One hand didn't clear the edge of the cleft and I screamed as flesh came free and finger bones snapped. The world spun some more, but then I came to rest on rough stones, staring up at that brilliant sky again.

I was out, thrown upward and free by that monster's convulsions.

All I wanted to do was lie on those hot stones and sleep until somebody found me, and at that point I didn't really care who it was so long as they were human. But then the memory of those searing red strands cut through my dozy delusions, and I was scrambling away from the hole. I didn't even look back until I had managed to put a hundred yards of mountainside between myself and that black crack. Nothing ever came out to follow me.

It was over.

Done.

7

Wakes stands staring at me, his cigarette nothing but an ash-capped filter.

"I eventually found my platoon on the mountainside," I say, my voice sounding empty and tired to my own ears. "I wouldn't let them go into the caves, and I wouldn't or couldn't tell them everything that had happened. When we got back and I was being debriefed, I tried my best to explain, but talking about it kept tying my brain up so I couldn't finish and couldn't speak for hours afterwards. By the time I decided to just write it all down, the Germans had contacted my CO with a lot of angry, confused questions. What I wrote is in that report, the closest thing I could do to honoring those men, and it's the truth."

I feel something wet on my cheek, something that isn't the cold sweat that crept over me when I talked about that thing in the cave. I don't know for sure why I am crying, but the tears feel honest, and now as much as ever, honest is what I am, so I don't bother to hide them.

"It's the truth," I repeat, and then take a couple steps away to just stare at the sky.

I stand there staring upward, my heart and brain wrung too dry for thought. After a little bit, I remember seeing Zorn praying and think that maybe I should have learned how to say a prayer before now. I am pretty sure I am in the same spot as he was, and I need something true to help me remember to be strong.

I don't hear Wakes moving up beside me, and so I jump a little when he suddenly speaks at my elbow.

"This might seem impossible," Wakes says as he stares through the fences beside me, "but your story is not the strangest thing I've ever heard, Lieutenant. It may be more truthful than some, but I am afraid you don't corner the market on terrible and weird shit that happens in the midst of a war."

That wasn't what I expected to hear, but it is neither good news nor bad news, so I don't know how to respond.

"It doesn't really make a difference to me what happens next, but I want you to know that I believe you," Wakes says without ever turning to look at me. "I believe every word of it, for a lot of reasons I can't ever tell you. Unfortunately that doesn't mean shit to my superiors, and it won't change the way this is about to go down."

I am too spent for an emotional seesaw, and it all washes over me in one even flood. He is still talking.

"There is going to be another investigator who is going to come, and he won't even talk to you, so don't bother trying. Then there will be a sequestered tribunal, where that investigator is going to say a lot of nothing to three old warhorses who aren't listening. Then those warhorses are going to get instructions from someone you can hope never to meet, and they will stamp whatever he tells them to. At best you are going to spend some time under psychiatric observation and then receive a discharge under ODPMC."

I didn't think I could feel anything or be hurt in any way by whatever he had to say, but damn, I feel that one. Other Designated Physical and Mental Condition. Six years, and the truth gets me that.

"And at worst?" I ask, the words falling out of my mouth before I can catch them. I really don't want to know.

Wakes turns back toward the door leading back inside, his voice falling back into that flat, bored tone that chilled me earlier.

"There is this town in Switzerland where some folks made up a bunch of rules," he says as if this bit is almost by rote. "Some people take those rules very seriously."

And please have your tray tables in the upright and locked position...

"Just like that, huh?" I wonder hollowly.

"Yeah, just like that."

Wakes knocks on the door and then waits as something clicks and clacks on the inside.

"How long do I have before that other investigator shows up?"

Wakes pauses, shrugs, and then calls over his shoulder as the door in front of him opens to Rawls's lovely face.

"A week, maybe less. It is going to go quick when it starts."

A week.

"Good luck, Lieutenant." Wakes says and then steps inside.

Rawls gives me an ugly grin and I decide I would rather look up at that beautiful sky.

———

READ on for sample chapters of War-Born, Book 1 of The Warring Realm Series.

WAR-BORN

THE WARRING REALM, BOOK 1

I had a good home but I left
I had a good home but I left, right, left

— • TOM WAITS, "HELL BROKE LUCE"

"...you *want* me on that wall. You *need* me on that wall."

— • COLONEL NATHAN R. JESSUP, A FEW GOOD MEN

"Have you news of my boy Jack?"
Not this tide.

— • RUDYARD KIPLING, "MY BOY JACK"

PROLOGUE

PAPERWORK

It was a cold autumn night—the kind of cold that reminded the city of Baumholder, Germany, that the oncoming winter was fast approaching, and it had teeth.

The Rock, as Baumholder U.S. Army Garrison Rheinland-Pfalz was sometimes called by its long term residents, looked out over the medieval town like a placid, albeit looming guardian. Baumholder itself was an old soul that had carried on beneath that shadow for more than 50 years, which was the proverbial blink of an eye in its long existence. The base sat on a slope that once held a legion of old trees, the likes of which only central Europe could grow, and the remains of those old woods cradled the housing that stood in neat rows. Beyond a maze of fences and switchback roadways, up a hunched hill that brooded over the tops of the trees, a series of gates led to a wide yard of concrete, punctuated by clusters of steel buildings squatting along a rail line.

A pair of soldiers stood in the gatehouse, sharing contraband snacks from the mess. Occasionally, they glanced at the security monitors displaying their less fortunate fellows moving along alleys created by the barn-like metal warehouses or checking to make sure doors were locked.

If they had been paying more attention, they might have noticed the spindly shadows creeping in at the corners of the screen, sidling up behind the soldiers dutifully patrolling the area.

Instead they bickered over who could do a better impression of their CO.

"No, no, man," one said before he finished gulping down a mouthful of stolen crackers and jam. "You gotta make it more, like, through your nose and shit. Listen, like this-"

He cleared his throat and then sounded off in a pinched, nasally tone.

"Who do you think you are, Private? Hugh Hefner?"

His compatriot snorted and then choked, his upraised hand only partially catching a spray of food.

"Dude!" the imitator barked as he winced away from the salvo of half-chewed food. "How am I going to keep boosting shit from the mess if I end up wearing it every time I'm on watch with you?"

The choker, breathless, gasped out "Sorry!" and then gave a hacking cough as his face began to redden. Lurching past his comrade, he snatched up a cup of lukewarm coffee and took a bitter mouthful to clear his throat.

"Wasn't even that funny," he finally grunted, blinking watery eyes. He happened to glance down at the gallery of monitors, nearly forgotten beneath the pilfered banquet.

"Yeah, sure," his friend drawled, folding his arms across his chest and leaning back against the guard station's tiny window. "Like to hear you do better, you gaggin' asshole."

The other man didn't reply. He was staring, bemused, at the security monitors.

"Come on then, let's hear it."

"Where's Winnfield?" the recovering choker wheezed.

"Man, that sounds nothing like- "

"Shut-up!" he snarled. "I can't find Winnfield!"

He jabbed a slightly shaky finger toward the offending monitor that had misplaced Private Winnfield. They both crowded around the bank of displays, eyes darting to every screen, probing pixelated shadows as realization dawned on them. None of the patrolling sentries were on camera.

The monitors only showed open alleys and bare yards between the metal warehouses. In the corner of one screen displaying the railyard, a pair of boots disappeared— dragged offscreen under the loading platform. After that, there was not a single sign of movement. There were no watchmen to watch, and stillness ruled every screen.

The pair exchanged nervous looks, jaws gaping open, no sound coming out. Before they found their voices, their bodies were already moving—reacting with the efficiency born of training's automation. Unsteady hands reached, digits were punched in with numb fingers, and then many things happened at once.

The soldiers found their world engulfed in darkness a second before the alarm, which had only just begun to warm to its song, was cut short. One of them heard a superior officer demanding to know why he was being bothered this late at night, and then the line went dead.

"Oh shit," one managed to breathe into the inky dark before a short set of squeals lost in a butchershop symphony of thunks and ripping sounds filled the guard station.

The dark would not clear inside the guard house for some minutes, but outside in the pools of lamplight, a quartet of crouched figures prowled among the warehouses.

Scuttling with a spider's graceless agility, they moved

quickly between the alleyways until they joined more dark creatures of similar proportions. In all, there were more than a dozen of them, all wrapped in layers of night-dark clothing that seemed to cover every inch of flesh except for eyes which reflected dark amber in stray lamplight. Even if they had stood upright, not one of them would have been even five feet in height.

"Big lads make li'l screams," one of them tittered to a fellow beside him, his voice like shattered glass in a dumpster. "I likes it when they scream louds."

The last statement drew chuckles from several of the surrounding figures—each laugh a jagged, nervous sound.

One figure whirled about and snapped back at the jokester with a peculiar sharpness of tone that was unique to matrons of most species.

"Shut yer gobdawin' hole, Fitch, or I'll make yer scream plenty loud when we get back."

"Sorry, Ma Grimple."

Fitch hunkered low, and the rest fell into subdued silence as they all moved to fall in behind Ma Grimple who was leading them to an open maintenance shed. The light above its gaping bay door was shattered; the darkness within was absolute. The black-shadowed congregation hunkered in front of the portal, squatting on their haunches as their leader shuffled a few steps forward and then reached inside her ragged vest.

Out came a thin, silver whistle in the shape of a bird's skull on a brass chain. Ma Grimple raised it up to her lips, and blew three short, clear notes.

The darkness rippled, and then, with one fluid step rolling into the next, a towering man sauntered out of the bay door, the crown of his head nearly scraping the lintel as he passed. Even in the dim twilight cast by the lamps of the warehouses on either side, the man's body glistened with the metallic solidity of burnished bronze, and the long-tailed vest he wore open across his chest glistened like woven onyx.

"Is everything in order, then?" he asked in a voice that was resounding and strong as a war trumpet in its timbre, if not in volume.

All the dark figures winced at the sudden sound.

"The guards be all dead, and none should come te bovver 'til yer done, Lord Nadder," Ma Grimple reported with a deferential bow that did not touch her sharp tone.

"Satisfactory, I suppose," the bronze man said with a slight frown at Grimple's obvious distaste. "Now just make sure you and your... family stay clear of the work teams and keep watch. It would be most unfortunate if your warren had to make recompense for anything lost to us."

Ma Grimple bristled, but kept her head bent low. "The Gloaming Court already be payin'. No need for threats an' the like."

"In my experience with your ilk, it is worthwhile to provide multiple incentives," he sniffed archly and gave a dismissive flap of his hand. "Scurry along now."

The smaller figures, many whispering nasty curses, darted along predetermined routes and slither-crawled up the sides of warehouses, taking up crouched positions upon corners and peaks. They watched as the burnished Lord Nadder strode forward to inspect the warehouse contents which lay open to the cold autumn night.

With bare fingers he pried open crate tops and peeled away plastic sheeting, revealing rifles, grenades, ammo boxes, and mortar shells. Covetously, his hands lingered over barrel and pin, and he seemed to breathe in the munitions' scent in heavy wafts. Slowly he dragged his attention from the plunder and beckoned toward the open bay door. There came the rumble of heavy, bestial grunts, and then the clink of chains as horns breached the pooling shadows.

It took US Army Captain Gerome Roux five minutes sitting in his office staring at his computer to decide to call the arms depot back.

After three failed attempts to raise the guard station, a stream of profanity was flowing freely from his mouth, and an uneasy sensation was settling into his belly. He closed the video chat without bidding adieu to the local woman that did not share his last name, and his mind went through all the terrible possibilities. Standing in front of his computer, one hand worked to mask his previous endeavors while the other thumbed across his phone contacts.

He raised the phone to his ear as his clean-up on the browsing history was finished.

He didn't even wait for the voice on the other end to finish its sluggish salutation before he was snarling into the phone.

"Rawls, shut the hell up and listen to me," he hissed, moving to the door of his office. "Get First Sergeant Abse's ass up and over to the depot with as many as he can."

There was silence for a second too long, and Captain Roux held the phone directly under his mouth.

"Rawls, give me some fucking confirmation, and then get your ass moving!"

Rawls muttered a brief "Yes, sir," and the call ended.

Roux was moving down the darkened corridors, desks and cubicles blurring past as he hustled into action. The squirmy feeling in his guts wouldn't go away, and when he burst through the garrison administrative office front door, the autumn air made him shiver and break out in goosebumps. He'd left his coat in his office, but for the moment he didn't care. He stared across the base up toward the hillock where the depot stood. Part of him knew it was stupid to expect to see anything, but in the back of his mind he kept repeating a mantra: "Don't explode. Don't explode. Don't explode."

When he finally met with Abse on that hilltop and learned of the empty warehouses and strange tracks which led to a single maintenance shed, he was still thankful for a lack of fireworks. But by noon the next day, he would find himself sitting in his office with a singularly unpleasant man called Officer Wakes, and Captain Gerome Roux would wish that the powers of the universe had not listened and just blown the whole thing to hell.

At least the paperwork for that would have been straightforward.

1

REFLECTIONS

I stood in front of the Eneukauf Baumholder, hands in my pockets, and watched people go about their business as the light of the sun faded.

The old woman shuffling out of the grocery with a single bag clutched to her chest; the young man jabbering on his phone and laughing as he toted a case of beer; a mother of three juggling this week's rations while drilling her offspring to parade march to the family car.

Human beings going about the necessary but commonplace parts of life, in a world where things made sense and everything operated in a civilized fashion, with obvious and deliberate rules.

Comfortable lies.

The anesthetizing effect of civilian facades had been clear to me by the time I had come back from my first tour of duty, so this was nothing new. But now more than ever the hollowness of it seemed so evident. Maybe it was because I was here in Germany rather than back home in the States, but here in Baumholder, the American and German way of life rub such close shoulders together, it wasn't far off. Here, as much as anywhere else in the civilized world, people carried out their merry lives in a kind of perpetual, self-restoring fog of comfortable assurance.

You can almost hear the quaint, little theme song: We eat our fill. We live in peace. And we sleep in soft beds of assurance that it will always be so. Probably because we deserve it.

I knew it wasn't intentional, and unlike some vets coming back from what is aptly called The Shit, I didn't resent them for it. After all, wasn't that what I fought for? Doing violence on behalf of others so that they can sleep sound and happy.

My eyes slid out of focus on the people within the market, and I saw my own reflection in the glass storefront. I was the absolute picture of the lonely, burnt-out war vet—a man standing under a streetlight in stolen civilian clothes. To go along with the oversized sweatshirt and loose fitting jeans, I might even have start growing a beard to give it some proper shades of homelessness.

Homeless. Was that what I was now? Maybe.

I had slipped off base, shaking my relentless MP shadow, and managed to get a ride with a delivery man into town. The guy had been chatty enough, spoke good English, and I had a sneaking suspicion he had helped more than one soldier in his day, letting them ride along for an AWOL walk around town.

"I almost say no," he confessed once I hopped in. "You looking like one of those refugees from Morocco or something."

"Huh," I grunted, unsure if he was referring to my skin color or my clothing.

"Lucky I let you talk, eh?" he said cheerily. "You talk like one of the boys on the base, not some North African. You even talk as well as the white boys."

"Lucky for me," I muttered.

He went on to say most of the "boys" he helped were just rambunctious kids looking for fun, and he was glad to let them spend their money and time in town. The guy was so helpful he even told me when his route would take him back by the base so I could bum another ride.

He told me to enjoy myself and drink a "Helles" for him after dropping me off. I thanked him and even managed a smile as his van trundled off.

The sun was already going down when I began my escape, and with night setting in, the temperature had been dropping sharply. I moved more to keep warm rather than because I had an actual plan for where I was going. I ended up meandering down quietly busy streets, the likes of which you would never believe until you'd been to a German city. I was just one among thousands who would happily mind their own business, not necessarily because they were a cold people, but because they were mostly content in their own little lives. It was the perfect place to be left to your thoughts and meander.

So I did for several hours. I walked and tried to think. It wasn't much good, but I had plenty of opportunity as I roamed the modern roadways interspersed with the old, narrow streets that had been laid before the U.S. was a twinkle in some uppity colonial's eyes.

I thought about my life, or what was left of it, and how I might drag it out a little longer. Officer Wakes had been clear. After my encounter in the caves of Afghanistan, the best I could hope for was to be sent to a mental hospital stateside after being served an ODPMC. Other Designated Physical and Mental Condition. I rolled each of those words over and over in my mind, but no matter which direction I turned them, they all fit together to mean six years killing for Uncle Sam only to be shat out like a dirty MRE. I guess that's what you do with vets who come home talking about monsters—especially monsters responsible for murdering almost a dozen German soldiers and who knows how many insurgents.

For nearly thirty minutes I mulled and muttered over this pitiful, unfair fate. I probably spent so long brooding over it because the only alternative was so much worse.

If I wasn't going to be labeled certifiable, I was going to be tried for war crimes and found guilty of killing a squad of allied soldiers. I'd rot in a cell for a little while before being executed as a traitor and a monster, and all that was assuming that some shadowy branch of my government didn't swoop in and drag me away. Then I might be wishing that I *had* been executed.

And all this because I had the decency to tell the truth about how some brave men had died. Truth only sets you free when people want to hear it, and the truth is never more unwelcome than when it dares to contradict what people believe. After all, how do you sleep so soundly when you know that there are honest-to-God monsters in this world? I know I hadn't for the better part of six months. How many times can you wake up screaming, searching the dark corners for four red eyes, before sleep just doesn't seem worth it? For me, it was somewhere around month three or four.

I dug my hands into my pockets and felt the wad of cash I had scrounged. Quite a few fellas back at base would be pissed when they found out I had ransacked their foot-lockers and closets for every cent I could get a hold of, but they would get over it. I was a man looking for a last meal before the axe fell, and even if they wouldn't have given it willingly, it wasn't going to kill them.

I walked into the grocery and instantly felt a few eyes narrow in my direction.

My ride may have been a jolly friend of American soldiers, but I knew not every citizen of Baumholder felt that way. A few years ago, some enlisted boys had torn through the town in one drunken, vandalizing night, and I had heard there were still a few places that hadn't quite recovered. And even though I wore a slovenly disguise, these people had learned to spot a New World GI whether he was wearing BDUs or lederhosen.

One of the clerks gave me a glassy smile but never stopped watching me, even after I had walked by and moved toward the liquor aisle, hiking up my jeans as I shuffled along.

I'd never been a real big drinker, except for a few occasions before I dropped out of my first round of college, but vodka had always been a favorite so I snatched up a bottle with a label that looked Russian—you know, for authenticity. I moved through the store, aware of the looks I was getting, but not really caring as I grabbed some chips, then smoked sausage, and then some candy. On my way back through the store, I thought "why not" and picked up a second bottle of unpronounceable vodka.

Arms full, I went to the checkout clerk—a pretty young girl who stared at me with a mix of pity and disgust. The latter became more evident as she had to wait for me to pick through the wad of bills to find the necessary euros to cover the purchase.

I gave her a smile as I put the last note in her hand, and she pulled away wearing an expression like she'd sucked on a lemon.

I scooped up my bag of junk food and liquor, and headed out the door. I managed a half dozen steps or so, and then I felt every hair on the back of my neck stand at attention.

Something was wrong, and not like I forgot to get my change sort of wrong. You spend enough time in a place full of people who want to kill you, and you develop a knack for sniffing out trouble—even on a subconscious level. It wasn't foolproof. Sometimes the wind was just the wind after all, but you were a walking dead man if you didn't check that shit out every time.

My eyes searched well-lit streets and swept over a rank of decorative trees catty-corner from the grocery. Just outside a McDonalds across the street, I saw two men watching me. Our eyes met for a brief moment, and they began to move forward with quick, long strides. I felt my pulse quicken to that sharp tempo it gets right before things go dynamically sideways. One part thrill, one part terror, two parts insanity. My body knew what to do even as my brain wailed about the unfairness of it all.

I turned and began to jog along the side of the grocery store, wondering how MPs had found me so quickly. But if they were Military Police, they would have been with the local authorities. My stomach sank into my boots as I rounded the corner of the building, remembering all the things Wakes had offhandedly said about men with black bags.

I wasn't going to the stockade if they caught me. I was going away. Forever.

A small wooded patch sat behind the grocery store— probably less than four acres ringed by other commercial buildings.

I looked behind me and saw that the two guys had

almost made it across the street. They had started to jog. I didn't need to see the bulges at their sides to know they are armed.

I dropped the bag of food and shucked the brown sacks off the liquor, taking one in each hand.

Without another backward glance, I took a running leap and plunged into the timber.

2

PROMISES

Specialists Hawkes and Arn rounded the corner of the grocery to find that their quarry was already racing through the timbered parcel behind the store.

They both cursed, drew their pistols, and quickened their pace, trying to close the distance between themselves and the escaping man. They had been chasing down deserters together long enough to have developed a hatred for all the patches of brush and forest which peppered the town of Baumholder. It made this kind of work a bitch with heels, for certain.

Their target's trail was not hard to follow. In fact, he seemed to be making no attempt to hide his tracks at all. He must have thought speed alone would buy him some time, but he was a man on foot with no friendly resources in the area. He was just going to be out of breath when they eventually brought him down.

The two hunters stalked beneath the trees at a measured clip, their pistols held down and parallel to their right legs, their left hands warding off wayward branches here or there. The deeper they went, the farther they were from the streetlights, and they eventually had to draw flashlights to keep up their pursuit. The trail looked to be cutting a north-western route through the timber, which would put the target at the back of an Esso gas station.

"Think he might try to steal a car?" Arn asked, spying the haze of the gas station lights just at the top of a forested rise.

"Would be pretty ballsy," Hawkes huffed, He swept his flashlight left and saw nothing, but then swept back right, thinking he had heard a branch snapping in the dark. Nothing but the trees and the deepening gloom between their trunks. His eyes and ears strained at the mocking void. "Shit, I hate Baumholder and all its fucking trees!"

Arn advanced up the hill a little more and then stopped to gesture up at the gas station.

"If he does, this could get complicated quick."

Hawkes turned back to his left, pistol and flashlight tracking together through trunks. Nothing.

"Fine, get Fischer on the horn, and have the Kraut cops on alert," Hawkes snarled, never taking his eyes off the offending woods. He was sure he had heard something, even if the trail led up the hill.

"Fischer, we need you to put out the word for a runner," Arn began as he crept a few more steps up the hill, eyes hoping to see some silhouette cresting the slope. "I'm sending you his info now. No, no. This one goes under special considerations."

Hawkes stood rooted to his spot, pistol and flashlight probing the dark between tree trunks. It would be just like the bastard to double back and slip around them as they humped up that hill. He wasn't going to be made a fool of by some lying, deserting pussnut, no sir.

Out of the dark, something flew down the hill, spinning

and glittering in Hawkes' flashlight beam as it passed. He fired twice, shots ringing through the trees and drawing Arn's attention away from the gas station in the distance.

In the time it took Arn to look back, a man-shaped shadow detached itself from a tree just ahead and swung a bludgeon across the side of Arn's head. He staggered a step, and might have recovered had two more blows not bounced off his skull with the clunk of heavy glass. Specialist Arn collapsed to the ground in a boneless heap, and his pistol was in the hands of his attacker before Hawkes realized what had happened.

Hawkes spun around in time to catch two rounds in the chest. His vest took the brunt of it, but the sharp impact knocked the wind out of him. He staggered back a little, dazed. Three more shots hammered his chest and belly before he could coordinate the link from his brain to his trigger finger. By then, breathing was hard enough without trying to raise his arms to fire, and he tasted blood in the back of his throat with each ragged exhalation.

"Beretta's got a long first pull, remember," the shadow said, advancing on the wheezing hunter. "That's probably why you missed the bottle."

Hawkes tried to curse but only managed a pained cough.

"Guarantee you won't miss the second one, though," the shadow said, stepping into the light. He sauntered over to Hawkes and chopped the vodka bottle down on Hawkes' skull. Once, twice, three times.

A crack sprang up from the base of the bottle on the third blow, the sharp smell of alcohol mixing with the coppery tang of blood smeared on the glass.

The shadow collected Arn's pistol and some spare clips, and then checked the dropped phone, cursing at what he saw on the stream of past and incoming texts.

It seemed he had gotten the information to Wacht-meister Fischer of the Baumholder Stadtpolizei, and they were now on the look out for one Lieutenant Lucius "Luce" Bollham.

Fischer's officers moved quickly to their vehicles or assigned beats, and all of them wore some version of the same anxious look. The information had been sparse, but they knew an American soldier was abroad in their town, and even his gung-ho compatriots considered him armed and dangerous. A few drunken GIs had done enough damage with nothing but a give 'em hell attitude; what could one who was weaponized and hostile do?

The streets became more and more empty as people retreated from the cold, feeling a growing sense of unease as they noticed local law enforcement hustling about with suspicious vigor.

Shop owners locked up their establishments with a little more thoroughness, hoping the events of the past would not be repeated.

Amid the gathering of shadows and fears, a patch of black beneath the exposed roots of an old ash tree over-looking Baumholder began to seethe and boil.

Hardy woodland birds gave shrill warnings as they took flight while their earthbound neighbors chattered and chuffed as they retreated from the shivering tree. Whether it was a hatred for the unaccustomed intrusion or some ancient genetic memory from a time before two legs was the scourge of the wood, all living things, great and small, fled.

Within moments, the ground itself seemed to rebel against whatever was stirring in the bowels of the ash. The earth rippled and slid away in pebbly runnels, exposing more roots and the living dark which roiled between them.

Suddenly the tenebrous lesion swelled against the encasing roots, and centuries old moorings snapped in a series of sharp pops. The old ash, which had stood sentinel over Baumholder for more than 200 years, toppled backwards with a groaning crash. From the ruined tree, a long, segmented figure burst forth, its jagged, tusked head stabbing at the bare sky before swinging down to regard the human settlement below.

A shudder of what might have been revulsion ran along its coiling body, chitinous plates scraping against each other, as it beheld the feeble works of man. It spat contemptuously, and a gobbet of dark earth and phlegm landed, hissing upon the ground.

The Fiend drew a thin breath, tasting the air, and whispered to the wind.

"Luciusssss... "

For a few beats of its three hearts, nothing happened, but the wind remembered the old pacts and ancient promises between it and this creature's kith and kin. Sour and sluggish as an old gambler settling an overdue debt, the wind drew up the air of Baumholder and rolled it across the twitching face of the monster.

Among the many disagreeable smells of the dirt-roaming apes, the Fiend found the scent he had tasted beneath the White Mountains months ago. It had unfinished business with this creature and promises to keep.

Four red eyes turned toward Baumholder as the rest of its body seethed and piled out of the earth.

"Luciusssss... "

3

KEPT

I was so screwed.

There were police everywhere, and I had no idea why I was even running. I ran at first because people were chasing me, and it seemed like the thing to do. But now, as I flattened myself against the side of a building and tried not to breathe too loud, I wondered about the choices I'd made.

I was wearing stolen clothing. In my pockets, I had some money, a couple Berettas, three spare clips, and a phone—all of which I also stole—and I'd battered two American operatives into unconsciousness.

I held my breath as a Stadtpolizei vehicle passed by, wondering whether or not I killed either of those men in the woods. I think they were both breathing when I left, but I was in a hurry, and I hadn't been gentle. There was a good chance one or both had blood on the brain, and if left there long, they would be as dead as if I'd put a bullet in their heads.

Part of me was bothered by that possibility because, after all, they were soldiers like me, and they were probably just following orders, but another part of me refused to give two shits about their welfare. They knew the risks when they took the dime, that part of me said. I detached myself from the wall and moved deeper into the medieval part of Baumholder.

The other part of me answered back that, dime or no, you never really know the risks until you are there. After everything I'd been through, couldn't I at least admit that? I never imagined the risks included half the things I had to do in Afghanistan, and that was all before what happened in those caves with that...thing. You can't understand it until you're there, and by then, well it's just too damn late.

The narrow streets were not quite empty. I ducked past a few knots of people here and there, taking roads and side streets at random, trying to buy time to get my head on straight.

What was I going to do? Best I could figure, I had three options: give up, run, or hide.

If I ran, I would need a vehicle and more money, and all that meant stealing more, which posed problems. First of all, stealing more stuff increased the risk of being caught, and it would give my pursuers cause to expand and intensify their search efforts. Second, cavalier as I'd been about taking money from the soldiers on base, I knew it was wrong, and the thought of stealing from innocent civilians ate at me. If one of them tried to stop me, what would I do then? And even if all that worked out, where was I going to go? I had no identification, and therefore no way to get back on U.S. soil.

I knew now that giving up meant a black bag over my head and all the unpleasant things Wakes had talked about so blithely, so that was out. I had no intention of revisiting the world of enhanced interrogation, and certainly not from the other side of things.

So that left hiding.

Maybe, if I found a spot in Baumholder and hunkered down for a couple weeks, the heat would die down, and I could come up with a real plan for the steaming pile that was left of my life.

I looked around the buildings, which seemed to lean in over the streets, and saw the gallingly cheery signs of lights and life within each window I passed. Behind thin sheets of glass, in warmth and often the company of their fellow creatures, people laughed and lived, ate and drank. The scenes of comfort and light were cruel reminders to me as I moved with greater and greater speed from one street to the next. None of this would be mine, ever again.

I was ready to scream with mounting frustration when I turned down a sidestreet and then raced up a particularly wide alleyway, emerging onto yet another street. This one was far less lively than previous thoroughfares, however, with few streetlamps to punctuate the dark and not a single human presence to enliven the rows of close set shops and buildings.

It was my first glimmer of hope, however slim, and, with a few darting glances up and down the pavement, I stepped out to examine my prospects.

Many seemed to be old shops and businesses—the kind of structures that have been renewed and refurbished umpteen times since the Renaissance. While thankfully devoid of people now, they weren't going to do me much good come morning. Almost all of them showed signs of recent use. As I passed one after the other, I felt the frustration building again, but I was beginning to tire and I wondered how long before I just collapsed in surrender.

Did I really think I could just go on the run, like some secret agent badass?

My self-defeating musings were cut short as I rounded the curve of the road and spied something promising.

From the dancing pigs emblazoned on one panelled wall and the chubby children chasing them on another, I guessed that it might have been a butcher shop once. Yeah...Germans. Go figure.

It was uniquely dingy compared to the clean and cheery facades on either side of it. I got closer and saw that a peeling advertisement on the inside of a cloudy window— for something called knackwurst—was for nearly five years ago. It was worth a shot.

The front door was padlocked, and I didn't feel like trying to batter it off. There was an alley alongside the building that led past a loading dock behind the storefront, though. The bay door was locked as well, but beside it was a wide, shuttered window. With a little finagling, I got the shutter open and then the window.

I hopped up and made a less than dignified, wriggling entrance into the shop, before quickly drawing the shutters closed and re-latching the window. I turned around to take in the interior of my new hideout and felt the air rush out of my lungs.

Plastic sheeting hung like great curtains, and many still bore rusty stains which streaked down and between the folds.

Something cracked inside my head without a sound.

Like looking through bad 3D glasses—as if superimposed on top of reality—I saw the plastic curtains beneath the White Mountains and smelled the tang of freshly-spilt blood on the stale air. I felt the tiles of the butcher shop floor beneath me as I dropped to my knees, but I was still in those caves—still in the dark with that thing.

I grabbed for a flashlight I didn't have on a harness I wasn't wearing. I found one of the Berettas, and in that instant, it was close enough. Mechanical instincts chambered a round, and then I swept the barrel left and right in my shaking hands, wanting to run, to shoot, and to cry, but knowing that none of that would help me.

I took several long breaths and reminded myself that it wasn't real—that I was in Germany, on the run for my life—and I didn't have time to lose it now. My finger slid on and off the trigger nine times as my rational mind screamed for me to lower the gun before I ruined the one chance I had to hide. I rose from the floor, and, inch by inch, through sheer force of will, I lowered the pistol to my side.

"This is Baumholder," I whispered, the sound of my voice strange in my ears, tight and jagged. "I am in Germany. Not there. *Not* there... "

I don't know why, but that reminder was the most comforting thing to hear, so I just kept saying it. I watched the secondary image of the tunnels in Afghanistan melt and run down the butchershop curtains, disappearing like runoff in a tub.

I let out one long breath, and then it was over.

I was in Baumholder, Germany, in an abandoned business, hiding from the law. My whole life had gone up in smoke, but I felt loads better.

Stowing the pistol, I took stock of my situation.

No electricity and no water seemed to be running to the abandoned building, but as luck would have it, I found a stash of old tins of corn beef, cheap sausages, and other high sodium, high fat kinds of stuff that can keep you going for a good while if you pace yourself. Hell, they were just like MREs really. They just tasted a little better. I could sort out the lack of water tomorrow, but for tonight, everything seemed secure enough—at least on the ground floor. The door to the upstairs, labeled Bürotür, was locked, but judging from the dust on the floor and counters, no one had been up there for a long time. I decided to save that for tomorrow, too.

I checked every door to make sure the place was locked down tight. It was a bit more work to secure the window I had come in, but I found a splintery coat hanger in a break room and used a broken spur of that to jam the window shut. Anyone coming in here would have to make a lot of noise to do it.

That done, I thought about getting some sleep. My sleep had been spotty for some time, but with all the excitement, I suspected it wouldn't be too hard tonight. Besides, I needed to be well-rested if I was going to figure out what to do about water tomorrow.

As you can imagine, butcher shops are not known for having plenty of comfortable spots to lie down in, but I'd slept rough on the rocky hills of Afghanistan, so this was nothing. Sliding under a bare metal table, I curled up with one arm under my head.

One by one I told the host anxieties, aches, and other annoyances to shut up, as I settled in, breathing slow and steady.

Tomorrow would be better. Hell, it had to be.

At least the sweatshirt I'd taken was soft. My thoughts did a sideways shuffle into a thankful, empty sleep.

"Luciusssss."

There weren't supposed to be dreams. I was too tired. Why was I listening to some echoing murmurs from a floor drain?

"Luciusssss."

Why? Why couldn't I just rest?

"Luciusssss."

The third time finally penetrated the fatigue and denial, and my head whipped up sharp.

"No," I whimpered as I watched red filaments crawling up through the floor drain—ghostly strings of blood creeping across the floor.

"Luciusssss."

It sounded closer.

"No," I said again, my voice higher and tighter. I skittered back and away from the drain until my butt struck the cabinets behind me.

This couldn't be happening. I was in Baumholder, Germany. Not there—not with that thing.

"Not there," I whispered as my chest tightened. "Not there. Not there."

The incantation wasn't working. The drain was nearly overflowing with crimson silk. There was a sharp snap, and the aluminum crumpled. A second later the surrounding tile splintered.

"Not there," I sobbed, both pistols suddenly in my hands. Being discovered didn't seem so important right then.

"Luciusssss."

This time I could smell the roadkill breath as more tile broke away and a few dark points jutted up from the spreading nest of red. Like some kind of obscene birth, that tusked, spiny head emerged, little by little into the room. Half a heartbeat later four red eyes blinked open among the tusks, crinkling up with pleasure.

"Luciusssss."

I heard gunfire, one shot after another in rapid succession, and it took me second to realize I was the one pulling the triggers.

"Notthere, Notthere, NOTTHERE!"

I screamed over and over, but with crushing certainty, I knew it wouldn't matter. Like a nightmare, the bullets struck the monster without effect, falling squashed to the floor without leaving a single mark.

Too soon the pistols were clicking empty, and somehow it had gotten more of itself out of the hole than I had realized. Its shelled coils undulated on either side of me, bleeding raw shadow, closing me in with climbing walls of black. I could have plunged through the thickening darkness, but it wouldn't have done me any good. It was fast, and darkness was no impediment for it. There was nothing to do.

I was dead.

The pistols slid from my hands. I wanted to cry and scream, but that was just too much work right then. The desperate energy and adrenaline evaporated, and I was done. The end was heavy, and I was tired.

"I hoped I would never see you again," I sighed as my head rocked back to rest against the cabinets. They were cold.

"Hope," it hissed wetly, scoffing. "Hope is the first step to disappointment."

I laughed a little at that. A philosophical monster.

"Well I don't have any nails or any other metal to stick you with," I confessed, my hands spread in defeat. "Manage to find a butcher shop and there isn't even a damn meathook."

"I know," it growled venomously. "I would not have come otherwise."

For a second it almost sounded petulant, but I was past caring.

By now I was enclosed on all sides by darkness, trapped on an island of twilight creeping in from street-lit windows. All I could see was the triangular head, covered in a nest of stabbing points around its four eyes.

"You've caused me no small humiliation, and I would wish you the agony of hosting my spawn, but I have promises to keep."

It said the last words in a liquid snarl, and my eyes watered from the smell.

"Get on with it then," I shrugged, head sinking forward onto my chest. "Get it over with."

"Oh, Luciusss," it purred, "It is far from over."

Its head began to quiver and split. I had seen this before, but it was just as disgustingly fascinating to watch as before. Quivering, wet sounds of splitting shell and flesh, another gush of stink. Then its head bifurcated into a gaping pit lined with bony hooks and slimy, black meat.

"Time to go."

My world was swallowed up in crushing darkness and the smell of carrion.

4

DELIVERY

Bryth stopped pacing the banks of Purllaeth and sought to gather her thoughts.

He should be here any minute.

Long fingers worked together into knots of nervous energy and unraveled to run over the fall of her orb-silk dress and then her long, silver hair. She would have preferred to greet the Aspirant in the garb of her father— the raiment of war she was accustomed to—but the Queen had forbidden it. Bryth protested respectfully at first, but then the Queen patiently explained. The Fiend's passage for the Aspirant would not be gentle, and if the Aspirant emerged to find a warrior arrayed for battle, he might well engage in violence before words of peace could be spoken. If Bryth were to serve the Gloaming Court, she must be both warrior and diplomat, harridan and princess, bound up within a single form.

So she had gone to the ladies of the Court, they had outfitted her in their finest, and she had strode down the Grand Stairs of Duanon's docks. There she boarded the

Queen's own pleasure barge under the chanted blessings of the entire Gloaming Court.

Now the elegant, broad-framed craft rested near the shore with two armed, but unarmoured knights of the Court at its rail. The elder of the two Tuatha bodyguards caught her nervous glance and gave her a smile and a wink. She returned her most gracious smile, hoping this would be good practice for when the Aspirant came.

She remembered the encouragement of the Queen when she had been about to embark.

"I would not have chosen you if I did not know you would succeed. You carry the hopes of the entire Court, my dear, but for my part you have something stronger and more certain than just hope. You, Bryth Lighttread, child of my heart—you have my trust. And I know you will not fail us."

With that, she had been sent out to win the man who would save her people, and it was a salvation that needed to be quick in coming. The Gythraul legions would not stay in their fortresses much longer, and since the fall of Paladin Toulouse Valoise, the Twilit Kingdom would not be capable of holding back their eventual advance. The Gloaming Court, for all their magical power, would be no match for the regimented waves of murderous Gythraul. And with the Paladin no longer uniting the Lords of Tirallanol, the hosts of the kingdom were scattered.

A new Paladin was needed, and the Aspirant would only take that mantle if she could convince him to do so.

Bryth looked up and measured the progress of Arianog, the silvery orb that illuminated the days here in Eileait, or Other-Realm, and with a shivering flutter, she realized the arrival of the Fiend was eminent.

Turning sharply on her heel, she walked from the

water's edge and down the trail that wound between the brilliantly hued fungal stalks of the Forlorn Forest.

Though the fungal towers had a kind of gaudy beauty, all in pulsing shades of emerald, azure, and fuchsia, this would not have been where Bryth would have chosen to meet the savior of her people and kingdom. For one, it was far too close to the waste waters that flowed from Duanon, the capital city of the Twilit Kingdom, and even the sweet spice of the fungal stalks could not completely mask the smell. Second, the Hombaths who dwelt in colonies on the stalks were notorious gossips and busybodies, and she hardly needed an audience when she first met the Aspirant. Third and finally, there was always the risk of meeting the various breeds of Goblin kind that wandered in from the waste water communities. For a Draoi'cogaidh, or battle-magus, like herself, they were no real threat, but the distraction was one she could ill afford.

But this was where the Fiend had chosen, and for some inscrutable reason, the wicked Darkling remained adamant that it be here.

Bryth came to a tight, circular glade where stood, at its center, a low-walled, stone well. All around her, the Hombaths murmured, and here and there, she saw small, jewel-bright eyes watching her from beneath mushroom caps clinging to the trunks of the fungal stalks.

"It had better be here soon," she pouted, feeling exposed and scrutinized as she waited at the mouth of the glade.

She knew it was just anxiety that drove her to distraction, her feet yearning to pace. But it would not do to present herself to the Aspirant looking so unsettled so she finally calmed herself to wait.

Her patience was rewarded after a few moments in the form of a wet, sucking sound from the well.

The Hombaths muttered excitedly, their toadstool tops rocking about as they gossiped. Another angry sound echoed up from the bowels of the stony portal, and they took turns shushing each other before finally falling silent. Bryth took a few steps forward and waited. She could feel something coming, feel it pressing against the tangled skein between the worlds.

Violently, like fabric being torn, Bryth felt the layers give way, and a rush of brackish water and black mud burst out from the well mouth. Amidst the spray was the dark, sinuous form of the Fiend, temporarily without its shadowy covering. Almost instantly, myrk began to seep from its ridged carapace, restoring its black, festering aura. Its trunk was distended and veiny, and its charcoal colored flesh stretched grotesquely between segmented plates. Something of considerable size had been forced down its gullet.

Without ceremony, the Fiend flopped its bulk over the lip of the well and slid its sinuous form onto the ground. Its usual, unsettling liquidity was gone, and its jagged head hung low to the earth.

The head parted in its revolting fashion, and the whole body began to shudder and heave. Even though Bryth knew what he was doing and marveled at the incredible power necessary to safely transport a mortal to the Other-Realm, she could not hide the disgust on her face.

The lumpen mass within the Fiend began to move up its body. A jet of bloody bile shot from its gaping mouth. Then a head, followed by shoulders, and finally, an entire man was vomited upon the grassy floor of the glade. The man, tall and likely considered strongly-built by members of his own race, flopped limply to his side. His body twitched a little and then spasmed into a fit of convulsions. Eventually, they subsided, the man heaving up a final throat-full of what looked like more bloody bile. He rolled onto his back, chest rising and falling with steady, labored breaths.

The Aspirant had survived passage to Other-Realm.

Bryth strode forward, then stopped when she saw the ragged punctures along the Aspirant's arms, chest, and neck. Outrage sparked, hot and white inside of her, and she felt the thrum of her battle magic ready to be unleashed.

"He was to be brought to us unharmed!" Bryth snarled, fierce as any wildcat.

The Fiend, its head joined together once more but still dripping ichorous effluence, regarded her with weary, hateful eyes.

"It was ... difficult," it breathed heavily. "Something powerful anchored the ape to his world. It nearly killed us both to bring him through. I had to keep a tight grip on him."

Bryth stepped closer and saw that the wounds, while deep enough to put a finger in, were not bleeding, and seemed to be shrinking before her eyes.

"You have worked healing spells over him?" Bryth asked, surprised that such a creature would even know healing magics.

"I had a promise to keep," it replied, and it turned its long body toward the fungal stalks. "It is finished."

"Yes," Bryth said, not even looking up from the Aspirant as she spoke, afraid he would stop breathing if she did. "Your service is completed, and your privileges to dwell and feed beneath Duanon are restored."

The Fiend did not respond to her. It slithered slowly away into the Forlorn Forest.

"Thank you," Bryth called after the Darkling, certain the nicety was lost on the creature.

As Bryth watched, the healing spell finished its work,

and though fresh scars whitened his dark skin, the Aspirant seemed stable—healthy even. His clothes were torn and still soaked with the bile of the Fiend, but even they seemed to be drying quickly as Arianog's light drew the filth out in faint wisps of smoke.

So absorbed was she in assessing the state of the Aspirant that Bryth did not notice the intruder until he was rushing toward her in a gibbering frenzy.

5

RABBIT

I didn't want to wake up, but there was a buzzing, gravelly sound that just wouldn't stop.

Like a hacksaw gouging rock, it kept up, and even all the horror that had pitched me into unconsciousness couldn't keep me from needing to shut that sound up. Hard.

I came to by degrees, my senses returning quicker than any muscular control. So as I lay on my back, unable to open eyes, I eventually recognized that what I was hearing was a voice. Like a rapid-fire auctioneer who'd lost his voice to throat cancer, it rasped and jibbered on, and before long, I could make out words.

"...tastytastycorpsypaygoodsIwills...nonono noyouwantsto wantssell noneed... "

Another voice, soft and feminine, with a bit of a husky whisper, tried to respond.

"No. Stop talking, and just listen to me," it insisted, but the other voice hadn't paused once.

"...nofightsnotricksnolies nonono no Kimblermakeyoudealmakeyouhappy fairtradefortastytastycorpsy... "

"No, damn you. He is not for sale. He is mine. My 'tasty-corpsy,' you relentless, little wr—"

"...peacepeacepeaceTuathaladyfair nofightsnonono nosellsittoKimbler selltastytastycorpsy sohungryis-Isohungry ... "

My muscles were responding now, and I managed to open one eyelid a fraction of an inch. Through that narrow slit, I saw a creature with a wide, squirmy mouth squatting over me, one three-clawed hand inching closer and closer. It was looking up at the other speaker, but she was beyond my limited field of vision. For a second, I just watched its curious mouth and realized that the squirming I perceived was its lips rippling back and forth—like a crowd doing *the wave*. Between those thin wrinkles of flesh that wriggled like wrestling worms, I spied rows of needle-sharp teeth.

"Tastytastycorpsy" suddenly registered, and I decided that, while I might not know how I had survived whatever had happened to me, I was damned if I was going to get eaten a second time in one day.

Sluggishness washed away in a surge of adrenaline. I reached out and snared the thing—Kimbler—by the wrist, pulled him to the ground, and punched him square in the face before he could scream. There was a horrible, rubbery feeling to his flesh and even the bones beneath, but I didn't have time to think about it. I scrambled to my feet.

Turns out Kimbler stood barely four feet tall— a hard thing to judge through one eye and flat on the ground. And though he was a solid, little bastard, once I had my feet under me, I used my grip on his wrist to spin him around.

There was a stunned exhalation as I released him, and then I was off. I ran the opposite direction from the two creatures who'd been arguing over who got to eat me, my boots making undignified squelching noises in the soft terrain.

Long tubes that felt like oversized pool noodles and glowed like neon decorations at a rave pressed in around me as I ran on, but they weren't hard to push aside, so I kept going. I heard shouts behind me, but I was determined to put as much distance as I could between us before I looked back.

My brain tried to make sense of all the sights, sounds, and smells that met me each way I turned. The tubes had the consistency of foam but were smooth to the touch, and when they swayed, the air smelled like cloves and ginger. Over the sound of my own wild flight, I could hear croaks and caws that just didn't sound right. They were too rhythmic and steady—like toads and crows speaking to each other.

All of this happened beneath a softly-pulsing glow of green, blue, and pink, which overshadowed the silvery light glinting between the feathered tops of the tubular forest.

I'm not sure how far I ran before the adrenaline wore off, but when it did, I found myself clutching at my ribs between ragged breaths. I felt like I had been on the wrong end of a blanket party, and the attendees had used broken bottles instead of soap in their socks.

Leaning against a sturdy tube the color of spring leaves in sunshine, I tried to slow my breathing and listen for the sounds of my pursuers.

All I heard were strange animal calls and just a hint of something else. The sound was so pervasive yet so soft, I wondered if it wasn't caused by the beating I'd taken—like ringing ears after a blow to the head. It sounded almost like wind whispering softly between branches, but there were no branches on these tall, swaying stalks—only clumps of big mushrooms. I held my hand out to check. There wasn't a hint of wind, either.

Where was I?

I began to walk through the alien forest and felt a growing sense of unease nestle in my belly. Nothing around me was nearly as terrifying as the thing that, I thought, had devoured me. But that monster had clearly been something wrong and nasty intruding on the world of humans. These weird, not-tree things that glowed and smelled like Christmas cookies, the mysterious sounds of gossiping wildlife, and even that Kimbler thing, had all seemed like part of the same world.

Could I be on another planet? Had that monster—that thing I would have called a demon if it hadn't sounded so silly—been an alien? Had I been abducted?

I staggered another step and reached out a hand to steady myself, my guts twisting and knotting.

My hand pressed into something firmer—meatier than the tubes, and I heard a soft grunt.

"Please!" warbled a muffled voice beneath my hand. "Please, don't eat me!"

I snatched my hand away and looked down to see a mushroom attached to the side of the tree give a shake of its button head. A light dust of ivory flakes fell as it wriggled, and, to my amazement, I could see a pair of garnet-colored eyes looking up at me from the dark hollow just beneath its cap.

"Oh, thank you, thank you," the mushroom said in a raspy voice. "I am sorry for being in the way."

I staggered back a step and swiped my hand over my face. I recoiled when I realized my hand had touched the mushroom and was covered in the little white flakes.

"Don't worry, sir, don't worry," the mushroom assured

me as it shuffled a little higher on the stalk to look me in the eye. "I'm as cleanly a Hombath as any could wish, just ask my neighbors."

A stream of other husky, murmuring voices joined in, and I realized I was surrounded by the things.

"Yes, a fine little spore—just fine."

"You'll never find one more cleanly and punctual."

"Without a doubt, but he tends to be a bit excitable."

"Oh yes, remember that one time with the Gremlin herder?"

"Bother, don't start in on that old line; it's been talked simply to death."

"Well, if you don't like it, you can just just shuffle on then."

"Shuffle on! How very rude."

Soon the mushroom mutterings had devolved into an argument about whether to tell some story concerning a Gremlin herder—whatever that was—and I was trying not to collapse in a fit of madhouse giggles. Glowing not-trees, talking mushrooms, and two creatures haggling over my corpse. This wasn't another planet. This was the other side of the damned looking glass! Now where the hell was my white rabbit?

A sharp screech, like a raptor's scream but deeper, cut through the ambiance and the ensuing argument like a jagged knife. If a sound could be hungry, this was it, and judging by the sudden silence that followed the cry, I guessed I wasn't wrong.

"Sir, you should run. Quickly!" the mushroom I had originally squished hissed urgently as it began to hunker down against the tree so its head was almost flush with the tube it clung to.

"Quite right," added another mushroom from a nearby stalk. "With all haste make for Purllaeth."

"What and where is that?" I whispered, trying not to think too hard about getting directions from a fungus.

"The river, silly. The river," answered one I couldn't see. "The River-Guard will keep you safe."

"Yes, make for Purllaeth."

"Quick, before they find you!"

Spurred on by the insistent chorus and the growing feeling of exposure, I took a deep breath and plunged deeper into the forest.

"No, no, silly. The other way. The other way!"

6

INTERVENTION

Lady Bryth Lighttread could have withered that little Gremlin wretch from crown to heel had he not scuttled off in terror as soon as she sprang to her feet.

Instead of chasing after him to administer the curses and blights he so rightly deserved, she went to find the Aspirant. His trail had been easy enough to follow at first, but as he went farther afield, some of the battered fungal stalks had shifted, agitated by the mortal's passing, making the erratic trail difficult to follow. Her progress slowed, she carefully picked her way along, peering intently at the soft ground between the twitching stalks.

Then she'd heard the poachers' hunting cry and was moving along as fast as she could now. The screech mimicked a gryphon on the hunt. The idea was to flush any game out of hiding, but Bryth knew she was not so lucky. Her father had kept a trio of gryphons in their family's spired estate, and she knew all their utterances intimately.

No, these were Goblins, and they would hardly be picky

about the quarry they pursued, whether it moved on two legs, or more.

Bryth raced through the forest, stirring up spells she thought might help, but with horror, she realized that somehow she had lost the tacks. Snarling in rage, she turned around and tried to see if she could spot anything back the way she'd come.

"Are you looking for the creature in funny clothes, Milady?" asked a soft voice behind her.

The Hombaths!

"Yes! He is tall and has brown skin," Bryth said, not bothering to find the exact mushroom that spoke to her. "Where is he? Quickly, please!"

"I told him to make for Purllaeth," it said, and almost instantly, Bryth set off toward the river.

"Wait! Apologies, Milady, but he went the wrong way."

Bryth stopped, trudging back to glare down at the huddle of cowering fungoids.

"Then where did he go?" she growled, unable to keep the edge from her voice.

"The waste waters, Milady," one of them squeaked.

Bryth turned sharply, gathering up the folds of her dress, and rushed off through the forest, heedless of the fungal stalks she left writhing in her wake.

"Naturally," she panted as she shouldered past another stalk. "Right into the mouth of the damn beast!"

Bryth came to the swampy ground where the Forlorn Forest gave way to the waste waters that descended from the hills beneath Duanon.

Here, in the stink, filth, and misty vapors, she found the Aspirant fighting for his life.

Noxious water sloshed about his calves as he spun

around to keep an eye on all his attackers. The strange, over-sized tunic he once wore was now bunched up in one fist, and he was using it to deflect the jabs of the Goblin poachers hemming him in. Judging by the red gashes in the thin shirt he still wore, the man had not been able to fend off every attack from the poachers' long handled gaffs and harpoons. The Goblins' armament marked them as flotsam Goblins, and Bryth found time to be relieved about that.

Flotsam Goblins didn't get off their floating trash heaps for food, but for sport. That fact had probably kept the Aspirant alive more than anything else.

"Playtime is over," Bryth breathed as she drew upon her magic, and her eyes shone with a fell light.

Stepping forward, she called upon ancient contracts that underpinned all life and sorcery in Other-Realm, and a ring of water around the Aspirant began to hiss and bubble. The poachers recoiled, looking around in mounting horror. Wicked and debased as these creatures may have been, they knew what such a display meant.

They scrambled away, a filthy spray springing up behind them, but it was too late. An eruption of boiling swamp water cascaded outward from the ring. Squealing and shrieking, the Goblins floundered about as the unnaturally-heated liquid worked its way over their blistering skin and under their ragged clothing.

The Aspirant stared, slack-jawed, as Bryth strode toward the scene, her feet resting atop the brackish swamp as though it were a marble floor.

"You dare to raise your hand against the chosen of Queen Meabh?" she thundered in her best regally-offended tone.

The Goblins mewled but made no coherent answer.

They cringed and bowed low enough that many of their long noses dipped into the water.

Bryth knew she was within her rights to slay them all, and besides, they were Goblins. Many would consider it a public service, but she glanced at the Aspirant and saw wonder and fear warring on his face. Perhaps mercy would keep the former in ascendance.

"Flee from here," she ordered, looking back at the humiliated poachers. "Flee and never set foot upon the Forlorn Forest or near Duanon again. Flee now, or I will have the swamp weed flay you alive!"

The Goblin poachers, sharp ears pointed downward and shoulders slumping, were gone in a matter of moments, leaving Bryth and the Aspirant alone in the putrid swamp.

Standing there with the man staring at her, Bryth realized how dishevelled she now looked after the urgent pursuit. Her dress was stained with earth at the hem, and her long, silver hair was cast about her shoulders and back, having fallen out of its sculpted plaits. She also realized she was still channelling her magics as the Aspirant stared into her witch-lit eyes.

She released the contracts and sank onto the spongy ground, her dress already soiled.

Tuatha grace alone kept her elegant as she padded across the soggy turf and into the marsh water to extend a hand to the gawking Aspirant.

"I am Lady Bryth Lighttread," she said with a bow of her head. "Welcome to Other-Realm, Lucius Bollham."

7

INTRODUCTIONS

I stood on the glossy deck of a broad-bottomed boat, drifting down an impossibly clear river that wound around a city of elegant spires and towering walls. The stink of the swamp was rinsed off my skin with sweet-smelling waters, and the few cuts I'd taken from those knife-eared, long-nosed creatures were swaddled in soft bandages that cooled and soothed as soon as they touched my skin.

I was no less confused than I had been when I first awoke following my abduction, but I thought that, so far, this was a vast improvement over the way things had been going.

The boat slid slowly across a river whose waters were as clear as those lapping at the beaches I'd seen in Mexico once upon a time. As I stood by the rail, I watched twisting, agile shapes dart beneath the water, and I could have sworn that some of them had human heads and arms.

"We can provide you with fresh clothes, should you desire," called my rescuer from beside a low table where she reclined on plush pillows.

I turned from the placid river and looked at the woman who saved me in the swamp.

The thin, glistening dress she wore did little to hide the muscles of her legs and arms, or the soft swells of her chest and hips. Her skin was light, with just the barest flush of color, and while her hair was silver, it was lush and thick and seemed to have nothing at all to do with age. Brilliant eyes the color of storm-tossed seas flashed up at me as I stepped toward the table beside her.

"Any reason I need to get dressed up?" I bent to pick up a fruit that might have been a cross between a pomegranate and nectarine. "You haven't exactly told me...well, anything, really."

Fluid as the ripples of her dress, the woman who'd introduced herself as Lady Bryth in the swamp rose to her feet as I began to peel the fruit.

I was struck by her stature, eye level with me and I stood half a head taller than most guys; she exuded strength. Her eyes met mine, she gave a smile, and stepped toward the rail.

"What do you wish to know?" she asked over her shoulder. "I will answer any questions I can."

The deep pink fruit was as sweet and tart as its flesh was vibrant, and I snatched up another one from the table before joining her at the side of the boat.

"You called this place Other-Realm, but what does that mean?" I leaned against the railing. "Is this another planet? Another dimension? Somethin' else?"

She considered the question for a second and then reached up to unfasten one of her earrings. She turned and held it up so I could see the jeweled pendant glittering between her long fingers.

"Your world—the dry world of mankind—is here," she said, tapping a sharply tapered nail to one facet of the jewel. "Eileait—Other-Realm—is here," she continued, tapping the other side. "They are ... mirrored realities of each other."

I stared at the pendant and then looked back at her, chewing things over in my head.

"So, your world is just a reflection of Earth?"

"Not just your Earth, but your entire cosmos. And we are not a reflection in that we come from you, but rather, our worlds are opposite sides of the same thing."

"Two sides of the same coin," I offered.

"In a way, yes. But the jewel is better because, just as it has more than two facets, there are more than just two realities." She pointed to the other sides of the gem in her hand.

"How many?" I was suddenly seized by a curiosity mixed with fear.

My conception of reality was getting a little stretched.

"I do not know, and as far as I know, no one else does either." She returned the earring to its rightful place. "We can only travel to your realm, and that is very difficult. We know different realms exist, only because my people, the Tuatha, came to Other-Realm many thousands of years ago from somewhere else. Another reality."

This close to her, I noted the leaf-like shape of her ears and the subtle peculiarities in her neck, jawline, and cheekbones which were both striking and unsettling. On the street, you'd think she was gorgeous, but up close, some part of you'd know she wasn't quite human. It wasn't any one thing, but rather a sum of many details—angles that were just too wide or slightly too sharp to be explained away.

"Where did they come from?" I tore my eyes away, setting to work peeling my second piece of fruit. "Your people, I mean."

Bryth turned her eyes to the water and shook her head.

"We do not know," she answered quietly, almost like it pained her to admit it. "Even the one among us who was alive when we first came to Other-Realm cannot recall anything from before."

A short silence lapsed between us.

I was trying to figure out how dimension-hopping beings fit with my admittedly limited understanding of the universe and its supposed laws. Magic. That hand-waved it all, didn't it. But then why would stuff like magic be seen as fiction or cheap tricks on Earth?

I remembered something she had said earlier.

"You said my world is dry," I flicked some peel over the railing. "But you know that there is plenty of water on Earth."

She chuckled softly—a pure sound, free of mockery.

"Yes, we know, but the dryness was not concerning water." She smiled as she turned to look at me. "The dryness I speak of is a drought of magic. I know it must be confusing."

"Try and explain it, and I'll let you know when I get lost." I grinned back at her, and she gave what I might have considered a snort, had it not sounded so musical.

"Magic flows freely through Other-Realm," she said, gesturing out across the river and up to the great city. "Something about this reality conducts magical energies and binds its contracts to the elemental pieces of this world. But where you come from, everything seems insulated against such energies. Magical creatures die of 'thirst' in your world; their energies bleed out, and even simple spells do not reliably activate the contracts that allow sorcery to work."

I looked across the shimmering surface of the river as

Other-Realm's silvery sun began to set. The sky turned shades of gold and scarlet that reflected across the waters.

"Look up there," Bryth said. I followed her outstretched arm to where a trio of immense birds soared through the gilded sky.

Only, they weren't birds, I realized as their flight brought them closer to the river. They had great wings—the biggest I think I've ever seen—covered in brown feathers, but their bodies looked more like those of a mountain lion, including a trailing tail tufted with grey fur.

"What are those things?" I whispered, not caring that I probably sounded like a child just then.

"Osphryns," she said at my shoulder. We watched their swooping passage over the river, their fierce, beaked heads scanning the water below. "Cousins of the mighty Gryphons. They are the kind of beast which could never live in your world, but they are common enough among the rivers and coasts of Other-Realm. Look now. That one has found something to eat."

One of the Osphryns peeled away from its mates and locked its eyes on something just beneath the surface.

Tucking its wings, the raptor plunged downward into the water. For a moment, there was nothing but a few ripples where it had disappeared, then an explosion of spray and writhing forms snapping and flailing at each other erupted. In the tumult, I could see the Osphryn clinging to the shoulders of a creature that looked like a scaled horse with a fin in place of a mane. The predator's beak was buried in its prey's neck, and for all the thrashing of its finned head and scaly tail, it was clear the struggle would not end in its favor. Within moments, the water horse floundered limply before collapsing lifelessly to float on the water's surface. The other Osphryns descended to share in the feast.

It was like watching a lion on some nature documentary, but somehow more beautiful, more incredible for the fantastical nature of the creatures composing the drama. I couldn't stop staring.

"Magnificent, aren't they?" Bryth sighed.

I nodded dumbly.

"Our world is full of wonders like this, Lucius," she said, and I could feel the intensity of her eyes upon me. "Marvels and miracles that your world knows only as legends, and things even your myths could not imagine. A world of magic is before you, but we need your help to save it. That is why you were brought here—to save this world."

I turned from the feeding Osphryns and tried to get my brain to process what she had just said.

"Wait, what?"

"Lucius, you are the Aspirant," she said her face alight with a fierce intensity. "You were brought here to help save Other-Realm from those who would conquer and despoil it. We need you."

Things started falling into place. Things that probably should have clicked a lot sooner.

"Wait a second," I growled. "Brought? Brought by what? You mean that ... that *thing* was yours?"

"We need you here," she pressed, not desperate but adamant. That made me angrier. "The Fiend was the only certain way to do it."

My hands shot out and grabbed her shoulders. I felt her toned muscles quicken in my grip, but my fingers dug in all the same.

"What the fuck did you just say to me?"

8

BLAME

Looking back, Bryth really kept it together. I mean, she just calmly kept trying to explain. Didn't fight, didn't pull out any of the glowy-eyed, sorcery stuff. Nothing. All of which was probably good, because, magic or no, I would have tossed her, ass over head, into the river and sorted it out from there. But she stayed cool and let her two bodyguards, who'd been discreetly maintaining their distance, pull me off of her.

I fought them a little, but not so hard that they felt the need to draw those swords they wore on their belts. I was pretty sure those things weren't just for show.

Bryth gave me some time to cool down. Pacing the deck up and down, I considered jumping and making a swim for it, but quickly dismissed it. Running hadn't gotten me shit so far, and I was still rational enough to remember the definition of insanity.

"Doing the exact same thing and expecting a different result," I mused, leaning forward on railing and indulging in a shout of anger.

I might have done that a few times already.

As I stood there, fingernails gouging the laquered wood, I felt the urge to vomit, realizing one of my worst fears had been true. All those men who died in those caves in Afghanistan died because of me. Even the insurgent bastards, who, as far as I was concerned, deserved to die for all the people they'd hurt, hadn't died for the right reason. They'd died because some people—hell, not even people— but Tuatha-fuckin-whatsits, had sent a monster to come fetch me.

I was sure they had some rationale—some reason for all this—but it didn't really matter. Everyone's got a reason. The only thing that *did* matter is that men, some of them good, brave men, died just to arrange my travel to this place.

"Unbelievable." I spat into the water, then paused as something rippled to the surface.

It looked almost like a child—boy or girl, I wasn't sure— but its eyes were far apart, and instead of ears, it had little spiny fins, which it waggled at me. It bobbed along, keeping pace with the barge, waving a thin, webbed hand. I tried to stay angry—to keep hold of the righteous indignation that burned in my belly. I was outraged with this place and everything in it! But those wide eyes just kept staring up at me, hoping for me to do what any kid wants when they wave excitedly at a passerby.

With a throaty sigh, I waved back.

The child-thing smiled broadly, sinking below the surface, only to burst upward a moment later with strong flick of its tail. Yep, my suspicions about merfolk had been well-founded.

"The Gythraul slaughter them," came a soft voice from behind me.

I knew it was Bryth, but I kept watching the merchild.

"Not for food or even for some kind of sport." She joined

me at the rail. "They kill them because they get in the way of their machines—their pumps and mills. Simple creatures. Especially their young. They are easily caught in the wheels and gears where their bodies clog their operations."

The sprightly merchild swam away, but it stopped every few seconds to turn around and wave at me again and again. I returned the waves, prompting another joyous leap each time.

"So rather than alter the construction of their machines or change where they are placed, they stretch barbed nets across the rivers and channels."

I couldn't see my watery friend anymore, but I still refused to look at Bryth, grinding my teeth as I fought with myself about what to do with that information.

"Whole schools of them are exterminated, their bodies left to rot on beaches and shoals."

I straightened and crossed my arms tightly across my chest. "Why are you telling me this?"

"Because you should know what is at stake," Bryth replied, moving to stand beside me. "No one can make you save us. But you should know, at least in part, what will be lost if you do not."

"Hoping that will make me forget the men your pet monster murdered to get me here." An edge of bitterness had crept back into my voice.

Bryth was quiet for a moment. I stole a sideways glance. I was surprised to see what looked an awful lot like genuine sadness on the Lady's face.

"Whatever the Fiend did was not because we willed it to do so," she said after a moment of reflection. "It is an old and powerful creature that we bargained with to bring you here. It was told not to harm you, but it apparently chose not to exercise that same restraint with others of your species. I am sorry."

Her apology did not change anything, but seeing her genuinely remorseful cooled the growing fire a little bit.

"Why not just ask?" I turned to face her fully.

Bryth's eyes met mine, and beneath the sorrow, I saw a resolve—a conviction solid as stone.

"For many reasons, but most of all, because it would not have worked. Traveling to your reality is possible, and we can even bring things—objects—back easily enough. But living beings—especially those with souls—cannot easily travel here. They are anchored to your solid world and all that insulates you from magic. Only a being of incredible power can bring a person from your world to ours safely."

"Something like the Fiend."

"Yes," she said with a nod. "And the Fiend feeds off of fear, so there would be no way to simply ask you to come. Not that I believe you would have come if something like that had asked. It was supposed to take you quickly and in the midst of battle, when there would have been much fear to fuel its magic."

"But I hurt it and ran away," I sighed, understanding settling over me like a leaden blanket.

"Exactly," she replied.

I couldn't stand to do anything but turn and look out over the river. It was still me the Fiend had been coming for. It was still *my* fault those men were dead.

"Lucius," Bryth said, and before I could stop her, she took my hand. "I am sorry for all the pain that the Fiend caused to bring you here...but still I am glad you are here. We need you."

I wasn't sure if I wanted any part of this, but, right or

wrong, her words and her touch on my hand made me willing to at least keep talking.

"Why me? Why choose me?" I muttered, as much to myself as Bryth, but she took it as a question to answer, all the same.

"As we have always done, we called on a powerful sorceress, Mother Gwiddon, to find a worthy Aspirant. Her magic has always found leaders and warriors who could help keep us from ruin."

She paused and took a breath.

"The Tuatha ... we are a people of magic, a people of power and fragile immortality, but that power also limits and confines us. We don't ... we can't innovate, can't adapt as your people and as the Gythraul do. As powerful as we are individually, we do not coordinate, do not plan as we need to if we are to win this war."

I heard every word, but just one thing stuck out in my mind; more magic. More powers beyond my comprehension. More things beyond a simple soldier.

"I'm just one man," I said to the river. "What can I possibly do in a world with sorcery and talking mushrooms?"

"Let me show you."

9

MEMORIES

The Hall of Remembrance, as this long, stone building was called, sat upon a narrow island in the middle of a broader part of the river. We did not come within sight of it until right before I fell asleep atop the pillows on the pavilioned deck. My dreams were dark and unsettling, but I didn't wake until first light. By then we were making berth.

The barge slid alongside a narrow quay, and the two Tuatha bodyguards moored the craft while Bryth and I went from the dock up flagstone steps to the Hall.

The entrance was a huge edifice of paired stone doors worked with silver tracery in a series of complex, inter-looping patterns. I doubted if even the two of us working together could push open one of the stone panels. I looked around for someone who might work there or some device to move the doors, but then my escort spoke a single word I didn't understand, and her eyes flickered with power. The silver traceries slid around and over each other like metallic serpents, and the doors slid open soundlessly.

The inside of the building was deeply shadowed except

where thin shafts of light shone from eyelet windows near the roofline. In the sparse lighting, I could just make out a series of statues separated by long, bas-relief carvings along the left-hand wall. The right side of the building was a stretch of black stone seamed with wavering lines of gold. There didn't seem to be a single living thing inside.

"The Hall of Remembrance was built shortly after the first coming of the Gythraul," Bryth said, moving toward the left wall. "We do not know how they came here from another realm, but by the time they were known to the Queen, they were legions of disciplined, deadly soldiers. Their forces were driven back by the Queen's armies at the siege of Duanon, but the Kingdom was in ruins. After the siege was broken, the Twilit Kingdom at last had time to evaluate the situation and bury their dead, who were beyond count. Generations of commoners were dead, and the eldest of our people had all fallen, save for the Queen."

A small relief just before the first statue depicted what looked like the great city Bryth described, its walls and towers battle scarred, and the river beneath it filled with long barges laden with human-shaped bundles. Bryth touched the relief, and, one by one, the little graven barges sprouted tongues of flame.

"The Tuatha of the Gloaming Court are mighty in magic and fierce in battle, but we are creatures of will and whim, and we have never been very...fecund. We felt every loss sharply, knowing that each life lost could not easily be replaced. The Gythraul are soulless and relentless. Their brutal discipline, combined with our fractious nature, meant that when they regained their strength, we would not be ready to face them. But the Queen had an idea."

Bryth stepped over to the first statue—marble accented with gold. It was a stoutly built man in classic Roman armor.

He had a stubborn set to his jaw and rested a broad hand on the sword belted to his waist.

"She knew that the mirror realm to ours was a dire place and accustomed to war," Bryth said, standing next to the statue. It only just came to the height of her shoulders. "She decided then that we would find men of war from your world to train and lead our people against our mortal foes. The first Paladin of the Pale Banner was a man from what was then Britannia, a warlord named Arcturus."

She left Arcturus' likeness and stood before the next relief.

"Under his direction, the armies of the Twilit Kingdom drove the Gythraul back from many holdings they had claimed with their initial invasion."

The relief showed what I can only assume was Arcturus, mounted on an honest-to-God unicorn, leading ranks of Tuatha knights mounted on a variety of mythical beasts after a mob of fleeing dark stone shapes with skull-like faces. Broken swords and shields littered the ground between the two armies. Bryth touched the corner of the carvings and Arcturus rode forward, parting the sea of skeletal shapes like Moses. He planted a banner in the spine of a fallen enemy. The flag was white with a downward-pointing sword of black, and it rippled in an imagined wind.

"With most of the Tirallanol, or Far-Holds, now secured and under their Lords, the Twilit Kingdom seemed secure from the Gythraul. It was hoped that, in time, what remained of their number would wither and die as they scratched out a living on the Blight Isles in the Forgotten Sea on the far side of the realm. Paladin Arcturus, not a young man when he came to us, lived out his days and was laid to rest when all the Twilit Kingdom was at peace. He would be the only one to take his rest when the Kingdom was not at war."

"You want me to lead your people to war?" Incredulity sharpened my words more than I intended. Bryth took it in stride.

"That, and more besides."

Bryth led me to the next statue. It was a taller, thinner man with sad eyes. He was clad in chainmail and a nasal helm, holding a kite shield with one hand and a longspear with the other. His statue was greyer—a less resplendent stone ornamented with brass.

"The Gythraul came again, having bound themselves with some of the fell powers that nestle in the bowels of this world, so another Paladin was sought to bring new ways to combat the revitalized threat. He was Tancred, a knight and devout man, and he marshalled the armies of the Twilit Kingdom to meet the oncoming Legions."

On the next relief, thousands of tiny figures stood arrayed against each other. The Gythraul, black, ant-like figures in square formations against wide ranks of soldiers in white, the hosts of the Twilit Kingdom. When Bryth stirred this one with her touch, I watched the ranks of Gythraul stall against the Twilit Army. Then, without warning, part of the white battle line peeled away from the fight and charged into another section of the white army. The scene ended with the battered Gythraul encircling a sizable chunk of the Twilit Army while the rest fled.

"Yet, for all his tactical acumen, Paladin Tancred forgot that he did not lead men of his own kind and faith, and the Tuatha Lords squabbled. Tancred would not win their trust or bind them to his will. His forces compromised over and over again. The Gythraul broke their exile and took hold of the lands which have never been recovered. In the end,

Tancred slew a great leader of the Gythraul and broke the main strength of their Legions, but he died of his wounds, and the fractured forces of the Twilit Kingdom could not capitalize on the victory. So, again, a Paladin was sought to unite us before the Gythraul returned."

I looked up from the enchanted carving and met Bryth's grave stare.

"You mean, I don't just have to lead an army of people I don't know, but I also have to play politics?"

Bryth looked back at the relief. There was something sad, almost ashamed, in her not-quite-human face. It was like she saw something personal—something painful—there in those miniscule, battling shapes.

"The Paladin must be a leader on and off the field of battle." The frown melted from her face, revealing that same grave conviction I had seen before. "Wish as any might that it were not so, the fact is that the very nature of our people works against itself."

"Have any of these Paladins actually succeeded at that?" I remembered the weight that settled over me the first time I commanded my platoon in the field. I had puked right before we went out on patrol.

"Some more than others." she cast a pitying look to the statue of Paladin Tancred. "Come and see."

I did.

One by one, I met all the former Paladins of the Pale Banner and learned of their victories and defeats. I learned how Paladin Baghtur nearly destroyed the Gythraul, but in his pride, led his army into a trap that got him killed and left the next two Paladins struggling to keep the Kingdom together. Paladin Khalid had restored some stability by establishing a network of fortresses to slow the assaults down. I saw their tactics and weapons of war advance and improve. Catapults became cannons, except the cannon balls in the carvings looked like fanged skulls. We passed a statue that had been shattered into hundreds of pieces, and the only comment Bryth made was that this Paladin had forgotten his place.

She spat on the pieces before leading me to more stories of this incessant war.

Finally, after learning of the exploits of the sly and ruthless Paladin Alula, we stood before a statue of a slight but fierce-eyed man. He wore an ornate breastplate and the flat-topped cap of a French officer at the beginning of the 1900s. He had binoculars in one hand at his side and the other raised in salute, palm out.

"Paladin Toulouse Valoise was the last to serve the Queen," Bryth explained. She led me to a scene that looked like something out of a World War I propaganda ad. Once activated by Bryth's touch, I watched a dashing Valoise stride before firing banks of field artillery, whose barrels were the jaws of dragons, while grim-eyed Tuatha waited in trenches in front of them.

"What he taught us of the warfare and weapons of your world almost a hundred years ago was incredible," Bryth said with no small amount of awe in her voice. I noticed something peculiar in the way she watched Valoise's figure stride across the relief. "He was the first Paladin I had the honor to serve, and because of him the Gythraul were held in check for many years."

She stepped away, and I realized that though the Hall went on, there was only a blank wall.

"But not anymore?" I asked as she walked across the open floor toward the other side of the Hall. "The Gythraul are coming back, like they have every time?"

"Yes, and to make matters worse, the current Lords and

Ladies of Far-Hold have refused to come to the Gloaming Court for some years now," Bryth explained as we came toward the right-hand wall of black stone. "You will have to not only train your forces quickly, but also renew the Oaths of Fealty before you can do so."

Despite the particulars of said Oaths, it seemed straightforward enough. But the one crucial piece of this whole thing still stuck in my head.

"And why should I?" I asked, giving voice to it, despite the fact that it felt sacreligious standing in this shrine to Other-Realm. "Why should I do this?"

Bryth stood facing the black stone wall and laid her fingers upon one of the golden seams. It flowed and rippled, and then the molten metal took the shape of letters in a language I did not understand. As the transformation worked its way across the entire seam, I realized I didn't need to know the language to recognize what they were.

Names.

I saw that the seams striped the wall from floor to ceiling, and my mouth went dry.

"Because I know something despite never having met you," Bryth said, looking away from the wall, teary-eyed. "I know in my heart that you are not a man who would allow so many to have died in vain. Not when you have a chance to make a difference."

10

DECLARATIONS

The Hall of Remembrance had been intimidating with its solemn, mystic air, but the city of Duanon, capital of the Twilit Kingdom, was mind-blowing.

I saw it from afar for the better part of two days, but as we drew closer, the size and splendor of the city seemed to grow exponentially. I knew it was big, but exactly how massive didn't sink in until we were gliding under the shadow of its walls.

The walls alone were impressive, soaring up 60 or 70 feet, even at their lowest points, and composed of fitted stone blocks the dimensions of a midsize sedan. I was no engineer, but the amount of work required to move hunks of rock that big must have been incredible. Each one fit so precisely with its neighbors that I'd have been surprised if you could have found a seam big enough to wedge a knife blade. The thickness of the walls was harder to judge, but here and there, I saw sharply crenellated gatehouses and redoubts jutting out from the wall and overhanging the water by 50 or 60 feet. I imagined the wall itself may have been nearly that thick, and if so, nothing short of bunker-busting munitions could have made a mark on the place.

Behind those immense fortifications rose sharp-peaked spires, more works of art than engineering, whose sloped sides glittered in the setting sun. Spanning gaps above the vertiginous chasms between some of the towering columns, graceful bridges formed woven thickets between the cloud-piercing towers. Some spires stood alone, their slender structures bastioned at regular intervals by what looked like castle fortifications. The tallest was at the northern end of the city, where we were headed currently. Its base was an entire section of the wall that bulged with fortified keeps. Nestled at the base of this citadel was a broad landing of stone from which descended an immense array of steps.

"The Grand Stairs of Duanon," Bryth said as I gawked at the tiered ranks of black and white stones dominoing down to the arms of an open quay.

"Built by my great grandsire, Manann Water-Loved," one of the bodyguards declared from behind us as he worked the pole, punting the barge toward the stairs. "The Water-Loved wished the Tuatha, their city, and their throne to be bound to Purllaeth, which has always been our friend."

Either more magic was at work, or Manann's great-grandson was scary strong, moving the barge like he did.

That was the first time either of Bryth's bodyguards had spoken to me, and that prompted a question that had been in the back of my mind for sometime.

"Bryth, how come you speak English?"

"We do not," she answered flatly. I stood there confused until I saw the ghost of a smile tugging at the corners of her mouth.

"Fine," I grunted, falling back a step with my arms crossed. "How silly of me to ask something like that."

Bryth laughed at my little display. It was rich, warm sound that made me sad when it stopped.

"Excuse my cheek." She reached up to touch one of her gently tapered ears. "We each hear the language that is closest to our hearts in Other-Realm. The fracturing of tongues that came about in your own world never came to this realm, or the magic that suffuses it mends the wound. I do not know your English, and neither do you know my tongue."

"Well, that's convenient at least," I nodded, chuckling. "Saves me having to discover how terrible I am at yet another language. First Spanish in high school. Then Pashto and Dari in the Army. I only managed to embarrass myself in all of them. This job is only slightly less impossible."

"Yes," Bryth agreed, and her smile fell to a stern stare. "You will be kept quite busy as things stand ... that is, assuming you will accept the Queen's command and become the Paladin of the Pale Banner. You have never said plainly what your choice will be."

It doesn't get more blunt than that.

I turned, looking at the stairs, and saw a flock of elegant figures moving down the steps toward the quay. They were arrayed in clothes ranging from regally archaic to ridiculously bizarre. Members of the Gloaming Court. Bryth told me they would be here to welcome and usher me to the Queen.

"Has any Aspirant ever refused?"

"Not so far," Bryth said. It was the first time i had heard her voice tighten with uncertainty—or was it a note of desperation? "Thankfully, all have seen the need of our people, as well as the honor in serving, and have chosen to take up the banner."

The contrary part of my nature—the part that had defied my self-important father at every turn—wanted to quip about there being a first time for everything, but I thought better of it. These were her people she spoke of, and even though she could plainly see their flaws, she loved and wanted to fight for them anyway. In some small way, that made her like every soldier I'd ever met that was worthy of the name. Could I really turn her down?

My own country had turned on me for telling the truth, but maybe here, where there were still wonders and miracles, I could find something worth fighting for.

The barge glided toward the quayside and I heard the sound of trilling pipes and rumbling drums. The Gloaming courtiers stirred on the patterned stairs, each straining to get a good look.

Most of the celebrants were like Bryth—pale, tall, and elegant—though they seemed to all have a flair for dramatic attire that Lady Lighttread did not share. There were impossible hairstyles and intricate dresses. Some wore garments more like jewelled body sleeves than actual clothing. Still others wore costumes that swayed and glittered over their lithe bodies of their own accord. Here and there, I caught glimpses of creatures that weren't Tuatha within the crowd. An inhumanly tall yet stooped woman, with a hooked nose and a smile that was wet, black, and wickedly sharp, looked out of place in her drab, patched robes. A bearded toad sat atop the shoulders of a creature whose face was set in his chest. A woman with a face of polished mahogany that bore carved, green sigils stood smiling, the flowers dotting her leafy hair rustling softly in the breeze.

These and so many other oddities—part fantastic dream

and part nightmare—took stately but eager steps forward to welcome me as I stepped off the barge with Bryth.

The courtiers were friendly; I had certainly never before received so many courtly bows, nor had so many flowery blessings thrown my way. To be honest, half of them were so ornate, I had no idea what they were meant to convey, though I assumed good intent.

After all such protocol and proper greeting had been observed, the sun had nearly set, and I was ushered through a massive, bronze-hasped gate. I found myself in a long corridor that felt and looked like a freeway tunnel—only this one was lit by faerie fire of blue and green rather than orange sodium lights.

The courtiers strode along around Bryth and I, all exuding a kind of powerful grace that the Tuatha seem born to. For my part, I felt more than ridiculous, still wearing the stained and torn clothes in which I had fled Baumholder. Bryth had offered clothes, but the pants looked more like tights than trousers, and I wasn't down with that game. No, and hell no.

So it was in such ragged attire that I stood before Queen Meadh.

In my head, I had envisioned all sorts of things, knowing that she was the only remaining survivor of the Unexpected Arrival when the Tuatha came to Other-Realm. Bryth explained that Tuatha do not age like humans, but when I saw the regal woman rising from a throne of silver and pearl, I was at a loss for words. She was beautiful and radiant like a sunset, tall and statuesque, so she seemed untouchable. When I looked at her deep, golden hair spilling down over tawny shoulders and the long, majestic cast of her uplifted chin upon her delicate throat, I felt unworthy—ashamed even.

Inexorably, my embarrassed eyes stole up to her face. More than by how unfathomably gorgeous that heart-shaped face was, I was trapped by her eyes—the most striking cerulean I'd ever seen. They weren't just pretty; they were powerful. Even the jeweled circlet crowning her head seemed meager compared to the majesty in those eyes. I could feel her great age when my gaze met hers, and as she looked at me, I felt as though she could see through me—to my bones and my soul. I felt stripped naked, laid bare, but curiously free in that honest, open regard—the kind usually reserved for true lovers. It was a look I'd never experienced so fully in my checkered, somewhat disappointing love life.

That's what it was. Love. I was in love with Queen Meabh.

Not in the romantic sense, though she was heart-stoppingly lovely. I was unequal to that kind of thing—unworthy. No, it was love like a man can have for his country or for an ideal. A love for something bigger than himself. She was greater than me, and for that greatness I would lay down my life or walk over a thousand dead enemies.

Right then and there, I knew my answer. All my anxieties washed away, replaced with a glowing certainty.

"Who comes now to our hall?" the Queen asked melodiously. It was a question free of challenge. She stood next to her throne atop a tiered dais, and at each level two massive figures clad in baroque armor stood guard. "Know that We are the Twilit Kingdom, and the Twilit Kingdom is Us."

"Behold the Queen," the courtiers intoned in the revenant drone of a ritual chant. "She is land, water, and sky."

"I come humbly before you, my Queen," Bryth answered, head bent low. "And with me stands the Aspirant, long sought."

"Lady Bryth, child of our hearth and heart, is the Aspirant ready to take up the banner and drive out the darkness?" Queen Meabh asked.

Bryth came to stand beside me, her head still bowed in deference.

"My Queen, Aspirant Lucius Bollham stands before you after having seen the Hall of Remembrance and hearing the voices of our war-torn past. He has come because he is not deaf to our cries, but he does wish to sp- "

"To speak to you, Queen Meabh," I interrupted, unable and unwilling to let Bryth voice any of my old doubts.

Galvanized by an electric euphoria, I strode toward the dias, ignoring the way the armored giants leaned forward menacingly, and took a knee before the Queen.

"I am yours," I said, clear and strong as I could with my head bowed. "I've spent years fighting wars for unworthy men and deceitful causes, but now, before you, my Queen, I swear to fight for the Twilit Kingdom until your enemies lie broken at your feet and there is peace once more. I, Lucius Arthur Bollham, give you my vow."

There was a moment of stunned silence, and I suddenly felt very small and very stupid for my bold, flashy words. I figured I'd probably said something wrong or improper, but then the room exploded into cheers and cries of joy. Out of the corner of my eye, I saw courtiers laughing, grinning— even crying. I raised my head to look at Queen Meabh, and the smile she gave me was worth more than all their cheers and blessings combined.

I had spoken well and she was pleased. That was all I needed.

"Bring the banner," the Queen commanded in her strong, carrying voice. The room quickly quieted.

From behind the throne stepped a creature like the

guards, except he moved with an authoritative bearing. In a fist bigger than my head, he held a long spear, from which hung the same banner I had seen in the carvings in the Hall of Remembrance.

The huge warrior stepped down in front of me, and I felt the floor shudder. His authority rippled through the court like distortions in the air above a hot stretch of blacktop. The metal-shod giant held out the banner.

"Rise up, Lucius, Paladin of the Pale Banner, and take your badge of office from our champion who shall now serve as your second," said the Queen.

I stood and took the smooth haft of the banner from the juggernaut. As I did, I looked up into the helmeted face and saw dark, glistening eyes looking down on me with obvious contempt. I guess no one cared about his opinion of this arrangement, and I might have been more concerned had the Queen not started talking again.

"Uzran is Captain of our Royal Guard and our loyal servant." She gestured to the glaring giant. "He shall attend to all that you need to prepare to defend our Realm and our people."

Uzran gave a stiff nod, but his smoldering glare never waned in its focus or intensity.

The Queen turned toward the rest of the courtiers and lifted her arms into the air.

"Rejoice and make merry, our faithful friends," she cried. "Our salvation is at hand!"

11

CONTINGENCIES

The throne room, one of three in the Queen's spire, emptied of all its courtiers an hour later, and the newly christened Paladin Bollham was taken to his new chambers. Bryth remained and went to sit at her Queen's side. A hob footman named Groog, a favorite of Meabh's, fetched a small but comfortable chair for Bryth as the Queen dismissed all but two of her guardians. Shortly after Bryth sat, Groog produced a little table and some refreshments before he disappeared in a puff smoke that smelled of woodfire and spruce needles.

"Well, that could not have gone better," Meabh said, taking up a small bowl to sip a dark wine. "Well done, Our dear one."

Bryth raised her own bowl to her lips, but then lowered it, her eyes downcast. Did she dare to even ask?

"What troubles you?" The Queen set her drink on the table and reached a hand to squeeze Bryth's shoulder. "Are you not pleased that another Paladin has stepped forward to save us, and all because of your persuasive entreaties?"

Bryth sat the bowl in her lap and looked into Meabh's overwhelming gaze.

"Why did you use glamours to ensorcell Lucius?" she blurted. She immediately blushed and looked down into her wine.

"Oh, We see," the Queen cooed soothingly, leaning forward on an elbow. "You fear that our new Paladin did not choose because of your success, but because of our magic. Is that it?"

"No," Bryth said a little sharply, placing the bowl on the table between them. "That did occur to me, but that is not really the problem."

"Then what is, dearest?" Meabh asked with deep concern.

"When you wrap yourself in such magic, especially with one as ignorant as a man from their world, how can he not succumb and want to be exactly what we want him to be? How can he not choose to be the Paladin?"

The Queen nodded knowingly and let her chin sink into her palm.

"Do you feel We have coerced Lucius?" Meabh asked after a quiet moment, her eyes never leaving Bryth's downcast face. "That We have used our glamour encourage him to do something other than what he wants?"

Bryth shook her head.

"I know that is not how glamour works," she said plaintively. "I know such magics can only enhance what is seen or felt, but I cannot help that my heart is troubled to know he was manipulated."

Bryth looked up. The Queen extended her hand with maternal affection, caressing her cheek. Bryth's stiff posture slackened some and for a moment, she savored the tender touch that had comforted her since she was a child.

"Child of Our heart, We are not worthy of your good spirit," Queen Meabh said, leaning forward to take both of Bryth's hands in hers. "It is so like you to be so concerned, for without such questions, how very wrong We could go. Though We are your Queen and also have loved you like your mother, it is still fitting that you ask these questions. After all, even We can make mistakes."

Bryth felt sure, gentle strength as the Queen's fingers squeezed hers reassuringly. Then the connection broke as Meabh let go and reclined upon her throne.

"I did not to mean to say that, my Queen," Bryth added quickly. "It is just that I am troubled, and not just about the coming war. My heart feels heavy in my chest."

"But why, child?" the Queen asked, bemused. "You have had nothing but success this day. Savor it."

Reflecting upon the day and Lucius's oath brought back memories of another time, when another Paladin knelt before the Court and was given the Pale Banner. The remembrance stung her, and she felt the weight on her heart double.

"I just want things to be different this time," Bryth confessed, her gaze drifting downward once more. "Different than Toulouse."

Meabh turned a knowing eye on Bryth. She took a sip of wine and shook her head.

"Dear one, you must forget that ugly business. It was not your fault, and besides, they are only mortal men. They need our guidance, but guidance is all we can offer. Do not carry the weight of their frailties. They are beneath you, Our child."

Bryth's body sagged forward, a sudden shudder momentarily wracking her body. Her lip trembled and her shoulders gave a single shake. She looked up and saw the Queen's eyes upon her. Her head shook and then rose, a fierce light shining through the moistness in her eyes. Decisively, she took up the bowl and drained it in a single, long gulp.

"It is the past," she said in a voice of feral intensity. "I must look to the future."

"Yes," Meabh purred, setting her bowl down and clapping her hands together. "There she is! There is the mighty daughter of Lughan Redfinger."

Bryth ran long fingers across her eyes and cast the offending tears aside.

"I remember the words you said to me the day my father took his rest," Bryth said. "You said that when I was ready, I would be your right hand, as he had been."

"As you have been, and you shall be," the Queen agreed, eyes twinkling proudly. "As We said, you have served Us well this day. Take pride in that and look forward to the great things you shall do with this new Paladin. Think on the words of Mother Gwiddon."

Bryth did think on them and she felt another tremor running through her, but this one left her spirit light—almost giddy.

"He is the one, my Queen. I know he is. I cannot say why, but in my heart, I know it is true. He is the one toward which every augury has turned with perfect clarity, born in every twist and ripple in the readings."

The Queen's beaming smile shone over the dark wine like a crescent moon over the deepest sea.

"Perchance, do you wish it so for other reasons?"

Bryth made to answer, and her pale cheeks flushed before she rose with a speed masked only by her smooth grace.

"No, not at all. So unless you need me further, I will attend to a few things before I retire to bed," she said hastily, making a graceful curtsey that set the torchlight dancing over her dress like strings of living fire. "Not least of which is removing myself from this rather impractical costume."

"It suits you, my dear," Meabh commented with glittering eyes. "Something We are sure even Lucius noticed."

Bryth retreated from the throne room, chased by her Queen's amused chuckling.

12

UNDERSTANDINGS

The map in front of me did not look like anything I had seen before.

First off, it was huge. I didn't have a tape measure on me, but it was easily bigger across than the entirety of the last apartment I rented stateside.

Second, it wasn't flat. Its surface rose from a recessed table top into a variety of layered textures that displayed what looked to be the better part of a continent, all worked out in miniature. Tiny roads the width of yarn strands wound through forests and mountains and over rivers and moors. Towns no bigger than my palm sprouted up here and there, but the primary points were various fortress cities that stood on key strategic points across the vast and varied landscape. Duanon, with its titanic walls and olympian spires, was faithfully depicted and was without a doubt the largest, but there were other places nearly as grand, if not so immense.

A minaretted citadel atop a frozen mountain; a squat, sunken hall within a swamp; a sharp-edged ziggurat of black stone ringed by jagged walls in the midst of an ashen plain; a chateau-style castle rising from a dark forest. They were both fanciful and dreadful, beautiful as they were menacing, and it only took a cursory glance to understand their function.

"Lynchpins and gates," I muttered, walking around the table, waiting for the others to join me. "Each one securing the direct routes."

All fortifications stood astride the best roads through the landscape and the quickest routes to Duanon. Anyone approaching from the west would have to pass through one of them, and more than likely, any large scale attack would have to pass through more than one.

Stretching westward from these protected domains were a few more outlying settlements, the largest of which was situated in the valley between two mountains—the last link in a chain that began with a citadel in the mountains far to the north east. That last settlement, composed of many tiny buildings and a solitary stone tower, stood alone at the edge of the Twilit kingdom.

Everything beyond it was darkness. The map's western edge was an expanse of black that occasionally flickered with angry vermillion glimmers, like tiny gouts of fire in a landscape of perpetual night. Even the ashen plains surrounding the ziggurat seemed more hospitable.

"So this is where they are coming from," I mused, walking around the encroaching dark that seethed over nearly the last third of the table.

Standing closer, I got the vague impression of a land-scape beneath the shadow—hills, plains, maybe a mountain near the distant coastline, and even a few islands punctu-ating the sea the utmost edge of the table.

It was an ominous view, and from all that Bryth told me,

the Gythraul were united in their apocalyptic vision of taking the rest of the Twilit Kingdom.

Taking it and feeding it to the dark that already devoured their land.

I remembered the Queen's words to me from her throne.

Take up the banner and drive out the darkness.

Well, there was the darkness and I'd taken up the banner. It stood in a sleeve of bronze anchored to the floor beside the table.

"I will drive out the darkness," I promised, the oath as heartfelt as the moment I swore it to the Queen. "That, or die trying."

"Promises, promises," rumbled a voice so deep I felt it reverberate in my chest.

I looked up from the map, my head whipping around, and beheld the massive creature standing by the door to the chamber. His shoulders were wide enough to fill double doors that four of me could walk through. He was not wearing the ornate suit of plated armour, but one look at his disdainful glare told me that this was my new right-hand man, or whatever he was.

Captain Uzran padded in on bare feet as big as my torso, each step heavy but frighteningly soft. He wore a pair of loose, dark trousers and an open, short-sleeved shirt the color of red wine. With every movement, I could see massive slabs of muscle shift and slide under thick blue-grey skin. He came to the table and rested a fist on the edge, drawing a ponderous groan from the wood.

"Aren't you getting ahead of yourself, though?" the giant growled around a pair of tusks like ivory hook knives. "Unless you plan to charge the Gythraul on your own, something I would love to watch, you have to assemble your army before you can do anything."

He wasn't wrong, but I got the feeling the clarification was not meant to be helpful. Uzran wouldn't be the first guy looking to tell me what to do with my rank and authority. Hell, even Sergeant Feng had been slow coming around, and before the Fiend I would have called him a friend, as well as a true brother-in-arms.

I knew how to handle this: straight on.

"You're wrong, big guy." I walked around the table toward him. "I won't be charging the Gythraul alone."

I stood in front of him now, and he loomed over me like a mountain of meat and bone, glowering in reply to my rebuttal.

"I won't be alone, because last I checked, you are my second, and that means you'll be charging right next to me."

A sound so deep and powerful it was positively tectonic resonated from Uzran's immense chest, but I refused to turn away from his flinty eyes. After one achingly long stare, the growl subsided, and I hadn't flinched.

"I serve at your command and the Queen's pleasure," he acknowledged roughly with an incremental nod. "So it behooves you to make sure she is pleased with your efforts, Paladin."

There it was.

To say I broke him was a gross exaggeration, but right there he spelled out his service, as far as he saw it. He would follow orders. Hell, I'd have bet he would even fight and die at my command, so long as it served the Queen. The second he believed I was acting counter to the Queen's wishes, all bets were off. It wasn't winning hearts and minds, but it helped me understand him, and sometimes, that is a victory in and of itself.

"Well then, Captain," I said, clearly enunciating his title,

"Please advise me as to how I'll go about assembling those armies to prevent our suicidal charge."

The giant maintained his stare a second longer, but then gave a snort, like a bull in a stall, and turned his eyes to the map table.

"The Twilit Kingdom is divided, as with any feudal realm in which power descends from the throne, amongst various vassals. Those vassals maintain the forces required for the defence of the realm. Duanon, as the capital and largest city, can summon sizable levies, but those levies will only be effective if they receive support and supplies from the vassals."

One thick finger pointed to the various fortress-cities I noticed earlier.

"Those," he said, indicating each one, "are the holds of each of the Lords of the Far-Hold.

"Have they started to send the goods in yet?" I asked, looking from one fortress to the next.

Uzran shook his boulder of a head. Light glinted across his bare, grey scalp.

"The protocols of allegiance have not been enacted," he replied with a shrug. "Until you go and perform them, they will send nothing to Duanon."

"So a war is about to start with your worst enemy, and those pricks are waiting for a damn invitation?"

I couldn't have kept the indignation out of my voice if I had tried.

"You will learn that many things in the Twilit Kingdom are not the same as in your world, little Paladin," he answered flatly. "There are laws and customs in Other-Realm as binding as your natural phenomena. Even if the Lords and Ladies of the Far-Hold wanted to send aid, it would be a wasted effort."

"Just Paladin is fine, *Captain*," I said, hoping to nip his authority-testing in the ass. "Bryth mentioned contracts being involved in magic. Is that what you are talking about? And where is she, anyway?"

"The workings of magic are not so simply explained, but for now it may help you to think of things that way."

Uzran stared intently at the map, his jaws working as though he were chewing his thoughts.

"As far as Lady Lighttread is concerned, I am sure she will be along whenever she is able. She is perhaps the most reliable of all the Tuatha I've known." He didn't look up.

My Second didn't seem interested in explaining things further, so I decided to wait for the more amenable Lady Lighttread to show up and do a little more sounding out of my new cantankerous right hand.

"So, what are you, exactly?" I winced internally at my inability to segue politely into asking someone about their species. "I mean, you are not Tuatha, obviously, and other than them, I've only met Gremlins, Goblins, and Merfolk. So who are your people?"

Uzran, in resentful procrastination, refused to lift his eyes from contemplating the map.

"My people are the Ogres," he said without preamble or explanation. His eyes narrowed into obsidian razors.

"Did you come to this world like the Tuatha?" I hoped to at least sound like I'd been listening to all the history that had been flying at me since I arrived.

"We dwelt within this realm before the Tuatha, when we lived as barely more than animals fighting for survival against the tyrannies of the Darklings. We were first to ally with the Tuatha when they declared war upon them."

I saw it in the way his shoulders slid back and he raised his head, chin forward. Pride. This wasn't just a job or just a thing he happened to be good at. This was tradition, and from the sound of things, it was a tradition older than the country I came from. Probably older than the country *my* country came from.

"Are all Royal Guards Ogres, like you?" I remembered the inhuman size and stature of the other armored sentinels I'd seen around the Queen.

"Some," he said, keeping his eyes obstinately fixed on the table. "The trials to join the Royal Guard often prevent some of the weaker peoples from joining. A human, for example, would not make it past the second trial."

And now you are taking orders from one. I thought about suggesting he step down, or of asking the Queen to replace him, but I discarded these ideas as soon as I had them. I was supposed to unite the kingdom—to rally the army. If I dismissed one of their champions out of the gate, it would send the wrong message. I was stuck with the sour giant.

"You boys getting along?" Bryth strode into the room. "I am glad to see that the Paladin has found some clothes to his liking. Breeches and tunic—simple tastes, I see?"

If not for her strong, husky voice, I might not have recognized her when she walked in. The elegant dress was gone, in their place was a shirt and skirt of glimmering mail. Her elegant tresses from before had been exchanged for a single, tight braid. A sable tabard emblazoned with an ivory sword lay across her chest and a leather belt hung with a sword encircled her waist. She looked strong, beautiful, and undoubtedly lethal.

Bryth stopped in her tracks and met my stare. "Is something the matter?" Bemusement crept across her face.

"The human is gawking at you, Bryth," Uzran rumbled.

"I would have thought that after the last one, you would be used to it."

Bryth's pale face flushed, but there was steel in her eyes as she regarded the hunched Ogre. "That is quite enough, Captain," she responded icily. She about-faced sharply. "Come. We have much to talk about, and it would be best if we were somewhere you could see the obstacles you will face now that you've gotten a glimpse of what is at stake."

She set off toward the hallway outside the map room, her footsteps striking with firm purpose.

"Aren't we going to at least talk about the map?" I called after her, but she dismissed the question with a wave of her hand, without turning around.

"There is time for that later."

Uzran rose to his full height and bared his tusk-like teeth in a rare smile as he made to follow. "That, Paladin, is what's called a well-executed retreat."

13

PLANS

I t was strange walking through the halls of the Royal Palace.

If I hadn't known better, I would have said that the halls shifted and aligned to speed our stroll from the map room, which had been at river level by my guess, to a hall whose looming double doors opened onto to a wide veranda overlooking the city.

It should have taken us some time and required a certain amount of exertion to climb to such a height, but, other than traversing the gradual slope of one hallway and a single, short stairwell, we had made no great ascent. It was a little unnerving, until I reminded myself that I was in a land of magic, and that such things were probably commonplace.

Smooth stone pillars ran down the center of the room, stretching up to a ceiling dozens of feet above even Uzran's head, and each one stood nearly a dozen feet from another in an evenly-spaced row. Huge tapestries hung from the tops of those pillars, stretched across the spaces between, their hems just above our heads. Well, Uzran's head. All the tapestries had a similar design.

The top of each tapestry was an ornate, stylized rendering of a figure that went to about the waist. From there, the figures' clothing bloomed into scenes and land-scapes in which the crowning individual could be seen in full miniature, taking part in myriad activities with other creatures and people.

While the overall layout was similar, each tapestry was different in color, tone, and subject matter. At a glance, I saw one depicting what looked like a beautiful girl enclosed within a wall of glass—or maybe ice. Another showed a hunting party bringing prey to ground, but it was hard to tell which was man—or at least manshaped—and which was beast.

"These are Lords of the Far-Hold, and these tapestries are the embodiment of their allegiance to Queen Meabh and to the Twilit Kingdom," Bryth said with a grand sweep of her arm.

I took a few steps back to look down the length of the hall, noting all four banners, along with two bare spaces between three pillars toward the end.

"So these are the leaders I have to win over to get the army I need, huh?" I wondered aloud, feeling an odd famil-iarity with this kind of process. "Not so different from Afghanistan, really, when I think about it. You had to get familiar with the different local and tribal leaders if you wanted to be effective. I guess war looks the same, no matter where you fight."

"After you face the Gythraul in battle, we will see if you feel the same," Uzran snorted behind me, piledriver arms crossed over his huge chest.

It irked me, but he had a point. I was going to be dealing with an unknown enemy in a battlefield where the rules of reality were more like guidelines. I had to be careful that I didn't rely too heavily on my human experiences. I needed to keep my mind and eyes open.

"I have already planned and sent messengers ahead to announce our arrival to each of the Lords," Bryth explained at my shoulder. "I will introduce you to them. Is that acceptable, my Paladin?"

How the hell should I know? was my first thought, but I held it back and just nodded.

"First is Lady Aneira'Tywys, who rules the northern hold of Chillspire." Bryth gestured to a tapestry of a very pretty woman, almost childlike in her proportions, with light blue skin and a gown of silvery white. From beneath the rippling folds of her gown, scenes of her entrance into the cold fortress were woven onto the map. In other scenes, she found shadowy, shaggy creatures who produced glowing jewelry and other gifts to adorn the Lady's petite frame. In the penultimate scene, the creatures bowed before her even as they encased her within—I was leaning more toward ice, now.

"Lady Aneira'Tywys shall be first, because she is unlikely to require much convincing. She was the Queen's former ward, and the Arch-Monger who serves her will explain how the weapons we have taken will be adapted."

"Weapons? Taken?" The pair of words tumble out of my mouth.

"Yes," Bryth said without flinching. "The Arch-Monger will adapt the weapons taken from your garrison. The details and methods of the process you will have to discuss with him."

It didn't seem like making a big deal about stealing a bunch of weapons from the United States Army was going to be useful, but the shock of that realization made the rest of the incoming information hard to process.

I looked at the tapestry and pointed a finger at the frosty woman-child.

"So, wait, am I meeting with her or the Arch-Monger? I'm confused."

"Both," Bryth answered. "Lady Aneira'Tywys is liege over the Arch-Monger, and as such, you need her approval to utilize his expertise to adapt your weapons to our world and to employ his forges to equip the armies."

"So, he is the useful one, but I have to make her happy first."

"Very diplomatically put, Paladin," Uzran snorted again. "Make sure you mention that when you meet the Lady."

"Thanks for the advice, Captain," I replied dryly. "Anything I need to know about the frozen Lady?"

Bryth shot me a little smirk and directed my attention to the final scene of the tapestry.

"The Lady was encased in the Glass Tomb hundreds of years ago, the result of extreme paranoia that has plagued her since she took command of the fortress and its denizens. The Daerg are not the most kindly or honorable of creatures, but their skills as craftsmen and arcano-engineers are matchless. It is only by the Lady's hard and suspicious mind that they are kept in check and made useful to the rest of the kingdom."

The inky, hairy creatures seemed sinister enough, encroaching in on every scene from the dark borders of the tapestry. The artist had certainly captured their shiftiness in the weave. When I looked at the small figure encased in the Glass Tomb, I felt a twinge of sympathy.

"Poor girl," I sighed.

"Lucius," Bryth said, and I looked down at a hand on my arm that quickly retreated to the Tuatha's side. "I mean, Paladin, while your sentiment is noble, I would be remiss if I did not remind you that, though the Lady looks to be a very young woman to your eyes, she is a creature with nearly a millennium of experience manipulating and scheming. While meeting with her, you must remember: she is not a child, but a wily ruler, who is ever on the lookout for an advantage while constantly trying to sniff out treachery and deceit. Do not underestimate her."

"And don't lie to her," Uzran chimed in, this time with what actually sounded like real advice. "She does not suffer deception, and without her support, the armies will be crippled far more than if you do not manage to secure the allegiance of the others."

"Why would I lie to her?"

"It is the habit of elders to lie to the young, or at least to those they think are young. Don't make that mistake," Uzran sniffed.

I supposed that was true enough. "Duly noted," I replied. "So, no pressure. I just need to convince a suspicious master manipulator to give me the keys to the armory. What could go wrong?"

"And she will probably be the easiest to appease of all the Lords," Uzran said flatly. I looked back to see his black eyes boring into me. "Lady Aneira'Tywys is controlling, but not particularly ambitious. She will be cautious, but in the end she knows she needs to help you."

In other words, if you botch this one Luce, you won't even stand a snowball's chance in hell with the others. And in that case, the kingdom falls, and an apocalyptic slaughter comes next.

The weight settled deep into my bones, but I squared my shoulders a little to match the Ogre's. With a grim nod, I turned back to Bryth.

"Tell me about the rest. Everything."

14

SUGGESTIONS

Captain Uzran came into the Royal Garrison commons in the earliest hours of the morning, rubbing his face with a massive hand as he muttered to himself. The internalized conversation had been going on since the Paladin dismissed him and Lady Lighttread from their crash course in the politics of the Twilit Kingdom.

" ... if Lord Bwyathardd doesn't eat him on sight, it will be a miracle as legendary as the Liberation Wars ... "

Something shifted on one of the lounges near the ember-littered hearth, and Uzran's hand quietly slid to a long knife under his tunic. His fingers relaxed from the bone hilt when he spied the drooping nose and glittering eyes of a familiar face peering over the cushions. A heavy sigh that became a groan passed between the Ogre's tusks as he realized how unlikely it was that he would get any rest before embarking later that same morning.

"Reinforcements, Cap'n?" the troll asked, raising a wine-skin that sloshed with appreciable weight.

"Droth to the rescue," Uzran chuckled heavily as he trod

across the room to take the proffered skin. "This is exactly what I need after a day like today."

The troll relinquished the skin and settled his bulk into the lounge. Long, simian arms stretched out to clutch opposite corners of the furnishing with clawed fingers.

"First day of coddling the human, done," Droth growled, wet and leonine, like the teeth that glistened behind his thin lips. "Oh, I hate taking orders from those li'l kak-apes." The troll's claws dug at the wood of the lounge frame, taking out his displeasure by perforating the furniture.

"Get used to it," Uzran grunted. He sat down on another lounge beside his old comrade, savoring the heady smell of the strong liquor before taking his first, long gulp.

"It's plain stupidity, Cap'n, and we all know it," Droth hissed, tossing his head toward the barracks behind him. "We should've abandoned this fool practice after the last disaster. We don't need any more human runts muckin' things up again."

Uzran sucked the last of the stinging liquid from his lips and took another swallow, buying himself time to think. He knew where Droth was headed, but he needed to let the troll go at it full steam.

"After Valoise went the Gorm's way, the Queen should've seen that this way ain't workin'. We're treadin' water, when we should be swimmin' to shore. I sees it, the Guard sees it, and more than a few of the Court sees it, too, Cap'n. Don't you doubt that."

Uzran lowered the skin and leaned forward so his elbows rested upon his knees. "Courtiers are talking now?"

Droth let his glistening eyes slide left, then right, and then gave his commander a sly wink.

"Don't you worry, Cap'n, not a word of any kind of plan —just suggestions, see? Some Tuatha princeling complains of this, some Courtier's mistress complains of that, and we lot make mention of the one who's always been here to protect the Kingdom. All off-handed, all spontaneous. But some of the Courtiers are whisperin' like Hombaths on a rainy day."

The Ogre nodded and sat back. "Planting seeds." Uzran hoisted the skin to his lips. "Putting ideas into their heads."

"Just so, Cap'n, just so. Pile the fuel around the ol' wyrm, I say, and don't be surprised when things get hot."

Uzran drained the rest of the liquor and let the sack flop into a corner of the lounge. He wiped his face with his other hand. The drink had been good—fortifying even—its heat spreading from his belly on up. He gave a rumbling growl to clear his throat and then met Droth's eyes steadily. "You're going to stop this, Droth. Stomp it out now, and keep it that way."

The troll's eyes narrowed for a moment, even as his large nostrils flared. "Come ag'n, Cap'n?"

"You heard me, Droth," Uzran's voice was level, low, and hard as stone. "No more whispers, no more schemes, no more suggestions. Much as I hate it—much as we all hate it —our oath is to the Queen and this is the Queen's will. It is not for us to question it."

Droth's fingers again dug at the wood but he said nothing for a long moment. He seemed to hang there, clutching the lounge, eyes narrowed and nose quivering. "Cap'n," he said slowly, his guttural voice barely more than a hiss. "If'n this is because o' what happ'n'd with yer clan ... "

The silence that followed hung like a gibbeted corpse between the two for several pained eternities before the troll finally yielded to the Ogre's relentless stare and looked over to the cold hearth.

"It's as good as done, Cap'n. You have my word," he said

with a sighing huff, his claws coming unmoored from the gouged lounge with a faint squeak.

Uzran nodded and rose with the flaccid skin in his fist.

"The wine was good, Droth." He nodded before moving toward his private chambers alongside the armory. "Thank you for that."

"Of course, Cap'n," the troll replied, staring into the vacant fireplace. "Always proud to be of service."

15

PATHS

I bounced along on the back of something that might have passed for a horse in bad lighting, if it weren't for the glowing red eyes and fanged snout. The sable-coated Diomedans, Bryth explained, were some of the fastest and most tireless creatures dwelling in Other-Realm, but they were also cantankerous flesheaters, so it was suggested that I guard my fingers and toes. My particular mount was a lovely gal, proportioned like a fair-winning clydesdale, but with exposed fangs longer than my middle finger. Her name was Rhoslyn, and if the way she looked at me hadn't seemed so...hungry, I might have admitted how her eyes were a very pretty shade of rose.

As it stood though, I sat back in the saddle and kept one hand near a holstered M4A1 I'd retrieved from the stolen arms.. There was also a sword and dagger on my belt, but truth be told, while I knew the basics of knife fighting, I was pretty sure I was more likely to stab myself with the sword than fight off my hungry mount.

Still, when Bryth gave them to me, I was amazed at the precise balance and heft I felt just holding the blades out before me. They were light yet solid in my hands, like they were eager to move with my arm; an extension of my own body. There had been a sergeant from another platoon rumored to be some kind of sword geek, who sometimes practiced with one when he was back in the green zone. I had thought the guy was a moron when I heard about him, but right then, holding those lovingly tailored lengths of metal, I understood that I may have misjudged that sergeant. There was something powerful and centering about just holding them.

"Do you even know how to use one of those?" Uzran asked gruffly, nodding at a hand I had let slide to the pommel of the sword at my waist. "Paladin Valoise said that the use of the blade was all but extinct in your world."

Even on the back of this huge animal, Uzran still had to lower his anvil chin to look me in the eye. I doubted anything short of a rhinoceros could have carried the big guy, but it didn't matter, because he strode along beside us without any sign of fatigue—or even effort.

"We did some bayonet drills and some simple combat-ives in basic, and since I was infantry, I picked up some extra training afterwards. But no, Captain, I've never trained with a sword. I patted the stick of my new carbine. "I've had plenty of training, and even more experience with this, though."

Uzran regarded the holstered weapon with a frown before shrugging his huge shoulders. "Hopefully the Arch-Monger and his cronies will have a suitable means of applying their witchery to that device."

I looked at the carbine and back at Uzran, a question forming on my lips. But the Ogre had sidled back to check on the weapons crates. They were being hauled along on wagons, pulled by what might have been oxen, except they had too many horns. In addition to the weapons stolen from Baumholder, there were also some traveling supplies in those crates, I was sure. And for all his assholery, the Captain took his duty seriously. Every half an hour or so, he moved back to check the caravan and speak to a few of the soldiers—other hulks from the Royal Guard, like himself.

"I know Captain Uzran is as crusty as an old boar, but he is diligent and loyal," Bryth said, guiding her Diomedan alongside mine. "He has served the Queen as Captain for more than two hundred years, and another hundred as a Royal Guard before that."

Rhoslyn snapped at the the other Diomeda, which shied a half step away. I almost hauled on the reigns to correct my monstrous mount, but I noticed that Bryth acted like her mount's side shuffle was nothing special, so I thought better of it. Maybe that kind of crap is normal for these things.

"Three hundred years," I muttered. "He looks good for a guy his age. He must work out."

Bryth smiled politely, knowing I had told a joke, but she didn't seem to understand, or she didn't find it funny.

"So," I grunted, clearing my throat, "are they going to walk the next 600 miles?" I nodded toward the Royal Guards who trudged along like Uzran. They had traded in their plated armor for studded leather coats which hung to mid-thigh, but knives, swords, and maces—all proportioned appropriately according to race—hung menacingly from belts and rested securely across backs. They also had packs that probably held rations and road gear slung across their shoulders. Though each had a different gait depending on his species, all maintained a vigorous pace, keeping up with the wagons. They were ready to travel steadily for a long time, but 600 miles was still one hell of a trek.

"Six hundred miles?" Bryth's face twisted with concern.

"Has our course changed, Paladin? We do not have the supplies to travel such a distance."

Now it was my turn to express confusion. "Bryth, you said we were going to see Lady Aneira'Tywys," I said slowly, keeping my tone even. "I saw the map. It's at least that far to her fortress."

As I spoke, the knot of consternation between Lady Lighttread's eyes unravelled, replaced by a look of exasperation. "By the Wyrms, he didn't tell you did he?" she snarled, her gaze cutting back toward the wagons, eyes boring into Captain Uzran.

I shook my head. No. No, he didn't.

"Yes, Chillspire is some distance from Duanon—far more than 600 miles, nearly a thousand I believe—but with the Paths in place, we will not have to travel such a distance."

I nodded, not because I understood, but because it seemed like the thing to do. I hoped she would explain this magical business about Paths, but I expected that even if she did, I wouldn't really understand any of it. The modus operandi for me here seemed to be "Learn by doing." I felt sure that I'd need to experience these Paths to get the hang of them.

"As I have mentioned before, magic suffuses all of Other-Realm," she began, gesturing toward the rippling fields of blue-tinged grass rolling away from Duanon and toward the edge of the forest we had been approaching for the past few hours. "This magic is governed by the Contracts, the knowledge of which enables a sorcerer to manipulate the reality of Other-Realm. In these Contracts, there are Elements and there are Fundaments. Elements are the natural materials that compose the world—things such as earth, water, air, and fire. Anyone with a knack for sorcery and a rudimentary knowledge of the Contracts can manipulate and control these Elements. Their manipulation accounts for nearly all magic in Other-Realm."

"Nearly?" I asked, wondering what it would be like to learn magic.

"The Fundaments—the other side of the Contracts—are the forces that anchor and give structure to the Elements—forces such as time, space, animus, and void. Controlling or altering the Fundaments is not nearly so easy, or even possible for most, and if done unwisely, it can obviously create all manner of horrible disruptions. The Contracts long ago laid out the manner in which the Fundaments may be affected—by a precise and inflexible set of blessings and curses. Time and Space may be bent only in certain ways and by certain methods. Animus and Void may be invoked in potent yet very constrained rituals. These are the Fundament Clauses of the Contracts, and even the greatest of arcane masters must abide by them, including the Queen. The Fundamental Clause of Paths is what will aid us now."

"How?"

She stood up a little in her saddle and pointed toward the tree line. "Once we reach the woods, I will invoke the Clause, and in the forest there will appear a Path—the prescribed route that will allow us to travel to the slopes of Chillspire. We should be within Lady Aneira'Tywys' keep before sundown."

Sundown? Today? How was that possible? I felt stupid for even thinking it, because, as Bryth had told me, the answer was all around me: Magic.

"So, with that Clause thingy, you could just zip around all over the place?" I wondered aloud, thinking about the implications of such a power. I had assumed we were going to be working at a much slower speed. I mean, our supplies were in horse-drawn wagons, but now we were talking about covering distances beyond what most modern overland troop movement methods could hope for. "Do the Gythraul have access to magic?"

"No, thankfully they do not. Direct sorcery is not possible for them. But if they were to capture a capable sorcerer, it would be possible for them to force the poor wretch to open a Path. It would be extremely dangerous, though, as the captive could end the magic prematurely. Such a disruption would likely kill all on the Path. Even if the captive could be trusted, the Queen has become adept at blocking unwanted uses of Paths within her domain.

"However, my Paladin," she paused for half a breath, measuring her words, "you must understand that the Clause does not allow you to travel wherever you like. These Paths have distinct points to which they are linked. Duanon is anchored to all the major fortresses, and those fortresses have Paths to vital areas within their domains and to neighbouring fortresses, but that is all. Other smaller Paths can be opened between those set points, but they can only carry a few at a time without being very taxing to the sorcerer. The Paths are a web of connections, but this web only has so many strands."

"Alright." I accepted the clarification and adjusted my estimation of strategic deployments. "I know we need someone who can do magic to use the Paths, but how many people can use a Path at one time?"

I turned in the saddle and made a quick count of our procession. Uzran, half a dozen of his warriors, as many wagons, including their hunched little drivers—goggle-eyed creatures Bryth had called hobs—and then myself and Bryth.

"It is not a question of numbers so much as time," Bryth

explained. "As many creatures can step onto the Path as would wish, once it has been opened. However, a Path only stays open for so long, and the length of time is dependent on the sorcerer who opened it. Even if the Queen were to open a Path, it would only last until the sun either set or rose, whichever came first after the time the Path was opened."

"And if we are still on the Path when it closes?" I felt I had a pretty good idea what the answer would be.

"We would be thrown out into the realm beyond reality and would be as good as dead."

I swallowed a little harder than usual at that and eyed our procession, which seemed to amble on with glacial slowness. "So, when you said we would reach the Fortress by sundown, you meant that we would get there by then or die trying. Great."

To my surprise, Bryth seemed stung by the complaint. Her shoulders drooped forward a little. "I would not lead you into danger, Lucius." Her voice carried an odd mix of defensiveness and pleading protest. "I have made the trip to Chillspire before. Even with our company and slowed by the wagons, we will have more than enough time to reach our destination."

"Especially if we hit it at a run," Uzran added, strolling up beside Bryth who shot him an ugly look. His scarred lips dipped sideways in a smirk.

"Think you can manage to run that long, big guy?" I asked, feeling a surge of chivalric sentiment heating the words on my tongue.

Uzran met my eyes, and for a second, I was pretty sure I knew how a seal feels when it sees the great white coming for it.

"I once ran for three days and three nights with neither

food, nor rest. In one arm, I held the Queen's consort, in the other, the Pale Banner," he said levelly. "On my back was lashed Toulouse Valoise."

With a thunderous bark, the Ogre took off at a rapid jog that his fellow guards soon matched, and the wagon drivers snapped their reigns. The forest edge was close enough to make out the individual trees, and at their pace, Uzran and the wagons would be under the eaves in a few minutes.

"Is that really true?" I asked Bryth. "I mean all of it?"

Bryth's look was cooler than I would have liked, considering I had been trying to come to her defence. "It most certainly is." She gathered her reigns and put heels into her mount. "The Queen's consort was my father."

16

SHAPES

Like the last time I witnessed Bryth using her magic, I felt a kind of crackling tension in the air—like the whole world was taking a breath.

Her fingers flexed and contorted. Her voice rose and fell with intonations that were not words or language, but they were not merely sounds, either. If a human woman had moved or spoken like that, it would have seemed unnatural—maybe even comical. But she was no human, and that reality wasn't lost on me as she worked her magic.

The final phrase of Bryth's incantation slid into my ear like a whisper, even as pounding hooves, tromping boots, and creaking wagons created a din.

I felt, as much as saw, the ripple of power issue from the Tuatha sorceress and race ahead toward where Uzran and the lead wagon were about to hit the treeline. A bitterly cold gust of wind burst from between the trees, and on its whistling tail came squirming coils of fog. Slithering snakes of animated vapor rushed to meet the charging Ogre and his wards.

One by one, the wagons and hulking guardians were devoured, disappearing into the grasping fog.

I had put my heels into Rhoslyn's flanks to keep up with Bryth, but now I wasn't so certain I wanted to go racing into that sinister mist, especially at literally breakneck speeds. I looked over at Bryth again and saw that her green eyes wept radiant tears. It was like the energies she was manipulating were so great, they were leaking—bleeding out of her in luminescent drops of raw light. She caught my stare as we galloped toward the fog, and then she spoke with a voice like a storm goddess racing down from on high.

"Come, my Paladin," she boomed in a voice too immense for her body. "Ride with me along the Path toward your first victory."

Well, how do you turn an invitation like that down?

"Hell yeah!" I roared back. Yeehaw-ing like a drunk Pony Express rider trying to beat a train to the crossing, I drove Rhoslyn hard into the mist, side by side with Bryth.

For a second, there was nothing but molten shades of white twisting on top of each other, but then the fog slackened, and I was in a world of shades and shapes. Or maybe it would be more accurate to say that they were the shades of shapes—impressions of what things could be on the other side of the veil.

I saw the forest, which had lain within the fog, or at least, I saw the shadows of the trees stretching out like dark stains among layers of white. As we raced on, we passed through and over the spectral forms of trees, but no branches scraped at us, and no sturdy trunks barred our advance. There was no path that I could see, but that didn't matter, because there was a subtle yet undeniable pull due north. The ground was a sheet of flat, vaporous chalk, and coupled with the near absolute silence, the land was ghostly and desolate. The only real and solid thing I could see was my galloping Diomedan and Bryth on her mount. Her eyes no longer dripped with magical energy, but they still shone with a pale light that made their emerald depths glimmer bewitchingly. I didn't know whether I wanted to draw closer or run away, but in that instant I found it hard to even look away from her lest I lose myself to the barren landscape.

"How do you navigate?" I yelled, my mind remembering the thunder of our wild ride into the fog. I suddenly realized everything was deathly quiet. Even the sound of our horse's hooves seemed like an echo of something happening far away. "I mean," I began again in a hushed tone that seemed appropriate for the weighty stillness, "how do you know the way?"

"There is only one way," she said in a soft, almost conspiratorial whisper. "As I told you, Lucius, each Path has a beginning and an end. Your direction doesn't matter, because you can only ever reach one place."

"So it only matters that we get to the end of the Path before times runs out?"

"Exactly," she smiled.

"Then let's make sure we don't have to be worried about that," I grunted and urged Rhoslyn to ever greater speed. She obliged, and I felt the layers of fog pass over my face and through my hair in tingling sheets. Bryth gave short peal of laughter and joined me in my galloping.

The shapes of trees, boulders, buildings, hills, valleys, and even a mountain, I think, fell behind us. True to the reputation of the Diomedans, Rhoslyn kept up an incredible pace with little sign of flagging or fatigue. As we rode on, I felt like the weight—the crushing heaviness that had rested on me ever since that time in the caves of Afghanistan—was sliding off of me. I still felt it tethered to me with strings of memory, guilt, fear, and duty, but the farther we went, the thinner those bonds seemed. I wondered if one day I would get to ride fast enough to sever them completely—to snap all the ties to an ugly existence and just run free in that world of empty, white shapes.

My reverie was broken and my grip on reality tightened once more when the first wagon took shape out of the foggy shadows. They were still rumbling along, but the dampening effect of the Path had made the rattle and clamour of the wagons a distant murmur.

One of the Royal Guard, a thick-necked, humanoid creature with ram horns, bowed its head as we passed. It raised a hand, laying its clawed fingers across an ornate bronze disk bound across its forehead with studded bands of iron. Bryth raised a fist in salute, and I did my best to do the same, hoping the quickness of our passing would cover any failures in form. The wagoneer also raised a knobbly hand at us and waved, though his face remained dour.

I was going to need Bryth to help brush up on my etiquette. These were my soldiers now, I needed them to respect and trust me. It couldn't hurt to learn the protocols and traditions that underpinned their military societies. Those kind of things matter more to some soldiers than others but I had learned that, lots of times, it was the little trappings of honor and order that stabilize a soldier—especially in the emotional chaos of war, and these people had been at war a long time.

The pace of our hungry steeds devoured the pale ground, and we soon passed more of the wagons, each with its complementary guardian. As we passed, we offered salutes to more of the convoy, though a few of the Royal Guards only begrudgingly returned the salute. I wondered if that wasn't in part due to a difference of physiology. As best I could tell, there were four different species that made up the Royal Guard. Some were the tall, powerfully built Ogres like Uzran, then there were the horned guys with bronze shapes on their foreheads. Another kind had long noses and ape-like arms. They were shorter than either the Ogres or the ram-heads, but still bigger than any human I'd ever seen. Lastly, there was a kind taller than even the Ogres, with skin as dark and gnarled as tree bark. Whatever their build or features, all kept up their relentless trot, and from the way their weapons sat on their belts you knew they were ready for trouble.

All of them answered to me. It was a heady, terrifying understanding—like the first time you call in the big guns to take out an enemy position. That kind of power at your command makes you feel invincible yet sick to your stomach at the same time. Except now there was no chain of command to check me. No superior officer who might countermand my orders. Apart from the Queen, I was it. I was the commander—the entire military's singular leader.

My stomach tightened even further as I remembered the number one rule of leadership: when you're on top and shit hits the fan, the only one to blame is yourself.

Bryth and I were pulling up level with Uzran and the wagon he guarded. Without waiting for Bryth, I threw a salute to the big guy. He turned around, regarding us with a scowl. The speed of Rhoslyn was pulling me away from the glaring Ogre and he still was not saluting. For an instant, I wondered if this constituted a breach of etiquette. Then I wondered if I was willing to discipline the Captain for not saluting, if it really came down to it. What would that even look like? There was so much I didn't know.

I was spared worrying about it much longer. Uzran gave

an obviously reluctant salute, just as I was about to turn back to the empty white of the Path again.

In the vast, ever-moving but never-changing expanse that was the Path, it was hard to keep track of time, or even your own thoughts. There was something about the muffled nature of the sounds there and the steady drumming of our Diomedans' hooves which lulled a person into this almost trance-like state. It wasn't sleep, and honestly, despite the craziness of my last few days, I felt no fatigue at all on the misty Path. It was something that made you feel beside yourself—an out of body experience, I guess. Eyes ahead, you watched everything unfold. Stride by stride. And it didn't really mean anything, because it was just more stirred fog.

It reminded me of a time when I was a kid. Before my dad took me out for "private tutelage," I used school computers that had those old screensavers that gave the impression of moving through space, stars zipping by—but you never got anywhere. Just more stars, all of them moving by so fast you barely registered their passing. I had once spent half an hour staring into them from my desk; it wasn't until the teacher came by and took my blank quiz that I realized how long I'd been lost in my journey to nowhere.

Somewhere in a distant part of my mind that still kept up the tedious business of thought, I wondered if it was possible to go too far on a Path and become lost in the vacuous mist.

Maybe it was because Bryth was beside me, or maybe it was one of the rules of magic, but the screensaver journey did not last forever. A single sharp point of light, a brazen red after so much white fog, cut through the mist just ahead of us. As we grew closer, that point swelled until, inside its brilliance, I could discern shapes and forms more real than the surreal shadows I had first seen on the Path. A singular peak rising above other jagged points of rock came into focus, then I saw that the piercing top of the peak was not the mountain itself, but the minarets of Chillspire stabbing into the bloody sky.

There was a growing sound of whistling and as we rode onward, our vision returned to normal, the tuneless song grew deeper and fiercer. Something cold struck my cheek. It was so sudden that it almost stung. I raised my hand to my face, fingers coming away wet. Within seconds, more sensations, chilly and liquid, pricked my face and hands, then I saw the little motes of white racing toward me out of the vanishing fog.

Snow. Snow on a strong wind.

I looked up into the crimson light and realized it was a late afternoon sun seeming to set early as a snowstorm rolled in with twisting, ribbon-like flurries. The white peaks glistened gorily in the dying light. The whistling had become the howling of the wind across the mountainside. It became deafening as the last of the mist from the Path vanished, taking with it the muffling stillness.

The hooves of our steeds clomped across the frigid earth and the ground began to slope upward. The sparse trees added the smells of pine and spruce to the air, layering the sweet scents with the biting cold. The touch of the snowflakes had been gentle in comparison to the keening wind that was coming on.

Bryth called on me to slow down, shouting over the wind, and I did so without much trouble though my hands were quickly growing numb. Looking back I saw that just past a few broken ranks of trees, the fog of the Path still seethed, unaffected by the roaring wind. Somehow, in the bleakness of our new setting, it seemed even more ominous.

"You have a cloak and other winter clothing in your saddlebag," Bryth shouted as she unfastened the clasp on one of her own. "It is not much farther to Chillspire, but it will be much slower going and very cold."

I looked up at the fortress and felt an almost giddy sense of wonder. Here it was—the hold of Lady Aneira'Tywys, nearly a thousand miles from where we had set out. We had reached it in a few hours. By horseback. It had been a few hours, hadn't it?

I found the saddlebag with the winter clothes and yelled to Bryth as I drew a cloak of sable fur around my shoulders. "It seemed like we were only in there a few hours, which would make it just past midday or so, but the sun seems much lower." I fished out a pair of dark leather gloves that fit remarkably well and were pleasantly lined with more soft, black fur. "What gives?"

Bryth was already swaddled in a hooded cloak of silver fur and for all the world looked like some impossibly elegant and strong Queen of the North. She wouldn't have looked out of place in a sleigh drawn by polar bears or something else worthy of a heavy metal album cover.

"The Paths bend time and space, so it is understandable that what we perceive is less than the actual time which has passed." She maneuvered her mount around and peered back into the fog. "I imagine that it is, in part, our material minds trying to cope with the drastic change. Deep within, we know such things are impossible, but to avoid breaking, they must cut things away, like a seamstress casting off broken threads."

I could believe it, my own brain still racing in equal portions manic delight and churning dismay. Magic—terrifying and yet so wickedly cool.

It took another five minutes or so, real time, for Uzran's

charge to emerge from the mist. The wheels gouged at the stiff ground, and the mountainside echoed with the rattle and clamor of the heavy wagon. Uzran, his breath steaming sheets in the air, slowed to a walk before crunching through the snow up to where Bryth and I stood.

"It seems you made it through, and no worse for wear," I observed with a smile, though having to shout probably made it sound less friendly than I had intended.

"And you are still here, Paladin," he replied sullenly, tectonic voice carrying through the wind with careless ease. "You should head up to the gate. We will gather the wagons and see that they are brought to the forges within the mountain. The Lady will not thank you for keeping her waiting."

I looked up to the fortress, seeing the switchback path which wound its way up to the immense gates that looked like they had been woven from the trunks of golden trees. Above the gates were crenellated ramparts bearded with icicles, but I couldn't see any sentries moving around up there. Many slitted windows decorated the upper portions of the wall and the minarets, but all were dark. If it had not been in such good condition, I might have guessed that the place was abandoned.

"Does she even know we're here?" I asked.

"She should have been informed of our coming." Bryth raised a finger toward a stand of pines a little way up the hill. "And if not, she knows now."

A pair of glinting eyes set in a squat, shaggy shadow gleamed in our direction before vanishing behind a tree.

17

ENCHANTMENTS

The first and last thing you need to know about the Daerg who live in Chillspire is that they are creepy as hell.

FROM THE SECOND Bryth and I walked through the stronghold's gates, I felt their beady, little eyes on us—hundreds of them—though we were greeted by just one of their number —a sinister little bugger calling himself Morth. I caught enough quick glances at the rest of the Daerg as they scuttled about our peripherals to know that the emissary seemed a typical member of his kind. They all seemed about the height of large children, but with thick, hairy bodies and glittering, dark eyes. They were all a uniform, sooty black—both their hair and what I took to be their skin —and looked something like how I imagined Sasquatch might. Their shaggy, hirsute appearance made reading any kind of expression nearly impossible.

AND WORST OF ALL—THEY whispered. Not the overloud whisper of someone being silly, or the reverent hush of whispering in a library. No, this whispering was more like a stalker talking to himself as he watches. Just loud enough to hear, but not loud enough to discern meaning; it was sickening. A continual, grating, breathy hiss. Even Morth, who was talking clearly enough for us to hear him, sounded like some stalker panting at the window.

"THISSS WAY TO SEE HER, come my Lord." He beckoned from the stairs of the main hall, a silver candelabra held in his woolly knuckles. He wore a leather apron about his waist, what looked like well-worn slippers on his feet, and nothing else. I guess there was reason to be glad for all the hair.

THE MAIN HALL was dark except where the last red light of the sun peeked in through high, narrow windows. What I could see of the floor looked like an intricate mosaic worked in polished stones of various shades and hues, but so much was in shadow that I couldn't even guess as to what was being depicted.

ALL AROUND US, the blackness of the hall hissed with whisperings of the lurking Daerg.

BRYTH HAD EXPLAINED to me on our way up that the Daerg were the greatest magical craftsmen in all of Other-Realm, able to bind and weave the Contracts into artifacts of incredible beauty and power. She had also told me that no one liked them. At all. They were deceptive, grasping, cruel, and full of schemes that made sense only to them. If they weren't capable artisans, no one would have had anything to do with them. As it was, they remained isolated to these mountains exclusively until Lady Aneira'Tywys had come to them. The exact details of how she claimed lordship over the slippery monsters is unknown, but ever since then the Daerg had become more reliable and their craftsmanship had become an integral part of the Twilit Kingdom. They were going to help outfit my army—just as they had done for all the Paladins before me.

As we moved up the stairs after Morth, I thought of at least one obvious reason why nobody would befriend these creatures. The cold. Would it have killed them to turn on the heat? Or the lights? We trudged up the stairs in the dark, still wearing our winter cloaks and gloves, our breath misting on the air.

Up the stairs and through an archway that looked like it was made of vines of red, gold, and white crystal we went, the blue flames of the candelabra glinting off walls smooth as glass and set with fantastically intricate geometric patterns.

The chorus of snake sounds from the hall was gone but as we moved past dark, branching corridors, I would spy the glimmer of a staring Daerg or hear another trickle of whispers. Just enough to keep a man on edge as he moves through a shadowy fortress to meet an ancient sorceress.

I DECIDED I needed something to occupy my mind.

"So, MORTH," I stepped closer to our guide, "how long have you served Lady Aneira'Tywys?"

MORTH DID NOT STOP MOVING, but he slowed for a second to look up at me. The layers of hair above his eyes crinkled with what I took for confusion before he turned back and picked up the pace.

"ALL MY LIFE, BLESSED ME," he answered. I had a hard time believing that last part wasn't sarcastic. "Ssince I spilled from the root to thisss very day, have I served her. Faithful Morth."

SPILLED FROM THE ROOT? Perhaps that was a euphemism I didn't want to understand. "So has your family always served the Lady?"

"MY FAMILY," he hissed the word slowly, as though it was strange on his tongue, "yesss, my clan wasss formed at her direction. I am the two hundred and thirteenth to serve as her steward."

THE STATEMENT SEEMED A HOLLOW FACT, not a declaration of pride—just a bland recitation of information.

"Quite a line of distinctive service." I hoped I sounded sincere as I tried to think of nonchalant questions to keep the conversation going. I was spared the effort when we reached a door constructed of intersecting bars of polished bronze that shone with a rosy hue in the candlelight. From between the bars stairs led

up toward soft, icy light.

"Here it isss," Morth breathed in what may have been relief. It wouldn't have surprised me to learn that Daerg don't do small talk.

Morth fished a small, black key from his apron and with hardly a click or a clack, he opened the door which swung smoothly and silently inward.

"The Arch-Monger awaits you at the top of the stairsss," our guide whispered, already creeping backward from the open portal. "He shall announce you to her."

"Thanks," I said, but then the candelabra was out, and not even Morth's beady eyes could be seen in the faint light coming from the stairs.

Up we went, Bryth and I climbing those smooth, stone steps. The light grew—an ambient, blue-white glow from the walls that had to be enchanted. My head swam with questions for Bryth about what to do and what to say but I still felt the oppressive presence of the Daerg, even if I couldn't see or hear them. It wouldn't do for them to all get the idea that I didn't know what I was doing, even if it was true. So we climbed the stairs in silence. It was a good thing I was still in fighting trim because it was a lot of stairs. The ascent left my legs burning and my back aching but eventually, we reached the top.

THE STAIRS OPENED INTO A WIDE, round room. It was bare except for a massive block of glass framed in black iron. It stood in the center of the room and reached nearly to the domed ceiling.

MIDWAY between where we emerged and the glass cube stood another Daerg. This one had a far nicer apron and coils of various metals woven into his beard. A cap of gold with a single inlaid ruby sat on top of his fuzzy head, gleaming just above above his brows.

THE DECORATED DAERG, which must have been the Arch-Monger, scuttled forward and bowed.

"WELCOME PALADIN BOLLHAM, welcome back Lady Light-tread," the Arch-Monger said in a voice that was far less hissy and whispery than the other Daerg. "I am most eager for you to meet our Lady so I may begin my work on your armaments. I have so many plans."

WHILE HIS UNABASHED enthusiasm caught me off guard, I was pleasantly surprised that there seemed to be at least one non-stalkerish Daerg in this place.

"SO YOU ARE familiar with the new weapons we brought?" I asked, curious.

"MOST CERTAINLY, GALLANT PALADIN," the Arch-Monger chuckled, sliding his hands into his apron pockets. "The concepts of combustion-propelled firearms has been with us for some time, but the new models—the M4 and the M240B—are fantastic improvements over the rifles we last took our...expertise to. The incredible rate of fire was particularly impressive. I believe that if we use impregnated manticore quarrels we will..."

"ARE We not to meet him first?" came a clear, high-pitched voice from the glass structure.

A STRANGE LOOK—PART embarrassment and part loathing—rippled across the shaggy face of the Arch-Monger and he turned toward the cube, bowing deeply. "My apologies, my Lady," he said in a voice of overdrawn politeness. "I present before thee Paladin Lucius Bollham and Lady Bryth Lighttread, come to seek your favor and friendship."

"APPROACH," came a tone too authoritative for a voice so small.

I GAVE Bryth one last worried glance, and she returned a comforting smile. We moved toward the center of the room.

EVEN THOUGH THE cube seemed to be made of glass, deep layers of frost covered its face in layers of rime so that everything within was obscured except for a small oval space facing the stairs. Within that window––the size of a bathroom mirror––stood Lady Aneira'Tywys.

IN HER TAPESTRY, she had been captured in that stage between woman and girl that existed for most mortal women somewhere between thirteen and eighteen, but in person she appeared much younger than the tapestry's portrayal. She was a child—as perfectly proportioned and pretty as any could dream to be—but she would never have passed for anything older than ten or eleven if she were human. Yet for all that, she dressed and appeared as a lady might, from the hem of her ornate, cobalt dress to the rosy colors of her lips and pale cheeks. She looked like a little girl playing an elaborate game of dressup, but the cool authority in her periwinkle eyes was nothing any child could possess. Everything she looked upon was hers, and the only thing youthful about such an imperious stare was the absolute conviction it held.

I THOUGHT EVEN Queen Meabh would have a hard time

matching that look, and for a second, I could think of nothing to say to the child-empress.

"You are duly smitten by our beauty," the Lady observed, her gaze weighing me up in a way no little girl's eyes could, "as it is with all who see Us."

"My L-lady," I stammered, trying to find my voice as I went to one knee before her, "it is my honor to stand before you now."

"Only you are kneeling, silly boy," Aneira replied as though she had begun to doubt my intelligence. "How strange."

Swallowing hard, I stood quickly and reminded myself what she was—old, cunning, and manipulative. I needed to take control of the conversation or she was going to play me like a fiddle.

"My Lady has a keen eye," I said straightening. "Keen enough also, I trust, to see the need the Twilit Kingdom has of her." Good, remind her of her obligations but make it clear she is needed, valued.

Lady Aneira'Tywys stared up at me, plainly undaunted despite the disparity of size between us.

"WE ARE." She gestured languidly toward the Arch-Monger beside me. "Our faithful servant has already begun preparing to arm the armies of Our beloved Kingdom."

OUT OF THE corner of my eye, I saw another weird expression twitch across the Daerg's face. The loathing was still there, I was pretty sure, but something else, too. Was it pride at being mentioned? Excitement at being noticed?

I SNAPPED my attention back to Aneira. I could figure out these people's jacked-up relationships some other time. For the moment, I was negotiating an arms contract.

"I AM PLEASE to hear this, as I am sure the Queen will be. Captain Uzran, my second, may even now be delivering the weapons that will serve as the templates for your workers to copy."

THE ARCH-MONGER GAVE a little choking sound. "Not copies, Paladin! No, much more than tha-"

"SILENCE," the Lady said sharply. "Such details are the business of you and your kind, Daerg. Do not trouble us with them now."

"Deepest apologies, my Lady," came the pitiable, miserable reply from the wilting Daerg.

"Now," Aneira raised her head and eyed me expectantly, "what *is* a matter of significance for Us to discuss is your worthiness to receive the gifts which Our servants shall provide. We are told you are a great warrior, a leader among your people, and We see now that you are indeed one of the more winsome creatures who has been chosen to serve as Paladin."

Bryth gave the slightest twitch at my side on that last remark, but I ignored it.

"Yet all of that means nothing when considering what We shall give to you. My Daerg shall take your mortal instruments and transform them into the armaments of gods. With such power, even the most noble of warriors may be tempted to abuse his station, pressing his advantage in self-deluded aspirations. He will forget that he is a servant when he is armed like a master, and he will never achieve all the great good he set out to do. So the question is not of your skill or your prowess, but the truth of your heart. Is your heart true, Paladin?"

How to answer that? I am no saint by anyone's measure in my world, and I barely understood the world I was in now.

"I AM GOING to do the best I can, Lady Aneira'Tywys." My voice was shakier than I wanted it to be. "For the Queen and for the Twilit Kingdom."

A DANGEROUS EDGE came into the mask of the little girl's face before me.

"THAT IS NOT ENOUGH. Declared intentions are not enough," she pointed a small, encarmined nail at me. "Is your heart true? Will you seek to serve and nothing more?"

I THOUGHT about trying to be clever, to make a play at some snarky turn of phrase, but then I felt her eyes digging into me, and I knew that would be a fatal mistake. Despite her appearance, she was an old hand at this game—older than any human could ever be—and she knew if I tried to be cute or cryptic or anything else, she would have me.

SO WITH NO REAL ALTERNATIVES, I was honest.

"NO ONE REALLY KNOWS WHO they are or what they'll do in a situation until it happens." My voice was a little heavy, even in my ears. "I know what I've set my mind to do, and I know what I plan to do, but until you trust me with this kind of power, I can't know how I will handle it. All I can tell you is that I've been faithful thus far to everyone I've served. I have no intention of being anything but that." I met the Lady's eye and put every ounce of sincerity I had into my next words. "I am a man, flaws and all, but I am the man that will save this Kingdom or die trying."

I STOOD THERE, feeling naked despite the layers of clothing covering my body, and hoped beyond hope that I hadn't ruined this thing before it even began.

"WE ARE... PLEASED," Lady Aniera'Tywys said at last. "But there is one last thing you must do before We give you Our blessing."

BESIDE ME, the Arch-Monger produced a red apple that fit snugly in the hairy cup of his coal-black hands. It was glossy and smooth—so perfect, it didn't seem real—and he held it out to me.

"TAKE THIS, and with one bite, prove the veracity of your words to Us," she said, a frigid smile on her red lips. "If you speak true, the enchantment shall pass over you like the shadow of a windblown cloud, but if you have spoken lies ... "

I GULPED and took the pristine apple in my hand. I knew what I said had been true, but was it true enough? Did I mean it enough, deep down? Was I true of heart?

I RAISED the apple to my lips, thinking about the time I first saw Queen Meabh. I had to trust that whatever she and her people saw in me was good enough to pass this test. Yet, as I sank my teeth deep into the skin of that apple, it was not any thought of the Queen, nor the grandeur of Duanon that came to mind. It was the innocent eyes of that merchild I remembered.

THAT WAS what I was fighting for, and that would have to be enough.

THE FRUIT WAS sweet at first, but as I swallowed, the taste soured into a cloying, bitter tang. With horror, I felt an icy numbness crawling up the back of my throat, chasing that taste away. My body began to shake, and I looked to Bryth, shame and fear welling up inside me but finding no voice. I had failed.

BRYTH'S EXPRESSION was stony and unflinching to my shuddering eyes.

I FELL to my knees as I stared at her, knowing that she must hate me for my failure—a failure which might doom her entire world.

I WANTED to say I was sorry, but I couldn't breathe. The cold had slid down my throat and was crystallizing in my lungs, crushing the life out of me.

THEN, just like clouds parting, the shadow of the poisonous enchantment slid away from me. I took a breath, and though it was cold, I relished the sensation of that sweet air tickling my throat. From my knees, I looked up and saw that Bryth was smiling, eyes beaming.

"IT SEEMS to Us that Mother Gwiddon has chosen wisely" Lady Aneira'Tywys sighed, her voice lilting with a child's disappointed pout. "Again."

18

PRACTICE

Bryth took hold of the rifle Luce had been using to teach her, rested the stock against her shoulder and sighted along the barrel toward a stand of trees where bristlecones hung from bowed branches.

She tried to remember the things Luce had told her. Aim through the target, breathe halfway out, squeeze the trigger, don't pull...

There was a shrieking hiss as the quill zoomed past a bristlecone, followed by a crack as it impacted a tree trunk behind it. It was enough for the Tuatha to feel a deep surge of frustration. It took all within her not to hurl the new weapon away. Instead, she settled for unleashing a magically-enhanced curse at an unlucky, nearby stone.

It flew apart in fragments.

She had missed again, but the failure itself did not gall her as much as the reason why. She had missed not because of a lack of skill, but a lack of focus. When she held the rifle to her cheeks, she remembered him leaning close to her, his voice soft and instructive. And when she remembered that, she remembered another man who had once held her close, too...

"Damnation and Wyrm-Fire!" she snarled, condemning feelings she would have given anything to exorcise.

"Wasting breath and wasting time," came a cavernous voice behind her. Bryth turned to see Uzran coming down the hill toward the impromptu shooting gallery. "What need do you have for such toys? You are still a battle magus, aren't you?" The Ogre inclined his head toward the few bits of stone left by her feet.

Bryth felt her cheeks color slightly at the evidence of her temper, but her hands tightened around the weapon. "I am, but these are fascinating creations," she retorted raising the rifle. "Mortal weapons have grown even more remarkable and deadly—able to fire with such precision and speed."

The Ogre crossed his arms and regarded the weapon with an incredulous glare.

"And the Arch-Monger has enhanced them further." She traced a hand across the modified barrel, magazine, and firing mechanism. "With the old rifles, we had replaced the humans' slugs with germinated Fire Flower seeds, but those were prone to violent misfires when jostled outside the chamber. They also had problems penetrating armor."

"I was there for all of this, you know," Uzran grunted.

"Yes, I know, but you weren't there when the Arch-Monger explained how these work now." With a quick release, she held up the magazine for inspection. "Now we are firing manticore quills impregnated with Deep Basilisk venom. The firing pin cracks the base of the quill where the venom reacts with the air, propelling the quill at incredible speeds. It becomes a piercing toxic missile that will dissolve inside the target. Even if it does not penetrate, it will burn handily on the surface."

"Elegant," the Ogre replied dryly, "yet, as impressive as that is, a squadron of war-magi could wreak far more havoc than a regiment of Bogguns and Hobbs."

"True, but not without risk, and it is far harder to train war-magi than rifle-armed Bogguns." Bryth rested a hand defensively upon the weapon. "Besides, it never hurts to have options."

Uzran gave a bovine snort and patted the broad blade at his side. "I need only one option."

"You might have been the salvation of the Twilit Kingdom, Uzran," Bryth said with a sigh, casting off his criticism and her own warring feelings. "If you just weren't so determined to be stuck in your ways."

"Perhaps." Uzran gave a rueful smile. "But then I wouldn't be me, and it is my duty to guard the Queen and her interests even if it be from herself and the consequences of her ... policies."

"Perhaps." Bryth parroted her old friend's rumbling tones. They shared a quiet chuckle before silence crept in and stretched on between them.

The wind was not howling as it had been on the day of their arrival, and the clouds had cleared away, displaying a crisp, blue sky. Despite this, fretful gusts speckled with snow, flitted across the mountainside and over the pair of them.

"We go to the savages next then?" Uzran frowned at the thought. "What is that look for?"

"I don't imagine that Lord and Lady Bwyathardd would appreciate the characterization. You do remember that our current endeavors are diplomatic in nature?"

"I don't see them or their misbegotten sycophants mewling about," the Captain said, shrugging. "And besides, Lord Bwyathardd knows what I think of him and has for years. If you'll remember, it was your father who talked him out of dueling me after he'd already posed his challenge. Bwyathardd is an impulsive fool."

"Bwyathardd is a formidable warrior," Bryth commented, part of her unwilling to dwell long on the memory of her father. "And his warbeasts are vital to the war effort."

"Debatable, but formidable or not, your father saved that fool of a Lord's life," Uzran rumbled, a fierce light coming into his black eyes. "I sometimes wonder if your father had not been so honorable, and if the duel had taken place, whether or not your father would have been granted Bwyathardd's realm. He was of proper rank and favored by the Queen. I cannot help thinking that, had he been Lord of Thistlebough, perhaps he would... well, things would have been different that day."

"If that had happened," Bryth swallowed around the lump in her throat, "you would not be here now. You would have died at the Breach of the Brittle Ridge. He would not have saved you, and you would not be here to see the coming victory."

"Do you really believe that victory is nigh? Truly?"

Bryth turned away, her face hardening incrementally even though her voice quivered. "The Queen says it will be so. I believe her."

A pained silence grew between them as more snow tumbled from the sky.

"The Queen talks of victory with each new Paladin," Uzran said after a pause. "My warriors and I have heard it so many times that it's almost a joke among us when we are alone in the barracks. Bitterness—not hope—sees us talking of the golden days to come, when the Human will save us all. I can't believe in him like you want me to, little one."

Bryth lowered the rifle to rest against an old stump and then took hold of the Ogre's massive hand. "Then what do you believe in, Ol' Stone?" she asked, using her childhood name for him.

Uzran drew in a heavy breath and squared his shoulders before looking down at her. "I believe that duty can stand, even when bitterness and despair have eaten everything else."

Bryth shook her head and squeezed the Ogre's war-roughened fingers. "There has to be more to it than that," she breathed, seeing the invisible weight that pressed down on Uzran's wide shoulders. "Duty without hope? That's a cold, lifeless thing, Ol' Stone. I know what happened to your clan—what you had to do—but that doesn't mean that you can't..."

Gently but firmly, he drew his hand away from her grip. "I have given everything to serve my Queen. I have nothing else but that. I need nothing else but that."

Bryth felt something on her cheek that was not the snow as she watched him trudge back toward Chillspire.

19

SAVAGES

The trip to Thistlebough, the estate of the Lord and Lady Bwyathardd, had been uneventful, though we were fewer in number now, with only Uzran and one other Royal Guard accompanying Bryth and me. The rest had stayed at Chillspire and would escort the newly modified weapons to Duanon, returning to fetch new batches as they were made. We didn't have the luxury of waiting around, but we stayed at Chillspire long enough for me to acquire a freshly-minted M-Core—the name I had given the modified battle-rifle holstered in my saddle.

The Path was strange and numbing as before, but the lands we rode into were as different from the mountains as night was from day. Everywhere was heavy, black-boughed forest. The trees stood close together, and the ground was blanketed by deep chartreuse and umber underbrush. It was also much warmer, and I was soon shedding my cloak and gloves, following Bryth down a narrow track to a clearing in the wood.

Thistlebough Castle sprawled across the wide meadow as one part curtain-walled fortress, one part garden palace.

Lush beds and lattices of blooming flowers were everywhere, and all seemed to be on the edge of overgrowth,
though they appeared all the more spectacular because of it.
The trilling hum of winged life, both bird and insect, was on
the air, and somewhere within the walls I heard the whin-
nying of horses. It might have seemed perfectly idyllic had it
not been set in such a dark, brooding forest.

The castle itself was welcoming, with a crushed stone
path that came up to the clearing edge. The gates of both
the curtain wall and central keep were opened wide in
preparation for our arrival. Hawk-helmeted sentries saluted
us from the gatehouse turrets, bayoneted rifles at their
shoulders. The picturesque scene was maintained even once
we were within the stately courtyard, with its artfully lithe
trees dripping with exotic, blooming flora. Well-dressed
grooms with doe eyes and small, spiky antlers greeted us in
the cool shade, their hands offering up cool water jugs.

I took the water gratefully and savored its coolness, even
though just hours ago I had been leaving the icy halls of
Chillspire. The domain of Thistlebough felt like it was in
the dead of a southern summer—like you found around
Fort Benning—sweltering and moist. After draining the jug,
I handed over the reins and dismounted. Rhoslyn snapped
her fangs playfully at me then gave a snort. I supposed that
the horse-monster might be beginning to like me.

Bryth stood next to me, and her face seemed to crinkle
with annoyance as she looked around.

"Everything okay?" I asked.

"She doesn't like it here," Uzran whispered none too
quietly behind me, "and neither do I."

"Let's just focus on the task at hand, shall we," Bryth said
tightly, eyes fixed ahead.

"Compared to the creeping Daerg, this place seems

awesome," I replied, smiling as a three foot tall hedgehog came to bow before us, dressed in hose and a currant doublet of velvet with puffed sleeves.

"Greetings and welcome, my Lords and Ladies," he squeaked as his quills rustled excitedly. "Please, follow me."

"Seriously," I gave my companions sidelong glances. "Not even a comparison."

"Just wait," Uzran rumbled dryly. "It gets better."

A pair of guards with porcine snouts sprouting bronze-capped tusks hauled open the doors to the central keep. Bryth and I walked from the smothering humidity into the relatively cool half-light of a torchlit hall. An assembly of humanoid species with various animal features lined the velvet carpet we seemed meant to walk upon. Each of them was dressed in a fanciful suit or gown. The whole thing looked like people going to a rave had tried to mix in some renaissance era garb. Each garish, ornately-clothed attendee bowed or curtseyed, making some kind perfunctory animal noise of greeting as we passed. I tried to look down the hall to where a pair of elaborate, high-backed thrones stood, but it was a long hall, and the constant hoots, howls, whinnies, and screeches were more than a little distracting.

Bryth put her arm in mine and pulled me forward. There was something warm and comforting about her touch, even through our armoured travel clothes. I gave her a quick sideways look, wondering if she felt something similar, but she was busy giving courteous nods to the zoo around us.

Uzran and his fellow Royal Guard stayed a measured pace behind us.

The crowd thickened as we drew closer to the head of the hall, but by that point, Bryth and I were moving briskly along, sparing only quick nods and smiles for the fawning creatures. They seemed perfectly happy with our pace, so long as they could make their obeisances. At last we mounted the stairs leading to a landing that lay just below where the thrones stood in looming, silent judgment. Coming up those steps, I received my first look of Lady Bwyathardd.

Stunning might be how I would first describe her, because as I came up those last few steps, I found myself dumbstruck.

Being around so many lovely people—and whatever else they were, the Tuatha were all beautiful—tends to put a a numbing gloss over the whole aesthetic, like a smell you get used to. When everyone was so damn pretty, then nobody was, or at least not in any way you'd notice. Some things stood out, of course; the strong, statuesque presence of Bryth, the overwhelming majesty of Queen Meabh, the clean, cold prettiness of Lady Aneira'Tywys. But most everyone else just blurred into this kind of white-noise, static.

But Lady Bwyathardd cut right through that static, like a red-hot signal from Lust's personal satellite.

She wasn't pretty or beautiful or lovely. She was hot. Scorning the fanciful and elaborate dress of her subjects, she lounged in a strapless party dress with high-slit sides that showed off her supple legs stretching out tantalizingly as she reclined. A pattern of thorny vines blooming with roses swirled across the dress, wrought in ruby thread, and each tendril seemed to caress a smooth, full curve of her body. I swear I am not a gawker, but something about this woman coerced my eyes into a long, hungry rove from her immaculately crimsoned toes to the black arched brow from beneath which dark, smokey eyes watched me with wicked delight.

Something in my stare must have amused her, because those wine-dark lips drew back into a knowing smile, and with a single voluptuous slither, she rose to her feet. Her hair—thick, dark, and wavy—was pulled back from her face and spilled down to her shoulders and across her bare back.

By the time she had taken a single step down from her throne, without thinking, I had dropped to one knee and lowered my head, but not enough to lose sight of her. She descended the steps with gratifying slowness. Incidentally, I had let go of Bryth's arm, and it took me a moment to realize that she was now standing stiffly beside me.

"Lady Bwyathardd," Bryth began, and the raucous room quieted some, "I present to you Paladin Lucius Bollham, champion of the Twilit Kingdom and faithful servant of Queen Meabh."

The sharpness in Bryth's tone cut through the sultry haze, and I found myself feeling a more than a little embarrassed as I remembered all the places my mind had wandered in the last five seconds. I guessed Lady Lighttread was not impressed.

"Stand, for I am thrilled to welcome you, brave Paladin," Lady Bwyathardd said in a soft, husky tone. "I had heard that you were a mighty warrior, having driven off a darkling such as the Fiend, but now I see that you are handsome as well. I am filled with wonder at our good fortune to have you, Paladin Bollham."

The surrounding crowd ooo-ed and ah-ed sympathetically, which was just as well because it helped cover the words Uzran muttered at my back. "And once she has you, you'll see she's a hard one to fill."

I felt my face warm, and Bryth couldn't have gotten any more rigid if her spine had been a ramrod, but I was pretty sure Lady Bwyathardd had not heard him.

"My Lady," Bryth said with deliberate clarity and volume, so as to be heard over the court. "As pleased as we all are to see you, I must ask where your Lord-husband is. The matters at hand concern him as well."

"Call him and spoil all the fun?" Lady Bwyathardd chuckled and gave me a conspiratorial wink that set the whole court to snickering. Bryth's cool silence would have given Chillspire a run for its money.

"Oh, don't worry, my dear. He will be here soon enough," Lady Bwyathardd cooed. She stepped onto the landing and gave Bryth a patronizing pat on the cheek, though she had to reach to do it. For all her massive sexual presence, the Lady of Thistlebough was one of the shorter Tuatha I had seen so far.

"In the meantime," Lady Bwyathardd purred, taking a step toward me, "perhaps the Paladin and I should get to know each other a little better. Strong and silent is all very alluring, but a lady needs a soft word now and then to keep her going."

I realized then I hadn't said a thing since coming into the hall, and my tongue felt like a wasted muscle gone limp in my mouth. "Uh, I mean, Lady Bwyathardd," I grunted, fighting to clear my throat. "As I am sure you know, or at least, I hope you do...um...but anyway, uh, war is coming, and the Queen has sent me to renew the fealties to prepare for the fight with the Gythraul."

"War, yes, we have heard." She almost whispered it, her eyes widening as their smokey depths caught fire. "The enemies of the Twilit Kingdom descend and you have come to save us. Such valor, such strength, such sacrifice. Oh, Lucius, it moves me heart and soul to know you come now to our rescue."

The bestial court sounded their agreement and affirmation. I most certainly was brave and strong, wasn't I?

She was now standing right in front of me, as I looked down into the those smoldering eyes I wanted to believe every word she said. Some distant, bloodless part of my brain was screaming at me to wise up, but the rest of me just burned to listen and believe.

"My Lady," Bryth tried to interject. "Perhaps we should wait until..."

"How could anyone ever repay such kindness?" Lady Bwyathardd ignored Bryth entirely. "How could I ever repay such sacrifice? What gift could I possibly give to you?"

I didn't have to really think about it too hard to realize I knew exactly what kind of gift she had in mind. Luckily I didn't have a chance to open my stupid mouth, because an incredible roar erupted from the entrance to the hall.

"YOU!!!"

I whirled around. Looming in the open doorway was a towering silhouette as regal as it was terrible. Half a head taller than an Ogre and corded with taut, lean sinew, this creature was every inch a predator. Loosely laced breeches of russet fabric covered his legs to just below the knee where they resembled the digitigrade limbs of a jungle cat, complete with partially unsheathed claws. His open-fronted silk shirt displayed a muscular torso and rippling abdomen that would have shamed an underwear model. Around his wide shoulders fell an honest-to-God mane of dark hair, shot through with highlights of deep gold. His face was handsome, strong, and cruel. Currently, his expression was a snarl that exposed leonine fangs. From each temple, a black horn framed the backward sweep of his hair. In one hand, he held an immense spear, its tip gleaming and stained with blood. It was levelled in my direction.

"Lord Bwyathardd," Uzran observed in his resonating voice.

Lord Bwyathardd. And here I was within inches of his wife, her breathing sweet bedroom whispers all over my mouthbreathing ass.

"Oh shit," was all I could manage as the monstrous Lord of Thistlebough stalked towards me, spear still upraised.

I found myself wishing I hadn't left my new rifle with Rhoslyn. My hands flew to my belt, and I laid fingers on the sword there. I felt strong fingers grab my wrist and snapped my head around to see Bryth holding me back from drawing.

"Wait," she hissed. We both turned back to the advancing Lord.

To my surprise and immense relief, Lord Bwyathardd did not run me through with his huge spear, but rather rammed it into the ground mere inches from Uzran's booted foot. Lord Bwyathardd thrust his face down into the Captain's impassive mug.

"You dare to come into my house, brute?" he roared in a voice like thunder. "Have all the blows to the head finally robbed you of what sense you had?"

Uzran didn't so much as blink.

"You really want to do this *again*?" he grumbled, the last words resounding off his tusks like a curse. "As much as I am sure you are keen to redress old wrongs, there is a war to be won. You know as well as I that picking a fight with me— impeding that war effort—would constitute a violation of your Oaths to Queen Meabh."

Lord Bwyathardd growled, and for a second, I thought he was winding up for a swing, but he twisted around and glared down at me.

"You!" he roared again, jabbing a clawed finger at me. "You brought this filthy beast into my house?"

All I could think to say as I watched the two glaring brutes was "Pot, meet Kettle," but Bryth spared me.

"Captain Uzran is Paladin Bollham's second, by order of the Queen," she said flatly. "By her will, he is bound to be at the Paladin's side."

Lord Bwyathardd roared once more, and I almost drew my sword again, for all the good it would have done me, but it was just a show of temper. He tore his spear from the cleft he had driven into the carpet—and even the stone floor beneath—and then ascended to his throne. Lady Bwyathardd had retreated there to her own, pouting during all the commotion.

She took turns casting venomous glances at her husband, then to Bryth, and back again.

"Well, whatever the business is, get on with it!" Lord Bwyathardd groused, settling into his throne.

"Now you know why I don't like it here," Bryth breathed out the corner of her mouth.

20

HUNT

"So, let's go over this one more time." I checked my holstered rifle, swatting away Rhoslyn's nipping fangs. "I have to go out into the woods with that psychotic monster and murder some unlucky critter to prove I am worthy of Thistlebough's help."

"Not quite," Bryth replied as she tightened my saddle. "Going on the hunt with Lord Bwyathardd is enough to technically secure the rights of fealty."

"Assuming you survive," Uzran commented from beneath the shade of a courtyard tree, arms resting across his chest. The other Royal Guard, one of the horned guys with a bronze disk on his forehead, waited by the gate out of the courtyard, supposedly to watch for when the Lord's hunting party turned up.

"Which is the reason the Captain is going with you." Bryth fixed Uzran with a piercing look.

The Ogre gave a shrug.

"Will he really try something?" I hated how small my voice sounded.

"Directly, no." Bryth was unperturbed. "To be honest, I

don't think, for all his bluster, that he has the stomach to put himself at risk like that. But on these hunts, he surrounds himself with other braggarts and bullies like himself, and if one of them happens to have an unfortunate mishap... well, again, that's why Uzran is there. They're scared of him."

I looked over at the captain, who met my gaze impassively, and I thought I understood what Bryth meant. Lord Bwyathardd was impressive and everything, but something about the way Uzran just stood there whispered "killer". He was a cold fire that could snatch the life out of someone in a moment and then return to a steady burn. All the snarling and roaring in Thistlebough couldn't match that.

Still, I wouldn't have minded having Bryth there too, for a whole host of reasons. "And why aren't you coming?"

"Lord Bwyathardd insists such hunts are the prerogative of the masculine. Therefore a delicate creature such as myself has no place among you." Bryth's caustic tone made it clear enough what she thought of Lord Bwyathardd's opinion. There had been an angry edge to Bryth since we had arrived in Thistlebough, and though I was curious, I hadn't had time to ask her about it. Right before riding into a forest full of monsters didn't seem like a great time for such conversations.

"Alright," I said, idly stroking the Diomedan's mane. "But what about the prize I have to bring back?"

Lord and Lady Bwyathardd had both been very specific on that point. I needed to bring back the carcass of something that was both impressive and terrible, at which point I would present it to the, um...affectionate Lady. Given what I'd seen of the native creatures, I was more than a little concerned with what they considered impressive and terrible.

"Going on the hunt may secure their service, but an

impressive trophy will shame them into cooperating fully," Uzran explained. He nodded toward his guard at the gate who was waving to signal the approaching Lord. "The Bwyathardds provide various beasts of burden and war, the results of Lady Bwyathardd's breeding programs and her husband's training regimes. The spirit of the oaths is that they will give their best, but they will only do so if they feel you are worthy of them."

"Worthy or not, don't they know that their people are at war?" I swung into my saddle and took up the reins. "I mean, whether I kill something impressive or not, the Gythraul are still coming, so isn't it in their best interests to help?"

"Even among our hotblooded people, the Bwyathardds are a fickle and nonsensical pair," Bryth answered, grinding the words between clenched jaws. "They are, in so many ways, what is wrong with the Twilit Kingdom. Rulers who are too powerful to displace, but unsuited for leadership."

Uzran grunted assent as he shifted away from where he was leaning against the tree. The plant gave an appreciative shudder—relieved to be free of his bulk. "Unsuited or not, they have something we want, and the only way to get it without starting a civil war is to play this game," He rolled his shoulders and twisted his neck one way then the other. "Lead on, Paladin."

"What if we don't find anything?" I asked taking up the reigns.

"In Thistlebough Wood?" Bryth gave an incredulous laugh. "It is less like hunting and more like brawling. Go now, and good luck, my Paladin."

Nodding farewell to her, I rode out of the gate with Uzran striding along behind me. The horned Royal Guard gave us a salute as we departed.

"Good hunting, Paladin," he called, his voice guttural but sincere.

"Uh, thanks," I said lamely over my shoulder, and then we were crunching down the path to where the rest of the hunting party waited at the gate to the curtain wall.

Lord Bwyathardd was, of course, the most impressive figure there, his previous garb now accompanied by a sleeveless leather long coat made from hides of various colors and textures. Judging from the curved, well-used blade he wore on his waist, it wasn't hard to guess how he got the material. He sat astride an immense, six-legged creature that looked like someone had crossed a rhino with an elk. The creature gave Rhoslyn and I a disdainful glare.

The rest of the hunters seemed like more of the animalistic humanoids from before, but they were all composites of predatory creatures; some I recognized, some I didn't. All of them––besides having fangs, claws, or talons––were armed with spears. They also were equipped with what looked like crossbow-flintlock pistols on their belts or saddles and were mounted atop rhino-elk like Lord Bwyathardd—though the rest of the hunting party's steeds were smaller, less impressive models.

"Fashionably late, little Paladin," Lord Bwyathardd sniffed as I rode up. "I am glad to see you didn't lose your nerve."

"He knows you weren't late," Uzran whispered before I could stammer out a protest. "Just trying to wrongfoot you."

I nodded and threw my head back, forcing out a hearty laugh. "Just wanted to give you ladies plenty of time to gather your nerve before we headed out." If they wanted macho bullshit, I could shovel it with the best of them.

There was a brittle heartbeat during which I met Lord Bwyathardd's eye, and I thought that I had pushed back too hard. Then the Lord of Thistlebough bared his razor-sharp teeth in a smile and gave a low, amused chuckle. "The Paladin has teeth, then," he barked, slapping his thigh.

On cue, the other hunter's laughed and gave general remarks of approval—a bunch of bullying sycophants falling in line behind their chief. I gave them my best devil-may-care grin and saw it returned across a range of bestial faces.

Out of the corner of my eye, I saw Uzran give me an almost imperceptible nod.

"Come then," Lord Bwyathardd roared suddenly. I had to fight to keep from flinching away from the sound. "Those brutes aren't going to spit themselves upon our spears."

The forests were as oppressive and sinister as Thistle-bough Castle was beautiful and idyllic. The trees were gnarled and black-barked, their leaves were so thick across the canopy that it felt like the sun had almost set, though it wasn't much past noon. All around, strange noises—croaks, growls, and shrieks—echoed from somewhere deep within the woods, and constantly, a sighing breeze rushed beneath the boughs, like the whole forest was breathing.

For their part, the hunting party seemed in good spirits, and besides singing occasionally—bawdy songs, whose lyrics were not nearly as clever as they supposed—they bragged about the terrible creatures they'd hunted and killed. When one got around to asking me if I ever hunted this, that, or the other, I laughed and told them I had taken down two at once, or something else just as ridiculous.

It was all barefaced lies anyway, I figured, or at the very least, exaggerations, so I didn't see the harm. Even Uzran seemed amused at my claims, his lips twitching into a brief smile once or twice.

The trek wound on, and little by little, the macho bull-shit faded. The trees pressed in closer, and the sounds of the forest echoed strangely. I noticed a subtle shift in Uzran, his meaty paw never straying far from his sword. We had passed some invisible division; the only thing missing was a rickety sign saying something like "Point of No Return" or "Here There be Monsters." Everyone in the party, even the mounts, could feel it.

We passed another fifteen or twenty minutes in this oppressive environment before Lord Bwyathardd's spear rose in his clenched fist, and the whole party stopped.

Then a crash of snapping limbs, followed by a snorting screech, invaded our retinue.

The hunting party whipped around like a pack of dogs all going on point at once. Their spears levelled and couched, Lord Bwyathardd's cronies leaned forward in their saddles.

"Well, well," the Lord gave purring, wet growl. "It seems you have the good fortune of facing a truly worthy quarry."

It took me a second to realize that he was referring to my purpose on this expedition, but then, with creaking slowness, the party turned their hungry eyes toward me.

Showtime.

"Surely, my Paladin, something as pitiful as a Muc'ros is no challenge for you," Lord Bwyathardd drawled. "After all, you have given us a great accounting of your many victories."

Glistening smiles broke out among the other hunters, lips peeling back to reveal teeth that looked like they belonged in the heads of wolves and sharks rather than Tuatha.

"Stand aside, then," I grunted, swallowing hard and nudging Rhoslyn into motion.

Uzran strode up beside me, hand on the hilt of his blade, eyes searching the countless tracks that snaked between the dark tree trunks.

"No," I said softly but firmly. "Stand here until I call you."

Uzran paused, and for the first time, something like surprise registered on his face. "As your second, it is my duty-"

"To do as I tell you, Captain," I said, a note sharper than I wanted. I don't know when I had decided it, but I was determined to face this alone. I was still learning the ropes around here, but I knew that if I wanted Uzran, Lord Bwyathardd, and the rest of the Twilit Kingdom to believe in me, I had to start getting heroic on this shit. And just maybe, I'd be able to believe it too.

I couldn't tell whether the Ogre had guessed my intent, but he gave a slow nod and cast a sidelong look at the hunters. His hand came away from his sword, but he leaned toward me and whispered, deep enough that I felt it between my ribs.

"Cochon'Rougir are thick-skinned and belligerent. Aim for belly and flanks."

I looked into his eyes. Maybe it was hope's delusion, but I thought there was a gleam of respect. His eyes returned to chilly disinterest and he pulled back to stand among the hunting party. I met the each of them in the eye and saw their expressions had changed. Gone were the jeering grins of a few moments ago; they had become serious and alert. Even Lord Bwyathardd raised his chin in subtle acknowledgment.

Now I just had to find out what a Muc'ros was.

I wondered sourly how it had come to this as I guided

Rhoslyn through the trees, out of the hunting party's sight. They had fanned out behind me, I guess to catch the Muc'ros if it trampled me making its mad dash out of the thicket. Maybe if the thing killed me outright, Uzran could step in and finish the job, and the whole thing wouldn't be a wash.

So there I was, nudging Rhoslyn forward with my heels, rifle drawn to my shoulder, reins wrapped around my left hand which I held perpendicular to the searching barrel. Despite all that the Daerg had done, the M-Core felt just like any old carbine. From the practice I had taken in the Chillspire mountains, I knew its firing mechanics were pretty much the same, though the sound of it was a little different. I found myself thankful for the little creepers' ingenuity. I figured I needed every advantage, and when the monster burst out of a knotted copse of trees, I found out how true that was.

It didn't go around or between the trees, but straight through them, jagged tusks tearing great gashes in the few trunks which stood between it and me. Snorting and howling with porcine fury, it charged, its muscular body bulging and bunching as cloven hooves tore across the ground. Its thorny skull was lowered, and I was pretty sure it could have fit me from head to kneecaps in that weaponized maw without much trouble.

Rhoslyn saved us both, shying to the left and spoiling my aim, but putting the bole of a tree between us.

The hippo-sized boar piled right into the tree, tearing it up by the roots with a horrible, ripping pop of snapping roots. It didn't even bother to shake the uprooted trunk free of its face before it charged again. It plunged past, its aim hindered by the tree stuck to its tusks.

As it passed, I saw a flutter of pale pink, and for a staggered second, I thought the thing had torn through some flowers. Then I realized that the fluttering petals were part of its body. Just over the hump of its great, green-black shoulders which bristled with thorny protrusions, a cascade of flapping, twirling petals draped across its back and along its flanks like a skirt of floral blooms. It seemed almost sacrilegious to fire off a pair of shots at something that looked so delicate and dainty, but when those hissing rounds sailed wide from my side-stepping Diomedan, I was reminded that the other had no care for my aesthetic sensibilities.

With a ferocious twisting of its head, the Muc'ros pitched the tree off its tusks, and the loosed trunk crashed through lower boughs before its own branches became entangled. It transfixed in a bouncing dangle over the forest floor. The flowery pig spun around and fixed me with baleful glare.

As it lowered its head for another charge, I levelled the M-Core and squeezed out three rounds straight into its skull. Hissing like super-sonic vipers, the quills punched into the thick, leathery face and the bony casing beneath. They began to smoke and splutter as the venom ate through the Muc'ros's flesh. The injuries were catastrophic, but as Uzran had warned me, the skull was thick, and the critter was ornery. I continued firing.

Rhoslyn tried her side-stepping again, and I tried to help by leaning with her movements, but through all its agony and rage, the Muc'ros had enough sense to watch for the trick. It kicked up and out with its back legs, spinning around to come alongside us, and broadsided us with a sweep of its head.

The Diomedan gave a scream of surprise and pain as it was thrown off its feet. I came up out of the saddle and hit the ground hard enough to knock the wind out of me, rolling through brush and bracken.

Wheezing and barely able to keep my hands on my rifle, I came up on a knee, trying to bring the barrel up as the Muc'ros bore down on me.

I was done for, but first I would put another round in the thing's shoulder—the best shot I could manage before those tusks spit me like a kebab.

The impaling stroke never fell. The boar's charge was suddenly arrested, and it lurched backwards with a frustrated squeal that stung my ears and made me cry out in pain. I was knocked onto my back as its chin connected with my forehead.

The swine floundered, and just over its freshly-sizzling shoulder, I saw that Rhoslyn had sunk her fangs into the monster's ankle joint and was gnashing and tugging.

With a snarling scream, the Muc'ros swiveled on the spot, tearing its wounded leg from Rhoslyn's jaws. Its huge, spiked snout clipped the her across the face, opening an ugly, wide gash.

A burst of rage flared to life if in my chest at the sight of my Rhoslyn bleeding, and with my lungs still screaming for more air, I lunged forward and began pumping shots into the exposed back and hindquarters of the boar.

First onto my knees and then up on my feet, I hammered round after hissing, searing round into the creature's haunches and spine. Blood spat and steamed from punctured flesh—a crimson mist festooning the soft blooms.

The Muc'ros swung toward me, squealing in rage, but even over the cracking hiss of my weapon, I could hear the rattling gurgle in its voice. Belligerent or not, there was only so much a living thing could take. Its legs staggered and wove together as it turned, bubbling blood coursing along runnels between the cloven hooves.It made a lunge at me, but its legs collapsed beneath it. It crashed hard into the churned-up ground, making a heavy thud as it landed.

With one final, frothing snarl, it stabbed upward at me with its tusks, but I was a gun barrel's length away. I drove four more shots into the puckered skull before the clip clicked empty.

21

LONGINGS

B ryth stood on the ramparts overlooking the parade field within the curtain wall of Thistlebough Castle, watching Paladin Bollham being toasted again by the gathered great and good of the domain.

Lucius raised his goblet in recognition, clanged the drink with Lord Bwyathardd's, and the feast went on. Behind the long tables that had been set upon the grass for the feast, the Muc'ros was still being turned slowly over a wide firepit. Whole hunks of flesh had been cut away from the carcass where the poison of the M-Core had blackened and soured the meat, but there was more than enough left to feed all at the celebration.

The Paladin had every right to be proud. By the standards of its own species, the beast had been impressive and would have been a formidable quarry even for a renowned hunter like Lord Bwyathardd. The decadent Lord and Lady of Thistlebough would have to bring the very best of their monstrous creations to serve under the Paladin, or find themselves condemned by their perverse sense of honor.

With each challenge, Lucius was proving himself more and more worthy of the charge he had been given.

The Pale Banner had been planted behind the table where the Paladin sat. He was pushing away another plate of food that Bwyathardd's servants were plying him with. The heavy fabric stirred a little in an evening breeze, and a chill went racing down Bryth's spine, though it had nothing to do with the cold. The banner truly had a new owner.

And in so little time. What had become of the last to bear the burden of Paladin—of her Paladin Valoise?

His screams—sharp and keening in her ears. They had stopped suddenly and then all she could hear was the sound of dripping upon the marble floor.

Bryth pushed the intrusive thoughts out of her mind and searched for the unmistakable form of Lady Bwyathardd. She needed something to hate right now, and the Lady of the Thistlebough was an easy target. But search though she did, she could not seen the brazen creature slinking about below. Her seat beside her lord-husband lay vacant.

"Really, my dear, we do have sentries for this sort of thing," came a throaty purr from the turret doorway.

"I am enjoying the fresh air, my Lady," Bryth said stiffly, refusing to turn and look at the Tuatha woman whom she wanted to hate from afar.

"Doubtful," Lady Bwyathardd sniffed archly, but then giggled softly, coming out onto the ramparts besides Bryth. "I am not sure anything in this castle will be fresh after all the swine flesh and wine is consumed. The whole estate will stink of the vengeful vapors issuing from those brutes down there for days."

The venom at the end of the declaration caught Bryth off guard, and she turned to regard her fellow Tuatha at last.

The seductive red and black dress, which had hugged the Lady's every curve, had been traded for a looser, flowing gown of green and gold. It still managed to display as much flesh or more, but at least it seemed that her garb was not so overtly sexual tonight. Bryth wondered if the legendarily amorous Lady of Thistlebough even realized anymore what she was expressing with her wardrobe. And, as Bryth looked at Bwyathardd's face, she wondered if the Lady even cared.

Her eyes, cast down on the field, were flat and hard; the coldness there struck Bryth mute.

"Have you ever wondered why we tolerate them?" Lady Bwyathardd's tone was conversational, even if her face told another, angrier story. "The brutish creatures that they are? We put up with their stupid posturing, their clumsy attempts at romance, and all their empty bids for nobility."

The last word came out dripping so much scorn, Bryth was surprised it didn't fall to the stone she leaned against. It was just as well, because the toxic utterance would have smoked and stunk as it ate through the rock.

"We put up with all of it," she said, her voice slower, more measured, "and fall in love with them for it."

Bryth had turned to look at hunters laughing and drinking in a loud, braying manner—the way males of many species do when they've been enjoying themselves too much. As much as she disliked the Lady of Thistlebough, she struggled not to see what Bwyathardd saw. Then that poignant little bit at the end caught her as soundly as a barbed hook and hauled her head around to stare at her hostess.

"I... am not sure I understand," Bryth managed limply, meeting the piercing stare of Lady Bwyathardd.

The sultry Tuatha's eyes glimmered with the reflected light of the bonfire below.

"I think you most certainly do, my dear," Lady Bwyathardd replied. The smile pulling at the corners of her mouth was positively vulpine. "After all, this is not your first stroll down the orchard lane."

Bryth felt a familiar, uncomfortable warmth bloom in her cheeks, and she was suddenly grateful for the deepening shadows.

"If you have a point to get to, my lady, perhaps you should make it." Bryth's words were cold and sharp. "I am tired and will retire soon."

The other Tuatha met her gaze with those eyes that only playacted at life—mummery absent true understanding.

"Poor thing," Lady Bwyathardd cooed, reaching up to stroke Bryth's cheek. "Did you think the tragic tale of your failed affair had been forgotten? Do you think we cannot all see what is happening again?"

Bryth pulled back then, as though Lady Bwyathardd's fingers had become something toxic.

"Again, my Lady, I ask you to speak plainly," Bryth said with stiff courtesy—as effective an armor as any she knew. "What is happening again? Who is we?"

The last question in particular was galling, but Bryth would be damned if she let this trollop know it.

"Oh, sweetling," the Lady of Thistlebough laughed, a high sound cold on the night air, "is this really how you treat an offering of help? Of counsel? Or are you just so simple that you can't see what is right in front of you?"

"I suppose I must be simple," Bryth snapped, the first real heat venting through the chinks in her armor. "Forgive me, my lady. It must be the intemperate blood of my mother and my lack of a courtly education, from which you have so clearly benefited. I simply do not understand what you are talking about."

Lady Bwyathardd's answering smile was perhaps the first true thing Bryth had ever seen emerge from the Tuatha, and it was terrifying to behold. Her red lips peeled back from her perfect, white teeth, and her eyes glittered darkly. Even though it was her husband that possessed the fangs, Bryth was far more fearful of being devoured by Lady Bwyathardd.

"Clever girl," Lady Bwyathardd purred, leaning forward, her shoulders flexing with a feline undulation. "Wrap that martyr's cloak tight about you, and with your impeccable manners and self-righteous duty, you are untouchable. A juggernaut. We were right to choose you."

"Again with this *we*," Bryth snarled, taking a sharp step backward. "I must be tired. If there is nothing else, my Lady, I shall go to bed."

The Lady of Thistlebough kept her hunkered-down position along the wall, and for the briefest instance, Bryth had the frightful thought that she might pounce forward like a cat upon a mouse. Bryth's hand strayed to the dagger at her belt, the intonations of a curse at the back of her throat. Her sword had been left in her room, as was custom, but she had been determined that she wouldn't need it. Lady Bwyathardd was never as dangerous on the field of battle as she was in...other domains.

"To bed then, chaste flower," the hostess said as her crouch dissolved into a lounge across the stone wall. "I understand that after surveying our stable tomorrow, you will leave the day after. You will need to keep up you strength."

Bryth turned smartly on her heel and marched off, Lady Bwyathardd's eyes shining hungrily as she watched the Queen's emissary depart.

22

BRUTES

The trip though the Thistlbough Stables—a sprawling complex two miles down a pebbled track from the Castle—was an overwhelming visit, due in large part to the stench. The musky smells of animals, the clinging spice of their feces, and the sharp tang of blood hung in the air like a blanket whose oily touch you felt, even if you couldn't see it. The smell must have been the reason for the timber-beamed, slate-roofed building being so very far from the Castle. It was probably twice the size of the fortified estate, but from the exultant tone Lord Bwyathardd had taken regarding his "pets," I imagined that if he had his druthers, the two would have been one and the same.

"Let the craven Daerg tinker and fiddle with their instruments," he roared over the raucous braying of a herd of those rhino-elk beasts he and his hunters had been riding. "The fruits of my labor shall be what carries you to victory." He swept both arms out in a grand gesture to the indoor arena. We looked down upon where the herd raced, other creatures waiting in wooden cages and pens.

The herd was being put through its paces by whip-snapping handlers who looked a lot like the Goblins who had first attacked me upon arriving in Other-Realm. Only their faces had been stretched to meet their long noses, creating a distinctly rodentious snout. With each snap of their hairy-skinned lashes, the handlers set the creatures—which I learned were called Sylvancerous—to turning and wheeling in another direction. The move was smooth as clockwork, despite the herd consisting of over thirty head. Each animal moved in perfect step with its fellows.

"Even over a forested mountain crag, they will not falter, and can hold a rider steadier on their broad backs than any equine mount—perfect for mounted soldiers who must pass over rough terrain."

I knew what the Lord of Thistlebough was aiming at, even without looking into his eager, willful eyes. Uzran, walking just a step behind, had filled me in on the finer points of Paladin Valoise's tactics during the feast. It sounded a lot like turn of the twentieth century trench tactics, meaning Valoise had made little use of Lord Bwyathardd's beasts for anything more than transportation and occasional reconnaissance. Bwyathardd was eager to see his many monsters being put to use in more aggressive roles, it seemed.

I just nodded along, trying to keep a catalogue running in my head of the most relevant traits. After the Sylvancerous came six-legged felines the size of german shepherds, each one black as pitch, with cords of sinew rippling beneath their thin pelts. Lord Bwyathardd explained that these Malks were not only exceptional hunters, but were also trained to follow detailed instructions. They could be relied upon to scent out an area for hostiles, harass an enemy without engaging, fetch things across a battlefield, or even capture enemies alive. With a single barked command, Lord Bwyathardd turned one of the Malks on an unlucky handler who screamed as the Malk ran him down. It pinned the handler to the ground, but halted the fatal clawstroke midswing at another command. The Goblin climbed shakily to his feet and fell back amongst the other handlers, his tunic sleeves torn and bloodied.

I was both impressed and more than a little disgusted by the display, if for no other reason than the fact that the other handlers stood by without so much as batting an eye, just another day at work for them. The demonstration, as well as the Malks' efficiency and discipline struck me, but I didn't have time to think on it for very long; more creatures were put on display.

Huge, bearish things with tusks and spiny shoulders—they were called Dread Morgs—displayed strength and resilience, hoisting boulders while being shot with crude muskets. The bullets bounced harmlessly away from their bristly hides. Then there were Rothwrenns—blood-colored birds that resembled ravens but were the size of a bald eagle. They operated much like the Malks, having been trained to follow all sorts of commands, but they could also speak in a croaking voice and were trained to make reports on enemy positions. I was told they were also more than happy to descend on vulnerable enemy soldiers in a flurry of talons and beaks.

On and on the weaponized menagerie went, with beasts the size of Welsh Corgis to animals larger than bull elephants. I knew that a lot of the mechanized, artillery, and air support options I was used to in the modern military were out of the question for the oncoming war. If Lord Bwyathardd's beasts were as reliable as he said, they would be vital for filling in the gaps. As an Army guy, and one in the infantry at that, I wholeheartedly believed that wars were won by the boys with their boots in the dirt, but even I knew that there were a lot of moving parts to the war machine. If Other-Realm required that we replace some machine parts with hairy ones, so be it.

"Needless to say, you are impressed beyond words," Lord Bwyathardd told me confidently as his rat-faced handlers collected the remaining creatures from the last demonstration—dog sized spiders who worked as watchdogs, shrieking when their webs were disturbed. "Yet, I have one last creation that will secure the Queen's confidence and your gratitude. It is my masterpiece—the culmination of my many centuries of selfless labor on behalf of our people."

Uzran made soft, disgusted sound, but the Lord of Thistlbough was too entranced in his own performance to be distracted.

"Wait here and refresh yourself, Paladin, for when I return, you will need all your strength just to stand before the glory of my achievement."

With that, Bwyathardd swept off and out of the arena. A few of his sombre servants stepped forward, offering us drink and various treats, which all seemed to be different kinds of undercooked meat. The servants looked like the gray creatures called Hobbs that I had met in Duanon, but their ears had been stretched and hung down alongside their faces, and fleshy jowls flapped next to their mouths; the similarity to Basset Hounds was inescapable.

I had gotten used to the stink of the place, but I was a long way from being hungry, so I just took a cup of the syrupy wine that Bwyathardd favored. Really wasn't too bad, especially served in a chilled goblet. The arena's shady interior was not as hot as it was outside, but I had still begun to sweat a bit while I watched the show. The wine was a welcome relief.

"Is Lord Bwyathardd blowing smoke up my ass, or can all these critters actually live up to his hype?" I asked Uzran. He was watching the handlers working with ropes, pulleys, and winches to clear the enclosed animals from the arena floor. Apparently the finale was going to need plenty of space.

"He is too proud for it not to be so," Uzran grunted as he came to stand next to me, plucking up fleshy snacks from his cupped hand. "He does not have the self-control for artifice or guile. That is solely the province of his wife."

I tried to shake off the thoughts of Lady Bwyathardd that arose. I hadn't had much of a chance to talk with her since we met, but the look she gave me each time we were close was increasingly ravenous. It evoked a combination of fear, thrill, and shame. Ever since puberty, I hadn't exactly lived the life of a monk, but I was a bit old-fashioned about matters of love and sex. If nothing else, my stance on such things may have been mostly out of spite for my dad's insistence that such things were all just brain chemistry. Still, when she looked at me like that—with naked want—I felt my scruples slacken, and I hated it. I didn't want to be involved in any kind of noble tryst—even ignoring the political ramifications to the war effort—but if it came down to it, I was afraid what I would do if given the chance.

"I am trying to plan things in my head. You know...strategize." I dragged my mind elsewhere by sheer force of will.

"I am told that commanders do that from time to time." Uzran's voice was acerbic in its nonchalance.

"Smartass," I snorted.. "So I am planning things, but something that remains problematic is not knowing much about the Gythraul. I mean, knowledge is power on the battlefield as much as any other place, but I haven't gotten a lot of intel about how the Gythraul operate. I know that they have been at war with you guys for a long time, and I know that they keep adapting to what each Paladin does, but other than that I have no idea."

The Ogre popped two more hunks of dripping meat into his mouth. He rubbed his hands together vigorously as he swallowed. "What do you want to, Paladin?" He fixed me with that chilly stare.

I thought for a moment. "What do they look like, for starters? Where I am from, I assume my enemies are human —like me—but that obviously isn't the case here. The murals in the Hall of Remembrance made them seem humanoid, but that was art, not a field report. Are they human-sized? Smaller? Bigger?"

Uzran considered the question, and for a second, I thought he was going to reply with something sarcastic. When he did finally speak, his voice was grave and deliberate.

"The Gythraul are similar in size to your kind and the Tuatha, though they are far tougher, their torsos being covered in a mesh of scales, and they are accustomed to harsh living. Ridges of bonier, horn-like scales run along their spines and small horns sprout from their brows, but they are of little use in actual combat. Still they are rugged and all wear full armor at all times on the field."

This vision of reptilian humanoids with metal-framed bodies was striking; it created more questions than it answered.

"Do they have any special magic, or...I don't know...powers? Besides just being tough? And when you say *tough* do you mean like, not prone to minor injuries, or do you mean like really hard to kill?"

"Well, they were never very hard for me to kill," the Captain said. It wasn't a boast, just a cold fact. "They are creatures of flesh and blood, and, by and large, they do not possess much in the way of magical traits. Heat and minor flames do not bother them much. Intense flames though—such as the fire seeds—will kill them as quickly as any other mortal creature. They have no sorcerers; the magic of the Contracts and Fundaments is beyond them."

I was still getting used to the mind-bending reality of magic's applications, and I was glad I wouldn't be facing it on the battlefield.

"So why have they been giving you guys fits for the last few millennia?" I asked, unsure of how to phrase the question any more delicately. "I mean, their abilities at war sound like small potatoes to a kingdom that has stuff like magic, Paths, and mad scientists that infuse mortal weapons with native flora and fauna. What makes them so dangerous?"

Uzran crossed his arms and looked past me into the middle distance, where I supposed both humans and Ogres must keep our memories, fears, and dreams.

Down in the arena, the last of the beasts were being dragged out of sight.

"Two things, Paladin. And the combination of these two things is what will keep the Twilit Kingdom at war to the end of time." His words rang with the final certainty of a funeral bell. "The first is that the Gythraul have a will to drown this realm in blood—theirs or their enemies. They will march entire cohorts into the line of fire, just to expend enemy ammunition, before an actual assault. They build ramps with their dead to climb over a shieldwall, a town's palisades, or even a castle's ramparts. Their will is not blind or stupid, for all its brutishness. They waste nothing—not least the lives of their legionnaires—but they do not balk at the costs of victory, no matter how ugly. They will make mistakes. They may even retreat if the battle is hopeless, but they will always come back, ready to shed every last drop of blood if it will bring victory. From the loftiest general to the lowest war-serf, they are committed to victory.

"Their determination would be challenging enough, but it would not be insurmountable were it not for the second thing. They are not sorcerers or eldritch beings, and so are bound to all the frailties and limitations of mortal flesh. All things mortal eventually fail—that is their nature. Their numbers are not limitless, and with time, we could exterminate them to the last spawnling. But that will never happen, because the second thing has nothing to do with them, but with Twilit Kingdom."

Uzran leaned back, suddenly seeming very old. Across his face a network of lines and scars that had been so easy to ignore on his craggy features now stood out, a testament to a veteran's life whose span I couldn't fully appreciate. He couldn't have looked more weathered if he'd been carved from a mountainside.

"Our rulers, the Tuatha, are a fractious and fickle people. When rallied behind that Pale Banner, following their Paladin, they can beat back the Gythraul—even when all hope seems lost. But true victory eludes them. With corpses still steaming on the field, they will squabble and scheme. They forget that war is not won with a few victories, and things fall apart. You see, Paladin, this war cannot be won, because each victory ensures that more of your forces will abandon you until you can advance no further. Then you will watch the Gythraul sharpen their swords just beyond your reach."

The last of the beast cages was sliding out of view,

making way for the grand finale that, according to the Lord of Thistlebough, was going to knock my socks off. I found myself hoping it would, because Uzran was hardly being the bearer of good news.

"Some are better than others—Lady Lighttread, her father, the Queen, and a few other courtiers—but most cannot be trusted to stay the course for more than a year or three. You balk at my centuries, but the Tuatha are ageless, and so without the enemy at their gates, they see no reason to hurry. For as much as we are different, most of them are stranger still, knowing that they will never need to fear age or decrepitude. They will always forget and then grow lax. The weapons gather dust, and then the Gythraul Legions return. This is the war that has no end, and I was born into it. I will die in it. It will continue on long after I am gone."

The animals gone, the arena was stiflingly quiet as Uzran finished. For several heartbeats, I just stood there, taking turns looking at him and the empty wine goblet I rolled between my hands.

I thought to ask, after that fatalistic speech, why *he* bothered to fight, but I dismissed the question. For him, it was duty and pride—the commitment to do what was expected and what he had said he would do. Beyond that, I dismissed the question for the same reason that I dismissed it when it occurred to me back in Afghanistan—it didn't matter. Why a man fights might matter to the soldier himself, his chaplain, his family members, even to the sheep-brained courts of public opinion, but in the midst of the ugly business of war, "Why" didn't—couldn't—mean anything to me. That he would fight, that he would kill, and that he would die was all that mattered; it was the only relevant factor in the brute arithmetic of large-scale violence.

"You'll have to get more specific on their tactics later." I shrugged off the oppressive silence. "But for now, can you tell me what the Gythraul home situation looks like? Do we know what their infrastructure is like?"

Uzran's eyes came back to rest on me, and a grim smile spread across his face.

"We've seen very little, and know even less for certain. What we *do* know is that all their resources go toward building or strengthening their war effort. We know that the highest ranking Gythraul—the Ceterum—act as governors of the lands they conquer. This intelligence comes from rumors and the ramblings of runaway slaves who manage to escape the Gythraul. Such information has proven unreliable in the past."

Well, you have to start somewhere.

"Then we will have to see about changing that." I looked up, hearing from above a great slithering of ropes and the dull clack of wooden boards stacking up on each other. "But now it looks like the finale is coming up."

The glare of daylight shone through as the beams and rafters of the arena roof swung up and out on great iron hinges. Above the mechanical sounds of the roof, I heard the cracks of whips and ponderous bestial groans. Then, coming from somewhere in the sky, there was a pounding, windy pulse.

A quintet of black shadows fell across the arena floor, each flapping in steady, majestic rhythm. Broad, leathery pinions stretched from sinuous bodies, each with a reptilian head crowned with backswept horns.

"Behold!" Lord Bwyathardd roared, standing in the midst of the arena where the shadows were descending. "My grand dreams made flesh! My masterpieces!"

A saurian bellow sounded above, carrying with it a terrible heat and the smell of ash.

23

HISTORY

"The fool has revived the line of Wyrms!"

Bryth's voice tore across the burbling swamp air.

She had been sitting beside the fire tended by Hurrahn, the Fomor Royal Guard whose name I had finally learned after thinking of him as the horned guy, when Uzran and I told her about Lord Bwyathardd's big reveal at the Thistle-bough Stables. We had not seen her the night we got back from the Stables, nor the next day, as we had been busy making arrangements for the first round of beasts to be taken to Duanon's mustering grounds. Shortly after that, we left by way of a long Path to Mistmire, the holdings of Mother Gwiddon.

Upon arriving in a bleak and fog-choked swamp, Bryth said that Mistmire could only be accessed at certain times. To avoid getting lost eternally in the fog, we needed to wait until dawn. After making camp seemed like a perfect time to share all the things that we had seen at the stables.

My excitement at having dragons on our side had not received the reaction I had anticipated.

"They are bastard offshoots, not even battle-trained yet," Uzran grunted dismissively. Bryth began to pace. "The results of interbreeding some drake degenerate with lesser beasts, at best."

"They were big, they could fly, and they could breathe fire," I said stubbornly. "A dragon by any other name."

I wasn't understanding nearly half of what was being thrown out here, but I was damned if Uzran or Bryth was going to spoil my getting to have pet dragons. It was the closest thing to a childhood wish I could remember having, other than actually knowing my mom, of course.

"I knew Bwyathardd was a fool, but I vastly underestimated the extent of his hubris," Bryth ranted as her feet tore tracks in the moist earth. "Even if they are some debased offshoot, they should have been put down at birth just on the off chance of one of them might escape and breed at Mount Vaul. I have half a mind to open a Path right now and ride to Duanon with news of this madness."

"He says they have all been gelded or sterilized," Uzran informed her in a tone so dry and wearisome, he sounded bored with her tirade. "If you ride to Duanon now, you will be doing the Paladin, the war effort, and your Queen a disservice, and all just to be told that, according to the Oaths of Fealty, Lord Bwyathardd is perfectly free to breed what he wishes on his lands."

"But they are Wyrmspawn!" Bryth snarled, whirling on him. "And since when are you so well disposed toward that oaf and his trollop? Did something else happen at Thistlebough that I don't know about?"

"I am only telling you things you already know," the Ogre replied coolly. "Stop your ranting and remember who you are."

Bryth, arcane energies gathering around her in unseen

waves of pressure and rage, advanced a stride toward the Royal Guard Captain. "Don't you try to tell me who I am!" she thundered in that magically augmented voice I had heard once before, in another swamp.

With frightening speed for a creature as big as he was, Uzran came to his feet. "It seems I am the only one here who remembers!" the Ogre bellowed with enough force and volume to make my teeth ache and my ears ring.

Hurrahn and I shared a bewildered glance as our eyes darted between the two. I got to my feet.

"That is enough from both of you." My voice was hard and uncompromising without being loud. More yelling was not going to do any good. "Before you two go after each other like a couple of bitchy teenagers, how about you tell me why this is a big deal? Why are dragons more dangerous than everything else in this realm full of magic and other crazy shit?"

Bryth and Uzran stood there glaring at each other, and I wondered if they had even heard me. Then Bryth threw up her hands and the magical tension went out of the air with a subaudible hiss.

"I am going to check on the Diomedans," she growled. With that, she stalked off, calling back without looking, "You explain it to him."

Uzran had snatched up a wineskin and was already walking off in the opposite direction. "I am checking the perimeter," he rumbled as he trudged into the marsh. "Hur-rahn, explain it to him."

Hurrahn looked from his Captain to me and back, then gave a defeated sigh as he returned to tending the fire. "My Paladin, would you like to sit and warm yourself?" he asked hopefully, his voice rough and gravelly. He ran a hand absently over the curl of his ram-like horns.

The night was not that cold, and the fire was putting off waves of heat, but I could tell the taciturn Royal Guard was doing his best to be courtly. Up to this point I don't think the Fomor had spoken more than a sentence to me.

Shaking my head a little, I moved alongside the horned giant and sat upon the waxed skins laid upon the soggy ground. "Alright, Hurrahn," I huffed, unable to keep the exasperation out of my voice. "Looks like you get the job of filling me in, so go on and spill it."

Hurrahn looked like he would rather swallow one of the embers he was stirring, but with a raspy clearing of his throat, he began.

"Lady Lighttread's mother was one of the Unbound—Tuatha who refuse to be a part of the Twilit Court or bow to the Lords of Far-Hold. They travelled about Other-Realm as they wished because they had made a pact with the Wyrms, the ancient dragons who are as old as the Darklings, who even the likes of the Queen regard as equals. To seal this pact, they promised to take time each year, travelling to Mount Vaul where they would tend the Wyrm Nests with the Ancient Dragon in hopes of one of their many cold eggs finally hatching. There have been only three Wyrms born since the Tuatha came to Other-Realm."

"Okay," I interrupted. "Bryth's mother helped dragons, so why does she want even dragon-like things dead?"

"Patience, please, Paladin," Hurrahn said, seeming almost pained. I felt a pang of guilt at my frustrated questioning and nodded for him to continue.

"Not long after Bryth was born, the Gythraul made another attack. In this attack, they took Mount Vaul, just as the Unbound were making ready for the Wyrm Nests to be tended. Hardly any of the Unbound were warriors of any renown, so they fled. The Gythraul took the mountain and then the eggs, whose fluids they used in strange alchemies. The wrath of the Wyrms was terrible, but it fell on the Unbound, whom they blamed for abandoning their sworn duty. Nearly all the Unbound, including Lady Bryth's mother, were slain by the vengeful dragons before her father and his retainers killed them all."

"So if all the dragons are dead and their eggs destroyed, how did Lord Bwyathardd breed those things Uzran and I saw?"

"The Wyrms—true dragons—can only be produced when a mated pair of dragons creates an egg together, but the egg itself can take centuries to hatch, if it hatches at all. In the meantime, Wyrms can breed with other, lesser creatures, creating debased animals called drakes. Far less powerful, and often less intelligent, they are still fearsome, and were far more numerous. Lady Bryth's father, Lord Lughan Redfinger, slew many of these as well, but some must have survived in the odd corners of the world."

"Okay, that makes things a little clearer," I admitted. "But why is she worried about the things getting loose and flying to Mount Vaul? Don't the Gythraul still hold that place?"

"Yes, they do," Hurrahn said, and for a second I could hear a spike of anger in his voice. "It is feared that, should any with Wyrm blood in them return to Mount Vaul, the magics instilled in the stones, combined with the alchemies the Gythraul work with the dragon eggs, could bring back the true Wyrms—or at least something close to what their kind were."

"Then they would be on the Gythraul's side," I finished for him, rocking back a little.

The weight of this latest bit of Other-Realm trivia settled across my shoulders, and though I wasn't ready to advocate for the extermination of Lord Bwyathardd's masterpieces, I realized what might be at stake.

"Well that sticks me in one hell of a situation," I growled irritably, rubbing at the headache forming in my temples. "Can't anything be simple around here? Use dragons—real damn dragons—but know they could set off some kind of apocalypse. Do you use a weapon that might win battles but could also lose the war?"

Hurrahn shrugged as he stared into the fire. "That's why I am glad that I am not the Paladin."

24

RIDDLE

After the majesty of Thistlebough Castle and the starkness of Chillspire, I was not prepared for Mistmire Hall. It was much smaller than the immense estate of Thistlebough, standing hardly more than three stories tall, and it was not even half the height of Chillspire. The entire structure was built from weathered beams and boards, many of which bore a shaggy pelt of gray-green moss. It was much less impressive than the adamant stone which had composed the two previous fortresses. But none of the other fortresses could walk.

I had awoken at dawn to an incredible groaning and creaking sound—like the world itself was stretching into wakefulness after a long night's sleep. Then there was the sound of sloshing water and slurping mud, followed by a deep thump that I felt through the ground and in my bones.

I was up, M-Core in my hands, looking around intently.

In the swamp, there was nothing but mist, stained orange and yellow by the pale sunrise.

Everyone else was up, except for Hurrahn, who lay next to the fire in his fur cloak, looking for all the world like a felled tree wrapped in bearskin. He had been on watch last night, and Uzran must have relieved him not long ago. That, or he was one hell of a hard sleeper.

I looked over at Bryth and then at Uzran, both standing side by side and staring impassively into the marsh fog. They must have worked through their little tiff, or moved past it while I slept, and I was glad of it, but right then, their absence of concern over the noise was causing me fresh distress. It sounded like a wooden skyscraper was pulling itself apart, and as I stood there, it sounded like it was getting closer.

Then I looked past Uzran and Bryth to see the shape forming out of the mist.

Like some green, furry tortoise, Mistmire Hall lurched along. It had thick, wooden legs—one on each corner of the squat, rectangular building. The movements were stiff, but coordinated; two corner legs held their position while the other two reached out to shuffle the hall forward. All manner of dangling cords and lengths of twine, attached to which were shells and bones, hung from the roof edge and clattered with each step.

It was an incredible sight, and despite my initial wariness, I found myself moving to stand beside Bryth, my rifle hanging down at my side. Some distant part of my brain wondered, as the walking hall came closer and closer, if we should give the structure a wide berth. I imagined the thing would be hard to park just where you wanted, but a look to the side showed that Bryth and Uzran weren't concerned— if anything, they looked bored.

Mistmire Hall came to within twenty yards of where we were standing, its forelegs emerging from the swamp water to punch their clawed toes into firmer ground. Then it began to sink down to the ground. The legs retracted with a deep groan until they were just the central anchoring pillars of each corner of the hall. With a heavy creak, Mistmire Hall settled to rest, its story-high double doors a few strides away.

The stillness of the swamp settled back in as the last hanging bits of bone stopped swaying, making a few final clicks and clacks.

Uzran looked over his shoulder at Hurrahn, and his shoulders sagged just a little as he saw the Fomor still slumbering beside the last cinders of the fire. "Royal Guard! Attend!" he boomed, turning back to face the doorway.

LIke he'd been stung, Hurrahn shot up, and, throwing off his cloak and taking up the Pale Banner from where it lay planted in the ground, he staggered toward his Captain, his gait straightening with each step.

"Good morning," I called as Hurrahn fell in beside Uzran.

The Fomor gave me a sheepish grin and touched his horns by way of salutation.

"Lead on, Paladin," Uzran rumbled. With a quick look at Bryth, who had no smile, but gave a quick nod, I walked toward the door and put out my hand to take hold of the corroded brass ring of the rightmost door.

Before I had touched the metal, the doors—which I only just noticed were carved with pictures of interwoven water plants and sharp-toothed little fish—moved of their own accord. Swinging inward with a prolonged creak, they opened to a dark hall, its boarded floor strewn with straw.

Days ago, I might have paused at that murky doorstep, but little by little, I was getting used to all the strangeness and theatrics of this weird world. Rifle shouldered, I strode into the darkness of Mistmire Hall.

For a moment, there was nothing but darkness and the sound of my boots scuffing across the floor. Then a few jagged snickers sounded in the darkness and something zipped past my head too fast to see. I took another step and felt something scuttle by, brushing past my leg.

"Is this how you greet a servant of the Queen?" I called sternly, refusing to pause as I walked forward in the darkness.

There were whispers now. Maybe Mother Gwiddon kept Daerg as well, I thought. But as I listened more closely, I realized these voices were higher-pitched—almost like the voices of children. But they were meaner somehow. Sharper.

. .

"Come now, thou hast had thy fun," croaked a brittle voice from somewhere in the darkness. With a splutter and whoosh, green light bloomed around the hall.

The emerald glow came from torches set in sconces attached to pillars running the length of the room. The hall itself seemed to be one single, large room, with paired pillars marching down the center. Here and there curtains and scaffolding between the pillars and walls created impromptu rooms and balconies. At the center of the hall, a pit had been dug where a blue-tongued fire burned beneath a bronze cauldron whose sides glowed with heat. Tendrils of vapor coiled up and out of the pot, dancing among the countless strings of shells, feathers, plant sprigs, and bones which hung drooping from the exposed rafters.

Presiding over the simmering pot was a surprisingly familiar figure.

It was the huge, bent woman from the crowd of courtiers who had greeted me when I came to Duanon. She still wore her drab, patched garments, and looked up as I approached. By the fitful light of the torches, her glistening, black smile spread beneath the shadow of a long, crooked nose. One long hand stretched out to run gnarled, jagged claws through the curling steam, and the other reached out and patted a stool beside where she squatted.

"Come, little children, come thou and sit with me," she creaked. "It is almost done. I've been up all night, poor Mother that I be, but it is nearly complete."

I looked over my shoulder to Bryth who gave me a nod of encouragement.

Of all the Lords of Far-Hold, the information she had given me on Mother Gwiddon had been the most vague, and the tapestry in the Hall of Fealty was so abstract that I had had no idea that the creature I had met on the Grand Stair was the same one I would be meeting today. Bryth had told me that Mother Gwiddon was the oldest creature living in Other-Realm besides the Darklings, and that she was not Tuatha. But in exchange for her aid in fighting the Darklings those long years ago, the Tuatha had given her the lands of Mistmire. She was eccentric and mysterious, but she mostly kept to herself. The only time she was ever heard from was when she used her strange ways to select the next Paladin—a process which none but the Queen and Mother Gwiddon fully understood.

In summary, Bryth had advised caution. As I stood in the wyrd light of that strange hall, it was easier than ever to see why.

Gingerly, I settled on the stool beside Mother Gwiddon.

This close, I noticed that the fire made no sound, and I realized there was no fuel for the fire—no wood or coals—just roiling blue flame. The pot's contents hissed and spat though, and despite looking like nothing but boiling water, there was a strong smell of spiced meat. There had been no breakfast this morning, and my stomach gave an approving burble, despite my head's stern warning to trust nothing from a hag's pot.

"Mother Gwiddon, I am Paladin Lucius Bollham," I began, feeling silly as I sat upon a stool next to a creature that stood as tall as Uzran even though she was bent nearly double.

"Oh, dost thou really think I know not who thou art," she cackled, dipping a talon into the pot, stirring. "Did yon little Lighttread not tell thee that it was I that found thee?"

"I was only trying to be courteous, my Lady," I said lamely.

"Well, cease with that 'Lady' nonsense, if courtesy be thy aim," she said in a soft, distracted tone as she stirred. "Mother will serve just fine." Mother Gwiddon drew her finger from the boiling pot and ran it beneath her hooked nose, sniffing deeply. She gave it a lick with a long, pointed tongue the color of a fresh bruise in the green torchlight.

"Very soon now," she said. Then she turned to look right at me, amber eyes glimmering like corroded nuggets of gold in her creased face. In the light of the green torches, her pale, withered skin seemed to take on a glowing, viridian tone. I fought the urge to look for a bucket of water in case she wanted my little dog too.

"Well, umm...Mother," I began, the word sounding strange in my mouth. "We've come on the business of renewing the Oaths of Fealty, though I am sure you knew this. I don't imagine you get many guests otherwise."

The hag gave a cracking honk of laughter and then showed me more of her sharp, black teeth.

"Thou might be surprised."

Around and above us came stifled giggles, and I swore I saw the flashes of eyes reflecting the torchlight before they disappeared behind pillars, rafters, and scaffolding.

The pot gave an incredible hiss and the turbulence in

the roiling water accelerated. "Here it comes," Mother Gwiddon whispered, breath whistling between her teeth.

There was a gathering charge in the air, like when Bryth uses her magic, only this was one was pulling inward rather than pushing out. It was more of an intangible suction than a pressure. Like the gathering of a great breath, the force pulled, and then, with a rush, it pushed out and the pot's contents erupted.

I pulled back, but not a single drop of the boiling rush fell on me. It spiraled and twisted around on itself, flowing upward. In the airborne jumble, I spotted glimpses of bone, scraps of warty skin, and what might have been the ragged finery of tattered butterfly wings. Steadily upward the concoction went, jangling the hanging ornaments in the rafters as it brushed past. Finally, the liquid struck the roof. Water sprayed in every direction, and with an incredible slurp, it drew back together and congealed into a small, solid shape.

This thick little blob plummeted down, landing in the empty, waiting pot with a splat.

Something splattered across my face, and when I wiped it away, I realized it was blood.

"Got thy face marked with afterbirth, eh?" Mother Gwiddon said with a lopsided grin, reaching over and into the pot. "Good luck, that is."

Afterbirth? I fought the urge to wretch as I used my sleeve to scrub at my face.

"Mother Gwiddon," Bryth said, "Is that what I think it is?"

Gingerly, the hag drew her hand out of the pot. "Depends upon what thou art thinking" she chuckled softly. "But if thou guessed a Bogle, then thou art right."

Out she scooped, in her huge, knobbled claw, a creature no bigger than an infant. It was struggling to free itself from clinging strands of bloody flesh. It had the rounded head and long, fleshy body of a salamander, but its forelegs were the hairy hands of a raccoon, and its legs looked like those of a jack rabbit. It flopped this way and that, mewling sleepily, and then the last sheet of meat fell away to reveal three pairs of comically undersized butterfly wings which ran down the length of its rubbery body.

"Oh, he is a handsome one," Mother Gwiddon cooed, stroking the Bogle's back with one crooked claw. "Alright, come on out and greet thy little brother. Gentle now, he's fresh."

With the rush of dozens of wings and whispering voices, a host of of glittering eyes sprang up around us. A hundred different varieties of hodgepodge creatures—amalgamations of dozens of recognizable animals, all no bigger than the fresh Bogle—gathered around Mother Gwiddon. A few even pushed or slid by Bryth and I to see.

"Pretty boy," one whispered in that sharp, almost childish tone.

"Shut up," another hissed. "You scare him."

"Wishing I has wings," groused a voice in the mob.

"Then you be stupid high and low," snickered one of them as it fluttered by.

"Hush now, my little dears," Mother Gwiddon chided as she turned, shuffling on her squatting haunches to face me. WIth her free hand, she brushed an open spot among the gathered Bogles and then softly deposited the fresh one.

The Bogle looked around with pale grey eyes and drooping, sleepy lids.

"Rise and shine, sleepyhead," I chuckled, I leaning forward to look at the little thing.

The Bogle raised its head and looked right at me, lids raising a little, staring.

"Me...Sleepyhead?" it croaked quizzically with a soft, raw voice.

"It will do as well as any other," Mother Gwiddon said. I looked up to see her smiling. "And who is this before thee, little Sleepyhead?"

With one hooked claw, Sleepyhead pointed at me, waddling forward. "Master?" it asked. "Master Paladin."

Mother Gwiddon nodded down at the Bogle and ran the back of one claw across its bowed back soothingly. "Good. Very good," she said. Then she looked up and her smile was gone, only deadly seriousness in its place. "Little Lighttread can tell thee all concerning Bogles and their many uses, but before this is done, thou must answer me some questions."

"Is this a test?" I asked, half laughing to ease the weight of her stare.

"Most certainly," she replied, and I thought I caught a hint of a grin in her wrinkles.

"Now lies this child, my flesh and my bone, that I give to thee and to thee alone," she said in a sing-song voice. "Yet, questions have I, thou must answer me, and no help thy companions may offer to thee."

"Do I have to answer in rhyme?" I crossed my arms across my chest. "Because that is going to slow down my response time. A lot."

This time, I knew I caught a fleeting smile.

"Answer how thou wilt, but of this, take thee heed. Speak truth for my help or leave with thy need. For lies and deceptions be worth less than scum; answer true, or to thee, my aid will never come."

It took me half a second to translate, but once I got it, I nodded.

"I understand."

"A riddle I have then to pose—a solution thy soul must disclose:

What holds the sword when fingers fail?

What bids thee stand when bravery sets sail?

It ties king to serf and mother to child

And keeps warrior hands from running wild.

When heart is gone and soul flees its shell,

What holds the promise, even unto hell?

It blinds, it ties, and enslaves the soul

Yet in ballads, its virtues the bard doth extol—

An impoverished mistress with no silver or gold,

Yet is treasured by she who the throne doth uphold."

I sat on that stool with the eyes of Mother Gwiddon and dozens of her "children" staring at me. For a time, I just sat there, mulling over the words, sniffing for any traps or tricks. I once took a class in college about medieval literature that had talked about how lots of riddles had twists and turns of phrase that made their answers appear like one thing, only to be another when given context and all the little details. There was a particularly dirty one that convinced you it was about a penis until you looked at the whole picture and realized it was an onion or something.

Leave it to my college education to leave me with little more than centuries-old dick jokes.

Well, my musings revealed no trapdoor in the riddle, so I let my eyes wander the room. Part of me wanted to believe I was searching for inspiration, but the more honest part knew I was stalling. Nothing was coming to me and my temper was rising—not least of all because I was having to solve this crap on an empty stomach.

This was bullshit! These people were going to base whether they helped me win a war—their war—on my ability to pass these ridiculous tests? Did they even want to win? Was all this worth the risk of losing the war and seeing themselves exterminated? If they weren't going to help save themselves, why the hell should I? Why should I eat an enchanted apple, hunt a monster, or answer some stupid-ass riddle?

It was then that my eyes fell across Uzran who stood there like a statue, Hurrahn beside him with the Pale Banner. Both standing at attention, ready even now, I knew, to live and die at a word from me. Me—a puny human who had been in their crazy world less than a month, and barely knew which way was up. How could they follow someone like me?

And right there I had the answer to the riddle.

"Duty," I said.

Mother Gwiddon's long, ebony fangs shone cheerfully in the green light.

Out stretched her hand, fingers uncurling from the flat blue stone that lay cupped in her palm.

25

EARS

Uzran stood by the witch's pot and stared into the empty bowl. The blue flames were gone, but green torches still burned in the hall, their guttering light shining on the bare bronze.

Bryth and the Paladin were wandering about the swamp; the Tuatha was teaching the human about Bogles and the vast information network that existed in the form of the lowest Fey creatures which infested Far-Hold. Excluding the lands sterilized by the Gythraul, there was hardly a glade, gully, or hillock in all this world that did not house at least a few Pixies, Pucks, Grindles, and yes, Bogles. The Ogre had heard there was a debate about whether such creatures were native to Other-Realm or if they had come from another place, but such things did not concern him. The only thing that mattered was that such creatures were excellent spies, and with the faithful service of one of their number, a knowledgeable individual could gain access to countless tiny informants.

He supposed that the Paladin was most certainly not knowledgeable, but Bryth was working to correct that.

Thinking on the Paladin, the Captain found himself wondering at the strange look the man had given Hurrahn and himself just before he answered Mother Gwiddon's riddle. Had it been respect? And why had that mattered to him? Why had he felt his shoulders square a little more as martial pride straightened his spine? What made Lucius Bollham any different than the last three Paladins who had come before?

"He is still just a human," he grunted softly to himself, turning away from the empty pot to find himself staring into the glittering eyes of Mother Gwiddon.

Uzran's hand did not fall to the blade at his side, but the muscles of his arms and shoulder twitched with longing. The Captain did not fear any creature that walked, crawled, swam, or flew through Other-Realm—not even the dread Darklings—but Mother Gwiddon made him uneasy. She defied explanation or expectation. She may have been Invaluable to the Queen and loyal to the Twilit Kingdom, but she was known to be inventively cruel when crossed or even inconvenienced. She was an unquantifiable threat, and Uzran had made it his business to quantify and be ready to nullify any and all threats to his Queen.

"Thou doest not care for me," the hag stated simply, never taking her eyes off him.

"No," he replied, though it had not been a question.

"But thou wisheth to ask me a question, still."

"Yes," he said, again answering without a query.

"Well," she sighed, shuffling past him and squatting down next to the pot. "The little ones are away with Sleepy-head, so ask thy questions without fear. My children shall inform me shouldst they wander back."

Uzran did not wonder at her intuitions, having spent too long among sorcerers like the Tuatha, but again he looked at the pot and wondered what asking the question would cost him.

Mother Gwiddon waited, long arms crooked and elbows hanging at her sides while her immense hands rested upon her knees. Her eyes glimmered, but otherwise she was motionless.

"Why must the Paladin always be human?" he asked at last, and felt a stab of guilt tighten in his stomach before the words even left his lips. It was not his to question such things. What had he told Droth? What kind of answer could she give that would really satisfy him, anyway?

Mother Gwiddon nodded slowly, nose nearly tapping the tops of her knees as she did so.

"Thou wants to know why thou must serve under such as them? Thou who has served thy Queen for centuries, made to serve a creature who is not of this world, and whom thou could crush beneath thy boot like an insect."

Uzran had begun to nod, but caught himself, giving his head a sharp shake.

"It is not just about personal skill, and you know that," he growled, eying the hag suspiciously. "I have been fighting the Gythraul since before that child's grandsires were a shine in their father's eyes. I have ended the lives of more enemies of this Kingdom than days he has lived, and I know who that enemy is. I have fought them on every field, and I know their every ploy and stratagem."

"And yet, they still stand," Mother Gwiddon observed. "For all thy victories and experience, thou hast never driven out the Gythraul completely."

"Nor have the Paladins," Uzran pressed angrily. "Two millennia and they have never claimed that victory either. New ways, new gadgets, new schemes, and still the same result. The blood of both armies watering one burnt field or another. This Paladin will be no different."

"How doest thou know this?"

"Because, he is the same as all the others!" Uzran bellowed loud enough to set the bones rattling on their strings above. "He is another soft human who is arrogant enough to believe that he will save us. He will win a few victories, the Court will shower him with praise, and he will either grow indolent and become useless, or grow rebellious, and the Queen will deal with him as she has done with those before. Regardless, he will not have the will to bind the Court together so that we could actually finish this war."

"Perhaps thou art wrong?" Mother Gwiddon mused. "Perhaps this Paladin shall be different than all the others."

"Are those the words of a seer, or just the deflections of a charlatan who does not want to lose her place by the royal ear."

Something amused, yet dangerous shimmered in the witch's eyes.

"I have heard that when angry, thou tends to speak thy mind more freely than thou shouldst," she said in low, painfully soft tones. "And though I put little stock in courtly niceties, I would advise thee to weigh thy words with more caution. The truth of what thou hast seen and what thous has done does not buy thee license to speak treason."

"Treason?" the Ogre snarled, and with a stride he was glowering into the hag's face. "With all your spies and your prophetic brews, you should know better than to suggest such foolishness. I have given everything for the Queen."

Mother Gwiddon did not flinch from his snarling face.

"Not everything. Not yet," she whispered to his face with a smile, "but our ears have heard of a bold Ogre who now stands with no clan and no kin. Dost thou know how such a thing came to be for so sorry a creature? One would think that such a wretch might be a desperate thing—tormented and unpredictable—but tell me, what do thou think?"

Uzran's eyes, formerly simmering with barely-contained rage, grew cold. The hard stare that remained held the witch's gaze as her head listed slowly left and then right, her eyes never leaving him.

"It had to be done," the Captain said flatly. "I serve— same as any faithful soldier."

Mother Gwiddon's eyes sparkled and she laid a single, long finger against the side of her nose.

"Let thee hope it is so."

The Ogre stood a moment longer, and then with hardly a sound, he turned and began to walk out of the hall. He was a single stride from the doors when they swung inward and Bryth Lighttread came in, surrounded by a gaggle of Bogles, all flitting, hopping, and scurrying around her. The Bogles whispered and giggled, and from her twinkling eyes to the easy smile on her face, it was plain to see that Bryth was quite enjoying the antics of her diminutive entourage.

"Captain," she said, her smile faltering slightly as she saw the grim countenance advancing toward her. "Hurrahn is still with Luce—I mean—Paladin Bollham. They are watching some marsh Goblins sport with a Mireshell, if you wish to join them."

"I go to make ready for our departure," Uzran continued toward the door, not even slowing as Bryth stepped clear of his advance. The Bogles only just managed to avoid being crushed under his boots.

"I did not think we planned to leave until the morning?" Bryth called after him.

The Ogre did not look over his shoulder as he trudged into the marsh beyond the doorway.

"Then we shall be well prepared by tomorrow."

Bryth frowned after him, then one of the Bogles tugged at her fingers, and she looked down into a Badger pup's stripped face atop the shoulders of a monkey. One simian hand still held her fingers while the other worried and picked at it's scabby rat tail.

"No want Lady to go," it chirped. "Stay here. Stay in Mistmire."

Bryth gently freed her fingers to rub the top of the Bogle's head, and then gingerly picked out a small twig she found tangled in its furry scalp.

"As lovely as that would be," she said softly, kneeling, "I have a mission still to complete and a Paladin to serve. Don't be sad though. I will probably see you—all of you—again, when the war starts. We will need brave creatures like you to be our eyes and ears."

"And who else can get words from the cranky, ol' Grindles, but us brave Bogles?" asked a weasel-headed Bogle, aloft on a pair of sparrow wings.

The crowd of Bogles cheered, turning flips, spiraling through the air, and running in tight, little circles. "To war!" they cried jubilantly. They began to march around Bryth in a lopsided, raucous parade.

Bryth found herself smiling again.

"Now, now," Mother Gwiddon clucked, and the Bogles quieted immediately, as though spellbound. "Off with the lot of ye, whilst little Lighttread and I hold quick council."

A few of the Bogles' mouths opened as though to protest, but no sound came forth, and like vermin scattering from daylight, they fled—some exiting through the open doors, other scuttling or flapping to the rafters and scaffolding about the hall.

"Thou said that the Paladin watches the marsh Goblins hunt." Mother Gwiddon rose from her squat beside the pot. "What does he hope to learn there, I wonder?"

"At first, he was learning to use the Hagseye you had given him." Bryth leaned against a pillar near the center of the room. "Using Sleepyhead and the Hagseye, he scouted the area south of here and found the Goblins stalking toward the Mireshell's nest."

Mother Gwiddon shook her head slowly as she began to pace toward the back of the hall.

"The human may not know it, but thou art well aware that, for good or ill, Goblins possess audacity in excess of prudence," she said. "But thou said 'at first,' so what then was second?"

"After finding the Goblins, I had him practice on using Sleepyhead's connections with the other Bogles and a few nearby Grindles to watch the their hunt from different angles."

Mother Gwiddon's wrinkled eyelids raised a little in surprise at this, and she craned her long neck back toward Bryth. "On the first day? The lad must be a natural with such things." She rubbed her hands together.

"Well, he did keep forgetting he was not seeing with his own eyes," Bryth chuckled. "More than once, he strode waist deep into the marsh, cursing as he tried to get the Bogle or Grindle to move forward. It was more than a little humorous to watch."

"No doubt," Mother Gwiddon said with a smile. Then she prowled toward the back of the hall where a tattered curtain hung from the right hindmost pillar to the wall. The thing looked as though it were made of the same material as the garment draped over Mother Gwiddon.

Bryth followed the witch a few paces behind.

"Why didst thou leave, then?"

"Most of what he will need now is practice, not teaching," Bryth shrugged. "And he had ceased to listen to my instruction anyway. He was engrossed in the hunt he was watching, and I could tell it was more than just the sport of it. I think he may have been developing some sort of plan."

Mother Gwiddon stopped at the curtain and laid a hand on the curtain hem, but did not enter yet. "Why doest thou think so?"

"As I watched his face, something changed. He seemed...inspired."

The witch sniffed and nodded, her lips curling in a smile. "Let thee hope it bodes well."

"I explained to the Paladin what great magics go into the making of a Bogle—magics of which only you have knowledge, and that even the Queen and all the previous Paladins did not possess their own personal Bogles. I do not think that he fully grasped the enormity of what you have done for him."

Mother Gwiddon chuckled, the sound thick and tumorous. "The young rarely ever do." She, drew back the curtain to reveal several small tables and shelves covered with jars, jugs, and bowls, all made from clay and filled with various strange contents.

"I hope it is not impertinent of me to wonder why?" Bryth came to the shadow of curtain as the hag began to shuffle the earthen vessels about the space.

"It most certainly is," the hag said over her shoulder as she cleared a spot on a table for a bowl heaped with indigo frogspawn. The jellied strands of embryo oozed and dribbled on the splintery tabletop.

"But why now?" Bryth pressed, stepping within the curtain to rest a hand on a table edge that came to her chin. "Why do you feel compelled to give tools you have held back for millenia?"

"I can change my mind, can I not?" Mother Gwiddon asked offhandedly, probing the contents of a jar with a fingertip. "Such is a mother's prerogative, I am told."

Bryth ground her teeth quietly in frustration, but refused to let her irritation at the witch's flippancy show. "Most certainly you do, but as emissary of the Queen and one chosen to aid the Paladin anyway, your reasons may be important for me to know."

Mother Gwiddon unstoppered a jug, took a sniff, and, wincing a little, lowered it to the table beside the bowl of amphibian eggs. "Is all thy talk of the Queen and emissary supposed to impress me, child?" She began to count the shelves on the far wall. "One, two, three up. One, two, to the left." The hag's long arm reached into a wood-framed cubby, where she felt about, her nails grating and scratching upon wood and what sounded like parchment.

"No, Mother Gwiddon," Bryth replied cautiously. "I know better than that."

"Doubtful," the witch sniffed, drawing her arm out and glancing at the leaflet of parchment she held. She let it drop and plunged her arm back into the cubby. "Thou art hardly seasoned enough to know the difference between thy pert little quim and a Grindle hole."

Bryth bared her teeth in an angry grimace and opened her mouth to give a retort, but the words never came. She shut her mouth hard enough to make her teeth click and stood there slowly breathing in and out. Mother Gwiddon had found her desired scrap of parchment and with it in hand, she gathered the bowl and jug from the table in her arms, turning to look at the Tuatha standing before her.

"Well?" she asked Bryth, a little impatiently.

More ichorous fluid dribbled from the jug of frogspawn onto the floor, black in the green torchlight.

"You are trying to make me angry. Seeing how I take such treatment," she stated in a steady, calm voice.

"Yes, of course," Mother Gwiddon sighed with exasperation. "Now move thyself before I am standing in a puddle."

Bryth took a step back and then two to the side to allow the hag to pass before following her back to the pot at the center of the hall. "So this was...some kind of test?"

"Everything is a test," the witch said with a grunt, lowering the jug and bowl to the floor and taking up her squat beside the fire pit. "Everything."

"Is this part of what Lady Bwyathardd began at Thistle-bough?" Bryth asked, standing opposite Mother Gwiddon on the far side of the pot.

The hag paused, blinked twice, and then stared at the Tuatha.

"What makes thou think I truck with that leaky slut?" she asked, though her voice held none of the venom her words implied.

"You both serve the Queen and both seem intent on being discourteous and boorish," Bryth stared unflinchingly, emerald eyes defiant before Mother Gwiddon's amber stare. "Perhaps the Queen wishes to make certain I am fit for the task given me, or perhaps as her subjects, you feel it is your responsibility to test me and make certain I will not falter."

Mother Gwiddon's whole body began to shake, violently hunching and quivering. Then a gargling sound that wheezed deep in her bony chest spilled out as she threw her head back.

"Precocious little thing," she warbled, flapping her crooked arms and knocking her knees together. "Thou art very certain of thy significance."

Bryth suddenly felt very small and foolish, but refused to blink or demure even as the hag cackled in her face. "Then you are saying I am wrong?" Bryth asked, back straight and stiff to steady herself.

"Oh, I am certain that Lady Bwyathardd would not say a single word of consequence to thee without the Queen putting it in her well-used mouth," Mother Gwiddon snickered, then raised a finger. "But for my part, I keep my own counsel. I simply wished to know what thou thought of thyself."

Bryth was surprised by that, but fought to keep it from her face. "And what have you learned?"

The hag chuckled some more and tapped the side of her nose. "As I told thee," she said, eyes gleaming wickedly, "I keep my own counsel."

26

ASH

After multiple abortive attempts to get Rhoslyn not to eat Sleepyhead when he sat on her back, I decided to have the Bogle ride on my shoulder. When the Diomedan tried to snatch a snack off of my shoulder, she got a snout full of my fist and quickly decided it was more trouble than it was worth. For his part, Sleepyhead seemed to appreciate the closeness, wrapping his long, plump body across the back of my neck, nestling his head in the hollow of my throat. I had given him a light scratch on the back of his round skull which elicited a soft gurgle of pleasure. I didn't need Uzran's disgusted glare to tell me I was smiling like an idiot.

I had to say that, so far, Bogles were some of my favorite critters in Other-Realm.

We left Mistmire the morning after I received Sleepyhead, and as we rode the Path to Cinderstone, our final stop in Far-Hold, my head was buzzing with ideas that had been brewing since the last afternoon.

As Bryth had taught me to use the Hagseye—the seemingly innocuous, blue stone given for answering Mother

Gwiddon's riddle—I had used Sleepyhead's eyes to spy on some marsh Goblins hunting something that looked like a cross between a crab, a lamprey, and a snapping turtle, grown to the size of a minivan. The six Goblins, most barely four feet tall and armed with crude spears of sharpened wood and bone, seemed totally outmatched. Even if there had been three times their number, the monstrous turtle-crustacean looked like it could have clipped them all in half with its claws before slurping them up in its wide, tooth-lined mouth. Part of me wanted to keep watching just because I wanted to see the shifty bastards get eaten, but even if that hadn't been the case, Bryth had seen the hunt as a learning opportunity.

I guess all Wee Folk—small magical creatures, of which Bogles are artificial, but recognized members—have a constant sense of each other. Even when they use their natural magical talent to camouflage themselves, or turn totally invisible, other Wee Folk still know they are there. Even more than that, with permission, these critters can share their senses with one other, letting others of their kind see, hear, feel, smell, and even taste what they are experiencing. They also have a kind of crude telepathy, allowing them to convey simple concepts and bits of information. Thanks to my magical stone, I could sense things through Sleepyhead, and thanks to his connection to other Wee Folk in the area, I had access to a huge amount of sensory information. With Sleepyhead acting as an envoy, I could move into an area, and within minutes establish a network of informants and remotely view developing situations in real time.

Any soldier knows that intel can make all the difference in the world, and now I had the keys to one of the most advanced surveillance systems ever conceived.

But as fantastic and invaluable as that was, it was not what had kept me up last night.

I remembered the Goblins as they worked around their monstrous quarry, an erratic flurry of movement and teasing attacks that all seemed to work together without actually looking like they'd planned anything. They hollered, hooted, and shrieked whether they were running for their lives, ducking down between the muddy roots of a swamp tree, or lunging in for an ineffectual stab at the armored body of the Mireshell. For a long time, I thought they were just insane and extremely lucky. They kept on, never seeming to do much harm, yet never managing to suffer any themselves. It might have almost become boring, until I started using the other Bogles in the area to get multiple perspectives of the hunt.

That is when I saw it.

For every blind, screaming rush, two subtler stabs jabbed weapons at joints and seams, worrying the shell and rubbery flesh, producing thin, leaking wounds. Each frantic retreat worked the creature into ever thicker, clinging vegetation. Not directly, but like a sailor tacking alongside the wind, they worked the Mireshell by gradual angles further and further back. Then, when I managed to gain the eyes and ears of a particularly grouchy Grindle, I saw a cohort of pole-armed Goblins crouching alongside a craftily concealed pit filled with sharpened logs. It was a masterful strategy, and despite my bias against its creators, I was finding myself more and more impressed.

If the clawed beasty kept fleeing in the direction it was going, it would find itself plunging to its doom. Its own bulk would most likely impale it on the jagged stakes. If it decided to give up the confrontation and run away, it had been given enough wounds and been led deep enough into the tangling morass of water vegetation that retreat would be just as costly. It would struggle and bleed to death, collapsing in the mud. Really, its best option now would be to hunker down and try to kill any of the hunters that came near—try to break the Goblins' spirit before its body gave out. But even that was no guarantee as the Goblin pack's numbers and nimbleness made every attack and retreat more costly to the Mireshell than it was to them. The creature was mad and determined to kill its tormentors. Its will for victory and revenge would not let it back down.

I remembered Uzran talking about how the Gythraul had a will of iron. Maybe I could use that to my advantage, playing a deceptive game of tag to goad that will. If I matched that with an unwillingness to engage in pitched battles, maybe I could prick that pride of theirs enough to seize the initiative and cripple them before Uzran's other warning came to pass. I knew a little bit what it was like, fighting a war unsupported by the homefront, but at least this time I wasn't going to have to keep trading hats between nation-builder and soldier. Once I finished this last Oath of Fealty, I was going to be the man of war—the meateating, lifetaking, bonestomping son of Hell that Uncle Sam had always wanted me to be.

As I rode the misty Path to Cinderstone, I hoped that would be enough.

Cinderstone was the most barren place I'd ever seen in my life, and I'd seen some pretty desolate places—from the moon-dusted crags of Afghanistan, to Death Valley during a trip I'd made when taking some leave stateside. At least in those places, the light of the sun had been bright, and it shone on stone and sand in such a way as to suggest that there was still hope for beauty and life somewhere. Cinderstone was gray on black, with the silvery light of Illaeth, Other-Realm's sun, shaded by overcast, ashen skies that rumbled ominously with the fury of thunder and no respite of rain.

Apart from a few nobby hills where black stones were piled in neolithic cairns, the land was mostly flat and featureless. Here and there, cracks in the parched ground glowed with an angry red ripple of heat or spat a stiff jet of smoke. Nothing growing or green touched the earth, and though I think I spied something with too many legs skitter between the rocks as we passed, no obvious sound of fauna met my ears, either. Looking across the expanse, the eye saw nothing of any real consequence, until it settled on the ziggurat. It sat at the center of the bare, endless plain and was enfenced by a low curtain wall of rough, black stone.

Looming huge and dark, tiered and sharp cornered, it was like some kind of obsidian altar to a vengeful god lurking just behind the ash and clouds above. I could almost imagine that the stones had been white marble when it was built, but after eons of bloody sacrifice to that hungry, glowering deity, they had become eternally stained.

As we rode toward the ziggurat, I felt in danger of being overawed, then a thought occurred. Looking at the soaring structure in that scoured land, with all of its scorched black, made me think of a fictional landscape that was well known back in my world, and as I looked over at Uzran and Hurrahn trudging along, I couldn't help but laugh.

"Well, all we're missing is Mount Doom," I chuckled. "But, then you two would really would be in trouble."

The Ogre and Fomor both raised their heads to stare at me, the latter, bemused, and the former, annoyed.

"How so, my Paladin?" Hurrahn asked with genuine concern.

"Because," I began, still in danger of giggling, "one does not simply walk into Mordor."

I burst into a fit of laughter that startled Sleepyhead into flight, and drew confused stares from all present. The weight of their incomprehension dragged my levity back down to the dust-choked ground, and I muttered an apology to all present. I tried to compose my face into a more sober expression as we neared the black fortress.

It seemed meme-based humor was not appreciated in Other-Realm.

"Master Luce," Sleepyhead gurgled just above me, "we no alone."

Uzran, Hurrahn, and Bryth came to a halt immediately, and I was obliged to join them as they moved into a rough approximation of a fighting square. WIth one hand, I drew my M-Core from the saddle holster, and in the other, I took up the Hagstone which hung around my neck on a leather braid. I raised the stone and pressed its hard edges against the orbit of my eye socket.

"Show me," I ordered, squeezing the other eye shut and feeling the magical rock adhere to my socket with a prickling tingle.

There was a flicker of images like a film reel going off kilter, then things stabilized into an aerial view of the expanse of bare plain where we now huddled. The strangeness of seeing myself from another's eyes was still new, but I concentrated on looking for threats. At first glance, there seemed to be nothing. Then I spied a few little puffs of dust behind a hill we had just passed. I couldn't see what was making the disturbance, but something was moving just beyond that mound.

"Higher," I said in a hoarse whisper, feeling my mouth go dry, and not just from the ash on the air.

Sleepyhead climbed upward, and I could see more little puffs of dust, but still couldn't tell what was making them. As Sleepyhead panned his view, I noticed more stirring dust coming from a crack in the ground, and then another from behind a different cairn-topped hill. All dust plumes triangulated, with us at the center. My belly sank as I watched the sweeping view of the churned ash clouds that were closing in.

"Keep up there with an eye out, and find any more Wee Folk that can help," I instructed my Bogle. As I opened my other eye, the Hagseye fell from my socket.

I blinked my eyes a few times, vision returning to normal, and looked up to see Bryth and Hurrahn staring out at the landscape with worried looks. Uzran stood his ground, glowering outward with one hand on the sword at this belt.

"Lucius," Bryth said, her voice already thickening with gathering magic. "What is out there?"

I pointed at the positions of the encroaching puffs of dust that could barely be seen at a few hundred yards out. "I'm not sure, but whatever it is, it's moving toward us." Shifting the carbine stock to my shoulder, I wondered if I should dismount as I felt Rhoslyn twitch beneath me. "And I think that we've got more than one of them. They're surrounding us as they close in."

Uzran cocked his head a little and half-turned to give me a sidelong glance. "So you saw dust moving, but no actual creature?" he asked. I couldn't tell if it was genuine concern or sarcasm I heard in his voice.

"Yes." I was about defend what I'd seen, but the Ogre nodded sharply, drawing his sword in one fluid motion.

"Arcghuls," he said grimly, his sword's edge glinting in the wan light.

"What?" I asked, watching the plumes of dust grow closer.

"Scavengers," Bryth explained, her voice now fully resonating with sorcerous power. "No more than pests, usually, but they can make themselves invisible for short periods of time. In numbers, they can be dangerous."

"Lord Arawn is supposed to keep their numbers down," Hurrahn growled, hefting a mace with a barbed, triangular head.

"Many more coming, Master Luce," Sleepyhead called, swooping down to deliver his message before flapping madly to regain altitude.

"I guess he needs a better exterminator." I bare my teeth in a fierce smile. Sighting down the barrel of my rifle at the dust plumes, I put a trio of shots downrange.

The first two kicked up ash in a hillside beyond, but one found something, because a high, keening hiss cut the air, and a spindly figure materialized out of the air like an alien peeling off his cloaking field. It was like someone took the worst attributes of a dog, a spider, and a human victim of famine and mashed them into one nightmare package.

Digitigrade legs shuddered and twitched along with a curled whip of a tail, while long, dangling ears flapped around a face with too many eyes and curved mandibles. It danced on its hind legs, clawing at the smoking wound in its abdomen then collapsed, twitching in the dust.

The rest of the encroaching dust clouds didn't so much as slow down.

"Well, at least they're ugly," I observed before pumping two more shots out, revealing another spasming corpse. "That's something."

"Does that make it easier to kill them?" Bryth asked, a

sword out in her hand now, and with a single, forceful sylla-ble, the length of the blade erupted with flame.

"I think so," I said with another manic grin.

Bryth laughed, and it was like I had amused a storm goddess—an elemental deity of fire and thunder. Her laughter grew into a roar, and her Diomedan reared back with restrained bloodlust. Then the Tuatha swept her flaming blade in front of her in a wide, searing arc.

A crackling wave of flame curled, surged, then crashed upon the invisible tide of Arcghuls. Nearly a dozen reared back and danced wildly, silhouettes of agony in the curtain of fire. I peppered the line along the outskirts of Bryth's pyrotechnics and was rewarded with the sight of three more emaciated shapes dying in a cloud of stirred ash.

Still more were coming; their numbers seemed only to swell as their invisible feet trampled their dead.

"Hurrahn and I will cut an opening that you will ride through. Make for Lord Arawn's citadel!" Uzran bellowed over the crackle of flames as Bryth unleashed another sweep of magical fire. "We will keep them busy once you are away."

"Hell no!" I shouted back, firing off another long burst. "We cut an opening, and we all make a run for it. None of this brave, last stand shit. The war hasn't even started."

I put my heels to Rhoslyn and hauled on the reins, swinging the Diomedan around to come alongside Bryth.

"We are going to start riding in a wide circle, hopefully dividing them," I shouted, feeling the horde closing in like a growing pressure at the back of my skull. "You two pair up and punch through where the line is thinnest, then start waving that damn banner to give us a point to head for."

The captain looked like he was going to argue, but the Arcghuls were close enough that the sound of all their clawed feet was raising a ruckus, and with a defiant cry, Bryth and I were off.

I am not sure if it was the exertion of springing the trap or just the time it took them to close, but the Arcghuls were becoming visible by the time we rode alongside the first wave of them. Glistening eyes and skeletal claws reached after us. Bryth and I wheeled hard left, pelting those fast enough to make a lunge at us with manticore quills and gouts of arcane flame.

The crack of the rifle was punctuated by the sharp wail of a fallen scavenger. There were so many, and they were so close that I couldn't miss. Bryth's fiery sword immolated handfuls of the creatures at a stroke. Over my shoulder, I caught a glimpse of the two hulking Royal Guards plowing into their own mass of Arcghuls, each sweep of their inhumanly large weapons scattering the hacked and pulped remains of numerous foes. They were like juggernaut threshing machines chewing through so much chaff on their rampage.

The horde split and doubled back on itself. The Arcghuls got in each other's way as they fought to choose their preferred targets. As Bryth and I wheeled this way and that at a mad gallop, I saw some of the creatures turn on each other with stabbing, fanged mandibles.

It seemed like my plan might work after all.

Then my carbine clicked empty, and one of the Arcghuls sprang at me. I managed to crunch the butt of the rifle into the thing's face, bursting eyes and breaking what passed for its nose, but its clawed digits dug into my mailed sleeves and dragged me forward and down. Rhoslyn fought to keep her balance, heavy cords of muscle standing out along her neck as I swung over the horn of the saddle.

More of the scavengers piled on, even as the one with

the smashed face fell away, clawing and pulling with surprising strength despite their weedy frames. Rhoslyn began to buck and spin, knocking some loose, but more leapt onto her as well. I cracked another across the side of the head with the rifle stock before they tore me bodily from the saddle.

The ground rushed up to meet me, and I tried to roll as I fell, tearing free from snaring claws. One of them must have been beneath me, because I heard a crunch as I hit, but felt only a dull thud from the impact. Then I was using the momentum of my roll, clearing space with my armored elbows and the butt of the carbine so I could get to my feet.

A mob of the creatures had formed a circle around Rhoslyn and I. As I slapped a hand down to grab a fresh magazine from my belt, I watched the Diomedan tear the head off the last of the Arcghuls that was clinging to her shoulder like a deer tick. Her fangs clamped down on its bristly, lumpen skull, and with a sharp shake, its head came free. A moment later, its body followed, crumpling to the ground.

The spent magazine landed softly in the ashen dust as I slammed the fresh one in. I began snapping off shots, spinning to level the barrel at the circling targets, one after another. Rhoslyn turned with me, her teeth, hooves, and muscular bulk driving back the onrushing creatures. We kept moving, even though I knew it was only a slice of time before my magazine ran dry, and we could ill-afford the spare seconds required to reload.

My faithful Diomedan drove her forehooves down through the chests of two Arcghuls she had staggered with a sweep of her sinewy flank, and I put my last quill through an opportunistic scavenger that lept toward her lowered head. Another Arcghul pounced on me, and we grappled with the spent rifle between us. I managed to snake a hand down to the knife at my belt and ram the blade up under the scrabbling fangs that stretched toward my face.

I tore the blade free and let the corpse and rifle fall away as I rushed to meet next spidery, dog-eared monster. I perforated another with a mad rush of stabs, nothing but frantic energy driving the gore-slick dagger in and out, over and over.

I saw more of them, and screamed in primal rage and defiance. "Want some?" I roared. "Get some!"

The Arcghuls were about to oblige, when a blanket of fire descended on them, and their bodies twisted in paroxysm of flaming rapture. Bryth's steed leapt over the crackling corpses, and she rode forward, one hand holding her burning sword, the other held out to me. I reached back and snagged the sling of my carbine just as we gripped each other's forearms. I swung up onto the back of her saddle.

"What did you say about last stands?" Bryth roared in her divine voice. Blood and ash were smeared across her pale face, but she looked like the most beautiful thing I'd ever seen.

"Do as I say," I hollered. "Not as I do."

She laughed, eyes flashing like emerald lighting.

Bryth swept her blade down, and a lash of fire whipped out in front of her, blasting more Arcghuls as droplets of fiery bronze descended like tiny falling stars. Wherever they landed, tiny eruptions of fire burst up to sear and blind more enemies. Without slowing, we rode them down. Their bony chests and spines snapped under our mount's hooves.

I was fitting a fresh magazine into my M-Core when I remembered Rhoslyn. I felt a sudden stab of panic, fearing she had been overwhelmed and borne down under the tide of claws and fangs.

And then I saw her plunging toward us, blood glistening on her legs and flanks from a dozen shallow cuts, but her rosy eyes burned with a fierce light. This was what she was bred for. This was home.

I cheered her on, clinging to Bryth's strong back, pumping rounds out left and right, one-handed with the carbine.

We beat a retreat along the amorphous edge of the Arcghuls and headed toward the Pale Banner flapping on a hilltop. Uzran stood in front of a pile of black stone, heaps of Arcghuls falling away from his dripping sword edge. Hurrahn waved the banner with mechanical speed and strength, never pausing, even when taking a moment here or there to squash the occasional Arcghul that managed to make it around the Ogre's blade.

We mounted the slope, and even the sturdy Diomedans had to struggle over the slick ground that was bloodied and thick with fallen Arcghuls. Eventually, Bryth pulled along-side Uzran, and I leapt down and rushed toward him.

"This doesn't look like a way out, Captain," I shouted before turning and spraying a tight formation of shots at more creatures creeping up the slope. "You were supposed to make for the citadel! What part of my orders was hard for you to understand?"

"But why bother, when the citadel comes to you?" came a soft, dark voice that managed a conversational volume despite the clamour of the fight.

It was then I realized there was someone else on the hilltop.

A gaunt-faced man with a dark beard rose from where he had sprawled languidly among the stones of the cairn. He was a just over six feet tall, putting him a few inches shorter than me, and garbed in a full-length coat of midnight blue. It was richly embroidered with gold and silver thread, and hung heavily across his compact, muscled frame. Even though I had seen this same getup on the tapestry in the Hall of Fealty, I didn't recognize who he was until I saw the crimson sclera of his amused eyes.

"Lord Arawn," I said with a quick bob of my head. "I had hoped we would meet under better circumstances. I am Paladin Lucius Bollham."

Lord Arawn strolled casually toward me, looking me up and down with his red eyes. Uzran swept past us and took the heads off of three more Arcghuls, limp bodies tumbling down the hill where more of their ilk were gathering.

"I suppose this will serve to seal the Oath as well as anything else," he commented, turning his bored stare from me to the gathering horde below. "It wasn't my plan, but it will do. I appreciate that your Bogle saw fit to draw my attention to the spectacle."

I looked up to see Sleepyhead flitting about overhead.

"Hope that okay, Master Luce." he warbled down.

I gave the Bogle a smile and a thumbs up. No longer a heartbeat from death, but not much more, I suddenly felt exhausted.

"My lord, why have these scavengers been allowed to grow to such numbers?" Bryth called from atop her mount after sending another jet of flame along the base of the hill.

"I have been otherwise occupied," the Lord of Cinderstone replied coolly. He watched the mustering mob of scavengers, which, even after all the damage we had done, looked to be nearly a hundred strong.

"I suppose we should clean this up, though." Lord Arawn turned his gaze on me. "After all, you have a real war to fight."

Stepping past us, the Tuatha raised his hands into the

air, and I felt the gathering pressure of magic. The creatures below must have felt it as well, because they suddenly seemed uncertain, milling around and snapping at each other. An incredibly deep and malevolent chuckle reverberated out from Lord Arawn, and then, with two eldritch words that stung my ears, he plunged his hands down into the ashen ground. A subtle, nearly imperceptible ripple rolled down the hill from where he stood, across the entire hillside and the plain below. The earth began to boil.

The Arcghuls began to scatter and scramble like freshly illuminated roaches as the Lord of Cinderstone rose and turned back toward us.

"Shall we retire for refreshment?" he asked, dabbing at a small trickle of blood at the corner of his mouth.

Below, an Arcghul gave a sharp death cry which was soon joined by more shrieks from his fellows as skeletal hands burst up from the ground to rip and tear.

27

SLAVES

"Y ou will find that though I am Tuatha, I differ quite distinctly from most others of my kind," Lord Arawn said. He reclined in his high-backed chair with nothing but a small bowl before him on the gilded table of black stone that stretched nearly the entire length of his dining hall.

I sat at his right hand, in a plush high-backed chair of my own, and Bryth was seated next to me. Neither of us had been given a chance to clean ourselves after the fight, so we sat sipping wine from small bowls and nibbling black bread and hard cheese, still stained with ash and blood.

"The Gloaming Court, all its squabbles and intrigues, and even the jockeying of the other Lords of Far-Hold have never much interested me." He pickied up the bowl and took a quick sip. "Of course, it could be that I am simply no good at such business, but regardless, such things require the pomp and ceremony of etiquette to keep them all under control. After all, without their little rituals and manners, they would have to admit what a bunch of squabbling curs they are."

Bryth stiffened a little at that, and though he may have been right, especially given what Uzran had told me and what I'd observed, the Lord of Cinderstone rubbed me the wrong way. Maybe it was the way he had of talking about others with such sneering condescension while believing himself to be an objective observer. Just like dear old dad —the prick.

"So," Lord Arawn continued. "The fact is that much of the courtly niceties and other wastes of time you may have come to expect will be circumvented here. Honestly, I hadn't expected to ask you to complete the Oath of Fealty, but if the old traditions must be observed, we can say that the affair with the pestilential Arcghuls should stand in for any request I could have made."

"That is very generous of you, my Lord," I commented dryly.

"Quite," Lord Arawn said, taking another sip and waving his free hand, beckoning someone out of the corridors behind his seat at the end of the hall.

There was the soft whisper of slippered feet on the stones of the hall floor, and three women in more fitted, less elaborate versions of the Lord's coat came to stand on the left hand side of the table. Each woman was identical to the others, all with sharp, striking features, raven hair, and eyes as red as arterial spray. In their hands, they each held a small iron cauldron by ring handles. Stamped upon each cauldron was the image of a skull whose mouth hung open. Out of the skeletal mouth poured curls of smoke or clouds.

"These are my daughters," Lord Arawn said with a sweep of his hand. "They hold the Black Caulders, which will give you the power to enslave the bodies of the dead."

I remembered Bryth telling me about this, and at first I had wanted nothing to do with enlisting the help of Lord

Arawn. As creepy as zombies were, they hardly seemed useful in battle, except perhaps as cannon fodder, and even then, it would only be in the pitched battles that I wanted to avoid. Then Bryth had explained that the dead were rarely used for actual fighting. She said that the ages of war had taken their toll on the Kingdom's population, so all able-bodied creatures were needed to be ready to stand as soldiers, and that still left many other jobs to do. Individuals in low-skill positions that keep an army moving and well-supplied—porters, labourers, ferriers, and the like—could all be creatures which would never complain and never needed to rest.

It all seemed too perfect, and that was why I invariably set about questioning a good thing.

"Thank you, Lord Arawn." I shifted forward in my seat. "But I have a question or two before I accept this generous gift."

He cocked a thin eyebrow, but nodded his assent.

"You say that these caulders enslave the dead," I began, trying to weigh each word carefully. "Can you help me understand what that entails? Am I actually enslaving the spirits or souls of the dead?"

Lord Arawn stared at me for a few long heartbeats, his face an impassive mask, but then a smile twitched beneath his beard.

"Bones and dead flesh have no souls—no spirits—to enslave, as useful as that would be," he explained. "The magic I have worked into the Black Caulders resonates with the trace energies remaining within the corpus. This resonance is then placed under the command of the caulder-holder, and it is manipulated to bind the unliving flesh to the will of that person. Thus the dead are enslaved, but perhaps that is the wrong term. Without the energies of the caulder, they have no animation at all. It is a matter of manipulating a physical body, just like a puppeteer—simply on a far grander scale."

It was all good, I guess, making sense as much as anything else in Other-Realm. Here, mushrooms gossip and flame-throwing swords are a thing. Still, that first little bit about enslaving souls gnawed at my mind. Enslaved souls? Useful?

I swallowed the sharp questions I wanted to put to the Lord of Cinderstone, deciding a full-blown ethical debate in a world where I barely understood the rules of reality was not the best decision. Besides, I was tired. I needed some rest; I needed to hammer out the last details of Lord Arawn's "support," check on Rhoslyn's injuries, and speak with Bryth and Uzran about our next step. I wasn't sure in what order those would all take place, but I imagined that the most important thing on that list was going to be the last thing I would get to.

No rest for the wicked.

I eyed the Black Caulders suspiciously.

I left Rhoslyn in the stables, sure she would be fine after watching her bite the hand off the lifeless Hobb groom that impassively continued grooming her even as she threw back her head and gulped down the last of his left hand's fingers.

I had freaked out at first, but then, as if waiting for that exact moment, one of the daughters of Lord Arawn had emerged and told me not to be concerned. The groom, like all her father's servants, was dead. When I saw how little blood dripped from the wound and the creature's complete lack of response, it began to sink in. The Hobb's face was waxy and pale, his eyes clouded. With some reluctance, I let her lead me from the stable which sat within the ground level tier of the ziggurat.

She told me her name was Wrenneth, and apologized for following me since I had left her father's presence.

"Why were you following me?" I asked as we stepped beneath an archway that was carved to look like a crescent moon stabbing down into two spiralled columns.

Inside, the ziggurat was well lit. Candles lined the trenches along each wall just above head height, and large chandeliers dangled at regular intervals. Yet, for all that light, the black stone of the citadel seemed to suck the life out of everything, leaving it a dour, cheerless place.

"I wanted to know." Her red eyes met my own before looking quickly away. "That is, I was curious as to what sort of man you were. I have served many Paladins, each one has been different."

"Trying to figure out what the new boss is like, huh?" I said. "I get it."

"I pray you will not take offense." Her eyes did not meet mine. "I meant no impertinence, of course. I would never wish to displease you. None of us would. My sisters and I, I mean."

Something in the way she spoke, with the barest hint of a fearful tremor, made the hairs prickle along my arms. Something insidious—some notion that perhaps more than just nerves flavoured this Tuatha's words—sparked internal warnings that I had no name for, but which I had learned to trust.

"You say you worked for other Paladins before," I said cautiously. "How do I measure up so far?"

Wrenneth seemed unsure of how to respond at first, and for some time, we walked down the passageway in silence. I was just about to change the subject, when she began her tentative response.

"You are... gentler..Many others have been harder, crueler men. They looked too boldly at my sisters and I, or they spoke harshly to us, and once we were on the campaign trail, they were even more...brutal. I do not see the same in you, if I may say."

"I *did* ask you." I wondered if this kind of war needed harder men than me. Running a hand along the ledge of a candle alcove, fingers skidding along the stone, I broke the silence again. "What about the last one, Paladin Valoise? Was he one of those cruel men?"

"No," the red-eyed Tuatha said quickly. "Paladin Valoise was not like those men, though he seemed to have little desire to be near us. He seemed...uncomfortable around us."

I could understand that, but kept it to myself.

"He cold be cold at times, but never cruel, not of his own design. He paid no attention to my sisters and I, but I imagine that was because of the time he spent with Lady Lighttread. They grew quite close during the time he served the Queen, until he was bound by the Pact. Then he had no time for such things."

"Wait, what?" I managed, fighting to process the information that was just dumped on me. I mean, I know that there had been a few hints about Bryth and Paladin Valoise, but this seemed like a pretty solid confirmation, and what the hell was this business about a Pact?

Wrenneth stared up at me as we stopped near the stairs that lead up to the rooms that had been prepared for Bryth, Uzran, Hurrahn, and myself. "Have I offended?" Her voice was high and tight. "I meant no offense, my Paladin! Please forgive me!"

"No, Wrenneth, just calm down," I said, seeing the panic spilling out of her eyes.

I reached out to give her shoulder a steadying, comforting squeeze, but the second my hand came up, she flinched away. My hand hung in midair, then I let it fall limply to my side. I wondered what she was seeing, because I was pretty sure it wasn't me. Something big and terrible built over years was glowering down at this poor woman, and there was nothing I could do about it. Just being near me seemed to push her close to a mental breakdown.

"Wrenneth, I am going to promise you one thing," I said solemnly, bending down a little to meet her downcast eyes.

Something in my voice must have reached her, because she looked up, though her whole body seemed ready to collapse in on itself.

"I will never try to hurt or take advantage of you or your sisters." I said the words with slow determination. "My only goal is to win this war and save this kingdom. You'll never have anything to fear from me."

I held her gaze a second longer, and then, in a burst of movement that took me off guard, she rushed forward and wrapped her arms around my chest. Shocked, unsure what to do or say, I stood there wondering how bad I smelled with blood, dirt, and sweat still crusting my body. I managed to return the embrace with a gentle pat on either shoulder. Then she tore herself away from me and raced down the hall.

I watched her go.

"What was that?"

I turned to find Bryth standing on the stairs looking down at me with a slight frown. Her eyes flashed with the same lighting I'd seen in the fight earlier in the day, but it was somehow a hotter, smaller fire that brightened her stare now.

"Uh, it seems," I began, but stopped as I met her gaze. Was that jealousy? Was I really going to have to deal with this kind of stuff along with trying to fight a war? "It seems that the dead aren't the only slaves around here." I shouldered past her to climb the stairs. "Come on. We have work to do."

28

SYMBOLS

Hurrahn and Uzran had made themselves as comfortable as they could in the common room that connected to the rooms arranged for the Paladin's traveling party.

They had decided without saying a word that they would spend the night there, taking turns keeping watch. They had waited for the Paladin and Lady Lighttread to go to bed, then they pushed aside the sparse furnishings. Bedrolls came out, and they settled down with their broad backs against the wall opposite the stairwell to the rest of the ziggurat. They had already asked the Paladin's Bogle to search for secret passages and spyholes, and to the best of their knowledge, Lord Arawn's disdain for politicking bore out with the arrangements he had made for his guests.

The Lord's peculiarities were the subject of the two guards' conversation as they shared some bread and a rasher of bacon brought to them by a dead Boggun servant.

"It makes me uneasy," Uzran grumbled around a mouthful of black bread. "The Tuatha are what they are.

Scheming and intrigue are part of them all. Lord Arawn must have some other designs."

Hurrahn peeled off hanks of bacon and gave his captain a quizzical look. "What about Lady Lighttread and her father?" He popped the crisp meat into his mouth.

Uzran shook his head and reached over to take some of the bacon for himself. Drips of cooling grease struck the stones before the Ogre laid the meat across the last of his bread. "She schemes in her own way, and her father was hardly what I'd call guileless. It was all honorable and done for the good of the Kingdom, no doubt, but a scheme is a scheme. After all, it was Redfinger who first won the Queen's favor when he brought the Gormstone to her."

Hurrahn finished chewing and took a swallow from his wineskin, nodding. "Do you think that Lady Lighttread will tell the Paladin about the Gormstone?"

The Ogre shook his head as he ground the food between his teeth with excessive force. He held his frustrations in his jaw, determined to tear them into more palatable chunks. At last, he gave up the crushing exercise, jaw aching, and held out a hand for the wineskin. "No, not after the last time," he sighed, licking the sweet, stinging liquor from his lips. "She is still very young, but I believe what happened with Valoise has taught her the right lesson."

Hurrahn frowned, looking down toward the stairwell. He remembered the stiffness between Lady Lighttread and the Paladin when they had come up the stairs together. The nuances of romance for the smaller creatures of Other-Realm were still a mystery to a Fomor like him, who had little experience with such things even among his own kind. Though in his many years of service, he had learned a few things from watching over others. Affections breed resentments, certain as stone, and serving in the Gloaming Court among the hot-blooded Tuatha, he had more than one occasion to witness, or even intervene, when the fiercest of loves ran sour. He knew that such affections could run from fair to foul and back again, all within the space of a smile or a word. Though such whiplash emotions were befuddling, they were all too common among the Tuatha. Given what he had seen of all the Paladins he had served under, the same went for humans.

This led inevitably to the Fomor's suspicion that Lady Lighttread had not learned the lesson the Captain hoped. He considered saying as much, but decided against it. Uzran could be temperamental when it came to Lady Lighttread.

They finished the last of the food, and the wine would shortly be gone as well. The night deepened. Soon they would begin sleeping in shifts. Both knew the expectation, and the inevitable duty would be on them as soon as the last drop was squeezed from the wineskin.

Either the heady wine or the excitement of the day's fight drove Hurrahn's mind to wander. The dark stone was unadorned by decoration or art, besides the raw skill it took to build in stone so precisely. Each block adjoined its neighbor exactly. He was unsure if such work required mortar because he certainly did not see any.

The furniture of the common room was equally plain—two short couches, sized for humans or Tuatha, and two padded stools sized for the Royal Guards. There they had all sat after the Paladin returned with Lady Lighttread in tow. Sitting around the low-burning fire, they had planned their return to Duanon, where the Paladin would begin the rapid training of the mustered forces of the Twilit Kingdom. The Paladin had laid out his plans to reorganize the old regiments and to introduce new elements into the army—points about which he had been somewhat evasive. The Captain had grumbled some, but not as much as Hurrahn had expected.

As he stared at a glowing spur of wood in the fireplace, he was reminded of Lady Lighttread's sword in the fight with the Arcghuls, and thought he knew the reason for Uzran's subdued criticism. With a grunt, Hurrahn rose to his feet and went to the fireplace to throw a few more logs on the flagging flames.

"The Paladin did well today," the Fomor said. "He did not balk."

Uzran stared straight ahead, the spout of the wineskin held in his fist.

"Brave and fierce, even for how small he is," Hurrahn continued, slowly turning around. "Already, he seems the equal of the last two Paladins."

The Ogre's voice came out of lips that barely seemed to move, and his eyes continued their sentinel stare at the portal. "That was barely a skirmish with feral scavengers. But yes, he did well. Though, if he had been a better horseman and knew how to use a sword, Lady Lighttread would not have had to save him and thus put herself at risk."

Hurrahn nodded, knowing better than to argue with him. "Yet, he learns quickly. Before he came to us, he had never ridden a mount. Perhaps if he were schooled in such things, he would be less of a burden."

Uzran's eyes flicked from the stairs to see the lopsided grin on Hurrahn's face. "Are you suggesting that I train the Paladin?"

Hurrahn's smile did not falter, even as his Captain's eyes narrowed. "You could teach him the blade, and you are not on unfriendly terms with Lady Durnsted, one of the finest cavaliers among the Tuatha."

Uzran took a drink of the slackening wineskin and

licked his lips. "These battles will not turn upon whether the Paladin can wield a sword well or drive a charge," he huffed dismissively, crossing his arms. "The Wyrd help us if they do."

Hurrahn shrugged and set about worming under the covers of his bedroll. "Perhaps," he sighed, resting his horned head upon his bundled cloak, "but the Paladin, as best a simple soldier like me can see, has always been about being a symbol—just like the Pale Banner. That is why we do all this running around, gathering forces, stirring hearts and minds to remember old oaths and glories. Symbols need to be seen, and you can't see one very well if it is constantly getting dragged off the back of its mount."

Uzran looked down at the Fomor, his brow furrowing. "I told you reading those books in the Guardhouse Library was bad for you," he growled, but there was no menace in the captain's voice. "Now, get some sleep. I'll wake you when it's your watch."

Hurrahn had already closed his eyes, and like any veteran, was asleep in moments, his breath whistling steadily from his nostrils.

In the firelit common room, the Captain of the Royal Guard sat and thought on the day and on the meaning of symbols.

29

FOUNDATIONS

I stood on a scaffolded platform in a freshly-cleared field outside of Duanon before an assemblage of motley banners. Dozens of inhuman faces stared up at me. Beneath each banner stood the officers of the regiments those banners represented—a collection of pale, unassuming Hobbs, leathery, sour-faced Bogguns, and squat, toad-like Gremlins. They were veterans of previous conflicts in Other-Realm, though to look at them, you'd think they represented a ragged, discombobulated timeline of the Twilit Kingdom's military history. Some wore helmets that looked like what you might have expected to see bobbing around the hellish trenches of Europe at the turn of the twentieth century. Others sported tricorn hats with garish, tattered feathers. One Boggun, his face a mass of scars, stood rigidly in the full armored glory of a roman centurion, crested helm tucked under one arm.

Since returning from Cinderstone, my world had been a flurry of planning and organizing as I tried to get things in place so that I could begin training the regiments all at once. It took nearly two exhausting weeks to ensure we had all the supplies, arms, and provisions necessary. Then another week coordinating with the painfully accommodating daughters of Lord Arawn to ensure that the dead could get everything where it needed to be when it was needed. In the past few days, the last of the old regiments and their new recruits had been sorted into camps around the capital, and plans had been made for everyone to assemble on this field.

So I stood on the platform after nearly a month of preparation, Bryth and Uzran behind me. Uzran held the Pale Banner in his huge fist and was decked out in his full armor. I barely had any idea how I was going to explain what I wanted to these soldiers, because what I wanted was so different from the way of thinking that they had been operating under for so long. I needed them to help me realize a bold vision. Having once been an officer just like them, knew that if these changes were going to be effective, I would need their input.

Now I just needed to actually convince them. "I called you here today," I began, my voice stronger and clearer than I expected, "because the Gythraul are coming. And rather than hold them off, I plan to destroy them."

Dramatic, I know, but I needed their attention, and with that bold proclamation, I began to understand how I was going to convey what I needed to say to them. I couldn't see much response, but I sensed a general increase in interest among the assembled troops. I'd gotten some attention beyond what was required by the occasion; now, I had to keep it.

"You heard me right, soldiers!" I pumped every ounce of gusto I could manage into the words. "I am not talking about stemming the tide, holding the line, or manning the ramparts. You've been asked to do that for too long. The days of defending yourselves is over. Starting today, you stop defending your homes, and you start killing your enemies."

I felt the weight of more eyes on me, and a few soldiers leaned forward. It might have been because I was ranting like some looney human, but at least they were listening.

"There is a saying where I come from." I began to pace, my heels bouncing off the wood as the vigor of the speech flowed through my body. "'The best defense is a good offense,' and I couldn't agree more. You are not going to save your Kingdom—your people—by standing guard. No. The time for that has ended. Hell, it was over a long time ago! No, you are going to take back your lands by doing just that. *Taking.* And you are going to start by taking things from your enemy.

"Those bastards—the Gythraul—marched into your world and took it from you! Oh, I know that the borders have gone back and forth. I know that when your armies pushed them onto those islands, you thought you'd gotten your world back. But I am here to tell you that you didn't— not since the first of those monsters set foot here. And I'll tell you how I know that. If this world was yours, you wouldn't have to keep mustering for the same old war! You and your fathers and your fathers' fathers wouldn't have had to march to war against the same enemy bent on the same aim. You would not have had to learn the ways of war from humans brought here by the Queen. If this was your world, you wouldn't need me! But it isn't your world, because the Gythraul have held it hostage for over a millennium! They've robbed you of brothers, sisters, parents, and children, and from many of you, they've even taken your hope for something better than this never-ending war!

"So much has been taken from you, and now it is time to take it back."

Scores of eyes were watching my every movement, and I was sweating and tired already, but momentum propelled me forward.

"We are going to start by taking the battlefield from the Gythraul," I declared, my hand snatching at the air as though I was literally pulling it from the enemy's clutches. "We are not going to fight in pitched battles, trading hits like punch-drunk boxers. We hit them hard, hit them where they are weakest, and then we're gone. We are going to be mobile, we are going to be unpredictable, and we are going to be deadly. Every time they try to gather their forces, we won't be there, and every time they think they have room to breathe, we will be there to shove our fists down their throats. To do this, we are going to retrain and restructure. We are no longer ranks of marching ants, but packs of prowling wolves, fangs sharp and running circles around the enemy."

I could tell some of them were concerned when I talked of restructuring, but most were still edging forward unconsciously, like it was just the thing they had been waiting to hear.

"Next, we will take the Gythraul's confidence from them," I said, a lupine smile on my lips. "We are going to take everything they think they know about how we operate and use it against them. We are going to use coordinated independence. Each company, each platoon—hell—each squad will have operational freedom to innovate and intelligently engage targets while attachments help coordinate those efforts. I am asking you to stay fast and think on your feet, but you are going to see that once we start, the Gythraul will be left reeling, and opportunities for you to kick those bastards right in the sack will open up all over the place. Using the Wee Folk, along with your own initiative, we'll leave the Gythraul wondering what is coming for them next."

"Finally, we are going to take the Gythraul's will from them." I laughed savagely as my clutching hands crushed imaginary spoils. "I've been told our enemy has a will of iron, and I am here to prove that such untempered stuff will prove too fragile to withstand the reckoning we'll bring. With adaptability we will make each action cost them dearly. When they press on, we are going to let them charge right over a cliff. When they dig in, we will bury them. We are going to let them become their own worst enemy.

"And then, when they are broken, scared, and lost, we'll finish the job. With your enemies in chains or burning on the pyre, you will take back your Kingdom, your world, your home!"

Hungry faces looked up at me, and I knew right then and there that they were mine—my soldiers.

"Are you tired of holding the line?" I roared.

A ragged cheer rose in answer.

"Are you ready to start taking?" I bellowed.

A sharp, fiercer affirmative arose in reply.

"Are you ready to kill?" I screamed.

The strength and intensity of their affirmation was beyond what their numbers should have been able to produce. They were desperate for it.

"Orders will be waiting in your camps," I called over the last hollering cries, arm raised in salute. "See them done, and tomorrow we start sharpening those teeth. Dismissed!"

Another savage cheer came up from ranks of soldiers who moments before had been staring dully into the emptiness of another campaign's drudgery. I hoped that the fire I had lit would be enough to last to when we actually fought the Gythraul. Then we would see if I knew what the hell I was talking about.

I stepped back and faced Bryth and Uzran. Bryth, who'd been rather cool toward me since CInderstone, smiled and nodded approvingly. Uzran's face remained as immovably grumpy as ever. Mount Rushmore emotes more freely.

"You certainly convinced me that you believe you can do it," Bryth said, stepping forward so she didn't have to shout over the departing regimental commands. "But you spoke of wanting to institute other changes. New forces. What do you need from us?"

I pointed to Uzran, who turned his dark eyes down toward me. His tusked mouth slid into a deeper frown within the confines of his helmet.

"I need you, Captain, to gather the entire Royal Guard, or at least as many as can be spared from their duties of guarding the Queen. Have them assemble on this field tonight."

Uzran nodded, the sun glinting off his armored shoulders and head.

"As for you, my Lady," I turned to Bryth. "I need you to find me whatever passes for leadership in the Goblin community around here."

Bryth did a poor job of hiding her shock. "But, why?" Her brow furrowed as her eyes narrowed.

"Recruitment."

That afternoon, I found myself picking my way down the crowded fairways of Duanon's underside docks. If I spared a look across moored riverboats and the Purllaeth River, I could see the swampy ground that lead to the Forlorn Forest, where I had first met Goblins.

Flotsam Goblins, I had learned. I had since been introduced into the various breeds and cultures of Goblins which inhabited Other-Realm. It seemed that the differences had mostly to do with where they lived, along with the occasional physical quirk. Also, they were universally reviled and mistrusted by most beings in Other-Realm, regarded with as much suspicion as the sinister Daerg, perhaps even more since the Daerg were so reclusive. They were viewed as second-class citizens at best, and a verminous infestation at worst.

And they were just the people I wanted to see.

Uzran had been busy carrying out my orders, but I was assigned a detail of two Guards. One was Kroog, a simian-proportioned troll, and the other was Julen, one of the giant treemen called Sylvankin. They accompanied Bryth and I down what passed for the seedy underbelly of Duanon, the docks which sat along the waterline beneath the great city's walls.

We were given as wide a berth as the folk who lived along the squalid streets could manage, but it was still a chore to shuffle around stalls and bundles of goods jutting into the narrow streets.

Hobbs, Bogguns, Gremlins, occasional varieties of Wee Folk, and yes, Goblins—skittered and scrambled to get out of our way, to stand and gawk form a safe distance. I smiled and waved to a few, but very few returned the niceties, so I gave up.

"So this Grimple Guthook...She has worked for the Queen in the past?" I skirted a pyramid of dried fish in reed baskets.

"Yes." Bryth led me down a flight of plank stairs to an alleyway that must have been below the waterline. Algae clung to the moist stone walls. "She coordinates with the Queen and other members of the Court who need clandestine operations completed. Most often, these are matters of personal or political importance."

"So why not use them to come get me instead of that monster, the Fiend?" I asked, being careful to watch my step so as not to take a tumble on the slick boards.

"Such Goblin teams, sometimes called Fingers, are not wholly reliable. They are susceptible to bribery and, um...renegotiation," she said over her shoulder.

As we continued downward, things began to darken. The stairs gave a squeaking groan behind me.

"They are just Goblins after all, my Paladin," Julen remarked in a slow, windy voice. "Treachery is in their blood."

"Cut 'em, and they bleed black," Kroog added from behind the tall, arboreal guard. "Clear mark as any."

I frowned and turned to see that Bryth had paused just above the last few steps. She was shaking her head up at the Royal Guards. "Those are rumors and apocryphal myths, at best," she chided, before stepping onto a floorboard where the river sloshed just beneath.

"What rumors?" I moved to stand next to her in the alleyway. It looked like it was nearing dusk despite the bright afternoon sunlight just above.

Bryth led us toward an alcove over which hung a corroded bronze lantern. As we neared, I could see a small door set into the stony archway.

"Some very old and highly unreliable accounts of the time when the Tuatha first came speak of the Goblins serving the Darklings, or even being a kind of debased offspring." She paused before stepping up to the door. "But even if those accounts are true, mentioning them within will be a sure way to spoil whatever you hope to accomplish here."

"WIth your permission," Julen intoned, setting the butt of his spear to rest against the boarded floor with a thump. "We shall stand guard out here."

Looking at the small door set in the alcove, I didn't seen any option that didn't involve some serious renovations to the entrance. "Good call, Julen," I remarked dryly before nodding to Bryth. "Lead the way, my lady."

We went inside, ducking to fit through. I don't know what I expected, but when I saw a single candle burning on a small table in a bare stone room, I was surprised. No cantina-style drinking den with a bunch of shady Goblins, no masses of dirty, long-nosed faces with hungry eyes. Just a shadowy room, empty of everything except a table, a candle, and a single creature squatting on a stool.

Dressed in a drab, dark tunic and apron with a leather skullcap sitting between knife-like ears, this creature hardly looked like some kind of Goblin kingpin. The Goblin's eyes —a deep amber color—glittered in the candlelight. One sharp-nailed hand worried at a braid of slate gray hair that swept from the back of the cap to hang over its left shoulder.

"Won't yer come and talk a spell?" came the rough, vaguely feminine voice of the seated Goblin.

There were no other chairs or stools, so Bryth and I stood next to the table.

"You are Grimple Guthook, I presume?" I made a small bow. This elicited a cruel chuckle from the Goblin.

"Aye, that be me," said Grimple. "What can a humble creature such as I do fer the lofty likes o' Paladin Lucius Bollham?"

"I am looking for soldiers."

Another cutting laugh. "Last I checked, yer had yourself a countryside full o' those. Besides, I know yer new here 'bouts, but I think even the like o' yerself knows not to trust our lot."

"The Paladin comes to change that," Bryth placed a hand on my shoulder and leaned into the light of the candle. "To help change the way you and your people are seen by the entire Twilit Kingdom."

"And what makes yer think I give a sow's bunghole what the Kingdom thinks?" the Goblin asked levelly.

"It is not about what they think," I cut in, "But it *is* about what they do. Help me, and I will get the Queen to grant rights and lands to you and yours."

Grimple's eyes narrowed suspiciously.

"So that we can be puppets, toiling to raise tithes on some backwater moor?" she spat, fingers leaving her braid to dig at the table's surface.

I shook my head and met her stare, unflinching. "No, not at all," I opened a hand on the table like the lands were right there in my palm. "We'll give you your pick of the lands taken back from the Gythraul—they'll be yours. You and the other Goblin underbosses, who I hear are all scared of you, can decide how to manage the place. Like the other Far-Holds, you will have an Oath of Fealty, but other than that, your business is no one else's. Build a brothel with the realm's best Ogre belly dancers, for all I care, but help us now."

Grimple Guthook stared at me—long enough that I became uncomfortable—but she didn't pounce or sink her needle-like teeth in my face like I feared she might. Instead, she looked from Bryth to me and then tapped a sharp nail against the table.

"We ain't goin' to be yer slaves or dregs, dyin' just so our corpses can trip the Gythraul."

"Far from it," I assured her. "That would be an utter waste of what your people can offer."

Grimple gave me a sidelong look. "And what might that be?"

"Deviousness, stealth, and a killer's instinct," I answered, hoping I wasn't over playing my hand.

Grimple's eyes narrowed to slits, then, without warning, she extinguished the candle with a pinch of her fingers. The room was plunged into darkness.

"Well," I heard Grimple's voice call in the dark. "What do yer think, boys?"

Suddenly the empty dark around Bryth and me was filled with snickering voices.

"Sounds like fun."

"Why not?"

"Can we make those scaly buggers scream?"

30

WARNINGS

L ady Bryth Lighttread stepped into the Queen's audience chamber. It felt like it had been years since she was last there, rather than a matter of months. It brought back familiar, if not necessarily welcome, sensations and feelings. She wondered if the years she felt were time lived backwards. She stood here to speak with the Queen about the Paladin and the war effort, her head awash with conflicted feelings, just as it had been with another mortal man nearly a century before.

There was a warm flutter in her belly as she remembered Lucius giving his impassioned speech, declaring he would become the next Paladin. Superimposed on top of that memory, the image of another man with a sharp, knowing smile flashing beneath his moustache. He too had spoken to some of the same people about the same war. Like a spider's web, that image had trapped her—snared her within the icy, numbing memories of screams and the sound of blood slowly dripping onto the floor.

The floor of that very room.

"Bryth, child," Queen Meabh called from her throne, "how long do you plan to keep us waiting?"

Bryth shook off the memories as best she could and mounted the steps to take her seat beside the Queen. Bowls of wine sat upon a table between them, just as before, when Bryth had been dispatched to aid the Paladin in obtaining the Oaths of Fealty. She did not see Groog, but she imagined the Hobb was lurking nearby in case he was needed.

Queen Meabh looked Bryth up and down as she sat, her eyes gleaming with a peculiar light the young Tuatha did not understand at first.

"It has gone well then," she said, smiling with such pride, she was positively radiant. "Our trust in both of you has been well-rewarded."

"Yes," Bryth said, feeling at a loss for words. She was suddenly uncertain how many of her thoughts the Queen could read in her face. "The Oaths are restored, and your Paladin has already begun to reshape the army. Soon the Gythraul will be laid low."

"I hear his plans are quite ambitious." Meabh gestured for Bryth to take a bowl. "Perhaps, we should drink to the young man's success. Such radical changes will, I trust, be for the best, but nothing is certain in these dark times. I hope his ambitions are not wrecked by the cruel fates which seem to rule these days."

"Lucius knows what he is about, your Majesty," Bryth took the bowl of wine. She was surprised by the forcefulness of her tone but unable to stop the words. "This way of war is akin to methods used in his world to defeat armies and enemies of all sizes."

The Queen cocked an eyebrow and gave Bryth a side-long glance over her own bowl. "Tactics and stratagems to break the teeth of Fate and Wyrd itself?" she wondered, smiling. "My, my. Mother Gwiddon has chosen our champion well this time."

Bryth felt embarrassment color her cheeks but shook the feeling off as she took a drink. Internally, she was determined to hold onto hope and the vision that Lucius had given her—an army victorious, an enemy driven out, and a kingdom at peace. Uzran might be fatalistic and the Queen might be skeptical, but she, Bryth Lighttread, would cling to hope hard enough for all of them.

"If his dreams are realized, the Gythraul will have no idea what hit them," she insisted. "His plans are so simple in philosophy—a soldier's innovation aligned with a commander's perspective. In practice, their complexity, when viewed from our enemy's viewpoint, will seem inscrutable. Training is already underway, and the old regiments, now divided into company platoons, are adapting very well. Luce says that it helps that so many of our forces are veterans and that they have soldiers' souls, even if they must change their way of thinking."

"Luce?"

"Oh," Bryth said, not realizing she had used the Paladin's preferred nickname. "Paladin Bollham prefers that those of us on his war council refer to him as such. For discipline among the rank and file, he is 'Paladin,' but when meeting amongst ourselves, he prefers a degree of informality."

"And who composes this war council?" Meabh asked.

"Myself, Luce, Uzran, the company Leaders, those that had once commanded the regiments, and Grimple Guthook." Bryth recalled each face as she counted them off, remembering then that she had left one out. "Also, Sleepyhead."

"The Bogle?" the Queen laughed as Bryth nodded affirmation. "And Guthook is a Goblin surname, is it not?"

Again Bryth nodded, lowering her bowl from her lips.

"That is quite the assortment of characters our Paladin has assembled."

"Luce is not done yet." Bryth was unable to mask the satisfaction in her voice. "Once Grimple's Finger teams are trained, he would like to bring in the other underbosses and their teams as well."

"How could they turn down the opportunity We have so generously afforded them?" the Queen wondered aloud. Something in her voice gave Bryth pause.

Bryth looked at Meabh for a moment, searching the ageless, inscrutable face. "Does it displease you that Luce has asked for such an incentive to win the service of the Goblins?"

The Queen nodded, taking a small sip from her bowl before replacing it on the table. Her fingers interlaced and she met Bryth's stare with her own. "Not if you tell Us that this is the path to victory, child," she said solemnly, as though each word was heavy. "Our concern does not truly lie with Goblins and the war, but on matters far closer to us. We beg you to speak truthfully now; is there something growing between you and the Paladin?"

Bryth had supposed this question would come, and though she had tried to come up with an answer since she was summoned, she could find no way to aptly put it into words. "The truth is, I do not know," she said honestly. "At first, I feared what I was beginning to feel, after the way things...well, the way things had gone before."

"And none was more broken-hearted for you than We were," the Queen said sympathetically, reaching out a hand to grip Bryth's fingers, which had begun to tremble.

Bryth swallowed hard and fought the urge to search for bloodstains on the stones at the base of the stairs to the throne. There was nothing there, she knew, but the thought that she might look and see them anyway kept her staring resolutely past the Queen's shoulder. "As I spent more time with him and saw the passion he had to serve a world that was not his, I found myself drawn in again." Bryth remembered the look in Lucius's eye as he had taken the apple in Chillspire, and the sound of his voice as he answered Mother Gwiddon's riddle.

Then there was the way he had looked at her on the plains of Cinderstone.

"So...does he return this affection?" the Queen asked, releasing Bryth's hand, but watching her intently.

"I do not know," Bryth said. She laughed despite herself, though in truth, she found nothing funny about it. "There are times—the way he acts, the way he looks at me—I think maybe he does indeed feel something, but then other times, he seems intent to push me away."

She remembered the way he had coldly shouldered past her in Lord Arawn's citadel, and how, in their meeting that night, he had hardly looked at her. Then she remembered the jealousy that had sharpened her tone when she saw Lord Arawn's daughter embracing him. Perhaps she was the one who was driving *him* away.

"Regardless, I am unsure of what to do." Bryth shook her head as though the movement might dislodge her doubts. "I do not wish to be a distraction to him, and our work is too important to put at risk with personal entanglements. He needs my help, but I cannot help feeling the way that I do."

"Oh, child of Our heart," Meabh began, laying a hand against Bryth's cheek. "We think We see more than just an interest in that human's eyes, and We are certain that with time and attention, it can bloom into something incredibly beautiful. Instead of fearing distraction, think of dedication.

How much more fiercely will he fight for our Kingdom if he counts his love among its people? How much more determined will he be to save us if he is saving the desire of his heart?"

Bryth couldn't mask her surprise.

"Even after everything that happened? Even after..." but she found her voice failing. She could not continue with the thought. The wine was sour in her stomach—a lurching, fluid mass that tugged her insides downward. She placed the bowl as far from her as she could on the table and then drew her clenched fists into her lap.

"Dear child, We understand," Meabh cooed soothingly, stroking the younger Tuatha's hair. "It hurts to even think of loving again, but think of what is to be gained if you dare to do so: your own heart's desire, our Paladin's undying loyalty, and the defeat of our age-old enemies. You have everything to gain."

"And so much to lose," Bryth whispered.

"Much must be risked," the Queen said softly, though just beneath the words, Bryth felt something hard and unyielding. "Even our very hearts—to save what is most precious."

The air in the room changed suddenly, cutting off further questions or protests from Bryth. The shadows deepened, and the air took on a queasy thickness. To the magically attuned senses of the Tuatha, the changes were even more drastic—as though a hot gush of corpse air had begun leaking from every dark corner.

"Darkling!" Bryth hissed. She drew her magical wards and curses to readiness around her through sheer, fear-rooted reflex.

"Peace," Queen Meabh said with a certain and immovable authority.

Something which bled night wormed its way from beneath the thin shadow cast by a step of the stairs. Serpentine, and with hundreds of wormy black cilia squirming across its length, the stain of living darkness slithered up the steps toward the throne.

Her initial terror subsiding, Bryth remembered the deal struck with the Fiend after its initial failure to obtain Lucius Bollham. The Fiend had promised the service of his spawn to the Gloaming Court in compensation for the extended time it had needed to capture the Paladin. Bryth had known that the Queen had been using the creatures to some effect—spying, sabotaging, and assassinating the Gythraul forces—but Bryth had never been in the presence of these particular abominations before. She had not enjoyed the idea of utilizing the short-lived monstrosities, even if it was for the noble cause of buying Luce more time.

Now face to face with one of their odious number, the notion was no more palatable.

The darkling-spawn coiled like a quivering, hairy snake before the throne and raised its head toward the Queen. Four round eyes the color of congealing blood stared above a mouth that looked like a ragged wound.

"Mistressss," the creature wheezed wetly, the folds of its gaping mouth showing off rows of its bony, hooked teeth, "the Gythraul come."

The Queen straightened at the pronouncement, her spine stiffening and her shoulders lifting with practiced, regal composure. Bryth felt her stomach clench again, knowing this was far sooner than they had expected.

"What happened?" the Queen asked evenly, her azure eyes flashing.

Bryth felt no pity for the infant monster, but she was

glad she did not have to bear the same look from Queen Meabh.

"Ceterum Cinis's forces were too many," it replied with an almost slurping disdain. "The Gythraul efforts were too large for our brood alone to prevent an invasion."

The Queen's eyes narrowed, but she did not say anything for a moment. Her whole form was poised as a statue of some great ruler of old. Bryth supposed, given Meabh's age, that she was indeed a ruler of old, her ageless hand still gripping the throne from which she had ruled for millennia.

"Shall their fleet make for Ystrddunn, as before?" the Queen asked at last.

The darkling-spawn reared back a little, some approximation of wounded pride playing across its expression. "No, thanks to the brood, they must disembark north of Ystrddunn, among the Grym Falls," it replied archly, its cilia stroking its own coils in nauseous self-congratulation. "They will march forth from there, one cohort of his legions heading south to secure Ystrddunn, while the others head east and northeast. Ceterum Cinis will lead the northernmost cohort."

"He is making for Chillspire," Bryth breathed, the Gythraul's aims plain to her. "If he can isolate and lay siege to Lady Aneira'Tywys, our soldiers will soon be without a means to fight."

The shadow-stained monster gave a contemptuous glare, it's strange eyes perfectly conveying disdain for what it deemed an unnecessary explanation.

"You are certain of this?" The Queen ignored the tension passing between Bryth and the Darkling.

"Absolutely," the creature said with a burp-like exhalation. "I extracted the information myself."

The Queen nodded. "He will need to take Luchath to secure the paths into the mountains," the Queen spoke, mostly to herself. "It will take him weeks to get there, even if he presses his Legions hard—which he will. We shall halt him there." Her gaze, which had wandered as she considered various plans and stratagems, snapped back to the coiled obscenity before her.

"Go. Inform the watch at Luchath to make ready to hold the town against any vanguard—even if they have to arm every last Boggun babe," her command came down with a force like a hammer blow. "Then continue to harass Cinis's forces. He may become suspicious if we just let him march there."

With only a bob of its head, the darkling-spawn oozed its way back into the shadow of the stairs and vanished.

"My Queen," Bryth began, "is that not a matter for the Paladin to decide?"

But Meabh swatted the question away with a toss of her head. "He serves *Us*, does he not? Tell him that within two weeks, he must be ready to move Our forces to Luchath. Within three weeks, he shall need to put Ceterum Cinis to rout. If the Paladin can do this, then perhaps he can defang this serpent before it truly strikes."

Bryth shook her head. Three weeks? The instruction of the raw recruits and the retraining of the veterans had been going on for less than half that time. They had planned not to engage the enemy for months—at least three, though they were hoping for more—in order to work out the kinks and iron out any unforeseen difficulties with the army's new operational structures before engaging in combat. Even then, their initial plan was to fight a few light skirmishes to get a feel for things before getting into the thick of war.

But now they had to be ready to engage Ceterum Cinis in three weeks?

"That is little time to make ready," Bryth whispered, disbelieving. "I will inform the Paladin at once." She made for the side corridor leading to the stables. She heard the Queen's stern voice pressing in on her as she walked, an invisible hand driving her onward, even as it bore down on her like a lead weight.

"See that you do, and impress upon him the seriousness of my command," the Queen said with utter finality. "His forces will learn quickly, and his plan will succeed, or soon, the entire Kingdom shall be set ablaze."

31

CERTAINTIES

"Three weeks." The words came out windily, as if I had taken a shot to the solar plexus. "Three weeks to get this shit show on the road."

"I am sure the troops would appreciate your new name for them," Uzran grunted with a grim chuckle.

I wanted to punch him in his snout, but I wasn't sure if I could reach it, and thought I might do more damage to my hand than to him. Ever since Cinderstone, the Ogre had, begrudgingly it seemed, tried to be more helpful. He had even given me a few pointers on swordsmanship. Not that I had had much time for personal improvement in the mad rush of retrofitting and reorganizing an entire army. But despite this new-found pseudo-friendliness, Uzran was still an asshole, and his commentary was doing little to ease my mind after such devastating news.

"Training and outfitting can only go on for two." Bryth said cautiously, seeming aware of how fragile my state of mind was becoming with each word. "After that, we will need to coordinate with the magi of the Gloaming Court to use the Paths to bring our forces into position."

"Well, isn't that just a kick in the sack." I paced in the field tent which acted as headquarters for the war council.

I had been instructing three platoons of the newly designated Echo company on the uses of bounding overwatch—when platoons needed to move toward an objective but expected enemy resistance—when Bryth had come riding up, her Diomedan in a lather, saying we needed to talk. I had picked up Uzran at the firing range—constructed by the Dead of our army—where he and a contingent of the Royal Guards were learning to use Daerg modified m240b machine guns. The big guns now fired from loops of Storm Djinn skein, instead of belts of 7.62s, heavy rounds replaced by bolts of earth shattering electricity. I had hollered for him to follow me to the command tent over the staccato crackle of chain lighting. With a frown, he had obliged after bellowing instructions to a troll named Druth to keep at it until they could stitch the outline of a Gremlin without the poor wretch getting blasted.

I had only a moment to pity the poor Gremlin who got roped into that job before we were in the tent and Bryth dropped the bomb.

Two weeks, and we were deploying. On the large central table, Bryth had unfurled a map of the region—a mountainous area whose valleys were laced with trade roads. The Gythraul would be using them to drive right up to the town of Luchath. From there, they would make a bid for Chillspire.

"I thought the Gythraul didn't have magi and so couldn't use the Paths." I eyed the distance between the Grym Falls and Luchath. "How are they going to cross that distance in such a short time? You said that the majority of their forces usually moved on foot."

"Even on foot, the Gythraul can cover near onto a

hundred miles in a day and a half," Uzran said stonily. "Especially if Cinis is willing to use the Legion's supplies of alchemicals to sustain his forces."

A hundred miles in a day and a half? On foot? I felt the urge to sit down, but settled instead for leaning against the table. "And Cinis," I said, forcing my overworked brain to keep moving before it just quit on me altogether, "who is he?"

Bryth looked up from the map, her mouth bent into a frown, an angry light burning in her eyes.

"Ceterum Cinis is the most recent rising star in the Gythraul hierarchy," she said venomously. "He took command after Paladin Valoise defeated Ceterum Yorn. It was he that staged the ambush that wounded the Paladin and killed my father, leaving the rest of the Legion's remnants to creep back to the Isles and lick their wounds."

I tried doing some math in my head, to work out the time period Valoise had come from, but I was too tired to get very far. "If he fought Valoise, doesn't that make him over a hundred years old? I thought Gythraul were mortal like me."

"Not all mortals are created equal." Uzran crossed his arms. "My people are mortal as well, but without war or disease, we can live for nearly a millennium. The Gythraul, as best we can tell, can live for at least three centuries."

"Great!" I exclaimed, hanging my head between my shoulders. "I get to square up against some badass who has been planning this campaign since before my grandfather was born." I looked from Uzran to Bryth and back again. "If we survive the next month, we are going to have a long talk about specifying terms and their meanings. Call me quaint, but living for a thousand years is not my idea of 'mortal.'"

The flap of the tent opened, and in Grimple strode, one

hand hanging free while the other spun the end of her grey braid. "So I hear we're goin' to war," she called cheerily, striding up to table. She was barely tall enough to see its surface. "Ah, Luchath. I should'a figured."

"How the hell did you find out?" I asked, stunned that she should know our strategic situation. I also felt a little embarrassed that I had forgotten to summon her to this meeting.

"I know shit," Grimple replied with a shrug before turning to eye the map. It rested just under the level of her nose "How much time they give us?"

"Two weeks," Bryth said.

Grimple gave a sucking hiss and squinted down at the map. She looked up at me. "Well, yer Fingers'll be ready enough by then, I s'pose," she said with another shrug. "Though I'd like 'em to get their mitts on some o' those Drake bile grenades first. Need to make sure the Fingers can use 'em without losin' their own digits, if yer follow me."

I wanted to balk at her claim, but admitted she was was probably right. Grimple Guthook, or Ma Grimple, as she was known to her Finger crews, had already shown that the kind of predatory game I wanted our soldiers to play was second nature to her and her ilk. With little to no encouragement, they assessed terrain, firing lines, enemy dispositions, and lines of sight, and they synthesized appropriate methods of approach, attack, and withdrawal. Their individual firing accuracy at first was mediocre, but it was rapidly improving. Plus, with their efficient coordination and execution of maneuvers, they could afford to miss a few shots here and there.

If I could combine their tactical acumen with their proclivity for stealth, they might be our best bet to get the Gythraul off balance first.

"How are the Malks working out?" I asked.

"Good." Grimple chuckled. "Pussycats only taken a few strips off the boys, but nothing vital. They should work nice for keepin' an eye out for anything the boys miss."

It had been my idea to run the Malks in pairs with the Finger crews, acting primarily as scouts. Of the skills the Malks had been taught, one was the ability to scent out Gythraul alchemical gizmos, including the landmines and boobytraps Uzran told me they were so fond of.

"Think you'd be up for sticking those Fingers in the Gythraul's eyes?" I asked the Underboss, tracing my finger along where the Gythraul vanguard would undoubtedly be coming.

"Oh, we can do the eyes for starters," Grimple answered, and I didn't need to look below the lip of the table to know that a nasty smile was spreading across her face.

With a groan, I sank into the embrace of my pallet, the crack of M-Cores resounding at regular intervals from the range. The carbines, along with Djinn guns and Drake balls —Grimple's name for the grenades—would keep up the auditory assault through the night. Some of the companies would be training through the night now. The revised schedule called for two eight-hour sessions of training for each rest session over the next week. The week after, we would slacken to let them get their wind back, but at the moment, we needed to cram as much training in as we could.

Two weeks, and then we were in The Shit.

The war council and I had made our slapdash plans in the command tent as quickly and thoroughly as we could, pulling the various company commands in as we altered their training regimens. I was prioritizing field movement and tactical training over company administration and procedural reporting—stuff that would help in long-term operations for sure, but which were lower in priority than making sure this new army could hit hard, fast, and with fluid cohesion. After all, if things went bad enough near Luchath, there would be no "long term."

I just hoped that I wasn't building a house of straw, because the wolf was at the door.

It was like I was making swiss cheese of the tactical standard operating procedure, hoping that the bits I was excising for time's sake wouldn't cause the whole thing to collapse in on itself. Communication was key, of course, but so was knowing the tactical procedures that kept you flexible and aggressive. I was praying to whatever passed for Heaven in this place that Sleepyhead could get cooperation from the Wee Folk in those mountain valleys so we could rely on some real-time communication—or as close as we could get—to make up for any deficiencies my hack and slash job had done to the command structure and supply lines.

By the time I had finished juggling all the different schedules and given a bit of corrective direction to some of the crash-course instructors I had picked out in the two initial weeks of training, I staggered to my tent in the dark. I got my boots unlaced and off, and shucked the Paladin's cuirass and tabard. That was as far as I got before sinking into a sitting position on my pallet. Earlier I had told Sleepyhead—who sleeps only for fun, as it turns out, and not out of actual need—to keep a watch over the training fields and wake me if some emergency arose.

I slept so deeply that, if I had any dreams, I wouldn't have remembered them, but I awoke after only a few hours, my stomach grumbling in protest at my neglectful treatment.

When was the last time I had eaten? I couldn't remember. I had been that busy.

I lurched to the flap of my tent and called for one of the Dead milling about outside the officer's tents to fetch me something to eat. I thought about going back to sleep after gobbling down whatever the Revenant brought, but as I sat there thinking about all that was to come, panic ripped away the notion of sleep with cruel glee. With a moan of blatant self-pity, I drew my cuirass and tabard back into place before searching around the floor of the tent for my boots.

I was on my knees fishing them out from under my pallet when I heard the tent flap stir, followed by the smell of my requested breakfast. The yeasty warmth of fresh bread and the smoky sweetness of seared ham filled my tent, and my mouth begin to water. Still on my knees, my stomach gave an audible grumble of eager interest.

"Watch out there, dead boy," I grunted over my shoulder as I retrieved one boot and then the other. "I think my stomach is falling in love with you."

I know it's weird, talking to animated corpses, but hey, Other-Realm is a weird place.

"Some would say that the sound of a hungry belly has nothing to do with love," came the husky reply that didn't belong to the mute zombie servants. "But, maybe things are different where you come from."

I waddle-shuffled around to look up at Bryth who stood just within my tent, a wooden tray held in front of her like an offering. Little wisps of steam rose from the meat, and at that moment I wasn't sure which was more beautiful—the sight of food or Bryth. My stomach gave another burble to remind me of its vote.

"I relieved the 'dead boy,'" she said with a shrug, "but if your stomach needs some time alone with him, I am sure he will come when called."

My back gave a few disgruntled pops and clicks as I stood, tossing my boots onto the pallet before taking the tray.

"I'm afraid my stomach is a bit of a player," I sighed in exaggerated disappointment. "Seems he'll take a liking to any pretty thing that brings him something to eat."

"The corpse with your food was missing half his face," she remarked dryly, as I settled onto the pallet with the tray on my lap.

"Beauty, my dear, is in the eye of the beholder." I tore a hunk of bread off the loaf and popped it into my mouth. I had to stifle an undignified moan of delight. It was amazing how good something could taste when you were hungry.

"Lucius." Bryth stood in front of me, hands curled into fists at her sides.

"Luce," I corrected around a strip of ham I had torn free with my teeth. They weren't big about dining utensils in Other-Realm. Adapt and overcome, I suppose.

"Luce, do you have a moment to talk?"

I paused my munching to notice the concern knotting Bryth's features, her whole body stiff and rigid.

"Yeah," I said, a little stunned, mopping grease from my chin where a beard had sprouted in the last few weeks. "Sit down and tell me what's up." I scooted down the pallet as Bryth sank down next to me. I took another bite of bread, but kept my eyes on her as I chewed quietly.

"I... I think that something... something more than comradely regard has sprung up between us," she began falteringly, refusing to look at me. "Something—some feelings, I mean—that might be regarded as...romantic."

The last word came out of her mouth in a rush, like her body was struggling to contain it. I put the bread down on the tray and swallowed the last bite.

Romantic? Was that what was going on between us? I thought back over the last two months of my life, remembering how nearly every waking moment was spent with this Tuatha battle-magus, from combat training to political lessons. I thought of the looks I sometimes caught her giving me, and how I kept finding my eyes lingering on her. I even felt a little anxious when she wasn't around. At first, I was sure it was because I was like a blind man learning to see with new eyes in this strange world, but could it be more than that?

I stared at her dumbly as she pressed on, eyes fixed on some part of the floor.

"I am sure this is hardly the time for such things, but...well, we are drawing close to battle, and I wanted things as settled in my mind as I can make them, considering the circumstance."

The words were picking up steam as they came out, gaining impetus with each syllable.

"Again, I know that we have only spent months together, and the differences between us are considerable, but I have come to care for you. Perhaps it is just because of my damn Tuatha blood that I so quickly fall into infatuation, but I cannot help what I am. I think I'm enamoured with you. I know this, not just because of how jealous I felt when I saw Wrenneth's arms around you, or how my heart positively burst with joy when you looked at me in victory on the plains of Cinderstone; I know it, certain as stone, because every day, I see you pour yourself out for a world and people that are not your own, because you see something worth saving—something beautiful—here. So tell me Luce. Tell me now, before we spend the next weeks preparing soldiers to die for that thing worth saving, if you see something beautiful in me—something...something you might grow to love?"

For one long heartbeat—one that thudded in my ear with tremendous force—I just sat there, my mouth hanging open, my tongue limp and useless behind my teeth. I felt the seconds slipping past with horrible slowness and knew the waste I was making of them was inexcusable. But try as I might to find the words—any words—nothing came out of my gaping mouth.

I saw tears form—tiny, swelling diamonds of uncertainty and pain—at the corners of Bryth's eyes.

My feelings and thoughts were stretched beyond the point of snapping, but as always, when things began to spin too fast, I fell back on what I was certain of. I was certain that I did not want to see Bryth cry, and I was even more certain that I didn't want those tears to fall because of me.

My mouth wouldn't cooperate, but my hand worked just fine.

Leaving the tray balanced on my knees, I reached over and took her hands in mine. Stiff at first, her fists opened with reluctant gratefulness, and before I could believe it, our fingers were intertwined.

"I think I see that," I whispered, my face leaning as close to her as I dared with my breakfast still suspended over my lap. "I see that and more."

Bryth let out a short sob that transformed into a hopeful smile. "Yes?" she asked, eyes shining.

"Yes," I said softly, feeling that inexorable gravity that draws two bodies together with scientific certainty.

Bryth must have felt the pull as well, because within the time it took an eye to close in pleasant expectation, she had leaned forward, her warm lips meeting my own. Soft but fierce, we held that kiss for an eternal, aching moment that vanished with bittersweet swiftness as our lips parted.

A deep longing surged up in me—something that had been waiting and smoldering in fitful, volcanic dormancy for so long—and if she hadn't stood right then, I might have tossed the breakfast tray aside without a second thought. But she did stand, our fingers still interlocked, and looked down at me, her war goddess face glittering with just a hint of a young lover's tears.

"Soon then," she said quietly, as though sharing a truth that was neither secret nor public. "Very soon, but first Luce, first we have a war to win."

She let go of my hands, and as they fell to my side, I felt the hungry longing settle into a slow burn—a low flame that would keep and keep. "Well," I sighed as the heat subsided into an undying ember and my hands came up to the tray. "I suppose I can't save the world on an empty stomach."

32

SNAFU

I watched Charlie and Delta companies move out, following their designated battle-magus as he conjured the Path to take them to the eastern slopes above Luchath.

In the two weeks that I had been given, I had managed to ensure that two and a half thousand of our initial five thousand troops were ready to be deployed, not counting the Goblin Finger teams or the Royal Guard attachments. The battle-ready companies were all veterans of the former editions of this age-old conflict—seasoned and determined old war dogs. The remaining three and a half thousand were mostly raw recruits who were still learning the difference between their ass and a hole in the ground, and I was holding them back with the instructors as reserves. They were to stay and train with the new levies that were being raised. I was desperately hoping I wouldn't have to call on them, at least not for this engagement, but I had left things in place that would see them organized as reinforcements if need be. The Paths, at least, made such things possible.

Assembled in tight knots of carbine-armed soldiers clustering around the hulking members of the Royal Guard that would provide suppression and command support, they looked almost like child soldiers marching to battle beside armored warlords. The image was hardly a comforting one. I remembered some of the stories I had heard when chewing the fat with some boys who had been forced to choose between the lives of their comrades and some twelve-year-old with an AK47. I had been thankful to never face that choice myself, at least never knowingly, but as I watched my soldiers, some with barely a month of training under their belts, I hoped they fared better than the twelve-year-olds from those stories.

"Do you ever wonder how they will die?" Uzran said, appearing at my shoulder. "Wondering if their last moments will be peaceful, bitter, or glorious?"

I followed his shark-eyed stare to the soldiers marching toward the Path.

"Sometimes," I confessed as they filed by, "but I don't like to think about it too much. Call me an optimist, but I prefer to think about all the hell they are going to give the enemy and how that all stacks up to victory."

Uzran's breath came out in a long, low sigh. "I suppose that might make it easier. But I have never been able to forget that the currency of war is the blood of soldiers. I am not sure I believe victory can be bought anymore. I've contented myself at times with the knowledge that spending their lives may buy us more time. It is not much; I only hope we spend them well."

I faced the Captain, his words settling over me like a weighted net. I fought the downward pull, drawing on years of gung-ho conditioning that half the time I knew was bullshit, but which let me do what needed to be done. Looking at this old warrior, at the way he watched fellow soldiers marching to what he knew was death, one way or another, well...my "give 'em hell" attitude just didn't seem up to snuff.

"That's a heavy weight to carry there, big guy," I said, looking up into his stony expression. "Makes the job pretty hard, doesn't it?"

Uzran looked down at me, a quizzical furrow crinkling his craggy brow. When at last he spoke, his voice was a low half-whisper—the softest sound I'd ever heard him make. "It is supposed to be hard," he said, the words weighted with centuries of experience. "When it stops being hard, that is when you are unworthy to lead."

Something deep and incredibly painful writhed under his expression—a shadowy silhouette passing just beneath the surface. There was no telling what it was, but given the fact that he had lived his long life with nothing but war to look forward to, it wasn't hard to imagine that he walked around with a whole lot of pain and loss.

"I suppose you're right," I replied, "But hard or not, they're the choices we have to make, and in making them, we aren't just buying a day here or a year there. As unlikely as it may seem, there is always a chance for victory—the real, foot-on-their-neck sort of winning."

"That sort of thing is for myths and legends," Uzran said with a sad chuckle grinding in the back of his throat. "Stories mothers tell their children about gods and heroes."

Standing there with my Ogre second-in-command watching my troops being led to war by battle-magi, I couldn't help but laugh, and laugh hard at Uzran's pronouncement.

"Well, you know what that means then," I said grinning madly up at the Captain. "Means we better go and be heroes."

"Something's wrong."

I could feel it, like a blade of ice tickling my spine. I was crouched amid a clump of evergreen bushes on a wind-blasted slope overlooking Luchath.

I should have been one of the first to go through the Paths when the companies started to move out for the northern climes, but there had been so many things to organize and orders to dole out that I thought it would be alright to have Grimple's Fingers and a few companies head out before me. After all, we had to secure at least twenty miles of valley, not to mention the town itself, and that was just to secure enough space to deploy along the rest of the valley and its various nooks and crannies.

But now, overlooking the valley that led to the stone-walled town with its sharply-peaked slate roofs, my guts twisted with apprehension.

I'd dispatched Sleepyhead with the first company to go make nice with the local Wee Folk and set up some kind of communication network, but I hadn't heard from him since I arrived, and the images I got from the Hagseye were dark flashes that made no sense. Sleepyhead wasn't responding to my questions. I could see Bravo and Charlie companies in position, flanking the first crook in the valley just a few miles southwest of Luchath, but there was little or no evidence that Alfa was securing the town. Delta had already moved farther down the valley, taking a position near the second crook in the valley's twisted furrow.

I didn't see any sign of the Finger teams, but I hadn't expected to, not just because of their covert nature, but because they were supposed to be moving down the valley to set up some surprises for the Gythraul. I would be getting a situational report, SITREP, from Grimple as soon as I got Sleepyhead to respond.

It was not that he never failed to respond, but this wasn't hanging around camp, and I was pretty sure he knew how serious things were.

I had Echo company with me and my command staff, and they were supposed to forge ahead to secure a site for us to bring Lord Arawn's daughters and the Dead along to set up some fallback and supply points along the length of the valley. Foxtrot and Golf would be along shortly to follow behind, and then eventually fan out and secure the valley beyond where Echo was positioned.

As soon as I set foot in the Valley of Luchath though, I had called for the company commanders in Echo to get their platoons into cover along the crest of the valley and hold. Now I was squatting among some bushes looking through a field glass and trying to figure out what was going on.

Luchath sat at the head of the valley looking not so dissimilar from the old, walled towns you see across Germany and other parts of Europe. The peaks of the houses seemed cartoonishly sharp, and instead of the odd tourist walking along its walls, regular sentries with old, bayoneted rifles at their shoulders paced. That might have seemed normal, or even expected, had I not dispatched all companies to make sure that the place was secure. I at least expected to see a few of the Alfa grunts in those blue tricorn hats they wore skittering about or hunkering down in positions overlooking the approach to the town, which was a broad, moss-fringed cobblestone road.

Two whole companies don't just disappear, and where was Sleepyhead? This was why I had him, after all—to create a communication network so I could get a SITREP from Alfa.

Echo had done a commendable job adjusting to my

orders quickly and efficiently, but our position was hardly ideal with such minimal intelligence. I had been watching for nearly fifteen minutes now, and each second that ticked by made me feel more queasy, and my gut twisted tighter.

I called over Echo's company commander, Zorr, the war-painted Hobb whom I had noticed during the address I gave to the regimental commands before we began training.

There was a puff of smoke, and the little guy materialized alongside me. Yeah, Hobbs can cover short distances, popping in and out of little gusts of smoke. Can't do it too often without getting smoke-sick, as they called it, so it wasn't as useful as you might think, but it certainly took some getting used to.

"What is the plan, Paladin?" he rasped in a voice too deep and rough for his slight frame. Seems at one point in his younger days, a legionaire had rammed a knife through the Hobb's throat, but that hadn't kept Zorr from blowing the Gythraul apart and living to fight another day. Still, it made him sound a little like some burly sergeant who had screamed himself permanently hoarse.

"Get a pair of messengers each to run down to them," I instructed, pointing down at Bravo and Charlie companies. "I want a report as to what they've seen since getting here. Something isn't right."

The Hobb nodded, his red-and-black streaked cheeks flexing around a grave frown. One look in his pale, grey eyes, and I knew he felt it too. He shuffled off and started to growl out orders.

I swept the field glass across the valley again, and something I saw in the corner of the image made me pause as I scanned Luchath. Raising my eye from the glass I caught a flutter of movement. Something small, about the size of a bird, was cutting through the air toward our position.

I raised the spyglass and saw the flutter of synchronized butterfly wings.

"Sleepyhead," I breathed and traded the spyglass for the Hagseye. The sense of dislocation came and went, then I was viewing the crest of the valley getting closer with each straining wingbeat. "Sleepyhead what is going on?"

"Trap, Master Luce, trap!" Sleepyhead gasped as he fought against the wind and gravity to gain altitude. "Soldiers shackled, Wee Folk dead, murder, murder!"

"Slow down, Sleepy, slo-"

Snaps of rifle fire rang out from far up the valley, followed by the dull *whump* of a detonation. Two more explosions, one after another—*whump...whump*—echoed amid more gunfire. I was guessing it was the sound of M-Cores.

"Incoming," a voice shrieked behind me.

I let go of the Hagseye and looked up to see molten orbs trailing blue and green flames arcing up from Luchath and sailing toward our position.

On reflex, I flattened and wormed away from the bushes to a lip of rock just behind.

The fireballs impacted across the slope of the valley just as I got the last of my damnably long body into cover. I stole a glance over the rocky ledge. The vast majority of the bombardment was falling short of our position, though some of it was impacting close enough to feel the rush of heat. Blasts of hot wind stung my eyes as curtains of flame fell and clung to the stony ground, lingering with a tenacity unnatural to its element. The sparse vegetation was consumed in seconds, and even after it had shrivelled to blackened husks, the flames would not release their hold on the rocks, which began to whine and crack.

"Zorr!" I roared. There was an exhalation of smoke, and

before my voice had died away, I found I was yelling into his face over the crackle of flames just below us. "Get everyone moving, now! We aren't going to be so lucky the next time around!"

Hunkering low, I raced along a narrow ridge that formed a cliff face, making for where Bryth and Uzran had deployed with the bulk of our forces.

War-painted members of Echo scrambled past as I found the Ogre and Tuatha shouting instructions for the various attendants of the command staff to get the lead out and follow Echo's third platoon up the mountain.

"The Gythraul vanguard must have taken the town before we got here," Bryth shouted when she saw me. "The rest of the Legion can't be far behind."

"Cinis has sprung a trap, again," Uzran snarled, reaching down and hauling a hapless Gremlin quartermaster to his feet. "I don't doubt those explosions we heard before were the Legion engaging with our forces further up the valley."

Another volley of alchemical projectiles was soaring through the air, but I breathed a sigh of relief. The company was clear of where they would land—if only just.

My relief was short-lived, though. Mist curled up from the ground, and I realized that Foxtrot and Golf were about to emerge from their Path right into the middle of the bombardment. Even if those firepots didn't come crashing down on their heads, they were going to be surrounded by sheets of flame, trapped and waiting for another salvo to finish the job.

I jammed the Hagseye into my socket and was glad to see that the Bogle was still flapping frantically toward me, intuitively adjusting his path to follow my movements.

"Sleepy, you said that the Wee Folk are dead, but are there any left alive in the area?" I asked, frantically switching perspectives between the Bogle's and my own as I moved with Uzran and Bryth.

"Few, yes," Sleepyhead answered, and I felt his supernatural sense reaching out and touching those tiny magical sparks of Wee Folk essence hiding from the fighting in the valley below.

"Get one to tell Charlie to give us cover with myrk-shells, confirmation   Sierra-Charlie-Romeo-Echo-Echo-November," I huffed, jogging over the rough terrain. "Then get one to direct Foxtrot and Golf's commanders, Mord and Valn, to get up into the mountains with us. After that, have Bravo put some tentative suppression on Luchath, confirmation Papa-Romeo-Oscar-Bravo-Echo."

I let the Hagseye drop as tendrils of Sleepyhead's consciousness reached out to his fellow Wee Folk.

"We are going to get out of this bombardment then sweep around the arm of the mountain to come down on top of Luchath," I said to Bryth and Uzran. We had paused beside a stone plateau, one of many forming rough tiers up the sheer slopes of the northernmost mountains framing the valley.

Down below us, I thought I spied the first of Foxtrot emerging from the mists, which recoiled and shrank from raging flames splashed across the slope. A second later, I saw a huddle of soldiers around two looming Royal Guards before hearing a chorus of dull percussions, then the sky between Luchath and our slope darkened with oily, black clouds.

The next round of artillery from Luchath was more scattered. Some of the fiery missiles extinguished themselves as they tore through the clinging myrk. An invention of the Daerg, the myrk was physical darkness and an excellent means of providing cover and disrupting an enemy's line of sight. I didn't like how it could compromise soldiers on the ground from seeing what was going on, but with Sleepyhead and the Wee Folk, at least I could get a look around the stuff when I needed to.

Or at least, I hoped I could after remembering what Sleepyhead said. Murdering Wee Folk just to blind us, huh? A fresh spike of anger came to a boil inside me. Up to this point, it had all been theoretical and mechanical—a kind of procedural thing—but the thought of innocent creatures like Sleepyhead being slaughtered stirred something hot and vengeful.

Uzran, Bryth, and I watched Foxtrot and Golf pick their way up the slope away from the flames, safe, except on the eastern flank, where two shells exploded next to a squad laboring up a scree-peppered ridge. Eight of them vanished in a blast of flame, and I couldn't stand to wait and see what was left of them after the fire burned down. I would get a report soon enough.

I looked down toward Luchath, my mind working feverishly on how best to approach the town without exposing ourselves to more bombardments.

I heard shells—banshee-shriekers, another Daerg invention—descend upon the town in a cacophony of keening wails. Bravo probably couldn't inflict much actual damage without good spotters in position, but they could give the Gythraul in the city some pause before they thought about exposing themselves in order to launch more fireballs our way.

"Approaching Luchath is too dangerous." Bryth hustled over to stand beside me. "The Gythraul are using the town's outmoded cannons to launch their munitions, but if we get any closer, they will use their skorpions to pin us along the ridge lines."

She pointed across the stretch of valley we would need to traverse, and I saw what she meant. The Gythraul skorpions, some kind of rapidfire launcher whose payload exploded in bursts of shrapnel, would halt any advance along that line. We could try and judge the distance between the skorpion's range and the cannons' to set up our mortar attacks, but it would be a hell of a risk. If we guessed wrong, the casualties we could suffer would be crippling.

As I thought about more intensive shelling of the town, I wondered where Alfa company was.They had deployed with the Finger teams and should have been, at most, an hour ahead of Bravo and Charlie. Could nearly three hundred soldiers really have been captured that quickly without the Fingers knowing it?

I remembered the sentries on the wall—Bogguns and Hobbs—and imagined a scenario in which Alfa company, thinking they were entering a town held by friendlies, moved into Luchath, only to find themselves surrounded— hemmed in on all sides by grinning, scaly faces. Now they were trapped there, probably bound and gagged, as their own army dropped wailing munitions on them and the rest of the town.

"Alright," I breathed, my back aching from my earlier dive for cover. "We need to keep Luchath pinned, but no advance for now. I need to know what is happening up the valley."

"Cinis is coming." Uzran pointed down toward the town. "He is going to march straight up the valley, his Legion sweeping in on both slopes. He plans to pin us between the mountains and Luchath."

"What if we pull back into the mountains on either side?" I asked, not liking the look of those bare, steep cliffs.

"And retreat before ever joining the battle?" Uzran snarled, whirling on me.

"Check yourself, Captain," I snapped back, not backing down. "No one's retreating, but sitting here waiting to get wiped out seems like a pretty piss-poor idea to me. I am considering our options for repositioning to launch a counter-attack."

Bryth moved toward me, stepping between us. "They will press us out of the zone of operation, and even if we are not blown off the cliffs, they will have a channel to funnel their forces to Chillspire. We would be scattered and fighting an even more difficult battle."

"Okay, I see that," I acknowledged, plans taking shape in my mind then being discarded in rapid succession.

"We should mobilize our forces in a pincer attack at Cinis," Uzran urged, his arms sweeping out and scissoring back together in illustration.

"A paired, massed charge?" I blurted in disbelief. "No. We don't do suicide missions. They have us on numbers, and besides, that is the exact opposite of what we have been training for."

A cold, hungry light shone in the Captain's eyes, and one hand flexed around the hilt of his sword. "Then what shall we do that does not involve running away?"

I didn't like the look he was giving me or the way he had so quickly shifted back to his old ways of thinking about war. Old dog, new tricks, I supposed.

"First, I am going to get ahold of Grimple," I said grimly as another volley of banshee-shriekers fell across Luchath. "We *think* we know what Cinis is doing, but we don't *know*, and before we make any stupid decisions, we should find out. In the meantime, one of you can tell Zorr to get us moving to support Bravo and Charlie."

Uzran gave a snarl of frustration, but threw up a salute and muttered something about getting the rabble moving.

"Thank the Wyrd," Bryth sighed. I thought she was talking about the departing Ogre until I saw her raise a finger toward a patch of open air above the valley.

"Sleepyhead!"

The dogged little Bogle fluttered down on a craggy spur in front of us and slumped down, panting. His thick, sausage-ish body was slick with some kind of film that must have been his equivalent of sweat, and one wing looked a little singed, but otherwise he seemed no worse for wear.

"Sleepyhead." I crouching down. "What happened? Why didn't you answer when I called?"

The Bogle raised his eyes to mine, and in them I saw such an innocent sorrow that my heart lurched a little.

"Sorry, Master Luce, so sorry," he gasped, his whole body shaking from exertion. "Went in with Alfa. Thought strange so few Wee Folk, many scared and hiding. Gythraul take Alfa in chains. Had to hide, play dead in pile of murdered Wee Folk in town square."

I imagined Sleepyhead, lying as still as he could in a pile of dead Pixies and Grindles, not daring to open an eye or whisper a word as the Gythraul moved around him.

"When cannons boom and Gythraul no look, left fast as could," the Bogle explained. "So sorry, Master Luce."

I laid a comforting hand on the little guy, not even caring about the oily residue that slid across my fingertips.

"You did good, Sleepy—real good—but things are just getting started. Can you reach any Wee Folk near Grimple or her Finger teams?"

Sleepyhead took a few steadying breaths and then his eyes rolled upward as he accessed the strange arcane network between all Wee Folk. "Y-yess," he said, shuddering a little.

"Good." I fit the Hagseye over my eye.

I found myself looking through the eyes of something being gripped in a huge, gnarled hand. I heard explosions and the crackle of carbine fire, but my view was limited to the hand and the wiry arm it was attached to. With sudden violent force, the arm flexed and the hand tightened. My view shook violently.

"Have yer gotten in touch with him or not yet, yer bleedin', foul, Grindle-shite?" snarled a familiar voice.

"Tell her I am listening," I told the poor Grindle Grimple had a hold of.

The stammering creature relayed my message, the view suddenly shifted, and I was treated to as close a view of Grimple Guthook's face as I would ever want. I guessed she had placed the creature on her shoulder, judging from the view of her in profile.

"Well, it's a right buggered mess," she snarled. Somewhere behind her I heard someone scream in pain.

"What does it look like at your end?"

"Weren't yer listenin'? I said a right mess," she chuckled humorlessly, and then the view moved again. She was moving, shouting over her shoulder. "Clear out, boys. She's goin' up quick."

More screams and sounds of M-Cores snapping off shots, then the rushing *floompf* of a fiery explosion. The Grindle's view wobbled as it clung desperately to Grimple's shoulder. At one point the little fellow looked behind him and saw a mass of tall, dark shapes falling and reeling in tendrils of flame and smoke. Wickedly glinting streaks hissed past and around, then my perspective swung again, to a vast scree-covered slope rushing up to meet me. I heard a piercing scream, and it took me a moment to realize it was the Grindle. Rock and dust flew as Grimple and her ride-along scramble-slid downward. Suddenly there was a vertiginous moment when the Grimple slipped into a crag that split the slope. The space was narrow, so much so that Grimple and the Finger team had to shuffle sideways, pressed flat against the wall.

They moved along, pausing every so often to stare up at the cleft of light above before continuing. From the Grindle's perspective, it was probably not nearly as claustrophobic as it was for the Finger team. Despite that and the nearness of enemy forces, I swear I saw glinting smiles on the sharp faces of the shuffling Goblins.

"Give me a SITREP on the go here, Grimple," I said, and waited for the Grindle to translate the message.

"The legion is marchin' up the valley, spread from slope to slope," she whispered breathlessly, squeezing through a tight spot. "Goin' to try and roll over anythin' between it and Luchath, and they got the numbers for it, too."

"Are your teams managing to slow them down any? How much time do I have?" Someone tugged on my arm, but I held on, determined to get the information I needed.

"Pissin' em off, more like," Grimple hissed. She looked up sharply as stone clattered from above.

Grimple and every Goblin around her paused, motionless but staring upward, and the

Grindle followed suit. The tug on my arm persisted, and I allowed my feet to start moving in the direction I was being lead.

"Yer've got maybe an hour before they are squeezin' around the final bend to Luchath," she said quietly. "I may be able to to turn it into two, but that'll be pushin' it—too much daylight and too many of 'em, and you promised no cannon fodder."

"Give me what you can, Luce out," I said and then dropped the Hagseye.

I woke up to a world on fire.

Bryth was doing her best to lead me around dancing patches of blue and green flame, and as the rest of my senses returned, heat prickled across my face as sweat poured from my scalp and neck. With dawning agony, I realized that the hand not being pulled on had been fire-kissed; there were ugly red welts striping the knuckles.

"They adjusted their aim," Bryth gasped. "The rest of company is gone, but you were tied to that damned stone."

I was going to have to find a way to be in two places at once, but in that moment I felt a thrill beyond simple adrenaline or terror. As I ran along the burning ridgeline, I had Bryth beside me, my hand in hers.

33

CLUSTER

I n the middle of a firefight, an hour can seem like an eternity. Then it comes to a crashing end, passing you so fast, you can't believe what happened.

ONE TIME IN AFGHANISTAN, patrolling a stretch of road looking for evidence of insurgents that, for whatever reason, were making their last stand near this blasted-out, little town that wasn't on any map. They had been poorly equipped and even more poorly trained, but they had a defensible position, and they outnumbered our platoon two to one. We needed to hold them down, but had no way of rooting them out without walking into a hail of bullets. So we waited for an hour, pinned along a stone wall in some field just outside of town. Eventually, support came in to punch enough holes to let us finish the job.

THAT WAIT BECAME one of the longest hours of my life, sucking moondust and watching stray rounds punch holes in the wall all around us. Finally the Stryker cohort appeared with their semi-portable toys, and we could finally mop things up. Their captain had given me crap afterwards about how we were bitching on the line for having to wait only an hour. Didn't we know what it took to get all the pieces moving around here?

To HIM, an hour was nothing. I don't think I really appreciated that until it was my turn to coordinate six companies to take on a force two to three times their size on rough terrain, all the while trading fire with a town controlled by pyromaniacs.

YEAH, an hour was an inconsequential blip, especially with Sleepyhead coordinating the rearrangement of the surviving Wee Folk across the valley. I still couldn't have pulled things together, even if the Wee Folk had acted like couriers instead of flapping, scuttling telecoms, or if Grimple had been able to give me two more hours instead of just an extra thirty minutes.

CETERUM CINIS's legion would have crushed anything in the valley, driving whatever might be on the periphery up and out.

I USED my field glass to sweep across the Gythraul's lines as the first banshee-shriekers came streaking down. The individual legionnaires looked like automatons of metal and horn, their bodies covered in full suits of hammered steel, except where those spurs of scale jutted out along elbow joints and shoulders. Their faces were enclosed in helmets shaped like snarling dragons, each century of soldiers bearing a unique version of draconic fury. They marched in staggered formation, those at the fore carrying rectangular shields that stretched from shoulder to shin, while those behind them carried weapons that looked like the guts of a grandfather clock got freaky with a crossbow. All had short, broad swords at their belts, and nestled in the midst of each formation, the dreaded skorpions. They were manned by two soldiers each—one legionnaire to tote the four-tubed, crank-turned business end, and another to lug a heavy pump on his back.

They might have seemed hilariously mishmashed if not for the fact that they would all gladly show me how lethal their tools of war were. War was their perpetual existence, and as the shells fell, I understood what that meant.

THE GYTHRAUL WERE READY, launching spinning lozenges from long brass tubes in hand-hauled wagons that rolled along between the blocks of ranked legionnaires. The lozenges hung in the sky, and just as screaming shells descended, exploded in streaming strands that filled the air above the Legion like cobweb clouds. The shells detonated, the sonic blast shredding the chaff overhead, but it hardly slowed the foot soldiers. But it did knock them slightly off balance, a few of them missing a step or two as they were rocked from the force of the explosion. For just a second, the battle line was out of sync. That was when the first companies pounced.

Foxtrot and Golf began leapfrogging squads down the north slope, taking turns firing stinging rounds into the nearest enemy formations as they closed.

The enemy casualties were nothing impressive, but the out-of-rhythm blocks of soldiers slid apart further, redirecting toward their tormentors. Banners waved and horns sounded as officers reoriented the formation. They didn't realize they were signalling their enemies as much as anything.

Delta company, the only Sylvancerous contingent I was fielding, had been skirting over the edge of the ridgeline on the south. When they heard the horns of the Gythraul, they came over the ridge screaming like cats on fire. One driver guided his mount down the slope while another—a gunner strapped to the beast's flanks—fired djinn bolts into the reforming enemy soldiers. The Gythraul swung their line around to face the foe, and that is when Golf and Foxtrot changed formation. Springing from their hunkered-down, potshotting position they formed a blistering firing line along a spur of stone above the furthest Gythraul legion.

I didn't know where Ceterum Cinis was, but he must have been getting things in order. Either that, or he had some phenomenal line officers. The most beleaguered formations sunk behind what cover the terrain and their shields could afford, stubbornly returning fire. Those behind moved to press around their pinned-down brothers, widening the front. I had hoped the abused centuries would charge after our distractions, but thankfully hadn't counted on it.

DELTA PEELED off before they could be surrounded, but more than one of their squad's gunners slumped over with bolts through their chests. Even a Sylvancerous pitched down the slope; the downed beast's driver and gunner were pincushioned in a heartbeat.

IT WAS the cost of war, the inescapable subtraction that any army—no matter how well led—must account for, but I didn't have to like it. I swore bitterly under my breath, cursing the legionnaires as I urged the rest of the company to get out of range.

AS FAST AS they were flying back up the slope, the Deltas probably would still have been torn to pieces as the encircling centuries opened fire, but those centuries had problems of their own. After launching that first mortar volley, Charlie company crept along the boulder-strewn valley floor beside the road. They sprang and punted Drake balls from their grenade launchers. The *whump* of explosions and fire, followed by eye-stinging smoke, threw the avengers into confusion.

CLOCKWORK CROSSBOWS *klik-klakked* and sent bolts whizzing among the rocks. The skorpions filled the air with storms of metal shards zinging and zipping like hellish wasps. Charlie was already down though, and the soldiers were pulling back to where they had dug in their mortars just in front of Luchath.

DELTA WAS clear but running up and seemingly out of the battle. If Cinis got too cocky, he would learn otherwise, though. They would skirt around the flank of the entire legion and drive some djinn bolts right up their asses, but not yet.

FIRST, Zorr's Echo company was going to try to pull off my first gambit.

WITH THE GYTHRAUL formations adjusting to the constant flux of assaults and retreats in the valley, the wagons full of the cobweb makers couldn't transition fast enough.

TO KEEP from getting entangled or overturned, they set themselves out of the flow of the century formations, and for just a second, as the legion broke into two fronts on the north and south slopes, the wagons were exposed. Echo sprinted into the gap from a canyon fissure we had learned about from a Pixie. They laid down fire to shred the poor wretches hauling the wagons. What the M-Cores couldn't perforate, Drake balls blasted apart.

ENRAGED at the audacity of the attack, the Gythraul line sharpened on either side and pincered in toward Zorr's boys who were already on the move, trading the cover of the valley floor for the speed of the road.

Seeing a chance to deal out some duly earned punishment, the Gythraul followed.

That is when the Royal Guards nestled among the boulders sprang up and unleashed a storm of thundering djinn bolts.

I saw Uzran below, blasting away with a fierce grin on his face as he and his behemoth brothers laughed and poured their hateful wrath on the surprised centuries. Legionnaires flew apart along the road as Echo raced toward the valley bend.

"Come on," I wished, watching the whole exchange through my fieldglass, the Hagseye in my other hand. "Take it! You know you want it."

After some initial staggering, horns blew, banners flapped, and the Gythraul line surged forward.

"Yes," I snarled joyfully and rammed the Hagseye in. "Open fire!" I was swept to Sleepyhead's perspective. I let the stone fall from my socket once I heard the words delivered.

I DIDN'T NEED the spyglass now to watch banshee-shriekers arcing into the clustering mass of the Gythraul. Bravo was keeping an eye on Luchath, but not so close an eye that they couldn't loose a salvo on the target I'd given them. They only had to give one initial volley, that was all they had munitions for after pressuring Luchath into silence, but by God, it was beautiful.

WITH NO COBWEB clouds to shelter under, the legionnaires got their first taste of the weaponized banshee cry. Those closest to the impact turned into dust devils—circling shades of grey, brown, and red. The rest of their fellows were knocked off their feet by the sonic bludgeoning of the erupting cry, many not rising as the flesh within their freshly pitted armor wrung out to leak onto the ground. Wherever the shells struck, dirty little cyclones spun out over withered corpses in corroded armor.

THE ARCH-MONGER HAD BEEN DISTURBINGLY happy about discussing the time dilating nature of refined banshee screams, but the particulars didn't matter to me. I just wanted to put corpses on the ground, and he had obliged.

FOXTROT AND GOLF had only a few mortar teams apiece, but those barked to life, and more shells came down in a brutal flurry. Echo spun around and came back snarling. All along the firing lines, M-Cores snapped and crackled like War's own skillet heating up. The legion was taking it on the nose, and I wasn't done yet.

Taking the descending shrieks as their cue, the riders of Delta sprang across the rear of the legion line. They weren't enough to rip open the back lines and fold the whole legion in on itself, but Cinis didn't know our strength, and for all he knew, there was another set of ambushes about to break on his rear if he tried to wheel around.

A few bursts of fire erupted on the flank opposite the side where Delta was advancing. There Grimple was using the last of her explosive munitions to sell the idea.

The Gythraul did what any group of hard bastards would do when hemmed in and in danger of getting pinned down —they were going to go through to get out, and "through" meant through us.

Just as I hoped, Cinis must have thought we were trying to surround and pin him against the crook in the valley, keeping him from Luchath. He didn't know that if he pushed back the way he came, we were made of paper. He was clever, and he was bold. I knew that from stories Uzran had shared, but boldness didn't mean he was clever enough.

The Gythraul centuries pressed forward over their dead, daring our shells to fall as they closed on our own forces. They were going to march over us, unleashing salvo after salvo in disciplined flurries, even as their brothers died to left and right. It was a strange combination of chilling and stirring to see exactly what Uzran said in action: a remorseless, brutal will.

THEY WERE COMING THROUGH, and we were going to let them.

MY COMPANY COMMANDERS held the firing line for as long as they dared, then they peeled off and made for the valley crook. Foxtrot and Golf were to funnel down the slope, passing under a sharp finger of rock jutting from the mountain and overhanging the valley floor. I stood on that finger of rock, watching the trickle of soldiers coming around the bend become a sizeable tide of retreating forces. Only the contingents of Royal Guards from all the companies, massed into flanking lines among the boulders, stood their ground and made the centuries pay for each step with more twitching, steaming bodies.

"JUST A LITTLE LONGER, BIG GUY," I growled, watching the first of the Royal Guards sink to a knee among the broken, scattered stones.

THE GYTHRAUL HAD TO COMMIT. That was the only way the last gambit would work. If they didn't, we were just going to delay an inevitable, grinding defeat.

THE LEGION, like a predator scenting fear on the wind, drove forward, barely noticing Delta pecking and pestering at their haunches. They were coming in force, the fore of their formations passing under the shadow of the mountain spur.

I SWUNG AROUND to where Bryth and the battle-magi who had brought us to the Valley of Luchath now stood in a tight circle. The air around them swam with pent up power, Contracts of Earth and Stone being extorted mercilessly as the mages dug at the heart of the rock on which we stood.

I WAS GOING to let Cinis charge into his grave, right before I buried him under a fucking mountain.

SOMETHING GAVE an incredible snap inside the circle of magi, and a seam opened in the center of the stony ground between them. The tension of the dammed-up magic coalesced over that crack, glowing with a mischievous green light.

BRYTH STEPPED AWAY from the circle as the other battle-magi relaxed, all for one tall male Tuatha with his shaven head inked in concentric rings of spidery sigils. Head bowed, he held both hands over the glittering seam as though warming them over a campfire. In the cool, bright sun of the north, sweat glistened on the symbols on his scalp.

BRYTH WIPED away blood leaking freely from her nose and lips as she stepped toward the cliff where I stood. Almost rushing over to her at the sight of blood, I stopped as I saw the other sorcerers also cleaning themselves up without fuss. I guess that kind of mojo gets a little messy.

"SIR FIAN HOLDS the enchantment in place for now." She gave a nod to the sweating, bald Tuatha. "At your word, he will release the spell. We had best get on the north side of that seam."

I SWUNG AROUND, expecting to see the Royal Guards making their withdrawal from among the boulders, pausing to fire a few bursts to keep the Gythraul pissed. Instead, the Gythraul closed in on the Royal Guards forming into a wedge among the rocks.

"WHAT IS HE DOING?" But with sinking surety, I already knew the answer.

SNATCHING UP THE HAGSEYE, I roared for Sleepyhead to connect me with the Puck attached to Uzran. A heartbeat later, I was among a forest of tree trunk legs, hearing Uzran's signature bellow thundering over the roar of the djinn guns.

"...HAVE never taken a step backward, and we will not start now! Draw blades with me, brothers! Cinis will not live to see his army broken by the mountain!"

"No," I screamed. "Tell that stupid bastard to get his ass back to the fallback point."

I DON'T KNOW if the Puck relayed my message as the Guards around Uzran gave a savage cheer and followed their Captain in a mad rush toward the Gythraul line.

I LET the Hagseye drop to my chest and spun to Bryth, watching the scene below unfold with horror.

"BRYTH," I grabbed her by the shoulder. "We need to get down there, fast!"

BRYTH TORE her eyes from my face, her attention darting between Uzran and Sir Fian. "There is no time... the spell..."

'BRYTH!" I took her hands in mine. "Fast!"

HER MOUTH OPENED AND CLOSED—ONCE, twice—then she nodded grimly.

34

HONOR

Bryth and the battle-magi, sans Sir Fian, got me down to the valley floor in style.

Reverberating eldritch words that made my bones ache flew from their mouths, and suddenly an incredible wind scooped us up and bore us to the ground. Arcs of lightning and razors of ice streamed down with and before us. As we fell, the Tuatha sorcerers drew their weapons—long-bladed swords and man-high spears—edges flashing with fire and crackling with electricity, or trailing streamers of icy fog. The tempest roared in my ears as I clutched the carbine across my chest and screamed a battle cry that was one part exhilaration, two parts terror.

The Royal Guard crashed into the Gythraul and scythed about with their huge blades and bludgeons, their djinn guns cast aside in their mad rush for revenge. Legionnaires died with each stroke, but they were many, and the Royal Guards were dragged down by sheer numbers. As we descended at breakneck speed, Uzran plowed at the fore of his warriors toward a knot of Gythraul in gold and red armor.

The fury of the storm raced ahead of our landing, scattering Gythraul like bowling pins and driving the nearest Royal Guards to their knees.

I hit the ground running, the last breath of the delivering tempest propelling me forward, battle-magi to my left and right.

Fire, lightning, and icy blasts drove like deadly fingers through the banks of Gythraul as I rushed forward, putting quills in the chests of any legionnaires in front of me until I was standing next to a horned giant holding the Pale Banner in one bloody fist.

"Royal Guard of Queen Meabh," I roared, stabbing my finger up at the flapping banner, now tattered and torn, "if you serve that banner and the Twilit Kingdom, get your asses up and moving to the fallback point. Now!"

I saw Hurrahn looking down at me from the slits of his helmet. One eye was nothing but a ragged wound, the other met my stare and there was odd shine to it. Glowing with pride, relief, or something less comprehensible, he bowed his head deeply before rising to his full height. Waving the banner back and forth, he threw back his head.

"Royal Guard!" he bellowed, as the rest of his brothers began to climb to their feet. "Withdraw! Close order! Move!"

The armored hulks stood, and each one looked to me, an internal battle raging within, no doubt, but dwarfed by the struggle around them. They could serve me and, by extension, honor their oaths to the Queen, or they could stand with the leaders they had fought beside, some of them for centuries. The hope of survival and fear of death didn't measure much on this scale, and I knew it when I looked into their eyes. More than life was at stake—something far more important than that.

Honor.

For one fragile second, I was afraid they would turn their backs and leap to their deaths in a sea of Gythraul. That second shattered, and with sharp salutes, they began their ground-eating lope toward the bend in the valley. Some bore up wounded comrades, but every Guard that had made it to the Gythraul lines withdrew, choosing to trust me for perhaps the first time.

If I survived, I might remember that as one of the proudest moments in my life, but I still had one more life to save.

That, or die trying.

The fury of the battle-magi managed to sow confusion in the Gythraul line, and as the centuries scrambled to reorganize themselves, I spotted Uzran.

A half dozen Gythraul soldiers lay dead on the ground, armor torn apart in gory rents. But the Ogre's armored body had sprouted more than one bolt, and he had sunk to one knee, gripping his sword for leverage, its point gouging he paving stones of the road. I was already running forward, rifle stock snapping to my shoulder as the remaining red legionnaires raised their weapons.

I snapped off shots in pairs—two to the left, two to the right—and felt a satisfied smile pull at my lips as two legionnaires fell with hissing craters in their chests. A bolt hissed over my shoulder, and I put a quill through the head of the soldier who had fired at me, the dragon on his helm spouting a different kind of smoke.

My feet cleared corpses I barely registered with my peripherals. My barrel tracked with my eyes to put down another legionnaire as I came close enough to peer around Uzran's shoulder. Two more legionnaires in red were waiting, crossbows braced against their body-length shields. But they weren't firing yet. Instead, they angled their bodies so I couldn't get a clear shot at the figure behind them.

I could hear the Gythraul reforming even as blasts of magical power lashed across the valley. My time was almost up.

"Uzran," I hissed as I stepped to his shoulder. "Get up, now!"

Uzran gave a pained grunt, even more bolts jutting from his breastplate. A human would have died five times over, but the Ogre just coughed up blood. It dripped from the faceplate of his helmet as he dragged himself to his feet.

"Impressive," hissed a rich, sibilant voice from behind the pair of red legionnaires.

The shields parted reluctantly, and a fireplug of a Gythraul was revealed, resplendent in alabaster armor trimmed in metal the color of rubies. He was a head shorter than me, but broad-shouldered and stout, with obvious strength in his heavy limbs. His dragon-faced helmet was not some snarling monstrosity like the others, but a majestic, reptilian king whose carmine eyes watched me and the rest of the world with regal disinterest.

"Ceterum Cinis," I called, drawing a bead on his face.

"Paladin." He cut a short bow, one hand clasped across his chest. The voice within the helmet was hardly muffled. It sounded more like the voice of a noble patriarch or a statesman. Not what I had expected.

The Gythraul didn't so much as twitch as he looked down the barrel of my gun, then raised his eyes to me.

"I wasn't certain the Queen had found you in time to be here for the first steps of our little dance," he said smoothly, not seeming to notice or care that Uzran was back on his feet now.

"I wasn't sure I was going to get lucky enough to start my

career by ghosting you, you son of a bitch," I snarled. Then I mumbled over my shoulder to Uzran. "I start shooting, you start running. No, bullshit this time, damn it."

"Withdraw now, and I promise you safe passage." Cinis sounded bored. "I don't want things to be over too quickly, now."

"I'd rather put you down now and leave time to kill the rest of the bodies you brought with you," I snarled, trying to make certain Uzran wasn't going to collapse before I began this bloodbath.

"Pity," Cinis clucked, then both of his red guards fired their crossbows.

Instinct alone got me out of the way of the first bolt, but the second took me in the shoulder. Pain blurred my vision, and I was spinning around. My shots sprayed wide, but got one of the legionnaires in the throat. He tumbled backwards as I lost my balance and fell to my knees. The other legionnaire almost finished me off, but Uzran let out a roar and swung his blade in a wide arc that split the Gythraul's helm and drove into his chest cavity.

Ceterum Cinis rushed forward, broad-bladed sword in hand, but Uzran's wild swing flung the corpse with the bifurcated skull into the oncoming commander. I staggered upward, trying to raise the rifle to finish Cinis off, but the point of the bolt ground into the meat of my shoulder. I couldn't raise the weapon. I strained harder, and it was all I could do to hold onto the thing. Cinis was on the ground, stunned, but there wasn't much I could do right then, and I heard the shouts of Gythraul officers.

The Gythraul centuries had marshalled and were marching toward us, coming in from all sides.

Uzran was on his feet, but barely, and I lurched up into a standing position, but I still couldn't use my arm. I tried to switch hands with the carbine, but a fresh jolt of pain sent it tumbling out of my fingers. It stayed with me only because of its strap slung over my shoulder. I hissed in pain as three more bolts zipped past. If we didn't move, we were as good as dead. Out of the corner of my eye, I saw Cinis limping, almost crawling away from us and toward the advancing legion.

Swearing six ways to Sunday, I grabbed the wounded Ogre's dangling arm with my good hand and hauled with all my might.

I may as well have tried to drag a semi out of park with a rope and a give-'em-hell attitude.

"Damn it," I snarled. "I better not have risked everything just for you to get lazy on me and get us killed."

Uzran ambled along with me, his bloody sword clinking along the paving stones as he used it like a cane. More bolts shattered around us, and I heard a sharp, whirring sound. My stomach turned to ice.

A skorpion's pumps. We were dead.

Then the world was wreathed in fire and smoke stung my eyes. The bodies of the recently killed Gythraul ignited around us.

I looked around, my exhausted and pain-rattled brain trying to make sense of things. Then the most beautiful sight in the world strolled up to us in the parting waves of flame.

"This is becoming habitual," Bryth said with a smile, sweeping her burning sword in a grand flourish.

"Yeah, well quit being so damned heroic," I laughed, moving toward her, one arm tugging futilely on Uzran. "You keep it up and it'll just be the expectation."

She laughed wildly—a gorgeous, though terrifying

sound that rang over the crackling flames. It faltered a little as her eyes fell on the limping Ogre.

"Still with us then, Ol' Stone?" she asked, her voice suddenly a rubbery imitation of levity.

Uzran leaned heavily enough on the sword that it split a paving stone, but his blood-smeared helm came up, and his black eyes glittered defiantly. He tried to straighten, but the effort drew a wince and another cough that spilled more dark blood.

"I am not done yet," he gasped, lurching forward.

"Damn straight," I swore. "Besides, you have to survive, 'cause I'm still going to kick the crap out of you when we get a spare second."

A weary, blood-clogged laugh rattled out of his chest. "Looking forward to it," he hissed between clenched teeth, taking a few more steps.

As much as we were making light of things, we were in trouble. I looked back and realized how close we were to the diminishing curtain of flame. At this rate, the fire would be out, and we would be pincushions before we got clear of the precarious mountain spur.

I thought about Sir Fian above us, sweat pouring from his scalp as he held the incredible energies in check. I wondered how long we had before his control failed. How much time before tons of stone began to slide free, burying everything beneath the shadow of these cliffs.

I looked back. Among the flames, figures ran toward us. At first I thought that some bold legionnaires had plunged through the blaze, but the silhouettes against the firelight were too tall and lithe to be the bulky, armored Gythraul. Then I spied the empowered weapons in their hands, much diminished but still humming with latent power. They were the battle-magi, returning from sowing chaos and buying us more time.

Crossbow bolts, smoldering from passing through the flagging flames, chased them across the ground.

"It is time we departed, Lady Lighttread," cried a willowy Tuatha, aiming her spear backward and launching a Parthian arc of lightning beyond the fire wall.

"Quickly then," Bryth called, and I felt the vibrations in my inner ear that signaled gathering magic.

The battle-magi pulled level with us as the last of the flames winked out, and tides of angry Gythraul came on. Some fired their weapons as they ran, but many of them, scorched and blistered, raced toward us with swords upraised.

We had less than thirty seconds before they were hacking us apart.

With a sudden, massive crack, I felt, as much as heard, Sir Fian release the spell. There was a long, low grinding noise, like the earth giving a yawn that wouldn't end. As magical stormwinds rose, the yawn sharpened into a growl. Looking up at the cliff face I watched it begin a slow, but accelerating plunge down and forward.

Shards of stone and chunks of rock bigger than me erupted outward from the point of impact, pulping anything in their path. I couldn't hold back a scream as a jagged boulder tumbled toward us, but then the stormwind was bearing us away. Dust in great billowing clouds chased us as we raced clear on the magical tempest.

The bulk of Cinis's legion were not so lucky

35

CASUALTIES

Lady Bryth Lighttread and Captain Uzran of Queen Meabh's Royal Guard stood atop the walls of Luchath, watching the Paladin make his frantic preparations to leave, part of which included the burial of Alfa company.

Hundreds of bodies had been carefully laid out in even rows along the road leading into the empty town.

"This will not end well." Uzran adjusted his stance and found a more comfortable position for the many bandages which showed under his armored traveling coat. The healing magics of the Tuatha could work wonders, but some injuries just took time to fully heal—if they ever did.

"He won't even talk to me," Bryth said, looking at the stones under her hands and feet. Slowly she raised her hands from the battlements, wrinkling her nose as she scented more of the darkling-spawn on the stones. The silent town positively reeked of their foul touch. She knew that Uzran and any others without magical sensitivities only felt a slight uneasiness and maybe a hint of foulness in the air, but to her and the other sorcerers, the effect was far more dramatic. The spoor of the Fiend's children left the entire town smelling like a butcher shop abandoned to rot in the heat of summer. A thick, charnel miasma lay across the place, and only fear of Luce's fury kept her here.

"Do you think you can get him to understand?" Uzran frowned. "With time, I mean? Maybe he could be made to understand that such is the way of things here?"

Bryth wanted to believe it was possible, but as she watched the Paladin doling out commands in a coldly burning fury, she knew there was no hope for such a thing. "No, I don't think so," she said with a defeated sigh, the exhaustion of the despair eating its way through her heart. "Those were soldiers under his command, and he will not let their deaths go unavenged."

Uzran shook his head, then winced as the movement pulled on one of a score of wounds. "Does he truly think that the Queen will punish the darkling-spawn for being what they are?" he muttered in frustration. "And what will he do when she tells him to be silent and continue the war effort?"

"It is on that last question that my heart is choking," Bryth whispered, hearing the invasive drip-drip of memories reminding her of the consequences of disagreeing with the Queen.

In his initial tirade against Lord Nadder, Lucius had made it clear what his thoughts were on the matter. As she had come to know him, Bryth learned he often said exactly what he meant.

"I'm not fighting this kind of war," he had raged into the smirking face of the tall Tuatha whose glamored skin gleamed like polished bronze. Then he had slammed his fist into Lord Nadder's face. It had taken several attempts to drag him off the stunned courtier.

In the rush to make ready for war, Lady Bryth had never taken the time to talk about Lord Nadder, the Queen's left hand, too seriously. Perhaps because the open secret of his existence in the Gloaming Court was something she found distasteful. Bryth had not wanted to tell Luce about the courtier who was known to be willing to do *whatever* the Queen asked. Bryth was convinced that the Queen only asked him to serve in the most dire situations and insisted his whispered exploits were greatly exaggerated. But the fact that he had recently become the darkling-spawn's handler did little to improve her opinion of him.

The second she had seen him standing in front of the gates of Luchath, sitting casually ajar, her heart sank. The town had fallen completely silent not long before Sir Fian released the landslide that shattered Ceterum Cinis's Legion, Bravo company had reported. Even with battle going on, they might have heard some screaming coming from the town, but, needing to maintain their position, they had not investigated.

It had been hours later, after ensuring Delta would harass the scattered remnants of the legion and drive them back toward the coast, and that Uzran would survive his wounds, that Bryth and Luce had met with Bravo before cautiously approaching the abandoned walls of the town.

Grimple and her teams, battle-weary but uncomplaining, had moved to offer support as the rest of their forces secured the valley, bringing mobs of the Dead to excavate the rockslide.

Luchath had been silent, the Fingers not able to spy a single living thing within as they skirted the cliffs around town. Other than wind rolling down from the mountains, not a sound was made, and everything was chillingly stilled until they came within shouting distance of the gates. Lord

Nadder had strolled out from the gatehouse with a jaunty wave of his hand.

Bryth had hurried to explain—in as sanitized a version as she could truthfully manage—who Lord Nadder was as they approached town. Within, they found nothing but death. Indoors and out, corpses of both Gythraul and residents they had kept alive to establish their ruse were being stacked on top of each other. Hobbs and Gremlins in watch uniforms lay atop the bodies of Gythraul legionnaires that had been manning the rusting cannons.

Despite the ragged wounds to throat, groin, and belly the dead displayed, there had been little blood, a detail Lord Nadder explained away with some mention of the "thirsty little darlings."

Luce's expression had been flat and stony, saying nothing until they came to the town hall. Outside the open doors of the hall lay a pile of butchered Wee Folk, and within could be seen the shackled ranks of Alfa company. All had met a similar fate to their captors, but in their chained thrashing, they had pulled each other into tortured shapes even more chilling than the limp poses of the legionnaires and false watch.

His whole body shaking, Luce had managed one word past his rage-locked teeth.

"Why?"

"Rather indiscriminate, aren't they," Lord Nadder had observed with a casual glance over the tangled dead within the hall. "Casualties of war, I suppose, but no great loss. The fools shouldn't have gotten captured."

And thus ensued Luce's assault and Bryth's attempts to keep him from murdering an emissary of the Queen with his bare hands.

In the days since, the Paladin had been hell-bent on returning to Duanon to demand an explanation of the Queen. When the war council pointed out that there were still Gythraul to the south, he had angrily waved it off. He stated that the companies could press south and engage on their own, piecemealing the cumbersome legions until they had more soldiers to attack directly. When Bryth had tried, in desperation, to call on him to hold to his duty and lead the army, Luce stormed out and had refused to speak to her since, except to tell her that if she would not open a Path to bring him to Duanon, he would have another battle-magus take him.

Lucius stood by a number of wagons drawn by thick-thewed Bovarines, directing the dead of Cinderstone to load Alfa company's remains into the same vehicles which had brought them to the valley. He would be leaving soon, and even if it broke her heart beyond mending, she was going with him to face the Queen.

"Hopefully, his temper will have cooled by the time we reach Duanon," she said, her voice betraying her doubts at her own words. "But either way, I need to get down there before he starts screaming for one of the others." She stepped away from the battlements and placed a hand on Uzran's bandage-swaddled arm. "Rest up, Ol' Stone."

"I am coming with," the Ogre said, looked down at her with pitying eyes. "Well or wounded, I am his second. I shall stand by his side as he goes before the Queen."

Bryth, looking up into her old friend's resolved face, did not have the heart to argue. In truth, she had hoped he would say so. As history repeated itself, it would help to have him standing with her. "Come on then." Her shoulders slumped forward as she took his hand and leaned against him.

Despite his wounds, he bore her weight with ease, and together they descended the steps toward the gate.

The audience hall fell silent only for as long as it took Paladin Lucius Bollham to step down from the doorway and stalk toward the throne. A stride behind him came Lady Lighttread and Captain Uzran.

The courtiers parted upon seeing the oncoming victor. Some began to clap and cheer. Many had begun celebrating only a day or so ago as news had reached them. Then they saw his grim countenance and the aggressive hunch of his shoulders. The cheers died on their lips, but the applause held on for one or two floundering seconds . Then only the sounds of murmurs and whispers ran the course of the hall.

From atop her throne, Queen Meabh watched his approach without a flicker of emotion. With a casual sweep of her hand, she preemptively bid her attending Royal Guards to take a step back and allow the stalking Paladin to stand directly before her throne's dais.

"Our Paladin," she said in a voice calm and clear. "Our congratulations to you on serving Us well, and leading Our armies to victory. Yet We sense you are displeased. How may We set things to right?"

"Your Majesty. I think you know exactly how this can be set right." Each word was a struggle for control.

"Please, elaborate," the Queen replied patiently.

"The Fiend's children are a cruel and careless weapon." He stared boldly into her face, his conflicted emotions washed away with his strong words. "They must be put down—exterminated for the murder of my soldiers—and I demand an oath from your Majesty to never again employ such creatures."

Meabh arched a single eyebrow, but when she spoke,

her tone was as even and longsuffering as ever. "We understand the loss of loyal servants is a sharp pain to bear, yet such is the burden of leadership. Surely, you have lost comrades and soldiers before, even to unfortunate and unforeseen situations on the field. Perhaps that perspective will ease your troubled mind."

Far from being dissuaded, Lucius snarled with pent up fury and jabbed a finger up at the Queen with a ferocity that made some of the more skittish courtiers cry out. "Don't you dare!" he shouted, finger quivering. "Don't you dare make this out to be an accident. You knew what the Fiend was like, you knew the damage it could cause, and you knew what its spawn are like after using them for months. You knew what they would do in Luchath, and you didn't care!"

The Royal Guards took a step forward, but with a gesture from the Queen, they withdrew.

"We knew what might have happened," She had an air of sad acknowledgment, but raised a slender finger. "Yet We also knew that Ceterum Cinis may have outmaneuvered you. We dispatched our agents to aid you in battle. You would not have been present for that battle if not for the intelligence gained by using the tools available to us, though they be cruel and sometimes careless."

The Paladin stared up at her, his expression souring from one of outrage to one of disgust.

"The soldiers of Alfa company, souls who'd survived centuries of fighting for you, died in chains, murdered by the demons you set loose. Three hundred and sixteen dead for nothing more than satisfying darkling bloodlust. I am confused, your Majesty, because I was told that your people already fought one war for freedom from those monsters. Why now do you let their bastard spawn feed on your loyal subjects?"

"Take care how you speak of such things," the Queen snapped in her first show of temper. "You speak of things which came about before your kind was even fully formed. You should return to the business that brought you to us in the first place."

"Not until I get what I came for," Lucius said, his voice low and hard.

"The Fiend's children are Ours to do with as We will," the Queen declared archly, squaring her shoulders. "We will not cast any tool aside which may yet be useful for securing our kingdom. We tell you once more: Go. Serve as you swore to, and leave the handling of such matters to Us."

Paladin Lucius Bollham stood for a moment, searching her face for something which he seemed to have lost. "No," he said at last, his searching done. "Oath or no, I won't wage war this way."

The murmurs in the court died, and all eyes shot from Lucius to the Queen. Lady Bryth had tears running silently down her cheeks, and Captain Uzran's head was bowed.

"You forswear your oath to Us?" she asked, a touch wearily.

"However you say I'm out, sure," the ex-Paladin said, crossing his arms. "Throw me in a cage or take my head or whatever the hell else you want, but you aren't getting any more help from me. If you are willing to throw away lives like that, you're no better than the Gythraul."

For one agonized moment, the silence in the hall was complete, then the Queen nodded solemnly and raised her voice, addressing the courtiers who looked on. "The Paladin has fallen," the Queen began with the measured cadence of an incantation. "What next shall come?"

Bryth began to sob openly as Lucius's face knotted with confusion.

"The Gorm is called," the courtiers replied in unison, eyes glittering with a cruel, voyeuristic interest. "Gauntlet of iron upon the hand of the throne."

"What the hell?" Luce managed to say before the Royal Guards rushed forward and took hold of him.

At their sudden grip he fought, but the huge, metal-shod hands held him like he was a belligerent child.

"The Gorm is called," the Queen cried, and from behind her throne stepped a bruised but leering Lord Nadder. He held an open chest wherein a shard of black stone glittered with a sickly green light.

"For the Paladin has fallen," responded the courtiers.

The Royal Guards forced Lucius to his knees. The Queen descended the dais, one hand held upward as arcane words slid from her lips. Invisible blades peeled the leather and cloth from Luce's chest so his bare torso lay exposed from clavicle to navel. Muscles stood out like taut cords under his chestnut skin as he fought futilely against the Guards.

"Majesty!" Bryth stepped forward even as she seemed about to collapse in on herself. "Meabh, please! Not again."

"Restrain her," the Queen spat, her eyes sharpening on Uzran.

The Captain put a hand on Bryth's shoulders and pulled her backward, but then took his own tentative step forward.

"My Queen," he began, eyes darting from where Lucius struggled and swore to the Queen and back again. "I..."

His voice failed him. The Queen gave him a cold glare as she reached to take the black stone from the small chest held by Lord Nadder.

"You would sacrifice your rebellious clan for us, your own flesh and blood," she said in mocking disbelief. "But this human—this mayfly ape—will see you forgetting your duty? Your oath?"

Uzran's eyes fell to the floor. He stepped back, gripping Bryth's shoulders as she wept.

"Oh, shut up, child," the Queen snarled as she turned her venomous glare on the young Tuatha. "If you had done as We bid you, this would not be necessary. We thought you had learned from the last, but it seems We thought too highly of you."

The words struck Bryth like a blow. With a final shuddering sob, she fell silent, though tears continue to fall.

Her chastisements through, the Queen held up the stone in front of Lucius's wide, terrified eyes.

"We make use of all at our disposal," she said in little more than a whisper. "Even when that tool is unwilling."

More words of power sprang from the Queen's lips and the flesh began to flay free of Lucius's heaving chest. He screamed and writhed, feet rapping against the floor, but armored hands held him fast.

Flaps of skin and cords of muscle were drawn back with surgical care until a sternum glistened gorily. Invisible drills gouged and sprayed tiny shards of bone as a cavity was excavated. Lucius's screams reached a new tenor of agony.

The Queen carefully fitted the stone in her hand into the shallow alcove created in Lucius's breastbone.

"The Gorm comes," she declared, but Bryth heard only the dripping of blood on the marble floor.

EPILOGUE

INEVITABILITIES

Mother Gwiddon's home swayed around her as it lurched through the depths of Mistmire.

It was supposed to be a hall and fortress against the Gythraul should they ever reach her swamps, but that had never mattered to her. It mattered only that she had some place to rest her weary bones—a retreat from the schemes she had been a part of for so very long. Here, by her bronze pot and fire, surrounded by her children, she did not feel so very old.

But she was old—ancient on a scale that boggled the mind of the sane and set the lunatic to giggling. With that age had never come decrepitude or frailty, as is the case with lesser mortal creatures, but it had brought fatigue. Sometimes in these most recent centuries, she had felt it pressing down with such terrible weight that she almost despaired and succumbed to slumber. That torporous swoon that had once taken ages from her until she had awoken in a world she did not know, overrun with upstart sorcerers who waged war with her veritable neighbors. She had no interest in awakening to such a mess again, and so she persevered, adjusting her schemes as needed to bring about her catastrophic goals.

It was one such adjustment she was making now, a Hagseye pressed to her socket as her house stomped along.

"I have learned that thy commander has met the Gormstone," the old witch said, waiting for the Bogle on the other end to relay the message.

"Should have listened to lil' Lighttread," came the muffled voice beside the Bogle's waiting ear. "But what does this mean fer the plan?"

Mother Gwiddon had to pause to remember what plan it was she was adjusting. She had so many going concurrently, plots and counterplots.

"Thy time will come sooner than thou thought," she said before the owner of the voice could become antsy and shake the Bogle, as it was wont to do. "So take care of thy kin so they are ready. Thy window of opportunity will be narrow."

"Don't yer worry about my side," the voice growled. "I just hope that all yer prophecies are up to snuff."

Mother Gwiddon smiled her sharp smile and gave a grating chuckle.

"Oh, my dear," she warbled from the very back of her throat. "When have I ever been wrong?"

ACKNOWLEDGMENTS

This is just the beginning, but beginnings are not easy things, and therefore there are many people to thank. My many family members, my friends, my children, and of course my exquisite wife. I also would like to note the people who have directly helped me to put this piece of work out in public. Anne Schneider, Elliot Eastin, and Lisa Eastin, for their contributions and assistance, taking something I'd made and making it shine. To Ms. Knorr for being convinced that I had something to give and to share.

And to you my dear reader for giving me the gift of your time and attention. Thank you.

-Aaron D. Schneider

JOIN THE WAR-COUNCIL

Be the first to learn about new releases, see covers fresh off the designer's desk, talk with Aaron and other fans of his work.

On Facebook search: The War Council: Reading Group for the Works of Aaron D. Schneider

or visit

www.aarondschneider.com

ABOUT THE AUTHOR

Aaron was born to parents who taught him two very important things: truth matters and imagination is not a crime.

Our protagonist has spent the rest of his life trying to live out those two maxims, much to the chagrin of every unfortunate around him (progenitors included).

As such, by age six or seven, he was writing stories about a dark, reptilian avenger who brought final, painful justice to the guilty- with unsettling illustrations to boot. His beloved and benighted parents realized that budding sociopathy would simply not do, and so they began introducing him to tales of great and good heroes. First the account of a certain carpenter, then a hairy-footed burglar, then a savior lion, and after that point our protagonists was plunging face first and arms out into a world of heroism both real and imagined. While far from a hero himself, he has endeavored to try and capture that same bowed but unbroken spirit that dwells in a dark and ugly world, because that as far as he can tell is what makes it all worth it.

Along this long, dreaming way he managed to find a woman he could bamboozle into loving him, and then even have children with, Lord have mercy on them all.

Now Aaron has managed to cram no few exciting jobs and

hair-raising experiences into his life so far, and God help him, he hopes for many more. It is these that drive his captured glimpses of something epic. If you have the time you should pull up a chair, grab a beer, light a pipe, or whatever your pre-literary consumption ritual may be and give them a look. It is been said they are truly monstrous, but as any true hero knows, monsters often guard treasure.

Sign up to Aaron's Newsletter to be the first to know about new releases!

Visit www.aarondschneider.com

Currently some of this hard won loot from Aaron's word-hoard is headed your way:

War-Torn (fall 2018)
War-Sworn (winter 2018)

www.ingramcontent.com/pod-product-compliance
Lightning Source LLC
Chambersburg PA
CBHW071739110726
47908CB00006B/1633